The Firm of Girdlestone

Sir Arthur Conan Doyle

DODO ● PRESS

THE FIRM OF GIRDLESTONE.

A. CONAN DOYLE

TO MY OLD FRIEND

PROFESSOR WILLIAM K. BURTON,

OF THE IMPERIAL UNIVERSITY, TOKYO,

WHO FIRST ENCOURAGED ME, YEARS AGO, TO PROCEED WITH

THIS LITTLE STORY,

I DESIRE AFFECTIONATELY TO

DEDICATE IT.

THE AUTHOR.

PREFACE

I cannot let this small romance go to press without prefacing it with a word of cordial thanks to Mr. P. G. Houlgrave, of 28, Millman Street, Bedford Row. To this gentleman I owe the accuracy of my African chapters, and I am much indebted to him for the copious details with which he furnished me.

A. CONAN DOYLE.

CONTENTS

CHAPTER.

CHAPTER I.

MR. JOHN HARSTON KEEPS AN APPOINTMENT.

The approach to the offices of Girdlestone and Co. was not a very dignified one, nor would the uninitiated who traversed it form any conception of the commercial prosperity of the firm in question. Close to the corner of a broad and busy street, within a couple of hundred yards of Fenchurch Street Station, a narrow doorway opens into a long whitewashed passage. On one side of this is a brass plate with the inscription "Girdlestone and Co., African Merchants, " and above it a curious hieroglyphic supposed to represent a human hand in the act of pointing. Following the guidance of this somewhat ghostly emblem, the wayfarer finds himself in a small square yard surrounded by doors, upon one of which the name of the firm reappears in large white letters, with the word "Push" printed beneath it. If he follows this laconic invitation he will make his way into a long, low apartment, which is the counting-house of the African traders.

On the afternoon of which we speak things were quiet at the offices. The line of pigeon-holes in the wire curtain was deserted by the public, though the linoleum-covered floor bore abundant traces of a busy morning. Misty London light shone hazily through the glazed windows and cast dark shadows in the corners. On a high perch in the background a weary-faced, elderly man, with muttering lips and tapping fingers, cast up endless lines of figures. Beneath him, in front of two long shining mahogany desks, half a score of young men, with bent heads and stooping shoulders, appeared to be riding furiously, neck and neck, in the race of life. Any *habitue* of a London office might have deduced from their relentless energy and incorruptible diligence that they were under the eyes of some member of the firm.

The member in question was a broad-shouldered, bull-necked young man, who leaned against the marble mantel-piece, turning over the pages of an almanac, and taking from time to time a stealthy peep over the top of it at the toilers around him. Command was imprinted in every line of his strong, square-set face and erect, powerful frame. Above the medium size, with a vast spread of shoulder, a broad aggressive jaw, and bright bold glance, his whole pose and expression spoke of resolution pushed to the verge of obstinacy.

1

There was something classical in the regular olive-tinted features and black, crisp, curling hair fitting tightly to the well-rounded head. Yet, though classical, there was an absence of spirituality. It was rather the profile of one of those Roman emperors, splendid in its animal strength, but lacking those subtle softnesses of eye and mouth which speak of an inner life. The heavy gold chain across the waistcoat and the bright stone which blazed upon the finger were the natural complement of the sensuous lip and curving chin. Such was Ezra, only child of John Girdlestone, and heir to the whole of his vast business. Little wonder that those who had an eye to the future bent over their ledgers and worked with a vigour calculated to attract the attention of the junior partner, and to impress him with a due sense of their enthusiastic regard for the interests of the firm.

It was speedily apparent, however, that the young gentleman's estimate of their services was not entirely based upon their present performance. With his eyes still fixed upon the almanac and a sardonic smile upon his dark face, he uttered a single word—

"Parker! "

A flaxen-haired clerk, perched at the further end of the high glistening desk, gave a violent start, and looked up with a scared face.

"Well, Parker, who won? " asked the junior partner.

"Won, sir! " the youth stammered.

"Yes, who won? " repeated his employer.

"I hardly understand you, sir, " the clerk said, growing very red and confused.

"Oh yes, you do, Parker, " young Girdlestone remarked, tapping his almanac sharply with the paper-knife. "You were playing odd man out with Robson and Perkins when I came in from lunch. As I presume you were at it all the time I was away, I have a natural curiosity to know who won. "

The three unhappy clerks fixed their eyes upon their ledgers to avoid the sarcastic gaze of their employer. He went on in the same quiet tones—

"You gentlemen draw about thirty shillings a week from the firm. I believe I am right in my figures, Mr. Gilray? " addressing the senior clerk seated at the high solitary desk apart from the others. "Yes, I thought so. Now, odd man out is, no doubt, a very harmless and fascinating game, but you can hardly expect us to encourage it so far as to pay so much an hour for the privilege of having it played in our counting-house. I shall therefore recommend my father to deduct five shillings from the sum which each of you will receive upon Saturday. That will cover the time which you have devoted to your own amusements during the week. "

He paused, and the three culprits were beginning to cool down and congratulate themselves, when he began again.

"You will see, Mr. Gilray, that this deduction is made, " he said, "and at the same time I beg that you will deduct ten shillings from your own salary, since, as senior clerk, the responsibility of keeping order in this room in the absence of your employers rests with you, and you appear to have neglected it. I trust you will look to this, Mr. Gilray. "

"Yes, sir, " the senior clerk answered meekly. He was an elderly man with a large family, and the lost ten shillings would make a difference to the Sunday dinner. There was nothing for it but to bow to the inevitable, and his little pinched face assumed an expression of gentle resignation. How to keep his ten young subordinates in order, however, was a problem which vexed him sorely.

The junior partner was silent, and the remaining clerks were working uneasily, not exactly knowing whether they might not presently be included in the indictment. Their fears were terminated, however, by the sharp sound of a table-gong and the appearance of a boy with the announcement that Mr. Girdlestone would like a moment's conversation with Mr. Ezra. The latter gave a keen glance at his subjects and withdrew into the back office, a disappearance which was hailed by ten pens being thrown into the air and deftly caught again, while as many derisive and triumphant young men mocked at the imploring efforts of old Gilray in the interests of law and order.

The sanctum of Mr. John Girdlestone was approached by two doors, one of oak with ground-glass panels, and the other covered with green baize. The room itself was small, but lofty, and the walls were ornamented by numerous sections of ships stuck upon long flat boards, very much as the remains of fossil fish are exhibited in museums, together with maps, charts, photographs, and lists of sailings innumerable. Above the fire-place was a large water-colour painting of the barque *Belinda* as she appeared when on a reef to the north of Cape Palmas. An inscription beneath this work of art announced that it had been painted by the second officer and presented by him to the head of the firm. It was generally rumoured that the merchants had lost heavily over this disaster, and there were some who quoted it as an instance of Girdlestone's habitual strength of mind that he should decorate his wall with so melancholy a souvenir. This view of the matter did not appear to commend itself to a flippant member of Lloyd's agency, who contrived to intimate, by a dexterous use of his left eyelid and right forefinger, that the vessel may not have been so much under-insured, nor the loss to the firm so enormous as was commonly reported.

John Girdlestone, as he sat at his square office-table waiting for his son, was undeniably a remarkable-looking man. For good or for evil no weak character lay beneath that hard angular face, with the strongly marked features and deep-set eyes. He was clean shaven, save for an iron-grey fringe of ragged whisker under each ear, which blended with the grizzled hair above. So self-contained, hard-set, and immutable was his expression that it was impossible to read anything from it except sternness and resolution, qualities which are as likely to be associated with the highest natures as with the most dangerous. It may have been on account of this ambiguity of expression that the world's estimate of the old merchant was a very varying one. He was known to be a fanatic in religion, a purist in morals, and a man of the strictest commercial integrity. Yet there were some few who looked askance at him, and none, save one, who could apply the word "friend" to him.

He rose and stood with his back to the fire-place as his son entered. He was so tall that he towered above the younger man, but the latter's square and compact frame made him, apart from the difference of age, the stronger man.

The young man had dropped the air of sarcasm which he found was most effective with the clerks, and had resumed his natural manner, which was harsh and brusque.

"What's up! " he asked, dropping back into a chair, and jingling the loose coins in his trouser pockets.

"I have had news of the *Black Eagle*, " his father answered. "She is reported from Madeira. "

"Ah! " cried the junior partner eagerly. "What luck? "

"She is full, or nearly so, according to Captain Hamilton Miggs' report. "

"I wonder Miggs was able to send a report at all, and I wonder still more that you should put any faith in it, " his son said impatiently. "The fellow is never sober. "

"Miggs is a good seaman, and popular on the coast. He may indulge at times, but we all have our failings. Here is the list as vouched for by our agent. 'Six hundred barrels of palm oil' —"

"Oil is down to-day, " the other interrupted.

"It will rise before the *Black Eagle* arrives, " the merchant rejoined confidently. "Then he has palm nuts in bulk, gum, ebony, skins, cochineal, and ivory. "

The young man gave a whistle of satisfaction. "Not bad for old Miggs! " he said. "Ivory is at a fancy figure. "

"We are sorely in need of a few good voyages, " Girdlestone remarked, "for things have been very slack of late. There is one very sad piece of intelligence here which takes away the satisfaction which we might otherwise feel. Three of the crew have died of fever. He does not mention the names. "

"The devil! " said Ezra. "We know very well what that means. Three women, each with an armful of brats, besieging the office and clamouring for a pension. Why are seamen such improvident dogs? "

His father held up his white hand deprecatingly. "I wish, " he said, "that you would treat these subjects with more reverence. What could be sadder than that the bread-winner of a family should be cut off? It has grieved me more than I can tell. "

"Then you intend to pension the wives? " Ezra said, with a sly smile.

"By no means, " his father returned with decision. "Girdlestone and Co. are not an insurance office. The labourer is worthy of his hire, but when his work in this world is over, his family must fall back upon what has been saved by his industry and thrift. It would be a dangerous precedent for us to allow pensions to the wives of these sailors, for it would deprive the others of all motive for laying their money by, and would indirectly encourage vice and dissipation. "

Ezra laughed, and continued to rattle his silver and keys.

"It is not upon this matter that I desired to speak to you, " Girdlestone continued. "It has, however, always been my practice to prefer matters of business to private affairs, however pressing. John Harston is said to be dying, and he has sent a message to me saying that he wishes to see me. It is inconvenient for me to leave the office, but I feel that it is my Christian duty to obey such a summons. I wish you, therefore, to look after things until I return. "

"I can hardly believe that the news is true, " Ezra said, in astonishment. "There must be some mistake. Why, I spoke to him on 'Change last Monday. "

"It is very sudden, " his father answered, taking his broad-brimmed hat from a peg. "There is no doubt about the fact, however. The doctor says that there is very little hope that he will survive until evening. It is a case of malignant typhoid. "

"You are very old friends? " Ezra remarked, looking thoughtfully at his father.

"I have known him since we were boys together, " the other replied, with a slight dry cough, which was the highest note of his limited emotional gamut. "Your mother, Ezra, died upon the very day that Harston's wife gave birth to this daughter of his, seventeen years ago. Mrs. Harston only survived a few days. I have heard him say that, perhaps, we should also go together. We are in the hands of a higher Power, however, and it seems that one shall be taken and another left. "

"How will the money go if the doctors are right? " Ezra asked keenly.

"Every penny to the girl. She will be an heiress. There are no other relations that I know of, except the Dimsdales, and they have a fair fortune of their own. But I must go. "

"By the way, malignant typhoid is very catching, is it not? "

"So they say, " the merchant said quietly, and strode off through the counting-house.

Ezra Girdlestone remained behind, stretching his legs In front of the empty grate. "The governor is a hard nail, " he soliloquized, as he stared down at the shining steel bars. "Depend upon it, though, he feels this more than he shows. Why, it's the only friend he ever had in the world—or ever will have, in all probability. However, it's no business of mine, " with which comforting reflection he began to whistle as he turned over the pages of the private day-book of the firm.

It is possible that his son's surmise was right, and that the gaunt, unemotional African merchant felt an unwonted heartache as he hailed a hansom and drove out to his friend's house at Fulham. He and Harston had been charity schoolboys together, had roughed it together, risen together, and prospered together. When John Girdlestone was a raw-boned lad and Harston a chubby-faced urchin, the latter had come to look upon the other as his champion and guide. There are some minds which are parasitic in their nature. Alone they have little vitality, but they love to settle upon some stronger intellect, from which they may borrow their emotions and conclusions at second-hand. A strong, vigorous brain collects around it in time many others, whose mental processes are a feeble imitation of its own. Thus it came to pass that, as the years rolled on, Harston learned to lean more and more upon his old school-fellow, grafting many of his stern peculiarities upon his own simple vacuous nature, until he became a strange parody of the original. To him Girdlestone was the ideal man, Girdlestone's ways the correct ways, and Girdlestone's opinions the weightiest of all opinions. Forty years of this undeviating fidelity must, however he might conceal it, have made an impression upon the feelings of the elder man.

Harston, by incessant attention to business and extreme parsimony, had succeeded in founding an export trading concern. In this he had followed the example of his friend. There was no fear of their interests ever coming into collision, as his operations were confined to the Mediterranean. The firm grew and prospered, until Harston began to be looked upon as a warm man in the City circles. His only child was Kate, a girl of seventeen. There were no other near relatives, save Dr. Dimsdale, a prosperous West-end physician. No wonder that Ezra Girdlestone's active business mind, and perhaps that of his father too, should speculate as to the disposal of the fortune of the dying man.

Girdlestone pushed open the iron gate and strode down the gravel walk which led to his friend's house. A bright autumn sun shining out of a cloudless heaven bathed the green lawn and the many-coloured flower-beds in its golden light. The air, the leaves, the birds, all spoke of life. It was hard to think that death was closing its grip upon him who owned them all. A plump little gentleman in black was just descending the steps.

"Well, doctor, " the merchant asked, "how is your patient? "

"You've not come with the intention of seeing him, have you? " the doctor asked, glancing up with some curiosity at the grey face and overhanging eyebrows of the merchant.

"Yes, I am going up to him now. "

"It is a most virulent case of typhoid. He may die in an hour or he may live until nightfall, but nothing can save him. He will hardly recognize you, I fear, and you can do him no good. It is most infectious, and you are incurring a needless danger. I should strongly recommend you not to go. "

"Why, you've only just come down from him yourself, doctor. "

"Ah, I'm there in the way of duty. "

"So am I, " said the visitor decisively, and passing up the stone steps of the entrance strode into the hall. There was a large sitting-room upon the ground floor, through the open door of which the visitor saw a sight which arrested him for a moment. A young girl was sitting in a recess near the window, with her lithe, supple figure bent forward, and her hands clasped at the back of her head, while her elbows rested upon a small table in front of her. Her superb brown hair fell in a thick wave on either side over her white round arms, and the graceful curve of her beautiful neck might have furnished a sculptor with a study for a mourning Madonna. The doctor had just broken his sad tidings to her, and she was still in the first paroxysm of her grief—a grief too acute, as was evident even to the unsentimental mind of the merchant, to allow of any attempt at consolation. A greyhound appeared to think differently, for he had placed his fore-paws upon his young mistress's lap, and was attempting to thrust his lean muzzle between her arms and to lick her face in token of canine sympathy. The merchant paused irresolutely for a moment, and then ascending the broad staircase he pushed open the door of Harston's room and entered.

The blinds were drawn down and the chamber was very dark. A pungent whiff of disinfectants issued from it, mingled with the dank, heavy smell of disease. The bed was in a far corner. Without seeing him, Girdlestone could hear the fast laboured breathing of the invalid. A trimly dressed nurse who had been sitting by the bedside rose, and, recognizing the visitor, whispered a few words to him and left the room. He pulled the cord of the Venetian blind so as to admit a few rays of daylight. The great chamber looked dreary and bare, as carpet and hangings had been removed to lessen the chance of future infection. John Girdlestone stepped softly across to the bedside and sat down by his dying friend.

The sufferer was lying on his back, apparently unconscious of all around him. His glazed eyes were turned upwards towards the ceiling, and his parched lips were parted, while the breath came in quick, spasmodic gasps. Even the unskilled eye of the merchant could tell that the angel of death was hovering very near him. With an ungainly attempt at tenderness, which had something pathetic in it, he moistened a sponge and passed it over the sick man's feverish brow. The latter turned his restless head round, and a gleam of recognition and gratitude came into his eyes.

"I knew that you would come, " he said.

"Yes. I came the moment that I got your message. "

"I am glad that you are here, " the sufferer continued with a sigh of relief. From the brightened expression upon his pinched face, it seemed as if, even now in the jaws of death, he leaned upon his old schoolfellow and looked to him for assistance. He put a wasted hand above the counterpane and laid it upon Girdlestone's.

"I wish to speak to you, John, " he said. "I am very weak. Can you hear what I say? "

"Yes, I hear you. "

"Give me a spoonful from that bottle. It clears my mind for a time. I have been making my will, John. "

"Yes, " said the merchant, replacing the medicine bottle.

"The lawyer made it this morning. Stoop your head and you will hear me better. I have less than fifty thousand. I should have done better had I retired years ago. "

"I told you so, " the other broke in gruffly.

"You did—you did. But I acted for the best. Forty thousand I leave to my dear daughter Kate. "

A look of interest came over Girdlestone's face. "And the balance? " he asked.

"I leave that to be equally divided among the various London institutions for educating the poor. We were both poor boys ourselves, John, and we know the value of such schools. "

Girdlestone looked perhaps a trifle disappointed. The sick man went on very slowly and painfully—

"My daughter will have forty thousand pounds. But it is so tied up that she can neither touch it herself nor enable any one else to do so until she is of age. She has no friends, John, and no relations, save only my cousin, Dr. George Dimsdale. Never was a girl left more lonely and unprotected. Take her, I beg of you, and bring her up under your own eye. Treat her as though she were your child. Guard her above all from those who would wreck her young life in order to share her fortune. Do this, old friend, and make me happy on my deathbed. "

The merchant made no answer. His heavy eyebrows were drawn down, and his forehead all puckered with thought.

"You are the one man, " continued the sufferer, "whom I know to be just and upright. Give me the water, for my mouth is dry. Should, which God forbid, my dear girl perish before she marries, then—" His breath failed him for a moment, and he paused to recover it.

"Well, what then? "

"Then, old friend, her fortune reverts to you, for there is none who will use it so well. Those are the terms of the will. But you will guard her and care for her, as I would myself. She is a tender plant, John, too weak to grow alone. Promise me that you will do right by her—promise it? "

"I do promise it, " John Girdlestone answered in a deep voice. He was standing up now, and leaning over to catch the words of the dying man.

Harston was sinking rapidly. With a feeble motion he pointed to a brown-backed volume upon the table.

"Take up the book, " he said.

The merchant picked it up.

"Now, repeat after me, I swear and solemnly pledge myself—"

"I swear and solemnly pledge myself—

"To treasure and guard as if she were my own—" came the tremulous voice from the bed.

"To treasure and guard as if she were my own—" in the deep bass of the merchant.

"Kate Harston, the daughter of my deceased friend—"

"Kate Harston, the daughter of my deceased friend—"

"And as I treat her, so may my own flesh and blood treat me! "

"And as I treat her, so may my own flesh and blood treat me! "

The sick man's head fell back exhausted upon his pillow. "Thank God! " he muttered, "now I can die in peace. "

"Turn your mind away from the vanities and dross of this world, " John Girdlestone said sternly, "and fix it upon that which is eternal, and can never die. "

"Are you going? " the invalid asked sadly, for he had taken up his hat and stick.

"Yes, I must go; I have an appointment in the City at six, which I must not miss. "

"And I have an appointment which I must not miss, " the dying man said with a feeble smile.

"I shall send up the nurse as I go down, " Girdlestone said. "Good-bye! "

"Good-bye! God bless you, John! "

The firm, strong hand of the hale man enclosed for a moment the feeble, burning one of the sufferer. Then John Girdlestone plodded heavily down the stair, and these friends of forty years' standing had said their last adieu.

The African merchant kept his appointment in the City, but long before he reached it John Harston had gone also to keep that last terrible appointment of which the messenger is death.

CHAPTER II.

CHARITY A LA MODE.

It was a dull October morning in Fenchurch Street, some weeks after the events with which our story opened. The murky City air looked murkier still through the glazed office windows. Girdlestone, grim and grey, as though he were the very embodiment of the weather, stooped over his mahogany table. He had a long list in front of him, on which he was checking off, as a prelude to the day's work, the position in the market of the various speculations in which the capital of the firm was embarked. His son Ezra lounged in an easy chair opposite him, looking dishevelled and dark under the eyes, for he had been up half the night, and the Nemesis of reaction was upon him.

"Faugh! " his father ejaculated, glancing round at him with disgust. "You have been drinking already this morning. "

"I took a brandy and seltzer on the way to the office, " he answered carelessly. "I needed one to steady me. "

"A young fellow of your age should not want steadying. You have a strong constitution, but you must not play tricks with it. You must have been very late last night. It was nearly one before I went to bed. "

"I was playing cards with Major Clutterbuck and one or two others. We kept it up rather late. "

"With Major Clutterbuck? "

"Yes. "

"I don't care about your consorting so much with that man. He drinks and gambles, and does you no good. What good has he ever done himself? Take care that he does not fleece you. " The merchant felt instinctively, as he glanced at the shrewd, dark face of his son, that the warning was a superfluous one.

"No fear, father, " Ezra answered sulkily; "I am old enough to choose my own friends. "

"Why such a friend as that? "

"I like to know men of that class. You are a successful man, father, but you—well, you can't be much help to me socially. You need some one to show you the ropes, and the major is my man. When I can stand alone, I'll soon let him know it. "

"Well, go your own way, " said Girdlestone shortly. Hard to all the world, he was soft only in this one direction. From childhood every discussion between father and son had ended with the same words.

"It is business time, " he resumed. "Let us confine ourselves to business. I see that Illinois were at 112 yesterday. "

"They are at 113 this morning. "

"What! have you been on 'Change already? "

"Yes, I dropped in there on my way to the office. I would hold on to those. They will go up for some days yet. "

The senior partner made a pencil note on the margin of the list.

"We'll hold on to the cotton we have, " he said.

"No, sell out at once, " Ezra answered with decision, "I saw young Featherstone, of Liverpool, last night, or rather this morning. It was hard to make head or tail of what the fool said, but he let fall enough to show that there was likely to be a drop. "

Girdlestone made another mark upon the paper. He never questioned his son's decisions now, for long experience had shown him that they were never formed without solid grounds. "Take this list, Ezra, " he said, handing him the paper, "and run your eye over it. If you see anything that wants changing, mark it. "

"I'll do it in the counting-house, " his son answered. "I can keep my eye on those lazy scamps of clerks. Gilray has no idea of keeping them in order. "

As he went out he cannoned against an elderly gentleman in a white waistcoat, who was being shown in, and who ricochetted off him

14

into the office, where he shook hands heartily with the elder Girdlestone. It was evident from the laboured cordiality of the latter's greeting that the new-comer was a man of some importance. He was, indeed, none other than the well-known philanthropist, Mr. Jefferson Edwards, M.P. for Middlehurst, whose name upon a bill was hardly second to that of Rothschild.

"How do, Girdlestone, how do? " he exclaimed, mopping his face with his handkerchief. He was a fussy little man, with a brusque, nervous manner. "Hard at it as usual, eh? Always pegging away. Wonderful man. Ha, ha! Wonderful! "

"You look warm, " the merchant answered, rubbing his hands. "Let me offer you some claret. I have some in the cupboard. "

"No, thank you, " the visitor answered, staring across at the head of the firm as though he were some botanical curiosity. "Extraordinary fellow. 'Iron' Girdlestone, they call you in the City. A good name, too— ha! ha! —an excellent name. Iron-grey, you know, and hard to look at, but soft here, my dear sir, soft here. " The little man tapped him with his walking-stick over the cardiac region and laughed boisterously, while his grim companion smiled slightly and bowed to the compliment.

"I've come here begging, " said Mr. Jefferson Edwards, producing a portentous-looking roll of paper from an inner pocket. "Know I've come to the right place for charity. The Aboriginal Evolution Society, my dear boy. All it wants are a few hundreds to float it off. Noble aim, Girdlestone—glorious object. "

"What *is* the object? " the merchant asked.

"Well, the evolution of the aborigines, " Edwards answered in some confusion. "Sort of practical Darwinism. Evolve 'em into higher types, and turn 'em all white in time. Professor Wilder gave us a lecture about it. I'll send you round a *Times* with the account. Spoke about their thumbs. They can't cross them over their palms, and they have rudimentary tails, or had until they were educated off them. They wore all the hair off their backs by leaning against trees. Marvellous things! All they want is a little money. "

"It seems to be a praiseworthy object, " the merchant said gravely.

"I knew that you would think so! " cried the little philanthropist enthusiastically. "Of course, bartering as you do with aboriginal races, their development and evolution is a matter of the deepest importance to you. If a man came down to barter with you who had a rudimentary tail and couldn't bend his thumb—well, it wouldn't be pleasant, you know. Our idea is to elevate them in the scale of humanity and to refine their tastes. Hewett, of the Royal Society, went to report on the matter a year or so back, and some rather painful incident occurred. I believe Hewett met with some mishap— in fact, they go the length of saying that he was eaten. So you see we've had our martyrs, my dear friend, and the least that we can do who stay at home at ease is to support a good cause to the best of our ability. "

"Whose names have you got? " asked the merchant.

"Let's see, " Jefferson Edwards said, unfolding his list. "Spriggs, ten; Morton, ten; Wigglesworth, five; Hawkins, ten; Indermann, fifteen; Jones, five; and a good many smaller amounts. "

"What is the highest as yet? "

"Indermann, the tobacco importer, has given fifteen. "

"It is a good cause, " Mr. Girdlestone said, dipping his pen into the ink-bottle. "'He that giveth'—you know what the good old Book says. Of course a list of the donations will be printed and circulated? "

"Most certainly. "

"Here is my cheque for twenty-five pounds. I am proud to have had this opportunity of contributing towards the regeneration of those poor souls whom Providence has placed in a lower sphere than myself. "

"Girdlestone, " said the member of Parliament with emotion, as he pocketed the cheque, "you are a good man. I shall not forget this, my friend; I shall never forget it. "

"Wealth has its duties, and charity is among them, " Girdlestone answered with unction, shaking the philanthropist's extended hand. "Good-bye, my dear sir. Pray let me know if our efforts are attended with any success. Should more money be needed, you know one who may be relied on. "

There was a sardonic smile upon the hard face of the senior partner as he closed the door behind his visitor. "It's a legitimate investment, " he muttered to himself as he resumed his seat. "What with his Parliamentary interest and his financial power, it's a very legitimate investment. It looks well on the list, too, and inspires confidence. I think the money is well spent. "

Ezra had bowed politely as the great man passed through the office, and Gilray, the wizened senior clerk, opened the outer door. Jefferson Edwards turned as he passed him and clapped him on the shoulder.

"Lucky fellow, " he said in his jerky way. "Good employer—model to follow—great man. Watch him, mark him, imitate him—that's the way to get on. Can't go wrong, " and he trotted down the street in search of fresh contributions towards his latest fad.

CHAPTER III.

THOMAS GILRAY MAKES AN INVESTMENT.

The shambling little clerk was still standing at the door watching the retreating figure of the millionaire, and mentally splicing together his fragmentary remarks into a symmetrical piece of advice which might be carried home and digested at leisure, when his attention was attracted to a pale-faced woman, with a child in her arms, who was hanging about the entrance. She looked up at the clerk in a wistful way, as if anxious to address him and yet afraid to do so. Then noting, perhaps, some gleam of kindness in his yellow wrinkled face, she came across to him.

"D'ye think I could see Muster Girdlestone, sir, " she asked, with a curtsey; "or, maybe, you're Mr. Girdlestone yourself? " The woman was wretchedly dressed, and her eyelids were swollen and red as from long crying.

"Mr. Girdlestone is in his room, " said the head clerk kindly. "I have no doubt that he will see you if you will wait for a moment. " Had he been speaking to the grandest of the be-silked and be-feathered dames who occasionally frequented the office; he could not have spoken with greater courtesy. Verily in these days the spirit of true chivalry has filtered down from the surface and has found a lodgment in strange places.

The merchant looked with a surprised and suspicious eye at his visitor when she was ushered in. "Take a seat, my good woman, " he said. "What can I do for you? "

"Please, Mr. Girdlestone, I'm Mrs. Hudson, " she answered, seating herself in a timid way upon the extreme edge of a chair. She was weary and footsore, for she had carried the baby up from Stepney that morning.

"Hudson—Hudson—can't remember the name, " said Girdlestone, shaking his head reflectively.

"Jim Hudson as was, sir, he was my husband, the bo'sun for many a year o' your ship the *Black Eagle*. He went out to try and earn a bit for me and the child, sir, but he's dead o' fever, poor dear, and lying in

Bonny river, wi' a cannon ball at his feet, as the carpenter himself told me who sewed him up, and I wish I was dead and with him, so I do. " She began sobbing in her shawl and moaning, while the child, suddenly awakened by the sound, rubbed its eyes with its wrinkled mottled hands, and then proceeded to take stock of Mr. Girdlestone and his office with the critical philosophy of infancy.

"Calm yourself, my good woman, calm yourself, " said the senior partner. He perceived that the evil prophesied by his son had come upon him, and he made a mental note of this fresh instance of Ezra's powers of foresight.

"It was hard, so it was, " said Mrs. Hudson, drying her eyes, but still giving vent to an occasional tempestuous sob. "I heard as the *Black Eagle* was comin' up the river, so I spent all I had in my pocket in makin' Jim a nice little supper—ham an' eggs, which was always his favourite, an' a pint o' bitter, an' a quartern o' whiskey that he could take hot after, bein' naturally o' a cold turn, and him comin' from a warm country, too. Then out I goes, and down the river, until I sees the *Black Eagle* a-comin' up wi' a tug in front of her. Well I knowed the two streaks o' white paint, let alone the screechin' o' the parrots which I could hear from the bank. I could see the heads o' some of the men peepin' over the side, so I waves my handkercher, and one o' them he waves back. 'Trust Jim for knowin' his little wife, ' says I, proud like to myself, and I runs round to where I knew as they'd dock her. What with me being that excited that I couldn't rightly see where I was going, and what with the crowd, for the men was comin' from work, I didn't get there till the ship was alongside. Then I jumps aboard, and the first man I seed was Sandy McPherson, who I knowed when we lived in Binnacle Lane. 'Where's Jim? ' I cried, running forward, eager like, to the forecastle, but he caught me by the arm as I passed him. 'Steady, lass, steady! ' Then I looked up at him, and his face was very grave, and my knees got kind o' weak. 'Where's Jim? ' says I. 'Don't ask, ' says he. 'Where is he, Sandy? ' I screeches; and then, 'Don't say the word, Sandy, don't you say it. ' But, Lor' bless ye, sir, it didn't much matter what he said nor what he didn't, for I knowed all, an' down I flops on the deck in a dead faint. The mate, he took me home in a cab, and when I come to there was the supper lying, sir, and the beer, and the things a-shinin', and all so cosy, an' the child askin' where her father was, for I told her he'd bring her some things from Africa. Then, to think of him a-lyin' dead in Bonny river, why, sir, it nigh broke my heart. "

"A sore affliction, " the merchant said, shaking his grizzled head. "A sad visitation. But these things are sent to try us, Mrs. Hudson. They are warnings to us not to fix our thoughts too much upon the dross of this world, but to have higher aims and more durable aspirations. We are poor short-sighted creatures, the best of us, and often mistake evil for good. What seems so sad to-day may, if taken in a proper spirit, be looked back upon as a starting-point from which all the good of your life has come. "

"Bless you, sir! " said the widow, still furtively rubbing her eyes with the corner of her little shawl. "You're a real kind gentleman. It does me good to hear you talk. "

"We have all our burdens and misfortunes, " continued the senior partner. "Some have more, some have less. To-day is your turn, to-morrow it may be mine. But let us struggle on to the great goal, and the weight of our burden need never cause us to sink by the wayside. And now I must wish you a very good morning, Mrs. Hudson. Believe me, you have my hearty sympathy. "

The woman rose and then stood irresolute for a moment, as though there was something which she still wished to mention.

"When will I be able to draw Jim's back pay, sir? " she asked nervously. "I have pawned nigh everything in the house, and the child and me is weak from want of food. "

"Your husband's back pay, " the merchant said, taking down a ledger from the shelf and turning rapidly over the leaves. "I think that you are under a delusion, Mrs. Hudson. Let me see—Dawson, Duffield, Everard, Francis, Gregory, Gunter, Hardy. Ah, here it is— Hudson, boatswain of the *Black Eagle*. The wages which he received amounted, I see, to five pounds a month. The voyage lasted eight months, but the ship had only been out two months and a half when your husband died. "

"That's true, sir, " the widow said, with an anxious look at the long line of figures in the ledger.

"Of course, the contract ended at his death, so the firm owed him twelve pounds ten at that date. But I perceive from my books that you have been drawing half-pay during the whole eight months. You have accordingly had twenty pounds from the firm, and are therefore in its debt to the amount of seven pounds ten shillings. We'll say nothing of that at present, " the senior partner concluded with a magnificent air. "When you are a little better off you can make good the balance, but really you can hardly expect us to assist you any further at present. "

"But, sir, we have nothing, " Mrs. Hudson sobbed.

"It is deplorable, most deplorable. But we are not the people to apply to. Your own good sense will tell you that, now that I have explained it to you. Good morning. I wish you good fortune, and hope you will let us know from time to time how you go on. We always take a keen interest in the families of those who serve us. " Mr. Girdlestone opened the door, and the heart-sick little woman staggered away across the office, still bearing her heavy child.

When she got into the open air she stared around her like one dazed. The senior clerk looked anxiously at her as he stood at the open door. Then he glanced back into the office. Ezra Girdlestone was deep in some accounts, and his brother clerks were all absorbed in their work. He stole up to the woman, with an apologetic smile, slipped something into her hand, and then hurried back into the office with an austere look upon his face, as if his whole mind were absorbed in the affairs of the firm. There are speculations above the ken of business men. Perhaps, Thomas Gilray, that ill-spared half-crown of yours may bring in better interest than the five-and-twenty pounds of your employer.

CHAPTER IV.

CAPTAIN HAMILTON MIGGS OF THE "BLACK EAGLE. "

The head of the firm had hardly recovered his mental serenity after the painful duty of explaining her financial position to the Widow Hudson, when his quick ear caught the sound of a heavy footstep in the counting-house. A gruff voice was audible at the same time, which demanded in rather more energetic language than was usually employed in that orderly establishment, whether the principal was to be seen or not. The answer was evidently in the affirmative, for the lumbering tread came rapidly nearer, and a powerful double knock announced that the visitor was at the other side of the door.

"Come in, " cried Mr. Girdlestone, laying down his pen.

This invitation was so far complied with that the handle turned, and the door revolved slowly upon its hinges. Nothing more substantial than a strong smell of spirituous liquors, however, entered the apartment.

"Come in, " the merchant repeated impatiently.

At this second mandate a great tangled mass of black hair was slowly protruded round the angle of the door. Then a copper-coloured forehead appeared, with a couple of very shaggy eyebrows and eventually a pair of eyes, which protruded from their sockets and looked yellow and unhealthy. These took a long look, first at the senior partner and then at his surroundings, after which, as if reassured by the inspection, the remainder of the face appeared—a flat nose, a large mouth with a lower lip which hung down and exposed a line of tobacco-stained teeth, and finally a thick black beard which bristled straight out from the chin, and bore abundant traces of an egg having formed part of its owner's morning meal. The head having appeared, the body soon followed it, though all in the same anaconda-like style of progression, until the individual stood revealed. He was a stoutly-built sea-faring man, dressed in a pea jacket and blue trousers and holding his tarpaulin hat in his hand. With a rough scrape and a most unpleasant leer he advanced towards the merchant, a tattoed and hairy hand outstretched in sign of greeting.

"Why, captain, " said the head of the firm, rising and grasping the other's hand with effusion, "I am glad to see you back safe and well. "

"Glad to see ye, sir—glad to see ye. "

His voice was thick and husky, and there was an indecision about his gait as though he had been drinking heavily. "I came in sort o' cautious, " he continued, "'cause I didn't know who might be about. When you and me speaks together we likes to speak alone, you bet. "

The merchant raised his bushy eyebrows a little, as though he did not relish the idea of mutual confidences suggested by his companion's remark. "Hadn't you better take a seat? " he said.

The other took a cane-bottomed chair and carried it into the extreme corner of the office. Then having looked steadily at the wall behind him, and rapped it with his knuckles, he sat down, still throwing an occasional apprehensive glance over his shoulder. "I've got a touch of the jumps, " he remarked apologetically to his employer. "I likes to *know* as there ain't no one behind me. "

"You should give up this shocking habit of drinking, " Mr. Girdlestone said seriously. "It is a waste of the best gifts with which Providence has endowed us. You are the worse for it both in this world and in the next. "

Captain Hamilton Miggs did not seem to be at all impressed by this very sensible piece of advice. On the contrary, he chuckled boisterously to himself, and, slapping his thigh, expressed his opinion that his employer was a "rum 'un"—a conviction which he repeated to himself several times with various symptoms of admiration.

"Well, well, " Girdlestone said, after a short pause, "boys will be boys, and sailors, I suppose, will be sailors. After eight months of anxiety and toil, ending in success, captain—I am proud to be able to say the words—some little licence must be allowed. I do not judge others by the same hard and fast lines by which I regulate my own conduct. "

This admirable sentiment also failed to elicit any response from the obdurate Miggs, except the same manifestations of mirth and the same audible aside as to the peculiarities of his master's character.

"I must congratulate you on your cargo, and wish you the same luck for your next voyage, " the merchant continued.

"Ivory, an' gold dust, an' skins, an' resin, an' cochineal, an' gums, an' ebony, an' rice, an' tobacco, an' fruits, an' nuts in bulk. If there's a better cargo about, I'd like to see it, " the sailor said defiantly.

"An excellent cargo, captain; very good indeed. Three of your men died, I believe? "

"Ay, three of the lubbers went under. Two o' fever and one o' snake-bite. It licks me what sailors are comin' to in these days. When I was afore the mast we'd ha' been ashamed to die o' a trifle like that. Look at me. I've been down wi' coast fever sixteen times, and I've had yellow jack an' dysentery, an' I've been bit by the black cobra in the Andamans. I've had cholera, too. It broke out in a brig when I was in the Sandwich Island trade, and I was shipmates wi' seven dead out o' a crew o' ten. But I ain't none the worse for it—no, nor never will be. But I say, gov'nor, hain't you got a drop of something about the office? "

The senior partner rose, and taking a bottle from the cupboard filled out a stiff glass of rum. The sailor drank it off eagerly, and laid down the empty tumbler with a sigh of satisfaction.

"Say, now, " he said, with an unpleasant confidential leer, "weren't you surprised to see us come back—eh? Straight now, between man and man? "

"The old ship hangs together well, and has lots of work in her yet, " the merchant answered.

"Lots of work! God's truth, I thought she was gone in the bay! We'd a dirty night with a gale from the west-sou'-west, an' had been goin' by dead reckonin' for three days, so we weren't over and above sure o' ourselves. She wasn't much of a sea-going craft when we left England, but the sun had fried all the pitch out o' her seams, and you might ha' put your finger through some of them. Two days an' a night we were at the pumps, for she leaked like a sieve. We lost the fore topsail, blown clean out o' the ringbolts. I never thought to see Lunnon again. "

"If she could weather a gale like that she could make another voyage. "

"She could start on another, " the sailor said gloomily, "but as like as not she'd never see the end o't. "

"Come, come, you're not quite yourself this morning, Miggs. We value you as a dashing, fearless fellow—let me fill your glass again—who doesn't fear a little risk where there's something to be gained. You'll lose your good name if you go on like that. "

"She's in a terrible bad way, " the captain insisted. "You'll have to do something before she can go. "

"What shall we have to do? "

"Dry dock her and give her a thorough overhaul. She might sink before she got out o' the Channel if she went as she is just now. "

"Very well, " the merchant said coldly. "If you insist on it, it must be done. But, of course, it would make a great difference in your salary. "

"Eh? "

"You are at present getting fifteen pounds a month, and five per cent. commission. These are exceptional terms in consideration of any risk that you may run. We shall dry dock the *Black Eagle*, and your salary is now ten pounds a month and two and a half commission. "

"Belay, there, belay! " the sailor shouted. His coppery face was a shade darker than usual, and his bilious eyes had a venomous gleam in them. "Don't you beat me down, curse you! " he hissed, advancing to the table and leaning his hands upon it while he pushed his angry face forward until it was within a foot of that of the merchant. "Don't you try that game on, mate, for I am a free-born British seaman, and I am under the thumb of no man. "

"You're drunk, " said the senior partner. "Sit down! "

"You'd reduce my screw, would ye? " roared Captain Hamilton Miggs, working himself into a fury. "Me that has worked for ye, and slaved for ye, and risked my life for ye. You try it on, guv'nor; just you try it on! Suppose I let out that little story o' the painting out o' the marks—where would the firm of Girdlestone be then! I guess you'd rather double my wage than have that yarn goin' about. "

"What do you mean? "

"What do I mean? You don't know what I mean, do you? Of course not. It wasn't you as set us on to go at night and paint out the Government Plimsoll marks and then paint 'em in again higher up, so as to be able to overload. That wasn't you, was it? "

"Do you mean to assert that it was? "

"In course I do, " thundered the angry seaman.

The senior partner struck the gong which stood upon the table. "Gilray, " he said quietly, "go out and bring in a policeman. "

Captain Hamilton Miggs seemed to be somewhat startled by this sudden move of his antagonist. "Steady your helm, governor, " he said. "What are ye up to now? "

"I'm going to give you in charge. "

"What for? "

"For intimidation and using threatening language, and endeavouring to extort money under false pretences. "

"There's no witnesses, " the sailor said in a half-cringing, half-defiant manner.

"Oh yes, there are, " Ezra Girdlestone remarked, coming into the room. He had been standing between the two doors which led to the counting-house, and had overheard the latter portion of the conversation. "Don't let me interrupt you. You were saying that you would blacken my father's character unless he increased your salary. "

"I didn't mean no harm, " said Captain Hamilton Miggs, glancing nervously from the one to the other. He had been fairly well known to the law in his younger days, and had no desire to renew the acquaintance.

"Who painted out those Plimsoll marks? " asked the merchant.

"It was me. "

"Did any one suggest it to you? "

"No. "

"Shall I send in the policeman, sir? " asked Gilray, opening the door.

"Ask him to wait for a moment, " Girdlestone answered.

"And now, captain, to return to the original point, shall we dry dock the *Black Eagle* and reduce the salary, or do you see your way to going back in her on the same terms? "

"I'll go back and be damned to it! " said the captain recklessly, plunging his hands into the pockets of his pea jacket and plumping back into his chair.

"That's right, " his grim employer remarked approvingly.

"But swearing is a most sinful practice. Send the policeman away, Ezra. "

The young man went out with an amused smile, and the two were left together again.

"You'll not be able to pass the Government inspector unless you do something to her, " the seaman said after a long pause, during which he brooded over his wrongs.

"Of course we shall do something. The firm is not mean, though it avoids unnecessary expense. We'll put a coat of paint on her, and some pitch, and do up the rigging. She's a stout old craft, and with one of the smartest sailors afloat in command of her—for we always give you credit for being that—she'll run many a voyage yet. "

"I'm paid for the risk, guv'nor, as you said just now, " the sailor remarked. "But don't it seem kind o' hard on them as isn't—on the mates an' the hands? "

27

"There is always a risk, my dear captain. There is nothing in the world without risk. You remember what is said about those who go down to the sea in ships. They see the wonders of the deep, and in return they incur some little danger. My house in Eccleston Square might be shaken down by an earthquake, or a gale might blow in the walls, but I'm not always brooding over the chance of it. There's no use your taking it for granted that some misfortune will happen to the *Black Eagle*. "

The sailor was silenced, but not convinced by his employer's logic. "Well, well, " he said sulkily, "I am going, so there's an end of it, and there's no good in having any more palaver about it. You have your object in running rotten ships, and you make it worth my while to take my chances in them. I'm suited, and you're suited, so there's no more to be said. "

"That's right. Have some more rum? "

"No, not a spot. "

"Why not? "

"Because I likes to keep my head pretty clear when I'm a-talkin' to you, Muster Girdlestone. Out o' your office I'll drink to further orders, but I won't do business and muddle myself at the same time. When d'ye want me to start? "

"When she's unloaded and loaded up again. Three weeks or a month yet. I expect that Spender will have come in with the *Maid of Athens* by that time. "

"Unless some accident happens on the way, " said Captain Hamilton Miggs, with his old leer. "He was at Sierra Leone when we came up the coast. I couldn't put in there, for the swabs have got a warrant out ag'in me for putting a charge o' shot into a nigger. "

"That was a wicked action—very wrong, indeed, " the merchant said gravely. "You must consider the interests of the firm, Miggs. We can't afford to have a good port blocked against our ships in this fashion. Did they serve this writ on you? "

"Another nigger brought it aboard. "

28

"Did you read it? "

"No; I threw it overboard. "

"And what became of the negro? "

"Well, " said Miggs with a grin, "when I threw the writ overboard he happened to be a-holdin' on to it. So, ye see, he went over, too. Then I up anchor and scooted. "

"There are sharks about there? "

"A few. "

"Really, Miggs, " the merchant said, "you must restrain your sinful passions. You have broken the fifth commandment, and closed the trade of Freetown to the *Black Eagle*. "

"It never was worth a rap, " the sailor answered. "I wouldn't give a cuss for any of the British settlements. Give me real niggers, chaps as knows nothing of law or civilizing, or any rot of the sort. I can pull along with them.

"I have often wondered how you managed it, " Girdlestone said curiously. "You succeed in picking up a cargo where the steadiest and best men can't get as much as a bag of nuts. How do you work it? "

"There's many would like to know that, " Miggs answered, with an expressive wink.

"It is a secret, then? "

"Well, it ain't a secret to you, 'cause you ain't a skipper, and it don't matter if you knows it or not. I don't want to have 'em all at the same game. "

"How is it, then? "

"I'll tell ye, " said Miggs. He seemed to have recovered his serenity by this time, and his eyes twinkled as he spoke of his own exploits. "I gets drunk with them. That's how I does it. "

"Oh, indeed. "

"Yes, that's how it's worked. Lord love ye, when these fust-class certificated, second-cousin-to-an-earl merchant skippers comes out they move about among the chiefs and talks down to them as if they was tin Methuselahs on wheels. The Almighty's great coat wouldn't make a waistcoat for some o' these blokes. Now when I gets among 'em I has 'em all into the cabin, though they're black an' naked, an' the smell ain't over an' above pleasant. Then I out with the rum and it's 'help yourself an' pass the bottle. ' Pretty soon, d'ye see, their tongues get loosened, and as I lie low an' keep dark I gets a pretty good idea o' what's in the market. Then when I knows what's to be got, it's queer if I don't manage to get it. Besides, they like a little notice, just as Christians does, and they remembers me because I treat them well. "

"An excellent plan, Miggs—a capital plan! " said the senior partner. "You are an invaluable servant. "

"Well, " the captain said, rising from his chair, "I'm getting a great deal too dry with all this palaver. I don't mind gettin' drunk with nigger chiefs, but I'm darned if I'll—" He paused, but the grim smile on his companion's face showed that he appreciated the compliment.

"I say, " he continued, giving his employer a confidential nudge with his elbow, "suppose we'd gone down in the bay this last time, you'd ha' been a bit out in your reckoning—eh, what? "

"Why so? "

"Well, we were over-insured on our outward passage. An accident then might ha' put thousands in your pocket, I know. Coming back, though, the cargo was worth more than the insurance, I reckon. You'd ha' been out o' pocket if we'd foundered. It would ha' been a case o' the engineer hoisted on his own Peter, as Shakspere says. "

"We take our chance of these things, " the merchant said with dignity.

"Well, good morning, guv'nor, " Captain Hamilton Miggs said brusquely. "When you wants me you can lay your hands on me at the old crib, the *Cock and Cowslip*, Rotherhithe. "

As he passed out through the office, Ezra rejoined his father.

"He's a curious chap, " he remarked, jerking his head in the direction which Miggs had taken. "I heard him bellowing like a bull, so I thought I had best listen to what he had to say. He's a useful servant, though. "

"The fellow's half a savage himself, " his father said. "He's in his element among them. That's why he gets on so well with them. "

"He doesn't seem much the worse for the climate, either. "

"His body does not, but his soul, Ezra, his soul? However, to return to business. I wish you to see the underwriters and pay the premium of the *Black Eagle*. If you see your way to it, increase the policy; but do it carefully, Ezra, and with tact. She will start about the time of the equinoctial gales. If anything *should* happen to her, it would be as well that the firm should have a margin on the right side. "

CHAPTER V.

MODERN ATHENIANS.

Edinburgh University may call herself with grim jocoseness the "alma mater" of her students, but if she be a mother at all she is one of a very heroic and Spartan cast, who conceals her maternal affection with remarkable success. The only signs of interest which she ever designs to evince towards her alumni are upon those not infrequent occasions when guineas are to be demanded from them. Then one is surprised to find how carefully the old hen has counted her chickens, and how promptly the demand is conveyed to each one of the thousands throughout the empire who, in spite of neglect, cherish a sneaking kindness for their old college. There is symbolism in the very look of her, square and massive, grim and grey, with never a pillar or carving to break the dead monotony of the great stone walls. She is learned, she is practical, and she is useful. There is little sentiment or romance in her composition, however, and in this she does but conform to the instincts of the nation of which she is the youngest but the most flourishing teacher.

A lad coming up to an English University finds himself In an enlarged and enlightened public school. If he has passed through Harrow and Eton there is no very abrupt transition between the life which he has led in the sixth form and that which he finds awaiting him on the banks of the Cam and the Isis. Certain rooms are found for him which have been inhabited by generations of students in the past, and will be by as many in the future. His religion is cared for, and he is expected to put in an appearance at hall and at chapel. He must be within bounds at a fixed time. If he behave indecorously he is liable to be pounced upon and reported by special officials, and a code of punishments is hung perpetually over his head. In return for all this his University takes a keen interest in him. She pats him on the back if he succeeds. Prizes and scholarships, and fine fat fellowships are thrown plentifully in his way if he will gird up his loins and aspire to them.

There is nothing of this in a Scotch University. The young aspirant pays his pound, and finds himself a student. After that he may do absolutely what he will. There are certain classes going on at certain hours, which he may attend if he choose. If not, he may stay away without the slightest remonstrance from the college. As to religion, he may worship the sun, or have a private fetish of his own upon the mantelpiece of his lodgings for all that the University cares. He may live where he likes, he may keep what hours he chooses, and he is at liberty to break every commandment in the decalogue as long as he behaves himself with some approach to decency within the academical precincts. In every way he is absolutely his own master. Examinations are periodically held, at which he may appear or not, as he chooses. The University is a great unsympathetic machine, taking in a stream of raw-boned cartilaginous youths at one end, and turning them out at the other as learned divines, astute lawyers, and skilful medical men. Of every thousand of the raw material about six hundred emerge at the other side. The remainder are broken in the process.

The merits and faults of this Scotch system are alike evident. Left entirely to his own devices in a far from moral city, many a lad falls at the very starting-point of his life's race, never to rise again. Many become idlers or take to drink, while others, after wasting time and money which they could ill afford, leave the college with nothing learned save vice. On the other hand, those whose manliness and good sense keep them straight have gone through a training which lasts them for life. They have been tried, and have not been found wanting. They have learned self-reliance, confidence, and, in a word, have become men of the world while their *confreres* in England are still magnified schoolboys.

High up in a third flat in Howe Street one, Thomas Dimsdale, was going through his period of probation in a little bedroom and a large sitting-room, which latter, "more studentium, " served the purpose of dining-room, parlour, and study. A dingy sideboard, with four still more dingy chairs and an archaeological sofa, made up the whole of the furniture, with the exception of a circular mahogany centre-table, littered with note-books and papers. Above the mantelpiece was a fly-blown mirror with innumerable cards and notices projecting in a fringe all around, and a pair of pipe racks flanking it on either side. Along the centre of the side-board, arranged with suspicious neatness, as though seldom disturbed, stood a line of solemn books, Holden's *Osteology*, Quain's *Anatomy*, Kirkes' *Physiology*, and Huxley's *Invertebrata*, together with a disarticulated human skull. On one side of the fireplace two thigh bones were stacked; on the other a pair of foils, two basket-hilted single-sticks, and a set of boxing-gloves. On a shelf in a convenient niche was a small stock of general literature, which appeared to have been considerably more thumbed than the works upon medicine. Thackeray's *Esmond* and Meredith's *Richard Feveret* rubbed covers with Irving's *Conquest of Granada* and a tattered line of paper-covered novels. Over the sideboard was a framed photograph of the Edinburgh University Football Fifteen, and opposite it a smaller one of Dimsdale himself, clad in the scantiest of garb, as he appeared after winning the half-mile at the Inter-University Handicap. A large silver goblet, the trophy of that occasion, stood underneath upon a bracket. Such was the student's chamber upon the morning in question, save that in a roomy arm-chair in the corner the young gentleman himself was languidly reclining, with a short wooden pipe in his mouth, and his feet perched up upon the side of the table.

Grey-eyed, yellow-haired, broad in the chest and narrow in the loins, with the strength of a bullock and the graceful activity of a stag, it would be hard to find a finer specimen of young British manhood. The long, fine curves of the limbs, and the easy pose of the round, strong head upon the thick, muscular neck, might have served as a model to an Athenian sculptor. There was nothing in the face, however, to recall the regular beauty of the East. It was Anglo-Saxon to the last feature, with its honest breadth between the eyes and its nascent moustache, a shade lighter in colour than the sun-burned skin. Shy, and yet strong; plain, and yet pleasing; it was the face of a type of man who has little to say for himself in this world, and says that little badly, but who has done more than all the talkers and the writers to ring this planet round with a crimson girdle of British possessions.

"Wonder whether Jack Garraway is ready! " he murmured, throwing down the *Scotsman*, and staring up at the roof. "It's nearly eleven o'clock. "

He rose with a yawn, picked up the poker, stood upon the chair, and banged three times upon the ceiling. Three muffled taps responded from the room above. Dimsdale stepped down and began slowly to discard his coat and his waistcoat. As he did so there was a quick, active step upon the stair, and a lean, wiry-looking, middle-sized young fellow stepped into the room. With a nod of greeting he pushed the table over to one side, threw off his two upper garments, and pulled on a pair of the boxing-gloves from the corner. Dimsdale had already done the same, and was standing, a model of manly grace and strength, in the centre of the room.

"Practice your lead, Jack. About here. " He tapped the centre of his forehead with his swollen gauntlet.

His companion poised himself for a moment, and then, lashing out with his left hand, came home with a heavy thud on the place indicated. Dimsdale smiled gently and shook his head.

"It won't do, " he said.

"I hit my hardest, " the other answered apologetically.

"It won't do. Try again. "

The visitor repeated the blow with all the force that he could command.

Dimsdale shook his head again despondently. "You don't seem to catch it, " he said. "It's like this. " He leaned forward, there was the sound of a sharp clip, and the novice shot across the room with a force that nearly sent his skull through the panel of the door.

"That's it, " said Dimsdale mildly.

"Oh, it is, is it? " the other responded, rubbing his head. "It's deucedly interesting, but I think I would understand it better if I saw you do it to some one else. It is something between the explosion of a powder magazine and a natural convulsion. "

His instructor smiled grimly. "That's the only way to learn, " he said. "Now we shall have three minutes of give-and-take, and so ends the morning lesson. "

While this little scene was being enacted in the lodgings of the student, a very stout little elderly man was walking slowly down Howe Street, glancing up at the numbers upon the doors. He was square and deep and broad, like a bottle of Geneva, with a large ruddy face and a pair of bright black eyes, which were shrewd and critical, and yet had a merry twinkle of eternal boyishness in their depths. Bushy side whiskers, shot with grey, flanked his rubicund visage, and he threw out his feet as he walked with the air of a man who is on good terms with himself and with every one around him.

At No. 13 he stopped and rapped loudly upon the door with the head of his metal-headed stick. "Mrs. McTavish? " he asked, as a hard-lined, angular woman responded to his summons.

"That's me, sir. "

"Mr. Dimsdale lives with you, I believe? "

"Third floor front, sir. "

"Is he in? "

Suspicion shone in the woman's eyes. "Was it aboot a bill? " she asked.

"A bill, my good woman! No, no, nothing of the kind. Dr. Dimsdale is my name. I am the lad's father—just come up from London to see him. I hope he has not been overworking himself? "

A ghost of a smile played about the woman's face. "I think not, sir, " she answered.

"I almost wish I had come round in the afternoon, " said the visitor, standing with his thick legs astride upon the door-mat. "It seems a pity to break his chain of thought. The morning is his time for study. "

"Houts! I wouldna' fash aboot that. "

"Well! well! The third floor, you say. He did not expect me so early, I shall surprise the dear boy at his work. "

The landlady stood listening expectantly in the passage. The sturdy little man plodded heavily up the first flight of stairs. He paused on the landing.

"Dear me! " he murmured. "Some one is beating carpets. How can they expect poor Tom to read? "

At the second landing the noise was much louder. "It must be a dancing school, " conjectured the doctor.

When he reached his son's door, however, there could no longer be any doubt as to whence the sounds proceeded. There was the stamp and shuffle of feet, the hissing of in-drawn breath, and an occasional soft thud, as if some one were butting his head against a bale of wool. "It's epilepsy, " gasped the doctor, and turning the handle he rushed into the room.

One hurried glance showed him the struggle which was going on. There was no time to note details. Some maniac was assaulting his Tom. He sprang at the man, seized him round the waist, dragged him to the ground, and seated himself upon him. "Now tie his hands, " he said complacently, as he balanced himself upon the writhing figure.

CHAPTER VI.

A RECTORIAL ELECTION.

It took some little time before his son, who was half-choked with laughter, could explain to the energetic doctor that the gentleman upon whom he was perched was not a dangerous lunatic, but, on the contrary, a very harmless and innocent member of society. When at last it was made clear to him, the doctor released his prisoner and was profuse in his apologies.

"This is my father, Garraway, " said Dimsdale. "I hardly expected him so early. "

"I must offer you a thousand apologies, sir. The fact is that I am rather short-sighted, and had no time to put my glasses on. It seemed to me to be a most dangerous scuffle. "

"Don't mention it, sir, " said Garraway, with great good humour.

"And you, Tom, you rogue, is this the way you spend your mornings? I expected to find you deep in your books. I told your landlady that I hardly liked to come up for fear of disturbing you at your work. You go up for your first professional in a few weeks, I understand? "

"That will be all right, dad, " said his son demurely. "Garraway and I usually take a little exercise of this sort as a preliminary to the labours of the day. Try this armchair and have a cigarette. "

The doctor's eye fell upon the medical works and the disarticulated skull, and his ill-humour departed.

"You have your tools close at hand, I see, " he remarked.

"Yes, dad, all ready. "

"Those bones bring back old memories to me. I am rusty in my anatomy, but I dare say I could stump you yet. Let me see now. What are the different foramina of the sphenoid bone, and what structures pass through them? Eh? "

"Coming! " yelled his son. "Coming! " and dashed out of the room.

"I didn't hear any one call, " observed the doctor.

"Didn't you, sir? " said Garraway, pulling on his coat. "I thought I heard a noise. "

"You read with my son, I believe? "

"Yes, sir. "

"Then perhaps you can tell me what the structures are which pass through the foramina of the sphenoid? "

"Oh yes, sir. There is the—All right, Tom, all right! Excuse me, sir! He is calling me; " and Garraway vanished as precipitately as his friend had done. The doctor sat alone, puffing at his cigarette, and brooding over his own dullness of hearing.

Presently the two students returned, looking just a little shame-faced, and plunged instantly into wild talk about the weather, the town, and the University—anything and everything except the sphenoid bone.

"You have come in good time to see something of University life, " said young Dimsdale. "To-day we elect our new Lord Rector. Garraway and I will take you down and show you the sights. "

"I have often wished to see something of it, " his father answered. "I was apprenticed to my profession, Mr. Garraway, in the old-fashioned way, and had few opportunities of attending college. "

"Indeed, sir. "

"But I can imagine it all. What can be more charming than the sight of a community of young men all striving after knowledge, and emulating each other in the ardour of their studies? Not that I would grudge them recreation. I can fancy them strolling in bands round the classic precincts of their venerable University, and amusing themselves by discussing the rival theories of physiologists or the latest additions to the pharmacopoeia. "

Garraway had listened with becoming gravity to the commencement of this speech, but at the last sentence he choked and vanished for the second time out of the room.

"Your friend seems amused, " remarked Dr. Dimsdale mildly.

"Yes. He gets taken like that sometimes, " said his son. "His brothers are just the same. I have hardly had a chance yet to say how glad I am to see you, dad. "

"And I to see you, my dear boy. Your mother and Kate come up by the night train. I have private rooms at the hotel. "

"Kate Harston! I can only remember her as a little quiet girl with long brown hair. That was six years ago. She promised to be pretty. "

"Then she has fulfilled her promise. But you shall judge that for yourself. She is the ward of John Girdlestone, the African merchant, but we are the only relations she has upon earth. Her father was my second cousin. She spends a good deal of her time now with us at Phillimore Gardens—as much as her guardian will allow. He prefers to have her under his own roof, and I don't blame him, for she is like a ray of sunshine in the house. It was like drawing his teeth to get him to consent to this little holiday, but I stuck at it until I wearied him out—fairly wearied him out. " The little doctor chuckled at the thought of his victory, and stretched out his thick legs towards the fire.

"This examination will prevent me from being with you as much as I wish. "

"That's right, my boy; let nothing interfere with your work. "

"Still, I think I am pretty safe. I am glad they have come now, for next Wednesday is the international football match. Garraway and I are the two Scotch half-backs. You must all come down and see it. "

"I'll tell you what, Dimsdale, " said Garraway, reappearing in the doorway, "if we don't hurry up we shall see nothing of the election. It is close on twelve. "

"I am all ready, " cried Dr. Dimsdale, jumping to his feet and buttoning his coat.

"Let us be off, then, " said his son; and picking up hats and sticks they clattered off down the lodging-house stairs.

A rectorial election is a peculiarly Scotch institution, and, however it may strike the impartial observer, it is regarded by the students themselves as a rite of extreme solemnity and importance from which grave issues may depend. To hear the speeches and addresses of rival orators one would suppose that the integrity of the constitution and the very existence of the empire hung upon the return of their special nominee. Two candidates are chosen from the most eminent of either party and a day is fixed for the polling. Every undergraduate has a vote, but the professors have no voice in the matter. As the duties are nominal and the position honourable, there is never any lack of distinguished aspirants for a vacancy. Occasionally some well-known literary or scientific man is invited to become a candidate, but as a rule the election is fought upon strictly political lines, with all the old-fashioned accompaniments of a Parliamentary contest.

For months before the great day there is bustle and stir. Secret committees meet, rules are formulated, and insidious agents prowl about with an eye to the political training of those who have not yet nailed their colours to any particular mast. Then comes a grand meeting of the Liberal Students' Association, which is trumped by a dinner of the Undergraduates' Conservative Society. The campaign is then in full swing. Great boards appear at the University gates, on which pithy satires against one or other candidate, parodies on songs, quotations from their speeches, and gaudily painted cartoons are posted. Those who are supposed to be able to feel the pulse of the University move about with the weight of much knowledge upon their brows, throwing out hints as to the probable majority one way or the other. Some profess to know it to a nicety. Others shake their heads and remark vaguely that there is not much to choose either way. So week after week goes by, until the excitement reaches a climax when the date of the election comes round.

There was no need upon that day for Dr. Dimsdale or any other stranger in the town to ask his way to the University, for the whooping and yelling which proceeded from that usually decorous building might have been heard from Prince's Street to Newington. In front of the gates was a dense crowd of townspeople peering through into the quadrangle, and deriving much entertainment from the movements of the lively young gentlemen within. Large numbers of the more peaceable undergraduates stood about under the arches, and these quickly made a way for the newcomers, for both Garraway and Dimsdale as noted athletes commanded a respect among their fellow-students which medallists and honours men might look for in vain.

The broad open quadrangle, and all the numerous balconies and terraces which surround it, were crowded with an excited mob of students. The whole three thousand odd electors who stand upon the college rolls appeared to be present, and the noise which they were making would have reflected credit on treble their number. The dense crowd surged and seethed without pause or rest. Now and again some orator would be hoisted up on the shoulders of his fellows, when an oscillation of the crowd would remove his supporters and down he would come, only to be succeeded by another at some other part of the assembly. The name of either candidate would produce roars of applause and equally vigorous howls of execration. Those who were lucky enough to be in the balconies above hurled down missiles on the crowd beneath—peas, eggs, potatoes, and bags of flour or of sulphur; while those below, wherever they found room to swing an arm, returned the fusillade with interest. The doctor's views of academical serenity and the high converse of pallid students vanished into thin air as he gazed upon the mad tumultuous scene. Yet, in spite of his fifty years, he laughed as heartily as any boy at the wild pranks of the young politicians, and the ruin which was wrought upon broad-cloth coat and shooting jacket by the hail of unsavoury projectiles.

The crowd was most dense and most noisy in front of the class-room in which the counting of the votes was going forward. At one the result was to be announced, and as the long hand of the great clock crept towards the hour, a hush of expectation fell upon the assembly. The brazen clang broke harshly out, and at the same moment the folding doors were flung open, and a knot of men rushed out into the crowd, who swirled and eddied round them. The centre of the throng was violently agitated, and the whole mass of people swayed outwards and inwards. For a minute or two the excited combatants seethed and struggled without a clue as to the cause of the commotion. Then the corner of a large placard was elevated above the heads of the rioters, on which was visible the word "Liberal" in great letters, but before it could be raised further it was torn down, and the struggle became fiercer than ever. Up came the placard again—the other corner this time—with the word "Majority" upon it, and then immediately vanished as before. Enough had been seen, however, to show which way the victory had gone, and shouts of triumph arose everywhere, with waving of hats and clatter of sticks. Meanwhile, in the centre the two parties fought round the placard, and the commotion began to cover a wider area, as either side was reinforced by fresh supporters. One gigantic Liberal seized the board, and held it aloft for a moment, so that it could be seen in its entirety by the whole multitude:

LIBERAL MAJORITY,

241.

But his triumph was short-lived. A stick descended upon his head, his heels were tripped up, and he and his placard rolled upon the ground together. The victors succeeded, however, in forcing their way to the extreme end of the quadrangle, where, as every Edinburgh man knows, the full-length statue of Sir David Brewster looks down upon the classic ground which he loved so well. An audacious Radical swarmed up upon the pedestal and balanced the obnoxious notice on the marble arms of the professor. Thus converted into a political partisan, the revered inventor of the kaleidoscope became the centre of a furious struggle, the vanquished politicians making the most desperate efforts to destroy the symbol of their opponents' victory, while the others offered an equally vigorous resistance to their attacks. The struggle was still proceeding when Dimsdale removed his father, for it was impossible to say what form the riot might assume.

"What Goths! what barbarians! " cried the little doctor, as they walked down the Bridges. "And this is my dream of refined quiet and studious repose! "

"They are not always like that, sir, " said his son apologetically. "They were certainly a little jolly to-day. "

"A little jolly! " cried the doctor. "You rogue, Tom. I believe if I had not been there you would have been their ringleader. "

He glanced from one to the other, and it was so evident from the expression of their faces that he had just hit the mark, that he burst into a great guffaw of laughter, in which, after a moment's hesitation, his two young companions heartily joined.

CHAPTER VII.

ENGLAND VERSUS SCOTLAND.

The rectorial election had come and had gone, but another great event had taken its place. It was the day of the England and Scotland Rugby match.

Better weather could not have been desired. The morning had been hazy, but as the sun shone out the fog had gradually risen, until now there remained but a suspicion of it, floating like a plume, above the frowning walls of Edinburgh Castle, and twining a fairy wreath round the unfinished columns of the national monument upon the Calton Hill. The broad stretch of the Prince's Street Gardens, which occupy the valley between the old town and the new, looked green and spring-like, and their fountains sparkled merrily in the sunshine. Their wide expanse, well-trimmed and bepathed, formed a strange contrast to the rugged piles of grim old houses which bounded them upon the other side and the massive grandeur of the great hill beyond, which lies like a crouching lion keeping watch and ward, day and night, over the ancient capital of the Scottish kings. Travellers who have searched the whole world round have found no fairer view.

So thought three of the genus who were ensconced that forenoon in the bow windows of the *Royal Hotel* and gazed across the bright green valley at the dull historical background beyond. One we already know, a stoutish gentleman, ruddy-faced and black-eyed, with check trousers, light waistcoat and heavy chain, legs widely parted, his hands in his pockets, and on his face that expression of irreverent and critical approval with which the travelled Briton usually regards the works of nature. By his side was a young lady in a tight-fitting travelling dress, with trim leather belt and snow-white collar and cuffs. There was no criticism in her sweet face, now flushed with excitement— nothing but unqualified wonder and admiration at the beautiful scene before her. An elderly placid-faced woman sat in a basket chair in the recess, and looked up with quiet loving eyes at the swift play of emotions which swept over the girl's eager features.

"Oh, Uncle George, " she cried, "it is really too heavenly. I cannot realize that we are free. I can't help fearing that it is all a dream, and that I shall wake up to find myself pouring out Ezra Girdlestone's coffee, or listening to Mr. Girdlestone as he reads the morning quotations. "

The elder woman stroked the girl's hand caressingly with her soft, motherly palm. "Don't think about it, " she murmured.

"No, don't think about it, " echoed the doctor. "My wife is quite right. Don't think about it. But, dear me, what a job I had to persuade your guardian to let you go. I should have given it up in despair—I really should—if I had not known that you had set your heart upon it. "

"Oh, how good you both are to me! " cried the girl, in a pretty little gush of gratitude.

"Pooh, pooh, Kate! But as to Girdlestone, he is perfectly right. If I had you I should keep you fast to myself, I promise you. Eh, Matilda? "

"That we would, George. "

"Perfect tyrants, both of us. Eh, Matilda? "

"Yes, George. "

"I am afraid that I am not very useful in a household, " said the girl. "I was too young to look after things for poor papa. Mr. Girdlestone, of course, has a housekeeper of his own. I read the *Financial News* to him after dinner every day, and I know all about stock and Consols and those American railways which are perpetually rising and falling. One of them went wrong last week, and Ezra swore, and Mr. Girdlestone said that the Lord chastens those whom He loves. He did not seem to like being chastened a bit though. But how delightful this is! It is like living in another world. "

The girl was a pretty figure as she stood in the window, tall, lithe, and graceful, with the long soft curves of budding womanhood. Her face was sweet rather than beautiful, but an artist would have revelled in the delicate strength of the softly rounded chin, and the quick bright play of her expression. Her hair, of a deep rich brown, with a bronze shimmer where a sunbeam lay athwart it, swept back in those thick luxuriant coils which are the unfailing index of a strong womanly nature. Her deep blue eyes danced with life and light, while her slightly *retrousse* nose and her sensitive smiling mouth all spoke of gentle good humour. From her sunny face to the dainty little shoe which peeped from under the trim black skirt, she was an eminently pleasant object to look upon. So thought the passers-by as they glanced up at the great bow window, and so, too, thought a young gentleman who had driven up to the hotel door, and who now bounded up the steps and into the room. He was enveloped in a long shaggy ulster, which stretched down to his ankles, and he wore a velvet cap trimmed with silver stuck carelessly on the back of his powerful yellow curled head.

"Here is the boy! " cried his mother gaily.

"How are you, mam dear? " he cried, stooping over her to kiss her. "How are you, dad? Good morning, Cousin Kate. You must come down and wish us luck. What a blessing that it is pretty warm. It is miserable for the spectators when there is an east wind. What do you think of it, dad? "

"I think you are an unnatural young renegade to play against your mother country, " said the sturdy doctor.

"Oh, come, dad! I was born in Scotland, and I belong to a Scotch club. Surely that is good enough. "

"I hope you lose, then. "

"We are very likely to. Atkinson, of the West of Scotland, has strained his leg, and we shall have to play Blair, of the Institution, at full back—not so good a man by a long way. The odds are five to four on the English this morning. They are said to be the very strongest lot that ever played in an International match. I have brought a cab with me, so the moment you are ready we can start. "

There were others besides the students who were excited about the coming struggle. All Edinburgh was in a ferment. Football is, and always has been, the national game of Scotland among those who affect violent exercise, while golf takes its place with the more sedately inclined. There is no game so fitted to appeal to a hardy and active people as that composite exercise prescribed by the Rugby Union, in which fifteen men pit strength, speed, endurance, and every manly attribute they possess in a prolonged struggle against fifteen antagonists. There is no room for mere knack or trickery. It is a fierce personal contest in which the ball is the central rallying point. That ball may be kicked, pushed, or carried; it may be forced onwards in any conceivable manner towards the enemy's goal. The fleet of foot may seize it and by superior speed thread their way through the ranks of their opponents. The heavy of frame may crush down all opposition by dead weight. The hardiest and most enduring must win.

Even matches between prominent local clubs excite much interest in Edinburgh and attract crowds of spectators. How much more then when the pick of the manhood of Scotland were to try their strength against the very cream of the players from the South of the Tweed. The roads which converged on the Raeburn Place Grounds, on which the match was to be played, were dark with thousands all wending their way in one direction. So thick was the moving mass that the carriage of the Dimsdale party had to go at a walk for the latter half of the journey, In spite of the objurgations of the driver, who, as a patriot, felt the responsibility which rested upon him in having one of the team in his charge, and the necessity there was for delivering him up by the appointed time. Many in the crowd recognized the young fellow and waved their hands to him or called out a few words of encouragement. Miss Kate Harston and even the doctor began to reflect some of the interest and excitement which showed itself on every face around them. The youth alone seemed to be unaffected by the general enthusiasm, and spent the time in endeavouring to explain the principles of the game to his fair companion, whose ignorance of it was comprehensive and astounding.

"You understand, " he said, "that there are fifteen players on each side. But it would not do for the whole of these fifteen men to play in a crowd, for, in that case, if the other side forced the ball past them, they would have nothing to fall back upon—no reserves, as it were. Therefore, as we play the game in Scotland, ten men are told off to play in a knot. They are picked for their weight, strength, and endurance. They are called the forwards, and are supposed to be always on the ball, following it everywhere, never stopping or tiring. They are opposed, of course, by the forwards of the other side. Now, immediately behind the forwards are the two quarter-backs. They should be very active fellows, good dodgers and fast runners. They never join in the very rough work, but they always follow on the outskirts of the forwards, and if the ball is forced past it is their duty to pick it up and make away with it like lightning. If they are very fast they may succeed in carrying it a long way before they are caught—'tackled, ' as we call it. It is their duty also to keep their eye on the quarter-backs of the enemy, and to tackle them if they get away. Behind them again are the two half-backs—or 'three-quarters, ' as they call them in England. I am one of them. They are supposed to be fast runners too, and a good deal of the tackling comes to their lot, for a good runner of the other side can often get past the quarters, and then the halves have got to bring him down. Behind the half-backs is a single man—the back. He is the last resource when all others are past. He should be a sure and long kicker, so as to get the ball away from the goal by that means—but you are not listening. "

"Oh yes, I am, " said Kate. As a matter of fact the great throng and the novel sights were distracting her so much that she found it hard to attend to her companion's disquisition.

"You'll understand it quickly enough when you see it, " the student remarked cheerily. "Here we are at the grounds. "

As he spoke the carriage rattled through a broad gateway into a large open grassy space, with a great pavilion at one side of it and a staked enclosure about two hundred yards long and a hundred broad, with a goal-post at each end. This space was marked out by gaily coloured flags, and on every side of it, pressing against the barrier the whole way round, was an enormous crowd, twenty and thirty deep, with others occupying every piece of rising ground or coign of vantage behind them. The most moderate computation would place the number of spectators at fifteen thousand. At one side there was a line of cabs in the background, and thither the carriage of the Dimsdales drove, while Tom rushed off with his bag to the pavilion to change.

It was high time to do so, for just as the carriage took up its position a hoarse roar burst from the great multitude, and was taken up again and again. It was a welcome to the English team, which had just appeared upon the ground. There they were, clad in white knickerbockers and jerseys, with a single red rose embroidered upon their breasts; as gallant-looking a set of young fellows as the whole world could produce. Tall, square-shouldered, straight-limbed, as active as kittens and as powerful as young bullocks, it was clear that they would take a lot of beating. They were the pick of the

University and London clubs, with a few players from the northern counties; not a man among them whose name was not known wherever football was played. That tall, long-legged youth is Evans, the great half-back, who is said to be able to send a drop-kick further than any of his predecessors in the annals of the game. There is Buller, the famous Cambridge quarter, only ten stone in weight, but as lithe and slippery as an eel; and Jackson, the other quarter, is just such another—hard to tackle himself, but as tenacious as a bulldog in holding an adversary. That one with the straw-coloured hair is Coles, the great forward; and there are nine lads of metal who will stand by him to-day through thick and thin. They were a formidable-looking lot, and betting, which had been five on four to them in the morning, showed symptoms of coming to five to three. In the meantime, by no means abashed at finding themselves the cynosure of so many eyes, the Englishmen proceeded to keep up their circulation by leap-frog and horse-play, for their jerseys were thin and the wind bleak.

But where were their adversaries? A few impatient moments slowly passed, and then from one corner of the ground there rose a second cheer, which rippled down the long line of onlookers and swelled into a mighty shout as the Scotchmen vaulted over the barrier into the arena. It was a nice question for connoisseurs in physical beauty as to which team had the best of it in physique. The Northerners in their blue jerseys, with a thistle upon their breasts, were a sturdy, hard-bitten lot, averaging a couple of pounds more in weight than their opponents. The latter were, perhaps, more regularly and symmetrically built, and were pronounced by experts to be the faster team, but there was a massive, gaunt look about the Scotch forwards which promised well for their endurance. Indeed, it was on their forwards that they principally relied. The presence of three such players as Buller, Evans, and Jackson made the English exceptionally strong behind, but they had no men in front who were individually so strong and fast as Miller, Watts, or Grey. Dimsdale and Garraway, the Scotch half-backs, and Tookey, the quarter, whose blazing red head was a very oriflamme wherever the struggle waxed hottest, were the best men that the Northerners could boast of behind.

The English had won the choice of goals, and elected to play with what slight wind there was at their backs. A small thing may turn the scale between two evenly balanced teams. Evans, the captain, placed the ball in front of him upon the ground, with his men lined all along on either side, as eager as hounds in leash. Some fifty yards in front of him, about the place where the ball would drop, the blue-vested Scots gathered in a sullen crowd. There was a sharp ring from a bell, a murmur of excitement from the crowd. Evans took two quick steps forward, and the yellow ball flew swift and straight, as if it had been shot from a cannon, right into the expectant group in front of him.

For a moment there was grasping and turmoil among the Scotchmen. Then from the crowd emerged Grey, the great Glasgow forward, the ball tucked well under his arm, his head down, running like the wind, with his nine forwards in a dense clump behind him, ready to bear down all opposition, while the other five followed more slowly, covering a wider stretch of ground. He met the Englishmen who had started full cry after the ball the moment that their captain had kicked it. The first hurled himself upon him. Grey, without slackening his pace, swerved slightly, and he missed him. The second he passed in the same way, but the third caught quickly at his legs, and the Scot flew head over heels and was promptly collared. Not much use collaring him now! In the very act of falling he had thrown the ball behind him. Gordon, of Paisley, caught it and bore it on a dozen yards, when he was seized and knocked down, but not before he had bequeathed his trust to another, who struggled manfully for some paces before he too was brought to the ground. This pretty piece of "passing" had recovered for the Scotch all the advantage lost by the English kick-off, and was greeted by roars of applause from the crowd.

And now there is a "maul" or "scrimmage. " Was there ever another race which did such things and called it play! Twenty young men, so blended and inextricably mixed that no one could assign the various arms and legs to their respective owners, are straining every muscle and fibre of their bodies against each other, and yet are so well balanced that the dense clump of humanity stands absolutely motionless. In the centre is an inextricable chaos where shoulders heave and heads rise and fall. At the edges are a fringe of legs—legs in an extreme state of tension— ever pawing for a firmer foothold, and apparently completely independent of the rest of their owners, whose heads and bodies have bored their way Into the *melee*. The pressure in there is tremendous, yet neither side gives an inch. Just on the skirts of the throng, with bent bodies and hands on knees, stand the cool little quarter-backs, watching the gasping giants, and also keeping a keen eye upon each other. Let the ball emerge near one of these, and he will whip it up and be ten paces off before those in the "maul" even know that it is gone. Behind them again are the halves, alert and watchful, while the back, with his hands in his pockets, has an easy consciousness that he will have plenty of warning before the ball can pass the four good men who stand between the "maul" and himself.

Now the dense throng sways a little backwards and forwards. An inch is lost and an inch is gained. The crowd roar with delight. "Mauled, Scotland! " "Mauled England! " "England! " "Scotland! " The shouting would stir the blood of the mildest mortal that ever breathed. Kate Harston stands in the carriage, rosy with excitement and enjoyment. Her heart is all with the wearers of the rose, in spite of the presence of her old play-mate in the opposite ranks. The doctor is as much delighted as the youngest man on the ground, and the cabman waves his arms and shouts in a highly indecorous fashion. The two pounds' difference in weight is beginning to tell. The English sway back a yard or two. A blue coat emerges among the white ones. He has fought his way through, but has left the ball behind him, so he dashes round and puts his weight behind it once more. There is a last upheaval, the maul is split in two, and through the rent come the redoubtable Scotch forwards with the ball amongst them. Their solid phalanx has scattered the English like spray to right and left. There is no one in front of them, no one but a single little man, almost a boy in size and weight. Surely he cannot hope to stop the tremendous rush. The ball is a few yards in advance of the leading Scot when he springs forward at it. He seizes it an instant before his adversary, and with the same motion writhes himself free from the man's grasp. Now is the time for the crack Cambridge quarter-back to show what he is made of. The crowd yell with excitement. To right and left run the great Scotch forwards, grasping, slipping, pursuing, and right in the midst of them, as quick and as erratic as a trout in a pool, runs the calm-faced little man, dodging one, avoiding another, slipping between the fingers of two others. Surely he is caught now. No, he has passed all the forwards and emerges from the ruck of men, pelting along at a tremendous pace. He has dodged one of the Scotch quarters, and outstripped the other. "Well played, England! " shout the crowd. "Well run, Buller! " "Now, Tookey! " "Now, Dimsdale! " "Well collared, Dimsdale; well collared, indeed! " The little quarter-back had come to an end of his career, for Tom had been as quick as he and had caught him round the waist as he attempted to pass, and brought him to the ground. The cheers were hearty, for the two half-backs were the only University men in the team, and there were hundreds of students among the spectators. The good doctor coloured up with pleasure to hear his boy's name bellowed forth approvingly by a thousand excited lungs.

The play is, as all good judges said it would be, very equal. For the first forty minutes every advantage gained by either side had been promptly neutralized by a desperate effort on the part of the other. The mass of struggling players has swayed backwards and forwards, but never more than twenty or thirty yards from the centre of the ground. Neither goal had been seriously threatened as yet. The spectators fail to see how the odds laid on England are justified, but the "fancy" abide by their choice. In the second forty it is thought that the superior speed and staying power of the Southerners will tell over the heavier Scots. There seems little the matter with the latter as yet, as they stand in a group, wiping their grimy faces and discussing the state of the game; for at the end of forty minutes the goals are changed and there is a slight interval.

And now the last hour is to prove whether there are good men bred in the hungry North as any who live on more fruitful ground and beneath warmer skies. If the play was desperate before, it became even more so now. Each member of either team played as if upon him alone depended the issue of the match. Again and again Grey, Anderson, Gordon, and their redoubtable phalanx of dishevelled hard-breathing Scots broke away with the ball; but as often the English quarter and half-backs, by their superior speed, more than made up for the weakness of their forwards, and carried the struggle back into the enemy's ground. Two or three time Evans, the long-kicker, who was credited with the power of reaching the goal from almost any part of the ground, got hold of the ball, but each time before he could kick he was charged by some one of his adversaries. At last, however, his chance came. The ball trickled out of a maul into the hands of Buller, who at once turned and threw it to the half-back behind him. There was no time to reach him. He took a quick glance at the distant goal, a short run forward, and his long limb swung through the air with tremendous force. There was a dead silence of suspense among the crowd as the ball described a lofty parabola. Down it came, down, down, as straight and true as an arrow, just grazing the cross-bar and pitching on the grass beyond, and the groans of a few afflicted patriots were drowned in the hearty cheers which hailed the English goal.

But the victory was not won yet. There were ten minutes left for the Scotchmen to recover this blow or for the Englishmen to improve upon it. The Northerners played so furiously that the ball was kept down near the English goal, which was only saved by the splendid defensive play of their backs. Five minutes passed, and the Scots in turn were being pressed back. A series of brilliant runs by Buller, Jackson, and Evans took the fight into the enemy's country, and kept it there. It seemed as if the visitors meant scoring again, when a sudden change occurred in the state of affairs. It was but three minutes off the calling of time when Tookey, one of the Scotch quarter-backs, got hold of the ball, and made a magnificent run, passing right through the opposing forwards and quarters. He was collared by Evans, but immediately threw the ball behind him. Dimsdale had followed up the quarter-back and caught the ball when it was thrown backwards. Now or never! The lad felt that he would sacrifice anything to pass the three men who stood between him and the English goal. He passed Evans like the wind before the half-back could disentangle himself from Tookey. There were but two now to oppose him. The first was the other English half-back, a broad-shouldered, powerful fellow, who rushed at him; but Tom, without attempting to avoid him, lowered his head and drove at him full tilt with such violence that both men reeled back from the collision. Dimsdale recovered himself first, however, and got past before the other had time to seize him. The goal was now not more than twenty yards off, with only one between Tom and it, though half a dozen more were in close pursuit. The English back caught him round the waist, while another from behind seized the collar of his jersey, and the three came heavily to the ground together. But the deed was done. In the very act of falling he had managed to kick the ball, which flickered feebly up into the air and just cleared the English bar. It had scarcely touched the ground upon the other side when the ringing of the great bell announced the termination of the match, though its sound was entirely drowned by the tumultuous shouting of the crowd. A thousand hats were thrown into the air, ten thousand voices joined in the roar, and meanwhile the cause of all this outcry was still sitting on the ground, smiling, it is true, but very pale, and with one of his arms dangling uselessly from his shoulder.

Well, the breaking of a collar-bone is a small price to pay for the saving of such a match as that. So thought Tom Dimsdale as he made for the pavilion, with his father keeping off the exultant crowd upon one side and Jack Garraway upon the other. The doctor butted a path through the dense half-crazy mob with a vigour which showed that his son's talents in that direction were hereditary. Within half an hour Tom was safely ensconced in the corner of the carriage, with his shoulder braced back, *secundum artem*, and his arm supported by a sling. How quietly and deftly the two women slipped a shawl here and a rug there to save him from the jarring of the carriage! It is part of the angel nature of woman that when youth and strength are maimed and helpless they appeal to her more than they can ever do in the pride and flush of their power. Here lies the compensation of the unfortunate. Kate's dark blue eyes filled with ineffable compassion as she bent over him; and he, catching sight of that expression, felt a sudden new unaccountable spring of joy bubble up in his heart, which made all previous hopes and pleasures seem vapid and meaningless. The little god shoots hard and straight when his mark is still in the golden dawn of life. All the way back he lay with his head among the cushions, dreaming of ministering angels, his whole soul steeped in quiet contentment as it dwelt upon the sweet earnest eyes which had looked so tenderly into his. It had been an eventful day with the student. He had saved his side, he had broken his collar-bone, and now, most serious of all, he had realized that he was hopelessly in love.

CHAPTER VIII.

A FIRST PROFESSIONAL.

Within a few weeks of his recovery from his accident Tom Dimsdale was to go up for his first professional examination, and his father, who had now retired from practice with a fair fortune, remained in Edinburgh until that event should come off. There had been some difficulty in persuading Girdlestone to give his consent to this prolongation of his ward's leave, but the old merchant was very much engrossed with his own affairs about that time, which made him more amenable than he might otherwise have been. The two travellers continued, therefore, to reside in their Princes Street hotel, but the student held on to his lodgings in Howe Street, where he used to read during the morning and afternoon. Every evening, however, he managed to dine at the *Royal*, and would stay there until his father packed him off to his books once more. It was in vain for him to protest and to plead for another half-hour. The physician was inexorable. When the fated hour came round the unhappy youth slowly gathered together his hat, his gloves, and his stick, spreading out that operation over the greatest possible extent of time which it could by any means be made to occupy. He would then ruefully bid his kinsfolk adieu, and retire rebelliously to his books.

Very soon, however, he made a discovery. From a certain seat in the Princes Street Gardens it was possible to see the interior of the sitting-room in which the visitors remained after dinner. From the time when this fact dawned upon him, his rooms in the evening knew him no more. The gardens were locked at night, but that was a mere trifle. He used to scramble over the railings like a cat, and then, planting himself upon the particular seat, he would keep a watch upon the hotel window until the occupants of the room retired to rest. It might happen that his cousin remained invisible. Then he would return to his rooms in a highly dissatisfied state, and sit up half the night protesting against fate and smoking strong black tobacco. On the other hand, if he had the good luck to see the graceful figure of his old playfellow, he felt that that was the next best thing to being actually in her company, and departed eventually in a more contented frame of mind. Thus, when Dr. Dimsdale fondly imagined his son to be a mile away grappling with the mysteries of science, that undutiful lad was in reality perched within sixty yards of him, with his thoughts engrossed by very different matters.

Kate could not fail to understand what was going on. However young and innocent a girl may be, there is always some subtle feminine instinct which warns her that she is loved. Then first she realizes that she has passed the shadowy frontier line which divides the child-life from that of the woman. Kate felt uneasy and perplexed, and half involuntarily she changed her manner towards him.

It had been frank and sisterly; now it became more distant and constrained. He was quick to observe the change, and in private raved and raged at it. He even made the mistake of showing his pique to her, upon which she became still more retiring and conventional. Then be bemoaned himself in the sleepless watches of the night, and confided to his bed-post that in his belief such a case had never occurred before in the history of the world, and never by any chance could or would happen again. He also broke out into an eruption of bad verses, which were found by his landlady during her daily examination of his private papers, and were read aloud to a select audience of neighbours, who were all much impressed, and cackled sympathetically among themselves.

By degrees Tom developed other symptoms of the distemper which had come upon him so suddenly. He had always been remarkable for a certain towsiness of appearance and carelessness of dress which harmonized with his Bohemian habits. All this he suddenly abjured. One fine morning he paid successive visits to his tailor, his boot-maker, his hatter, and his hosier, which left all those worthy tradesmen rubbing their hands with satisfaction. About a week afterwards he emerged from his rooms in a state of gorgeousness which impressed his landlady and amazed his friends. His old college companions hardly recognized Tom's honest phiz as it looked out above the most fashionable of coats and under the glossiest of hats.

His father was anything but edified by the change.

"I don't know what's coming over the lad, Kate, " he remarked after one of his visits. "If I thought he was going to turn to a fop, by the Lord Harry I'd disown him! Don't you notice a change in him yourself? "

Kate managed to evade the question, but her bright blush might have opened the old man's eyes had he observed it. He hardly realized yet that his son really was a man, and still less did he think of John Harston's little girl as a woman. It is generally some comparative stranger who first makes that discovery and brings it home to friends and relatives.

Love has an awkward way of intruding itself at inconvenient times, but it never came more inopportunely than when it smote one who was reading for his first professional examination. During these weeks, when Tom was stumping about in boots which were two sizes too small for him, in the hope of making his muscular, well-formed foot a trifle more elegant, and was splitting gloves in a way which surprised his glover, all his energies ought by rights to have been concentrated upon the mysteries of botany, chemistry, and zoology. During the precious hours that should have been devoted to the mastering of the sub-divisions of the celenterata or the natural orders of endogenous plants, he was expending his energies in endeavouring to recall the words of the song which his cousin had sung the evening before, or to recollect the exact intonation with which she remarked to him that it had been a fine day, or some other equally momentous observation. It follows that, as the day of the examination came round, the student, in his lucid intervals, began to feel anxious for the result. He had known his work fairly well, however, at one time, and with luck he might pull through. He made an energetic attempt to compress a month's reading into a week, and when the day for the written examination came round he had recovered some of his lost ground. The papers suited him fairly well, and he felt as he left the hall that he had had better fortune than he deserved. The *viva voce* ordeal was the one, however, which he knew would be most dangerous to him, and he dreaded it accordingly.

It was a raw spring morning when his turn came to go up. His father and Kate drove round with him to the University gates.

"Keep up your pluck, Tom, " the old gentleman said. "Be cool, and have all your wits about you. Don't lose your head, whatever you do. "

"I seem to have forgotten the little I ever knew, " Tom said dolefully, as he trudged up the steps. As he looked back he saw Kate wave her hand to him cheerily, and it gave him fresh heart.

"We shall hope to see you at lunch time, " his father shouted after him. "Mind you bring us good news. " As he spoke the carriage rattled away down the Bridges, and Tom joined the knot of expectant students who were waiting at the door of the great hall.

A melancholy group they were, sallow-faced, long-visaged and dolorous, partly from the effects of a long course of study and partly from their present trepidation. It was painful to observe their attempts to appear confident and unconcerned as they glanced round the heavens, as if to observe the state of the weather, or examined with well-feigned archaeological fervour the inscriptions upon the old University walls. Most painful of all was it, when some one, plucking up courage, would venture upon a tiny joke, at which the whole company would gibber in an ostentatious way, as though to show that even in this dire pass the appreciation of humour still remained with them. At times, when any of their number alluded to the examination or detailed the questions which had been propounded to Brown or Baker the day before, the mask of unconcern would be dropped, and the whole assembly would glare eagerly and silently at the speaker. Generally on such occasions matters are made infinitely worse by some Job's comforter, who creeps about suggesting abstruse questions, and hinting that they represent some examiner's particular hobby. Such a one came to Dimsdale's elbow, and quenched the last ray of hope which lingered in the young man's bosom.

"What do you know about cacodyl? " was his impressive question.

"Cacodyl? " Tom cried aghast. "It's some sort of antediluvian reptile, isn't it? "

The questioner broke into a sickly smile. "No, " he said. "It's an organic explosive chemical compound. You're sure to be asked about cacodyl. Tester's dead on it. He asks every one how it is prepared. "

Tom, much perturbed at these tidings, was feverishly endeavouring to extract some little information from his companion concerning the compound, when a bell rang abruptly inside the room and a janitor with a red face and a blue slip of paper appeared at the door.

"Dillon, Dimsdale, Douglas, " this functionary shouted in a very pompous voice, and three unhappy young men filed through the half-opened door into the solemn hall beyond.

The scene inside was not calculated to put them at their ease. Three tables, half a dozen yards from each other, were littered with various specimens and scientific instruments, and behind each sat two elderly gentlemen, stern-faced and critical. At one side were stuffed specimens of various small beasts, numerous skeletons and skulls, large jars containing fish and reptiles preserved in spirits of wine, jawbones with great teeth which grinned savagely at the unfortunate candidate, and numerous other zoological relics. The second table was heaped over with a blaze of gorgeous orchids and tropical plants, which looked strangely out of place in the great bleak room. A row of microscopes bristled along the edge. The third was the most appalling of all, for it was bare with the exception of several sheets of paper and a pencil. Chemistry was the most dangerous of the many traps set to ensnare the unwary student.

"Dillon—botany; Dimsdale—zoology; Douglas—chemistry, " the janitor shouted once more, and the candidates moved in front of the respective tables. Tom found himself facing a great spider crab, which appeared to be regarding him with a most malignant expression upon its crustacean features. Behind the crab sat a little professor, whose projecting eyes and crooked arms gave him such a resemblance to the creature in front that the student could not help smiling.

"Sir, " said a tall, clean-shaven man at the other end of the table, "be serious. This is no time for levity. "

Tom's expression after that would have made the fortune of a mute.

"What is this? " asked the little professor, handing a small round object to the candidate.

"It is an echinus—a sea-urchin, " Tom said triumphantly.

"Have they any circulation? " asked the other examiner.

"A water vascular system. "

"Describe it. "

Tom started off fluently, but it was no part of the policy of the examiners to allow him to waste the fifteen minutes allotted them in expatiating upon what he knew well. They interrupted him after a few sentences.

"How does this creature walk? " asked the crab-like one.

"By means of long tubes which it projects at pleasure. "

"How do the tubes enable the creature to walk? "

"They have suckers on them. "

"What are the suckers like? "

"They are round hollow discs. "

"Are you sure they are round? " asked the other sharply.

"Yes, " said Tom stoutly, though his ideas on the subject were rather vague. "

"And how does this sucker act? " asked the taller examiner.

Tom began to feel that these two men were exhibiting a very unseemly curiosity. There seemed to be no satiating their desire for information. "It creates a vacuum, " he cried desperately.

"How does it create a vacuum? "

"By the contraction of a muscular pimple in the centre, " said Tom, in a moment of inspiration.

"And what makes this pimple contract? "

Tom lost his head, and was about to say "electricity, " when he happily checked himself and substituted "muscular action. "

"Very good, " said the examiners, and the student breathed again. The taller one returned to the charge, however, with, "And this muscle—is it composed of striped fibres or non-striped? "

"Non-striped, " shrieked Tom at a venture, and both examiners rubbed their hands and murmured, "Very good, indeed! " at which

Tom's hair began to lie a little flatter, and he ceased to feel as if he were in a Turkish bath.

"How many teeth has a rabbit? " the tall man asked suddenly.

"I don't know, " the student answered with candour.

The two looked triumphantly at one another.

"He doesn't know! " cried the goggle-eyed one decisively.

"I should recommend you to count them the next time you have one for dinner, " the other remarked. As this was evidently meant for a joke, Tom had the tact to laugh, and a very gruesome and awe-inspiring laugh it was too.

Then the candidate was badgered about the pterodactyl, and concerning the difference in anatomy between a bat and a bird, and about the lamprey, and the cartilaginous fishes, and the amphioxus. All these questions he answered more or less to the satisfaction of the examiners—generally less. When at last the little bell tinkled which was the sign for candidates to move on to other tables, the taller man leaned over a list in front of him and marked down upon it the following hieroglyphic: —

"S. B.—. "

This Tom's sharp eye at once detected, and he departed well pleased, for he knew that the "S. B." meant *satis bene*, and as to the minus sign after it, it mattered little to him whether he had done rather more than well or rather less. He had passed in zoology, and that was all which concerned him at present.

CHAPTER IX.

A NASTY CROPPER.

But there were pitfalls ahead. As he moved to the botany table a grey-bearded examiner waved his hand in the direction of the row of microscopes as an intimation that the student was to look through them and pronounce upon what he saw. Tom seemed to compress his whole soul into his one eye as he glared hopelessly through the tube at what appeared to him to resemble nothing so much as a sheet of ice with the marks of skates upon it.

"Come along, come along! " the examiner growled impatiently. Courtesy is conspicuous by its absence in most of the Edinburgh examinations. "You must pass on to the next one, unless you can offer an opinion. "

This venerable teacher of botany, though naturally a kind-hearted man, was well known as one of the most malignant species of examiners, one of the school which considers such an ordeal in the light of a trial of strength between their pupils and themselves. In his eyes the candidate was endeavouring to pass, and his duty was to endeavour to prevent him, a result which, in a large proportion of cases, he successfully accomplished.

"Hurry on, hurry on! " he reiterated fussily.

"It's a section of a leaf, " said the student.

"It's nothing of the sort, " the examiner shouted exultantly. "You've made a bad mistake, sir; a very bad one, indeed. It's the spirilloe of a water plant. Move on to the next. "

Tom, in much perturbation of mind, shuffled down the line and looked through the next brazen tube. "This is a preparation of stomata, " he said, recognizing it from a print in his book on botany.

The professor shook his head despondingly. "You are right, " he said; "pass on to the next. "

The third preparation was as puzzling to the student as the first had been, and he was steeling himself to meet the inevitable when an unexpected circumstance turned the scale in his favour. It chanced that the other examiner, being somewhat less of a fossil than his *confreres*, and having still vitality enough to take an interest in things which were foreign to his subject, had recognized the student as being the young hero who had damaged himself in upholding the honour of his country. Being an ardent patriot himself his heart warmed towards Tom, and perceiving the imminent peril in which he stood he interfered in his behalf, and by a few leading questions got him on safer ground, and managed to keep him there until the little bell tinkled once more. The younger examiner showed remarkable tact in feeling his way, and keeping within the very limited area of the student's knowledge. He succeeded so well, however, that although his colleague shook his hoary head and intimated in other ways his poor opinion of the candidate's acquirements, he was forced to put down another "S. B." upon the paper in front of him. The student drew a long breath when he saw it, and marched across to the other table with a mixture of trepidation and confidence, like a jockey riding at the last and highest hurdle in a steeple-chase.

Alas! it is the last hurdle which often floors the rider, and Thomas too was doomed to find the final ordeal an insurmountable one. As he crossed the room some evil chance made him think of the gossip outside and of his allusion to the abstruse substance known as cacodyl. Once let a candidate's mind hit upon such an idea as this, and nothing will ever get it out of his thoughts. Tom felt his head buzz round, and he passed his hand over his forehead and through his curly yellow hair to steady himself. He felt a frenzied impulse as he sat down to inform the examiners that he knew very well what they were going to ask him, and that it was hopeless for him to attempt to answer it.

The leading professor was a ruddy-faced, benevolent old gentleman, with spectacles and a kindly manner. He made a few commonplace remarks to his colleagues with the good-natured intention of giving the confused-looking student before him time to compose himself. Then, turning blandly towards him, he said in the mildest of tones—

"Have you ever rowed in a pond? "

Tom acknowledged that he had.

"Perhaps, on those occasions, " the examiner continued, "you may have chanced to touch the mud at the bottom with your oar. "

Tom agreed that it was possible.

"In that case you may have observed that a large bubble, or a succession of them has risen from the bottom to the surface. Now, of what gas was that bubble composed? "

The unhappy student, with the one idea always fermenting on his brain, felt that the worst had come upon him. Without a moment's hesitation or thought he expressed his conviction that the compound was cacodyl.

Never did two men look more surprised, and never did two generally grave *savants* laugh more heartily than did the two examiners when they realized what the candidate had answered. Their mirth speedily brought him back to his senses. He saw with a feeling of despair that it was marsh gas which they had expected— one of the simplest and commonest of chemical combinations. Alas! it was too late now. He knew full well that nothing could save him. With poor marks in botany and zoology, such an error in chemistry was irreparable. He did what was perhaps the best thing under the circumstances. Rising from his chair he made a respectful bow to the examiners, and walked straight out of the room—to the great astonishment of the janitor, who had never before witnessed such a breach of decorum. As the student closed the door behind him he looked back and saw that the other professors had left their respective tables and were listening to an account of the incident from one of the chemists—and a roar of laughter the moment afterwards showed that they appreciated the humour of it. His fellow-students gathered round Tom outside in the hope of sharing in the joke, but he pushed them angrily aside and strode through the midst of them and down the University steps. He knew that the story would spread fast enough without his assistance. His mind was busy too in shaping a certain resolution which he had often thought over during the last few months.

The two old people and Miss Kate Harston waited long and anxiously in their sitting-room at the hotel for some news of the absentee. The doctor had, at first, attempted a lofty cynicism and general assumption of indifference, which rapidly broke down as the time went by, until at last he was wandering round the room, drumming upon the furniture with his fingers and showing every other sign of acute impatience. The window was on the first floor, and Kate had been stationed there as a sentinel to watch the passing crowd and signal the first sign of tidings.

"Can't you see him yet? " the doctor asked for the twentieth time.

"No, dear, I don't, " she answered, glancing up and down the street.

"He must be out now. He should have come straight to us. Come away from the window, my dear. We must not let the young monkey see how anxious we are about him. "

Kate sat down by the old man and stroked his broad brown hand with her tender white one. "Don't be uneasy, dear, " she said; "it's sure to be all right. "

"Yes, he is sure to pass, " the doctor answered; "but—bless my soul, who's this? "

The individual who caused this exclamation was a very broad-faced and rosy-cheeked little girl, coarsely clad, with a pile of books and a slate under her arm, who had suddenly entered the apartment.

"Please sir, " said this apparition, with a bob, "I'm Sarah Jane. "

"Are you, indeed? " said the doctor, with mild irony. "And what d'ye want here, Sarah Jane? "

"Please, sir, my mithar, Mrs. McTavish, asked me if I wudna' gie ye this letter frae the gentleman what's lodgin' wi' her. " With these words the little mite delivered her missive and, having given another bob, departed upon her ways.

"Why, " the doctor cried in astonishment, "it's directed to me and in Tom's writing. What can be the meaning of this? "

"Oh dear! oh dear! " Mrs. Dimsdale cried, with the quick perception of womanhood; "it means that he has failed. "

"Impossible! " said the doctor, fumbling with nervous fingers at the envelope. "By Jove, though, " he continued, as he glanced over the contents, "you're right. He has. Poor lad! he's more cut up about it than we can be, so we must not blame him. "

The good physician read the letter over several times before he finally put it away in his note-book, and he did so with a thoughtful face which showed that it was of importance. As it has an influence upon the future course of our story we cannot end the chapter better than by exercising our literary privilege, and peeping over the doctor's shoulder before he has folded it up. This is the epistle *in extenso*: —

"My Dear Father,

"You will be sorry to hear that I have failed in my exam. I am very cut up about it, because I fear that it will cause you grief and disappointment, and you deserve neither the one nor the other at my hands. "

"It is not an unmixed misfortune to me, because it helps me to make a request which I have long had in my mind. I wish you to allow me to give up the study of medicine and to go in for commerce. You have never made a secret of our money affairs to me, and I know that if I took my degree there would never be any necessity for me to practise. I should therefore have spent five years of my life in acquiring knowledge which would not be of any immediate use to me. I have no personal inclination towards medicine, while I have a very strong objection to simply living in the world upon money which other men have earned. I must therefore turn to some fresh pursuit for my future career, and surely it would be best that I should do so at once. What that fresh pursuit is to be I leave to your judgment. Personally, I think that if I embarked my capital in some commercial undertaking I might by sticking to my work do well. I feel too much cast down at my own failure to see you to-night, but to-morrow I hope to hear what you think from your own lips. "

"TOM. "

"Perhaps this failure will do no harm after all, " the doctor muttered thoughtfully, as he folded up the letter and gazed out at the cold glare of the northern sunset.

CHAPTER X.

DWELLERS IN BOHEMIA.

The residence of Major Tobias Clutterbuck, late of the 119th Light Infantry, was not known to any of his friends. It is true that at times he alluded in a modest way to his "little place, " and even went to the length of remarking airily to new acquaintances that he hoped they would look him up any time they happened to be in his direction. As he carefully refrained, however, from ever giving the slightest indication of which direction that might be, his invitations never led to any practical results. Still they had the effect of filling the recipient with a vague sense of proffered hospitality, and occasionally led to more substantial kindness in return.

The gallant major's figure was a familiar one in the card-room of the *Rag and Bobtail*, at the bow-window of the Jeunesse Doree. Tall and pompous, with a portly frame and a puffy clean-shaven face which peered over an abnormally high collar and old-fashioned linen cravat, he stood as a very type and emblem of staid middle-aged respectability. The major's hat was always of the glossiest, the major's coat was without a wrinkle, and, in short, from the summit of the major's bald head to his bulbous finger-tips and his gouty toes, there was not a flaw which the most severe critic of deportment— even the illustrious Turveydrop himself—could have detected. Let us add that the conversation of the major was as irreproachable as his person—that he was a distinguished soldier and an accomplished traveller, with a retentive memory and a mind stuffed with the good things of a lifetime. Combine all these qualities, and one would naturally regard the major as a most desirable acquaintance.

It is painful to have to remark, however, that, self-evident as this proposition might appear, it was vehemently contradicted by some of the initiated. There were rumours concerning the major which seriously compromised his private character. Indeed, such a pitch had they reached that when that gallant officer put himself forward as a candidate for a certain select club, he had, although proposed by a lord and seconded by a baronet, been most ignominiously pilled. In public the major affected to laugh over this social failure, and to regard it as somewhat in the nature of a practical joke, but privately he was deeply incensed. One day he momentarily dropped his veil of unconcern while playing billiards with the Honourable Fungus

Brown, who was generally credited with having had some hand in the major's exclusion. "Be Ged! sir, " the veteran suddenly exclaimed, inflating his chest and turning his apoplectic face upon his companion, "in the old days I would have called the lot of you out, sir, every demned one, beginning with the committee and working down; I would, be George! " At which savage attack the Honourable Fungus's face grew as white as the major's was red, and he began to wish that he had been more reserved in his confidences to some of his acquaintances respecting the exclusiveness of the club in question, or at least refrained from holding up the major's pilling as a proof thereof.

The cause of this vague feeling of distrust which had gone abroad concerning the old soldier was no very easy matter to define. It is true that he was known to have a book on every race, and to have secret means of information from stud-grooms and jockeys which occasionally stood him in good stead; but this was no uncommon thing among the men with whom he consorted. Again, it is true that Major Clutterbuck was much addicted to whist, with guinea points, and to billiard matches for substantial sums, but these stimulating recreations are also habitual to many men who have led eventful lives and require a strong seasoning to make ordinary existence endurable. Perhaps one reason may have been that the major's billiard play in public varied to an extraordinary degree, so that on different occasions he had appeared to be aiming at the process termed by the initiated "getting on the money. " The warm friendships, too, which the old soldier had contracted with sundry vacuous and sappy youths, who were kindly piloted by him into quasi-fashionable life and shown how and when to spend their money, had been most uncharitably commented upon. Perhaps the vagueness about the major's private residence and the mystery which hung over him outside his clubs may also have excited prejudice against him. Still, however his detractors might malign him, they could not attempt to deny the fact that Tobias Clutterbuck was the third son of the Honourable Charles Clutterbuck, who again was the second son of the Earl of Dunross, one of the most ancient of Hibernian families. This pedigree the old soldier took care to explain to every one about him, more particularly to the sappy youths aforementioned.

It chanced that on the afternoon of which we speak the major was engrossed by this very subject. Standing at the head of the broad stone steps which lead up to the palatial edifice which its occupiers irreverently term the *Rag and Bobtail*, he was explaining to a bull-necked, olive-complexioned young man the series of marriages and inter-marriages which had culminated in the production of his own portly, stiff-backed figure. His companion, who was none other than Ezra Girdlestone, of the great African firm of that name, leaned against one of the pillars of the portico and listened gloomily to the major's family reminiscences, giving an occasional yawn which he made no attempt to conceal.

"It's as plain as the fingers of me hand, " the old soldier said in a wheezy muffled brogue, as if he were speaking from under a feather-bed. "See here now, Girdlestone—this is Miss Letitia Snackles of Snackleton, a cousin of old Sir Joseph. " The major tapped his thumb with the silver head of his walking-stick to represent the maiden Snackles. "She marries Crawford, of the Blues—one o' the Warwickshire Crawfords; that's him"—here he elevated his stubby forefinger; "and here's their three children, Jemima, Harold, and John. " Up went three other fingers. "Jemima Crawford grows up, and then Charley Clutterbuck runs away with her. This other thumb o' mine will stand for that young divil Charley, and then me fingers—"

"Oh, hang your fingers, " Girdlestone exclaimed with emphasis. "It's very interesting, major, but it would be more intelligible if you wrote it out. "

"And so I shall, me boy! " the major cried enthusiastically, by no means abashed at the sudden interruption. "I'll draw it up on a bit o' foolscap paper. Let's see; Fenchurch Street, eh? Address to the offices, of course. Though, for that matter, 'Girdlestone, London, ' would foind you. I was spakin' of ye to Sir Musgrave Moore, of the Rifles, the other day, and he knew you at once. 'Girdlestone? ' says he. 'The same, ' says I. 'A merchant prince? ' says he. 'The same, ' says I. 'I'd be proud to meet him, ' says he. 'And you shall, ' says I. He's the best blood of county Waterford. "

"More blood than money, I suppose, " the young man said, smoothing out his crisp black moustache.

"Bedad, you've about hit it there. He went to California, and came back with five and twinty thousand pounds. I met him in Liverpool the day he arrived. 'This is no good to me, Toby, ' says he. 'Why not? ' I asks. 'Not enough, ' says he; 'just enough to unsettle me. ' 'What then? ' says I. 'Put it on the favourite for the St. Leger, ' says he. And he did too, every pinny of it, and the horse was beat on the post by a short head. He dropped the lot in one day. A fact, sir, 'pon me honour! Came to me next day. 'Nothing left! ' says he. 'Nothing? ' says I. 'Only one thing, ' says he. 'Suicide? ' says I. 'Marriage, ' says he. Within a month he was married to the second Miss Shuttleworth, who had five thou. in her own right, and five more when Lord Dungeness turns up his toes. "

"Indeed? " said his companion languidly.

"Fact, 'pon me honour! By the way—ah, here comes Lord Henry Richardson. How d'ye do, Richardson, how d'ye do? Ged, I remember Richardson when he was a tow-headed boy at Clongowes, and I used to lam him with a bootjack for his cheek. Ah, yes; I was going to say—it seems a demned awkward incident—ha! ha! —ridiculous, but annoying, you know. The fact is, me boy, coming away in a hurry from me little place, I left me purse on the drawers in the bedroom, and here's Jorrocks up in the billiard-room afther challenging me to play for a tenner—but I won't without having the money in me pocket. Tobias Clutterbuck may be poor, me dear friend, but"—and here he puffed out his chest and tapped on it with his round, sponge-like fist—"he's honest, and pays debts of honour on the nail. No, sir, there's no one can say a word against Tobias, except that he's a half-pay old fool with more heart than brains. However, " he added, suddenly dropping the sentimental and coming back to the practical, "if you, me dear boy, can obloige me with the money until to-morrow morning, I'll play Jorrocks with pleasure. There's not many men that I'd ask such a favour of, and even from you I'd never accept anything more than a mere timporary convanience. "

"You may stake your life on that, " Ezra Girdlestone said with a sneer, looking sullenly down and tracing figures with the end of his stick on the stone steps. "You'll never get the chance. I make it a rule never to lend any one money, either for short or long periods. "

"And you won't let me have this throifling accommodation? "

"No, " the young man said decisively.

For a moment the major's brick-coloured, weather-beaten face assumed an even darker tint, and his small dark eyes looked out angrily from under his shaggy brows at his youthful companion. He managed to suppress the threatened explosion, however, and burst into a loud roar of laughter.

"'Pon me sowl! " he wheezed, poking the young man in the ribs with his stick, an implement which he had grasped a moment before as though he meditated putting it to a less pacific use, "you young divils of business-men are too much for poor old Tobias. Ged, sir, to think of being stuck in the mud for the want of a paltry tenner! Tommy Heathcote will laugh when he hears of it. You know Tommy of the 81st? He gave me good advice: 'Always sew a fifty-pound note into the lining of each waistcoat you've got. Then you can't go short. ' Tried it once, and, be George! if me demned man-servant didn't stale that very waistcoat and sell it for six and sixpence. You're not going, are you? "

"Yes; I'm due in the City. The governor leaves at four. Good-bye. Shall I see you to-night? "

"Card-room, as per usual, " quoth the clean-shaven warrior. He looked after the retreating figure of his late companion with anything but a pleasant expression upon his face. The young man happened to glance round as he was half-way down the street, on which the major smiled after him paternally, and gave a merry flourish with his stick.

As the old soldier stood on the top of the club steps, pompous, pigeon-chested, and respectable, posing himself as though he had been placed there for the inspection of passers-by as a sample of the aristocracy within, he made several attempts to air his grievances to passing members touching the question of the expectant Jorrocks and the missing purse. Beyond, however, eliciting many sallies of wit from the younger spirits, for it was part of the major's policy to lay himself open to be a butt, his laudable perseverance was entirely thrown away. At last he gave it up in disgust, and raising his stick hailed a passing 'bus, into which he sprang, taking a searching glance round to see that no one was following him. After a drive which brought him to the other side of the City, he got out in a broad, busy thoroughfare, lined with large shops. A narrow turning from the main artery led into a long, dingy street, consisting of very high smoke-coloured houses, which ran parallel to the other, and presented as great a contrast to it as the back of a painting does to the front.

Down this sombre avenue the major strutted with all his wonted pomposity, until about half-way down he reached a tall, grim-looking house, with many notices of "apartments" glaring from the windows. The line of railings which separated this house from the street was rusty, and broken and the whole place had a flavour of mildew. The major walked briskly up the stone steps, hollowed out by the feet of generations of lodgers, and pushing open the great splotchy door, which bore upon it a brass plate indicating that the establishment was kept by a Mrs. Robins, he walked into the hall with the air of one who treads familiar ground. Up one flight of stairs, up two flights of stairs, and up three flights of stairs did he climb, until on the fourth landing he pushed open a door and found himself in a small room, which formed for the nonce the "little place" about which he was wont at the club to make depreciatory allusions, so skilfully introduced that the listener was left in doubt as to whether the major was the happy possessor of a country house and grounds, or whether he merely owned a large suburban villa. Even this modest sanctum was not entirely the major's own, as was shown by the presence of a ruddy-faced man with a long, tawny beard, who sat on one side of the empty fire-place, puffing at a great china-bowled pipe, and comporting himself with an ease which showed that he was no casual visitor.

As the other entered, the man in the chair gave vent to a guttural grunt without removing the mouthpiece of his pipe from between his lips; and Major Clutterbuck returned the greeting with an off-handed nod. His next proceeding was to take off his glossy hat and pack it away in a hat-box. He then removed his coat, his collar, his tie, and his gaiters, with equal solicitude, and put them in a place of safety. After which he donned a long purple dressing-gown and a smoking-cap, in which garb he performed the first steps of a mazurka as a sign of the additional ease which he experienced.

"Not much to dance about either, me boy, " the old soldier said, seating himself in a camp-chair and putting his feet upon another one. "Bedad, we're all on the verge. Unless luck takes a turn there's no saying what may become of us. "

"We have been badder than this before now many a time, " said the yellow-bearded man, in an accent which proclaimed him to be a German. "My money vill come, or you vill vin, or something vill arrive to set all things right. "

"Let's hope so, " the major said fervently. "It's a mercy to get out of these stiff and starched clothes; but I have to be careful of them, for me tailor—bad cess to him! —will give no credit, and there's little of the riddy knocking about. Without good clothes on me back I'd be like a sweeper without a broom. "

The German nodded his intense appreciation of the fact, and puffed a great blue cloud to the ceiling. Sigismond von Baumser was a political refugee from the fatherland, who had managed to become foreign clerk in a small London firm, an occupation which just enabled him to keep body and soul together. He and the major had lodged in different rooms in another establishment until some common leaven of Bohemianism had brought them together. When circumstances had driven them out of their former abode, it had occurred to the major that by sharing his rooms with Von Baumser he would diminish his own expenses, and at the same time secure an agreeable companion, for the veteran was a sociable soul in his unofficial hours and had all the Hibernian dislike to solitude. The arrangement commended itself to the German, for he had a profound admiration for the other's versatile talents and varied experiences; so he grunted an acquiescence and the thing was done. When the major's luck was good there were brave times in the little fourth floor back. On the other hand, if any slice of good fortune came in the German's way, the major had a fair share of the prosperity. During the hard times which intervened between these gleams of opulence, the pair roughed it uncomplainingly as best they might. The major would sometimes create a fictitious splendour by dilating upon the beauties of Castle Dunross, in county Mayo, which is the headquarters of all the Clutterbucks. "We'll go and live there some day, me boy, " he would say, slapping his comrade on the back. "It will be mine from the dungeons forty foot below the ground, right up, bedad, to the flagstaff from which the imblem of loyalty flaunts the breeze. " At these speeches the simple-minded German used to rub his great red hands together with satisfaction, and feel as pleased as though he had actually been presented with the fee simple of the castle in question.

"Have you had your letter? " the major asked with interest, rolling a cigarette between his fingers. The German was expecting his quarterly remittance from his friends at home, and they were both anxiously awaiting it.

Von Baumser shook his head.

"Bad luck to them! they should have sent a wake ago. You should do what Jimmy Towler did. You didn't know Towler, of the Sappers? When he and I were souldiering in Canada he was vexed at the allowance which he had from ould Sir Oliver, his uncle, not turning up at the right time. 'Ged, Toby, ' he says to me, 'I'll warm the old rascal up. ' So he sits down and writes a letter to his uncle, in which he told him his unbusiness-like ways would be the ruin of them, and more to the same effect. When Sir Oliver got the letter he was in such a divil's own rage, that while he was dictating a codicil to his will he tumbled off the chair in a fit, and Jimmy came in for a clean siven thousand a year. "

"Dat was more dan he deserved, " the German remarked. "But you—how do you stand for money? "

Major Clutterbuck took ten sovereigns out of his trouser pocket and placed them upon the table. "You know me law, " he said; "I never, on any consideration, break into these. You can't sit down to play cards for high stakes with less in your purse, and if I was to change one, be George! they'd all go like a whiff o' smoke. The Lord knows when I'd get a start again then. Bar this money I've hardly a pinny. "

"Nor me, " said Von Baumser despondently, slapping his pockets.

"Niver mind, me boy! What's in the common purse, I wonder? "

He looked up at a little leather bag which hung from a brass nail on the wall. In flush times they were wont to deposit small sums in this, on which they might fall back in their hours of need.

"Not much, I fear, " the other said, shaking his head.

"Well, now, we want something to pull us together on a dull day like this. Suppose we send out for a bottle of sparkling, eh? "

"Not enough money, " the other objected.

"Well, well, let's have something cheaper. Beaune, now; Beaune's a good comforting sort of drink. What d'ye say to splitting a bottle of Beaune, and paying for it from the common purse? "

"Not enough money, " the other persisted doggedly.

"Well, claret be it, " sighed the major. "Maybe it's better in this sort of weather. Let us send Susan out for a bottle of claret? "

The German took down the little leather bag and turned it upside down. A threepenny-piece and a penny rolled out. "Dat's all, " he said. "Not enough for claret. "

"But there is for beer, " cried the major radiantly. "Bedad, it's just the time for a quart of fourpinny. I remimber ould Gilder, when he was our chief in India, used to say that a man who got beyond enjoying beer and a clay pipe at a pinch was either an ass or a coxcomb. He smoked a clay at the mess table himself. Draper, who commanded the division, told him it was unsoldier-like. 'Unsoldier-like be demned, ' he said. Ged, they nearly court-martialled the ould man for it. He got the V. C. at the Quarries, and was killed at the Redan. "

A slatternly, slipshod girl answered the bell, and having received her orders and the united available funds of the two comrades, speedily returned with a brace of frothing pint pots. The major ruminated silently over his cigarette for some time, on some unpleasant subject, apparently, for his face was stern and his brows knitted. At last he broke out with an oath.

"Be George! Baumser, I can't stand that young fellow Girdlestone. I'll have to chuck him up. He's such a cold-blooded, flinty-hearted, calculating sort of a chap, that—" The remainder of the major's sentence was lost in the beer flagon.

"What for did you make him your friend, then? "

"Well, " the old soldier confessed, "it seemed to me that if he wanted to fool his money away at cards or any other divilment, Tobias Clutterbuck might as well have the handling of it as any one else. Bedad, he's as cunning as a basketful of monkeys. He plays a safe game for low stakes, and never throws away a chance. Demned if I don't think I've been a loser in pocket by knowing him, while as to me character, I'm very sure I'm the worse there. "

"Vat's de matter mit him? "

"What's not the matter with him. If he's agrayable he's not natural, and if he's natural he's not agrayable. I don't pretend to be a saint. I've seen some fun in me day, and hope to see some more before I die; but there are some things that I wouldn't do. If I live be cards it's all fair and aboveboard. I never play anything but games o' skill, and I reckon on me skill bringing me out on the right side, taking one night with another through the year. Again, at billiards I may not always play me best, but that's gineralship. You don't want a whole room to know to a point what your game is. I'm the last man to preach, but, bedad, I don't like that chap, and I don't like that handsome, brazen face of his. I've spint the greater part of my life reading folks' faces, and never very far out either. "

Von Baumser made no remark, and the two continued to smoke silently, with an occasional pull at their flagons.

"Besides, it's no good to me socially, " the major continued. "The fellow can't keep quiet, else he might pass in a crowd; but that demned commercial instinct will show itself. If he went to heaven he'd start an agency for harps and crowns. Did I tell you what the Honourable Jack Gibbs said to me at the club? Ged, he let me have it straight! 'Buck, ' he said, 'I don't mind you. You're one o' the right sort when all's said and done, but if you ever inthroduce such a chap as that to me again, I'll cut you as well as him for the future. ' I'd inthroduced them to put the young spalpeen in a good humour, for, being short, as ye know, I thought it might be necessary to negotiate a loan from him. "

"Vat did you say his name vas? " Von Baumser asked suddenly.

"Girdlestone. "

"Is his father a Kauffmann? "

"What the divil is a Kauffmann? " the major asked impatiently. "Is it a merchant you mean? "

"Ah, a merchant. One who trades with the Afrikaner? "

"The same. "

Von Baumser took a bulky pocket-book from his inside pocket, and scanned a long list of names therein. "Ah, it is the same, " he cried at last triumphantly, shutting up the book and replacing it. "Girdlestone & Co., African kauf—dat is, merchants—Fenchurch Street, City. "

"Those are they. "

"And you say dey are rich? "

"Yes. "

"Very rich? "

"Yes. "

The major began to think that his companion had been imbibing in his absence, for there was an unfathomable smile upon his face, and his red beard and towsy hair seemed to bristle from some internal excitement.

"Very rich! Ho, ho! Very rich! " he laughed. "I know dem; not as friends, Gott bewahre! but I know dem and their affairs. "

"What are you driving at? Let's have it. Out with it, man. "

"I tell you, " said the German, suddenly becoming supernaturally solemn and sawing his hand up and down in the air to emphasize his remarks, "in tree or four months, or a year at the most, there vill be no firm of Girdlestone. They are rotten, useless—whoo! He blew an imaginary feather up into the air to demonstrate the extreme fragility of the house in question.

"You're raving, Baumser, " said Major Clutterbuck excitedly. "Why, man, their names are above suspicion. They are looked upon as the soundest concern in the City. "

"Dat may be; dat may be, " the German answered stolidly. "Vat I know, I know, and vat I say I say. "

"And how d'ye know it? D'ye tell me that you know lore about it than the men on 'Change and the firms that do business with them? "

"I know vat I know, and I say vat I say, " the other repeated. "Dat tobacco-man Burger is a rogue. Dere is five-and-thirty in the hundred of water in this canaster tobacco, and one must be for ever relighting. "

"And you won't tell me where you heard this of the Girdlestones? "

"It vould be no good to you. It Is enough dat vat I say is certain. Let it suffice that dere are people vat are bound to tell other people all dat dey know about anything whatever. "

"You don't make it over clear now, " the old soldier grumbled. "You mane that these secret societies and Socialists let each other know all that comes in their way and have their own means of getting information. "

"Dat may be, and dat may not be, " the German answered, in the same oracular voice. "I thought, in any case, my good friend Clutterbuck, dat I vould give you vat you call in English the straight tap. It is always vell to have the straight tap. "

"Thank ye, me boy, " the major said heartily. "If the firm's in a bad way, either the youngster doesn't know of it, or else he's the most natural actor that ever lived. Be George! there's the tay-bell; let's get down before the bread and butther is all finished. "

Mrs. Robbins was in the habit of furnishing her lodgers with an evening meal at a small sum per head. There was only a certain amount of bread and butter supplied for this, however, and those who came late were likely to find an empty platter. The two Bohemians felt that the subject was too grave a one to trifle with, so they suspended their judgment upon the Girdlestones while they clattered down to the dining-room.

CHAPTER XI.

SENIOR AND JUNIOR.

Although not a whisper had been heard of it in ordinary commercial circles, there was some foundation for the forecast which Von Baumser had made as to the fate of the great house of Girdlestone. For some time back matters had been going badly with the African traders. If the shrewd eyes of Major Tobias Clutterbuck were unable to detect any indications of this state of affairs in the manner or conversation of the junior partner, the reason simply was that that gentleman was entirely ignorant of the imminent danger which hung over his head. As far as he knew, the concern was as prosperous and as flourishing as it had been at the time of the death of John Harston. The momentous secret was locked in the breast of his grim old father, who bore it about with him as the Spartan lad did the fox—without a quiver or groan to indicate the care which was gnawing at his heart. Placed face to face with ruin, Girdlestone fought against it desperately, and, withal, coolly and warily, throwing away no chance and leaving no stone unturned. Above all, he exerted himself—and exerted himself successfully—to prevent any rumour of the critical position of the firm from leaking out in the city. He knew well that should that once occur nothing could save him. As the wounded buffalo is gored to death by the herd, so the crippled man of business may give up all hope when once his position is known by his fellows. At present, although Von Baumser and a few other such Ishmaelites might have an inkling from sources of their own as to how matters stood, the name of Girdlestone was still regarded by business men as the very synonym for commercial integrity and stability. If anything, there seemed to be more business in Fenchurch Street and more luxury at the residence at Eccleston Square than in former days. Only the stern-faced and silent senior partner knew how thin the veneer was which shone so deceptively upon the surface.

Many things had contributed towards this state of affairs. The firm had been involved in a succession of misfortunes, some known to the world, and others known to no one save the elder Girdlestone. The former had been accepted with such perfect stoicism and cheerfulness that they rather increased than diminished the reputation of the concern; the latter were the more crushing, and also the more difficult to bear.

Lines of fine vessels from Liverpool and from Hamburg were running to the West Coast of Africa, and competition had cut down freightage to the lowest possible point. Where the Girdlestones had once held almost a monopoly there were now many in the field. Again, the negroes of the coast were becoming educated and had a keen eye to business, so that the old profits were no longer obtainable. The days had gone by when flint-lock guns and Manchester prints could be weighed in the balance against ivory and gold dust.

While these general causes were at work a special misfortune had befallen the house of Girdlestone. Finding that their fleet of old sailing vessels was too slow and clumsy to compete with more modern ships, they had bought in two first-rate steamers. One was the *Providence*, a fine screw vessel of twelve hundred tons, and the other was the *Evening Star*, somewhat smaller in size, but both classed A1 at Lloyd's. The former cost twenty-two thousand pounds, and the latter seventeen thousand. Now, Mr. Girdlestone had always had a weakness for petty savings, and in this instance he determined not to insure his new vessels. If the crazy old tubs, for which he had paid fancy premiums for so many years with an eye to an ultimate profit, met with no disaster, surely those new powerful clippers were safe. With their tonnage and horse-power they appeared to him to be superior to all the dangers of the deep. It chanced, however, by that strange luck which would almost make one believe that matters nautical were at the mercy of some particularly malignant demon, that as the *Evening Star* was steaming up Channel in a dense fog on her return from her second voyage, she ran right into the *Providence*, which had started that very morning from Liverpool upon her third outward trip. The *Providence* was almost cut in two, and sank within five minutes, taking down the captain and six of the crew, while the *Evening Star* was so much damaged about the bows that she put into Falmouth in a sinking condition. That day's work cost the African firm more than five and thirty thousand pounds.

Other mishaps had occurred to weaken the firm, apart from their trade with the coast. The senior partner had engaged in speculation without the knowledge of his son, and the result had been disastrous. One of the Cornish tin mines in which he had sunk a large amount of money, and which had hitherto yielded him a handsome return, became suddenly exhausted, and the shares went down to zero. No firm could stand against such a run of bad luck, and the African trading company reeled before it. John Girdlestone had not said a word yet of all this to his son. As claims arose he settled them in the best manner he could, and postponed the inevitable day when he should have to give a true account of their financial position. He hoped against hope that the chapter of accidents or the arrival of some brilliant cargoes from the coast might set the concern on its legs again.

From day to day he had been expecting news of one of his vessels. At last one morning he found a telegram awaiting him at the office. He tore it eagerly open, for it bore the Madeira mark. It was from his agent, Jose Alveciras, and announced that the voyage from which he had hoped so much had been a total failure. The cargo was hardly sufficient to defray the working expenses. As the merchant read it, his head dropped over the table and he groaned aloud. Another of the props which upheld him from ruin had snapped beneath him.

There were three letters lying beside the telegram. He glanced through them, but there was no consolation in any of them. One was from a bank manager, informing him that his account was somewhat overdrawn. Another from Lloyd's Insurance Agency, pointing out that the policies on two of his vessels would lapse unless paid within a certain date. The clouds were gathering very darkly over the African firm, yet the old man bore up against misfortune with dauntless courage. He sat alone in his little room, with his head sunk upon his breast, and his thatched eye-brows drawn down over his keen grey eyes. It was clear to him that the time had come when he must enlighten his son as to the true state of their affairs. With his co-operation he might carry out a plan which had been maturing some months in his brain.

It was a hard task for the proud and austere merchant to be compelled to confess to his son that he had speculated without his knowledge in the capital of the company, and that a large part of that capital had disappeared. These speculations in many instances had promised large returns, and John Girdlestone had withdrawn money from safer concerns, and reinvested it in the hope of getting a higher rate of interest. He had done this with his eyes open to the risk, and knowing that his son was of too practical and cautious a nature to embark in such commercial gambling, he had never consulted him upon the point, nor had he made any entry of the money so invested in the accounts of the firm. Hence Ezra was entirely ignorant of the danger which hung over them, and his father saw that, in order to secure his energetic assistance in the stroke which he was contemplating, it was absolutely necessary that he should know how critical their position was.

The old man had hardly come to this conclusion when he heard the sharp footfall of his son in the outer office and the harsh tones of his voice as he addressed the clerks. A moment or two later the green baize door flew open, and the young man came in, throwing his hat and coat down on one of the chairs. It was evident that something had ruffled his temper.

"Good-morning, " he said brusquely, nodding his head to his father.

"Good-morning, Ezra, " the merchant answered meekly.

"What's the matter with you, father? " his son asked, looking at him keenly. "You don't look yourself, and haven't for some time back. "

"Business worries, my boy, business worries, " John Girdlestone answered wearily.

"It's the infernal atmosphere of this place, " Ezra said impatiently. "I feel it myself sometimes. I wonder you don't start a little country seat with some grounds. Just enough to ask a fellow to shoot over, and with a good billiard board, and every convenience of that sort. It would do for us to spend the time from Saturday to Monday, and allow us to get some fresh air into our lungs. There are plenty of men who can't afford it half as well, and yet have something of the sort. What's the use of having a good balance at your banker's, if you don't live better than your neighbours? "

"There is only one objection to it, " the merchant said huskily, and with a forced laugh; "I have not got a good balance at the banker's. "

"Pretty fair, pretty fair, " his son said knowingly, picking up the long thin volume in which the finance of the firm was recorded and tapping it against the table.

"But the figures there are not quite correct, Ezra, " his father said, still more huskily. "We have not got nearly so much as that. "

"What! " roared the junior partner.

"Hush! For God's sake don't let the clerks hear you. We have not so much as that. We have very little. In fact, Ezra, we have next to nothing in the bank. It is all gone. "

For a moment the young man stood motionless, glaring at his father. The expression of incredulity which had appeared on his features faded away before the earnestness of the other, and was replaced by a look of such malignant passion that it contorted his whole face.

"You fool! " he shrieked, springing forward with the book upraised as though he would have struck the old merchant. "I see it now. You have been speculating on your own hook, you cursed ass! What have you done with it? " He seized his father by the collar and shook him furiously in his wrath.

"Keep your hands off me! " the senior partner cried, wrenching himself free from his son's grasp. "I did my best with the money. How dare you address me so? "

"Did your best! " hissed Ezra, hurling the ledger down on the table with a crash. "What did you mean by speculating without my knowledge, and telling me at the same time that I knew all that was done? Hadn't I warned you a thousand times of the danger of it? You are not to be trusted with money. "

"Remember, Ezra, " his father said with dignity, re-seating himself in the chair from which he had risen, in order to free himself from his son's clutches, "if I lost the money, I also made it. This was a flourishing concern before you were born. If the worst comes to the worst you are only where I started. But we are far from being absolutely ruined as yet. "

"To think of it! " Ezra cried, flinging himself upon the office sofa, and burying his face in his hands. "To think of all I have said of our money and our resources! What will Clutterbuck and the fellows at the club say? How can I alter the ways of life that I have learned? " Then, suddenly clenching his hands, and turning upon his father he broke out, "We must have it back, father; we *must*, by fair means or foul. You must do it, for it was you who lost it. What can we do? How long have we to do it in? Is this known in the City? Oh, I shall be ashamed to show my face on 'Change. " So he rambled on, half-maddened by the pictures of the future which rose up in his mind.

"Be calm, Ezra, be calm! " his father said imploringly. "We have many chances yet if we only make the best of them. There is no use lamenting the past. I freely confess that I was wrong in using this money without your knowledge, but I did it from the best of motives. We must put our heads together now to retrieve our losses, and there are many ways in which that may be done. I want your clear common sense to help me in the matter. "

"Pity you didn't apply to that before, " Ezra said sulkily.

"I have suffered for not doing so, " the older man answered meekly. "In considering how to rally under this grievous affliction which has come upon us, we must remember that our credit is a great resource, and one upon which we have never drawn. That gives us a broad margin to help us while we are carrying out our plans for the future. "

"What will our credit be worth when this matter leaks out? "

"But it can't leak out. No one suspects it for a moment. They might imagine that we are suffering from some temporary depression of trade, but no one could possibly know the sad truth. For Heaven's sake don't you let it out! "

His son broke into an impatient oath.

A flush came into Girdlestone's sallow cheeks, and his eyes sparkled angrily.

"Be careful how you speak, Ezra. There are limits to what I will endure from you, though I make every allowance for your feelings at this sudden catastrophe, for which I acknowledge myself responsible. "

The young man shrugged his shoulders, and drummed his heel against the ground impatiently.

"I have more than one plan in my head, " the merchant said, "by which our affairs may be re-established on their old footing. If we can once get sufficient money to satisfy our present creditors, and so tide over this run of bad luck, the current will set in the other way, and all will go well. And, first of all, there is one question, my boy, which I should like to ask you. What do you think of John Harston's daughter? "

"She's right enough, " the young man answered brusquely.

"She's a good girl, Ezra—a thoroughly good girl, and a rich girl too, though her money is a small thing in my eyes compared to her virtue. "

Young Girdlestone sneered. "Of course, " he said impatiently. "Well, go on—what about her? "

"Just this, Ezra, that there is no girl in the world whom I should like better to receive as my daughter-in-law. Ah, you rogue! you could come round her; you know you could. " The old man poked his long bony finger In the direction of his son's ribs with grim playfulness.

"Oh, that's the idea, is it? " remarked the junior partner, with a very unpleasant smile.

"Yes, that is one way out of our difficulties. She has forty thousand pounds, which would be more than enough to save the firm. At the same time you would gain a charming wife. "

"Yes, there are a good many girls about who might make charming wives, " his son remarked dubiously. "No matrimony for me yet awhile. "

"But it is absolutely necessary, " his father urged.

"A very fine necessity, " Ezra broke in savagely. "I am to tie myself up for life and you are to use all the money in rectifying your blunders. It's a very pretty division of labour, is that. "

"The business is yours as well as mine. It is your interest to invest the money in it, for if it fails you are as completely ruined as I should be. You think you could win her if you tried? "

Ezra stroked his dark moustache complacently, and took a momentary glance at his own bold handsome features in the mirror above the fire-place. "If we are reduced to such an expedient, I think I can answer for the result, " he said. "The girl's not a bad-looking one. But you said you had several plans. Let us hear some of the other ones. If the worst comes to the worst I might consent to that—on condition, of course, that I should have the whole management of the money. "

"Quite so—quite so, " his father said hurriedly. "That's a dear, good lad. As you say, when all other things fail we can always fall back upon that. At present I intend to raise as much money as I can upon our credit, and invest it in such a manner as to bring in a large and immediate profit. "

"And how do you intend to do this? " his son asked doubtfully.

"I intend, " said John Girdlestone, solemnly rising up and leaning his elbow against the mantelpiece—"I intend to make a corner in diamonds. "

CHAPTER XII.

A CORNER IN DIAMONDS.

John Girdlestone propounded his intention with such dignity and emphasis that he evidently expected the announcement to come as a surprise upon his son. If so, he was not disappointed, for the young man stared open-eyed.

"A corner in diamonds! " he repeated. "How will you do that? "

"You know what a corner is, " his father explained. "If you buy up all the cotton, say, or sugar in the market, so as to have the whole of it in your own hands, and to be able to put your own price on it in selling it again—that is called making a corner in sugar or cotton. I intend to make a corner in diamonds. "

"Of course, I know what a corner is, " Ezra said impatiently. "But how on earth are you going to buy all the diamonds in? You would want the capital of a Rothschild? "

"Not so much as you think, my boy, for there are not any great amount of diamonds in the market at any one time. The yield of the South African fields regulates the price. I have had this idea in my head for some time, and have studied the details. Of course, I should not attempt to buy in all the diamonds that are in the market. A small portion of them would yield profit enough to float the firm off again. "

"But if you have only a part of the supply in your hands, how are you to regulate the market value? You must come down to the prices at which other holders are selling. "

"Ha! Ha! Very good! very good! " the old merchant said, shaking his head good-humouredly. "But you don't quite see my plan yet. You have not altogether grasped it. Allow me to explain it to you. "

His son lay back upon the sofa with a look of resignation upon his face. Girdlestone continued to stand upon the hearth-rug and spoke very slowly and deliberately, as though giving vent to thoughts which had been long and carefully considered.

"You see, Ezra, " he said, "diamonds, being a commodity of great value, of which there is never very much in the market at one time, are extremely sensitive to all sorts of influences. The value of them varies greatly from time to time. A very little thing serves to depreciate their price, and an equally small thing will send it up again. "

Ezra Girdlestone grunted to show that he followed his father's remarks.

"I did some business in diamonds myself when I was a younger man, and so I had an opportunity of observing their fluctuations in the market. Now, there is one thing which invariably depreciates the price of diamonds. That is the rumour of fresh discoveries of mines in other parts of the world. The instant such a thing gets wind the value of the stones goes down wonderfully. The discovery of diamonds in Central India not long ago had that effect very markedly, and they have never recovered their value since. Do you follow me? "

An expression of interest had come over Ezra's face, and he nodded to show that he was listening.

"Now, supposing, " continued the senior partner, with a smile on his thin lips, "that such a report got about. Suppose, too, that we were at this time, when the market was in a depressed condition, to invest a considerable capital in them. If these rumours of an alleged discovery turned out to be entirely unfounded, of course the value of the stones which we held would go up once more, and we might very well sell out for double or treble the sum that we invested. Don't you see the sequence of events? "

"There seems to me to be rather too much of the 'suppose' in it, " remarked Ezra. "How do we know that such rumours will get about; and if they do, how do we know that they will prove to be unfounded? "

"How are we to know? " the merchant cried, wriggling his long lank body with amusement. "Why, my lad, if we spread the rumours ourselves we shall have pretty good reason to believe that they are unfounded. Eh, Ezra? Ha! ha! You see there are some brains in the old man yet. "

Ezra looked at his father in considerable surprise and some admiration. "Why, damn it! " he exclaimed, "it's dishonest. I'm not sure that it's not actionable. "

"Dishonest! Pooh! " The merchant snapped his fingers. "It's finesse, my boy, commercial finesse. Who's to trace it, I should like to know. I haven't worked out all the details—I want your co-operation over that—but here's a rough sketch of my plan. We send a man we can depend upon to some distant part of the world—Chimborazo, for example, or the Ural Mountains. It doesn't matter where, as long as it is out of the way. On arriving at this place our agent starts a report that he has discovered a diamond mine. We should even go the length, if he considers it necessary, of hiding a few rough stones in the earth, which he can dig up to give colour to his story. Of course the local press would be full of this. He might present one of the diamonds to the editor of the nearest paper. In course of time a pretty coloured description of the new diamond fields would find its way to London and thence to the Cape. I'll answer for it that the immediate effect is a great drop in the price of stones. We should have a second agent at the Cape diamond fields, and he would lay our money out by buying in all that he could while the panic lasted. Then, the original scare having proved to be all a mistake, the prices naturally go up once more, and we get a long figure for all that we hold. That's what I mean by making 'a corner in diamonds. ' There is no room in it for any miscalculation. It is as certain as a proposition of Euclid, and as easily worked out. "

"It sounds very nice, " his son remarked thoughtfully. "I'm not so sure about its working, though. "

"It must work well. As far as human calculation can go there is no possibility of failure. Besides, my boy, never lose sight of the fact that we shall be speculating with other people's money. We ourselves have nothing to lose, absolutely nothing. "

"I am not likely to lose sight of it, " said Ezra angrily, his mind coming back to his grievance.

"I reckon that we can raise from forty to fifty thousand pounds without much difficulty. My name is, as you know, as good as that of any firm in the City. For nearly forty years it has been above stain or suspicion. If we carry on our plans at once, and lay this money out judiciously, all may come right. "

"It's Hobson's choice, " the young man remarked. "We must try some bold stroke of the sort. Have you chosen the right sort of men for agents? You should have men of some standing to set such reports going. They would have more weight then. "

John Girdlestone shook his head despondingly. "How am I to get a man of any standing to do such a piece of business? " he said.

"Nothing easier, " answered Ezra, with a cynical laugh. "I could pick out a score of impecunious fellows from the clubs who would be only too glad to earn a hundred or two in any way you can mention. All their talk about honour and so forth is very pretty and edifying, but it's not meant for every day use. Of course we should have to pay him. "

"Them, you mean? "

"No, we should only want one man. "

"How about our purchaser at the diamond fields? "

"You don't mean to say, " Ezra said roughly, "that you would be so absurd as to trust any man with our money. Why, I wouldn't let the Archbishop of Canterbury out of my sight with forty thousand pounds of mine. No, I shall go myself to the diamond fields—that is, if I can trust you here alone. "

"That is unkind, Ezra, " said his father. "Your idea is an excellent one. I should have proposed it myself but for the discomforts and hardships of such a journey. "

"There's no use doing things by halves, " the young man remarked. "As to our other agent, I have the very man—Major Tobias Clutterbuck. He is a shrewd, clever fellow, and he's always hard up. Last week he wanted to borrow a tenner from me. The job would be a godsend to him, and his social rank would be a great help to our plan. I'll answer for his jumping at the idea. "

"Sound him on the subject, then. "

"I will. "

"I am glad, " said the old merchant, "that you and I have had this conversation, Ezra. The fact of my having speculated without your knowledge, and deceived you by a false ledger, has often weighed heavily upon my conscience, I assure you. It is a relief to me to have told you all. "

"Drop the subject, then, " Ezra said curtly. "I must put up with it, for I have no redress. The thing is done and nothing can undo it; but I consider that you have willfully wasted the money. "

"Believe me, I have tried to act for the best. The good name of our firm is everything to me. I have spent my whole life in building it up, and if the day should come when it must go, I trust that I may have gone myself. There is nothing which I would not do to preserve it. "

"I see they want our premiums, " Ezra said, glancing at the open letter upon the table. "How is it that none of those ships go down? That would give us help. "

"Hush! hush! " John Girdlestone cried imploringly. "Speak in a whisper when you talk of such things. "

"I can't understand you, " said Ezra petulantly. "You persistently over-insure your ships, year after year. Look at the *Leopard*; it is put at more than twice what she was worth as new. And the *Black Eagle*, I dare say, is about the same. Yet you never have an accident with them, while your two new uninsured clippers run each other down. "

"Well, what more can I do? " replied the merchant "They are thoroughly rotten. I have done nothing for them for years. Sooner or later they must go. I cannot do any more. "

"I'd make 'em go down quick enough, " muttered Ezra, with an oath. "Why don't you make old Miggs bore a hole in them, or put a light to a barrel of paraffin? Bless your soul! the thing's done every day. What's the use of being milk-and-watery about it? "

"No, no, Ezra! " cried his father. "Not that—not that. It's one thing letting matters take their course, and it is another thing giving positive orders to scuttle a ship. Besides, it would put us in Miggs' power. It would be too dangerous. "

"Please yourself, " said Ezra, with a sneer. "You've got us into the mess and you must take us out again. If the worst comes to the worst I'll tell you what I'll do. I'll marry Kate Harston, wash my hands of the firm, leave you to settle matters with the creditors, and retire with the forty thousand pounds; " with which threat the junior partner took up his hat and swaggered out of the office.

After his departure, John Girdlestone spent an hour in anxious thought, arranging the details of the scheme which he had just submitted to his son. As he sat, his eye chanced to fall upon the two letters lying on his desk, and it struck him that they had better be attended to. It did not suit his plans to fall back upon his credit just yet. It has been already shown that he was a man of ready resource. He rang the bell and summoned his senior clerk.

"Good morning, John, " he said affably.

"Good morning, Mr. Girdlestone, good morning, sir, " said wizened little John Gilray, rubbing his thin yellow hands together, as a sign of his gratification.

"I hear, John, that you have come into a legacy lately, " Mr. Girdlestone said.

"Yes, sir. Fifteen hundred pounds, sir. Less legacy duty and incidental expenses, fourteen hundred and twenty-eight six and fourpence. My wife's brother Andrew left it, sir, and a very handsome legacy too. "

John Girdlestone smiled with the indulgent smile of one to whom such a sum was absolutely nothing.

"What have you done with the money, then, John? " he asked carelessly.

"Banked it, sir, in the United Metropolitan. "

"In the United Metropolitan, John? Let me see. Their present rate of interest is three and a half? "

"Three, sir, " said John.

"Three! Dear me, John, that is poor interest, very poor indeed. It is most fortunate that I made these inquiries. I was on the point of drawing fourteen hundred pounds from one of my correspondents as a temporary convenience. For this I should pay him five per cent. I have no objection, John, as you are an old servant of the firm, to giving you the preference in this matter. I cannot take more than fourteen hundred—but I shall be happy to accommodate you up to that sum at the rate named. "

John Gilray was overwhelmed by this thoughtful and considerate act. "It is really too generous and kind, sir, " he said. "I don't know how to thank you. "

"Don't mention it, John, " the senior partner said grandly. "The firm is always glad to advance the interests of its employees in any reasonable manner. Have you your cheque-book with you? Fill it up for fourteen hundred. No more, John; I cannot oblige you by taking any more. "

The head clerk having made out his cheque for the amount, and having signed his name to it in a cramped little quaint handwriting, which reminded one of his person, was duly presented with a receipt and dismissed to his counting-house. There he entertained the other clerks by a glowing description of the magnanimity of his employer.

John Girdlestone took some sheets of blue official paper from a drawer, and his quill pen travelled furiously over them with many a screech and splutter.

"Sir, " he said to the bank manager, "I enclose fourteen hundred pounds, which represents the loose cash about the office. I shall make a heavy deposit presently. In the meantime, you will, of course, honour anything that may be presented. —Yours truly, JOHN GIRDLESTONE. "

To Lloyd's Insurance Agency he wrote: —"Sir, —Enclosed you will find cheque for 241 pounds seven shillings and sixpence, being amount due as premium on the *Leopard*, *Black Eagle*, and *Maid of Athens*. Should have forwarded cheque before, but with so many things of importance to look after these trifles are liable to be overlooked. "

These two epistles having been sealed, addressed, and despatched, the elder Girdlestone began to feel somewhat more easy in his mind, and to devote himself once more to the innocent amusement of planning how a corner might best be created in diamonds.

CHAPTER XIII.

SHADOW AND LIGHT.

John Girdlestone's private residence in Eccleston Square was a large and substantial house in a district which the wave of fashion had passed over in its westward course. It might still, however, be said to be covered by a deposit of eminent respectability. The building was stern and hard, and massive in its external appearance, but the interior was luxury itself, for the old merchant, in spite of his ascetic appearance, was inclined to be a sybarite at heart, and had a due appreciation of the good things of this world. Indeed, there was an oriental and almost barbarous splendour about the great rooms, where the richest of furniture was interspersed with skins from the Gaboon, hand-worked ivory from Old Calabar, and the thousand other strange valuables which were presented by his agents to the African trader.

After the death of his friend, Girdlestone had been as good as his word. He had taken Kate Harston away from the desolate house at Fulham and brought her to live with him. From the garrets of that palatial edifice to the cellars she was at liberty to roam where she would, and do what she chose. The square garden too, with its smoke-dried trees and faded lawn, was at her disposal, in which she might walk, or work, or read. No cares or responsibilities were imposed upon her. The domestic affairs were superintended by a stern housekeeper, who bore a quaint resemblance to Girdlestone himself in petticoats, and who arranged every detail of housekeeping. The young girl had apparently only to exist and to be happy.

Yet the latter item was not so easy as it might seem. It was not a congenial atmosphere. Her whole society consisted of the stern, unemotional merchant and his vulgar, occasionally brutal, son. At first, while the memory of her father was still fresh, she felt her new surroundings acutely, contrasting, as they did, with her happy Fulham home. Gradually, however, as time deadened the sting, she came to accommodate herself to circumstances. The two men left her very much to her own devices. Girdlestone was so engrossed in his business that he had little time to inquire into her pursuits, and Ezra, being addicted to late hours, was seldom seen except at breakfast-time, when she listened with awe to his sporting slang and cynical comments upon men and manners.

John Girdlestone had been by no means overjoyed upon the return of the Dimsdales from Edinburgh to learn that his ward had been thrown into the company of her young cousin. He received her coldly and forbade her to visit Phillimore Gardens for some time to come. He took occasion also to speak of Tom, and to assure her that he had received very serious accounts as to his spiritual state. "He is addicted to all manner of debasing pursuits, " he remarked, "and it is my particular wish that you should avoid him. " Learning that young Dimsdale was in London, he even took the precaution of telling off a confidential footman to walk behind her on all occasions, and to act either as an escort or as a sentry.

It chanced, however, that one day, a few weeks after her return, Kate found an opportunity of recovering her freedom. The footman had been despatched upon some other duty, so she bethought herself that a book was to be bought and some lace to be matched, and several other important feminine duties to be fulfilled. It happened, however, that as she walked sedately down Warwick Street, her eyes fell upon a very tall and square-shouldered young man, who was lounging in her direction, tapping his stick listlessly against the railings, as is the habit of idle men. At this Kate forgot incontinently all about the book and the lace, while the tall youth ceased to tap the railings, and came striding towards her with long springy footsteps and a smiling face.

"Why Cousin Tom, who would have thought of meeting you here? " she exclaimed, when the first greetings had been exchanged. "It is a most surprising thing. "

It is possible that the incident would not have struck her as so very astonishing after all, had she known that Tom had spent six hours a day for the last fortnight in blockading the entrances to Eccleston Square.

"Most remarkable! " said the young hypocrite. "You see, I haven't anything to do yet, so I walk about London a good deal. It was a lucky chance that sent me in this direction. "

"And how is the doctor? " Kate asked eagerly. "And Mrs. Dimsdale, how is she? You must give my love to them both. "

"How is it that you have never been to see us? " Tom asked reproachfully.

"Mr. Girdlestone thinks that I have been too idle lately, and that I should stay at home. I am afraid it will be some little time before I can steal away to Kensington. "

Tom consigned her guardian under his breath to a region warmer even than the scene of that gentleman's commercial speculations.

"Which way are you going? " he asked.

"I was going to Victoria Street to change my book, and then to Ford Street. "

"What a strange thing! " the young man exclaimed; "I was going in that direction too. " It seemed the more strange, as he was walking in the opposite direction when she met him. Neither seemed inclined to make any comment upon the fact, so they walked on together. "And you have not forgotten the days in Edinburgh yet? " Tom asked, after a long pause.

"No, indeed, " his companion answered with enthusiasm. "I shall never forget them as long as I live. "

"Nor I, " said Tom earnestly. "You remember the day we had at the Pentlands? "

"And the drive round Arthur's Seat. "

"And the time that we all went to Roslin and saw the chapel. "

"And the day at Edinburgh Castle when we saw the jewels and the armoury. But you must have seen all these things many times before? You could not have enjoyed it as much as we did for the first time. "

"Oh yes, I did, " Tom said stoutly, wondering to himself how it was that the easy grace with which he could turn compliments to maidens for whom he cared nothing had so entirely deserted him. "You see, Kate-well—you were not there when I saw them before. "

"Ah, " said Kate demurely, "what a beautiful day it is? I fancied in the morning that it was going to rain. "

Tom was not to be diverted from his subject by any meteorological observations. "Perhaps some time your guardian will allow the dad to take you on another little holiday, " he said hopefully.

"I'm afraid he won't, " answered Kate.

"Why not? "

"Because he seemed so cross when I came back this last time. "

"Why was he cross? " asked Tom.

"Because—" She was about to say that it was because she had been brought in contact with him; but she recollected herself in time.

"Because what? "

"Because he happened to be in a bad temper, " she answered.

"It is too bad that you should have to submit to any one's whims and tempers, " the young man said, switching his stick angrily backwards and forwards.

"Why not? " she asked, laughing. "Everybody has some one over them. If you hadn't, you would never know right from wrong. "

"But he is unkind to you. "

"No, indeed, " said Kate, with decision. "He is really very kind to me. He may appear a little stern at times, but I know that he means it for my own good, and I should be a very foolish girl if I resented it. Besides, he is so pious and good that what may seem a little fault to us would appear a great thing in his eyes. "

"Oh, he is very pious and good, then, " Tom remarked, in a doubtful voice. His shrewd old father had formed his own views as to John Girdlestone's character, and his son had in due course imbibed them from him.

"Yes, of course he is, " answered Kate, looking up with great wondering eyes. "Don't you know that he is the chief supporter of the Purbrook Street Branch of the Primitive Trinitarians, and sits in the front pew three times every Sunday? "

"Ah! " said Tom.

"Yes, and subscribes to all the charitable funds, and is a friend of Mr. Jefferson Edwards, the great philanthropist. Besides, look how good he has been to me. He has taken the place of my father. "

"Hum! " Tom said dubiously; and then, with a little pang at his heart, "Do you like Ezra Girdlestone too? "

"No, indeed, " cried his companion with energy. "I don't like him in the least. He is a cruel, bad-hearted man. "

"Cruel! You don't mean cruel to you, of course. "

"No, not to me. I avoid him as much as I can, and sometimes for weeks we hardly exchange a word. Do you know what he did the other day? It makes me shudder even to think of it. I heard a cat crying pitifully in the garden, so I went out to see what was the matter. When I got outside I saw Ezra Girdlestone leaning out of a window with a gun in his hands—one of those air-guns which don't make any noise when they go off. And there, in the middle of the garden, was a poor cat that he had tied to a bush, and he had been practising at it for ever so long. The poor creature was still alive, but oh! so dreadfully injured. "

"The brute! What did you do? "

"I untied it and brought it inside, but it died during the night. "

"And what did he say? "

"He put up his gun while I was untying it, as if he had half a mind to take a shot at me. When I met him afterwards he said that he would teach me to mind my own business. I didn't mind what he said though, as long as I had the cat. "

"Spoke like that, did he? " said Tom savagely, flushing up to his eyes. "I wish I saw him now. I'd teach him manners, or—"

"You'll certainly get run over if you go on like that, " interrupted Kate.

Indeed, the young man in his indignation was striding over a crossing without the slightest heed of the imminent danger which he ran from the stream of traffic.

"Don't be so excitable, Cousin Tom, " she said, laying her gloved hand upon his arm; "there is nothing to be cross about. "

"Isn't there? " he answered furiously. "It's a pretty state of things that you should have to submit to insults from a brutal puppy like that fellow Ezra Girdlestone. " The pair had managed by this time to get half-way across the broad road, and were halting upon the little island of safety formed by the great stone base of a lamp-post. An interminable stream of 'buses—yellow, purple, and brown—with vans, hansoms, and growlers, blocked the way in front of them. A single policeman, with his back turned to them, and his two arms going like an animated semaphore, was the only human being in their immediate vicinity. Amid all the roar and rattle of the huge city they were as thoroughly left to themselves as though they were in the centre of Salisbury Plain.

"You must have a protector, " Tom said with decision.

"Oh, Cousin Tom, don't be foolish; I can protect myself very well. "

"You must have some one who has a right to look after you. " The young man's voice was husky, for the back part of his throat had become unaccountably dry of a sudden.

"You can pass now, sir, " roared the constable, for there was a momentary break in the traffic.

"Don't go for a moment, " Tom cried, desperately detaining his companion by the sleeve of her jacket. "We are alone here and can talk. Don't you think—don't you think you could like me a little bit if you were to try? I love you so, Kate, that I cannot help hoping that my love is not all lost. "

"All clear now, sir, " shouted the constable once more.

"Don't mind him, " said Tom, still detaining her on the little-island. "Since I met you in Edinburgh, Kate, I have seemed to be walking in a dream. Do what I will, go where I will, I still have you before my eyes and hear your sweet voice in my ears. I don't believe any girl was ever loved more dearly than I love you, but I find it so hard to put into words the thoughts that I have in my mind. For Heaven's sake, give me some little gleam of hope to carry away with me. You don't dislike me, Kate, do you? "

"You know that I don't, Cousin Tom, " said the young lady, with downcast eyes. He had cornered her so skilfully against the great lamp that she could move neither to the right nor to the left.

"Do you like me, then, Kate? " he asked eagerly, with a loving light in his earnest grey eyes.

"Of course I do. "

"Do you think you could love me? " continued this persistent young man. "I don't mean all at once, and in a moment, because I know very well that I am not worthy of it. But in time don't you think you could come to love me? "

"Perhaps, " murmured Kate, with averted face. It was such a very little murmur that it was wonderful that it should be audible at all; yet it pealed in the young man's ears above the rattle and the clatter of the busy street. His head was very near to hers at the time.

"Now's your time, sir, " roared the semaphoric policeman.

Had Tom been in a less exposed position it is possible that he might have acted upon that well-timed remark from the cunning constable. The centre of a London crossing is not, however, a very advantageous spot for the performance of love passages. As they walked on, threading their way among the vehicles, Tom took his companion's hand in his, and they exchanged one firm grip, which each felt to be of the nature of a pledge. How sunny and bright the dull brick-lined streets appeared to those two young people that afternoon. They were both looking into a future which seemed to be one long vista of happiness and love. Of all the gifts of Providence, surely our want of knowledge of the things which are to come upon us is the most merciful, and the one we could least dispense with!

So happy and so light-hearted were these two lovers that it was not until they found themselves in Warwick Street once more that they came down from the clouds, and realized that there were some commonplace details which must be dealt with in one way or another.

"Of course, I may tell my own people, dearest, about our engagement? " Tom said.

"I wonder what your mother will say? " answered Kate, laughing merrily. "She will be awfully astonished. "

"How about Girdlestone? " asked Tom.

The thought of the guardian had never occurred to either of them before. They stared at each other, and Kate's face assumed such an expression of dismay that her companion burst out laughing.

"Don't be frightened, darling, " he said. "If you like, I'll go in and 'beard the lion in his den. ' There is no time like the present. "

"No, no, dear Tom, " she cried eagerly. "You must not do that. " It was impossible for her to tell him how especially Girdlestone had cautioned her against him, but she felt that it would never do to allow the two to meet. "We must conceal our engagement from Mr. Girdlestone. "

"Conceal our engagement! "

"Yes, Tom. He has warned me so often against anything of the sort, that really I don't know what he would do if he knew about it. He would certainly make it very uncomfortable for me to live with him. Remember I am nearly twenty now, so in a little more than a year I shall be entirely free. That is not very long. "

"I don't know about that, " Tom said doubtfully. "However, if you will be more comfortable, of course that settles the question. It seems rather hard, though, that we should have to conceal it, simply in order to pacify this old bear. "

"It's only for a time, Tom; and you may tell them at home by all means. Now, good-bye, dear; they will see you from the windows if you come nearer. "

"Good-bye, my darling. "

They shook hands and parted, he hurrying away with the glad tidings to Phillimore Gardens, she tripping back to her captivity with the lightest heart that she had felt for a weary time. Passers-by glanced back at the bright little face under the bright little bonnet, and Ezra Girdlestone, looking down at her from the drawing-room window, bethought him that if the diamond speculation should fail it would be no hardship to turn to his father's word.

CHAPTER XIV.

A SLIGHT MISUNDERSTANDING.

The revelation of the real state of the firm's finances was a terrible blow to Ezra Girdlestone. To a man of his overbearing, tempestuous disposition failure and poverty were bitter things to face. He had been wont to tread down before him all such little difficulties and obstacles as came across him in his former life. Now he encountered a great barrier which could not be passed so easily, and he raged and chafed before it. It made him still more wroth to think that the fault was none of his. All his life he had reckoned, as a matter of course, that when his father passed away he would be left almost a millionaire. A single half-hour's conversation had shattered this delusion and left him face to face with ruin. He lost his sleep and became restless and hollow-eyed. Once or twice he was seen the worse for drink in the daytime.

He was a man of strong character, however, and though somewhat demoralized by the sudden shock, he threw away no point in the game which he and his father were playing. He saw clearly that only a bold stroke could save them. He therefore threw himself heart and soul into the diamond scheme, and worked out the details in a masterly manner. The more he looked into it the more convinced he became, not only of its feasibility, but of its absolute safety. It seemed as though it were hardly possible that it should fail.

Among other things he proceeded to qualify himself as a dealer in diamonds. It happened that he was acquainted with one of the partners of the firm of Fugger & Stoltz, who did the largest import trade in precious stones. Through his kindness he received practical instructions in the variety and value of diamonds, and learned to detect all those little flaws and peculiarities which are only visible to the eye of an expert, and yet are of the highest importance in determining the price of a stone. With such opportunities Ezra made rapid progress, and within a few weeks there were not many dealers in the trade who had a better grasp of the subject.

Both the Girdlestones recognized that the success of their plan depended very largely upon their choice of an agent, and both were of the opinion that in Major Tobias Clutterbuck they had just the man that they were in want of. The younger merchant had long felt vaguely that the major's social position, combined with his impecuniosity and the looseness of his morality, as inferred from his mode of life, might some day make him a valuable agent under delicate circumstances. As to the old soldier's own inclinations, Ezra flattered himself that he knew the man's nature to a nicety. It was simply a question of the price to be paid. No doubt the figure would be substantial, but he recognized with a trader's instinct that the article was a superior one, and he was content to allow for the quality in estimating the value.

Early one April afternoon the major was strutting down St. James's Street, frock-coated and kid-gloved, with protuberant chest and glittering shoes which peeped out from beneath the daintiest of gaiters. Young Girdlestone, who had been on the look-out from a club window, ran across and intercepted him.

"How are you, my dear major? " he cried, advancing upon him with outstretched hand and as much show of geniality as his nature permitted.

"How d'ye do? How d'ye do? " said the other somewhat pompously. He had made up his mind that nothing was to be done with the young man, and yet he was reluctant to break entirely with one whose purse was well lined and who had sporting proclivities.

"I've been wishing to speak with you for some days, major, " said Ezra. "When could I see you? "

"You'll niver see me any plainer than you do at this very moment, " the old soldier answered, taking a sidelong glance of suspicion at his companion.

"Ah, but I wish to speak to you quietly on a matter of business, " the young merchant persisted. "It's a delicate matter which may need some talking over, and, above all, it is a private matter. "

"Ged! " said the major, with a wheezy laugh, "you'd have thought I wanted to borrow money if I had said as much. Look here now, we'll go into White's private billiard-room, and I'll let you have two hunthred out of five for a tinner—though it's as good as handing you the money to offer you such odds. You can talk this over while we play. "

"No, no, major, " urged the junior partner. "I tell you it is a matter of the greatest importance to both of us. Can you meet me at Nelson's Cafe at four o'clock? I know the manager, and he'll let us have a private room. "

"I'd ask you round to me own little place, " the major said, "but it's rather too far. Nelson's at four. Right you are! 'Punctuality is next to godliness, ' as ould Willoughby of the Buffs used to say. You didn't know Willoughby, eh? Gad, he was second to a man at Gib in '47. He brought his man on the ground, but the opponents didn't turn up. Two minutes after time Willoughby wanted his man to leave. 'Teach 'em punctuality, ' he said. 'Can't be done, ' said his man. '*Must* be done, ' said Willoughby. 'Out of the question, ' said the man, and wouldn't budge. Willoughby persisted; there were high words and a quarrel. The docther put 'em up at fifteen paces, and the man shot Willoughby through the calf of the leg. He was a martyr to punctuality. Four o'clock-bye, bye! " The major nodded pleasantly and swaggered away, flourishing his little cane jauntily in the air.

In spite of his admiration of punctuality, as exemplified in the person of Willoughby of the Buffs, the major took good care to arrive at the trysting-place somewhat behind the appointed time. It was clear to him that some service or other was expected of him, and it was obviously his game therefore to hang back and not appear to be too eager to enter into young Girdlestone's views. When he presented himself at the entrance of Nelson's Cafe the young merchant had been fuming and chafing in the sitting-room for five and twenty minutes.

It was a dingy apartment, with a single large horse-hair chair and half a dozen small wooden dittoes, placed with mathematical precision along the walls. A square table in the centre and a shabby mirror over the mantelpiece completed the furniture. With the instinct of an old campaigner the major immediately dropped into the arm-chair, and, leaning luxuriously back, took a cigar from his case and proceeded to light it. Ezra Girdlestone seated himself near the table and twisted his dark moustache, as was his habit when collecting himself.

"What will you drink? " he asked,

"Anything that's going. "

"Fetch in a decanter of brandy and some seltzer water, " said Ezra to the waiter; "then shut the door and leave us entirely to ourselves. "

When the liquor was placed upon the table he drank off his first glass at a gulp, and then refilled it. The major placed his upon the mantelpiece beside him without tasting it. Both were endeavouring to be at their best and clearest in the coming interview, and each set about it in his own manner.

"I'll tell you why I wanted to have a chat with you, major, " Ezra said, having first opened the door suddenly and glanced out as a precaution against eavesdroppers. "I have to be cautious, because what I have to say affects the interest of the firm. I wouldn't for the world have any one know about it except yourself. "

"What is it, me boy? " the major asked, with languid curiosity, puffing at his weed and staring up at the smoke-blackened ceiling.

"You understand that in commercial speculations the least breath of information beforehand may mean a loss of thousands on thousands. "

The major nodded his head as a sign that he appreciated this fact.

"We have a difficult enterprise on which we are about to embark, " Ezra said, leaning forward and sinking his voice almost to a whisper. "It is one which will need great skill and tact, though it may be made to pay well if properly managed. You follow me? "

His companion nodded once more.

"For this enterprise we require an agent to perform one of the principal parts. This agent must possess great ability, and, at the same time, be a man on whom we can thoroughly rely. Of course we do not expect to find such qualities without paying for them. "

The major grunted a hearty acquiescence.

"My father, " continued Ezra, "wanted to employ one of our own men. We have numbers who are capable in every way of managing the business. I interfered, however. I said that I had a good friend, named Major Tobias Clutterbuck, who was well qualified for the position. I mentioned that you were of the blood of the old Silesian kings. Was I not right? "

"Begad you were not. Milesian, sir; Milesian! "

"Ah, Milesian. It's all the same. "

"It's nothing of the sort, " said the major indignantly.

"I mean it was all the same to my father. He wouldn't know the difference. Well, I told him of your high descent, and that you were a traveller, a soldier, and a man of steady and trustworthy habits. "

"Eh? " ejaculated the major involuntarily. "Well, all right. Go on! "

"I told him all this, " said Ezra slowly, "and I pointed out to him that the sum of money which he was prepared to lay out would be better expended on such a man than on one who had no virtues beyond those of business. "

"I didn't give you credit for so much sinse! " his companion exclaimed with enthusiasm.

"I said to him that if the matter were left entirely in your hands we could rely upon its being done thoroughly. At the same time, we should have the satisfaction of knowing that the substantial sum which we are prepared to pay our agent had come into worthy hands. "

"You hit it there again, " murmured the veteran.

"You are prepared, then, " said Ezra, glancing keenly at him, "to put yourself at our orders on condition that you are well paid for it? "

"Not so fast, me young friend, not so fast! " said the major, taking his cigar from between his lips and letting the blue smoke curl round his head. "Let's hear what it is that you want me to do, and then I'm riddy to say what I'll agree to and what I won't. I remimber Jimmy Baxter in Texas—"

"Hang Jimmy Baxter! " Ezra cried impatiently.

"That's been done already, " observed the major calmly. "Lynched for horse-stealing in '66. However, go on, and I'll promise not to stop you until you have finished. "

Thus encouraged, Ezra proceeded to unfold the plan upon which the fortunes of the House of Girdlestone depended. Not a word did he say of ruin or danger, or the reasons which had induced this speculation. On the contrary, he depicted the affairs of the firm as being in a most nourishing condition, and this venture as simply a small insignificant offshoot from their business, undertaken as much for amusement as for any serious purpose. Still, he laid stress upon the fact that though the sum in question was a small one to the firm, yet it was a very large one in other men's eyes. As to the morality of the scheme, that was a point which Ezra omitted entirely to touch upon. Any comment upon that would, he felt, be superfluous when dealing with such a man as his companion.

"And now, major, " he concluded, "provided you lend us your name and your talents to help us in our speculation, the firm are prepared to meet you in a most liberal spirit in the matter of remuneration. Of course your voyage and your expenses will be handsomely paid. You will have to travel by steamer to St. Petersburg, provided that we choose the Ural Mountains as the scene of our imaginary find. I hear that there is high play going on aboard these boats, and with your well-known skill you will no doubt be able to make the voyage a remunerative one. We calculate that at the most you will be in Russia about three months. Now, the firm thought that it would be very fair if they were to guarantee you two hundred and fifty pounds, which they would increase to five hundred in case of success; of course by that we mean complete success, such as would be likely to attend your exertions. "

Now, had there been any third person in the room during this long statement of the young merchant's, and had that third person been a man of observation, he might have remarked several peculiarities in the major's demeanour. At the commencement of the address he might have posed as the very model and type of respectable composure. As the plan was gradually unfolded, however, the old soldier began to puff harder at his cigar until a continuous thick grey cloud rose up from him, through which the lurid tip of the havannah shone like a murky meteor. From time to time he passed his hand down his puffy cheeks, as was his custom when excited. Then he moved uneasily in his chair, cleared his throat huskily, and showed other signs of restlessness, all of which were hailed by Ezra Girdlestone as unmistakable proofs of the correctness of his judgment and of the not unnatural eagerness of the veteran on hearing of the windfall which chance had placed in his way.

When the young man had finished, the major stood up with his face to the empty fire-place, his legs apart, his chest inflated, and his body rocking ponderously backwards and forwards.

"Let me be quite sure that I understand you, " he said. "You wish me to go to Russia? "

"Quite so, " Ezra remarked, rubbing his hands pleasantly.

"You have the goodness to suggest that on me way I should rook me fellow-passengers in the boat? "

"That is to say, if you think it worth your while. "

"Quite so, if I think it worth me while. I am then to procade across the counthry to some mountains—"

"The Urals. "

"And there I am to pretind to discover certain diamond mines, and am to give weight to me story by the fact that I am known to be a man of good birth, and also by exhibiting some rough stones which you wish me to take out with me from England? "

"Quite right, major, " Ezra said encouragingly.

"I am then to tilegraph or write this lie to England and git it inserted in the papers? "

"That's an ugly word, " Ezra remonstrated. "This 'report' we will say. A report may be either true or false, you know. "

"And by this report, thin, " the major continued, "you reckon that the market will be so affected that your father and you will be able to buy and sell in a manner that will be profitable to you, but by which you will do other people out of their money? "

"You have an unpleasant way of putting it, " said Ezra, with a forced laugh; "but you have the idea right. "

"I have another idea as well, " roared the old soldier, flushing purple with passion. "I've an idea that if I was twenty years younger I'd see whether you'd fit through that window, Master Girdlestone. Ged! I'd have taught you to propose such a schame to a man with blue blood in his veins, you scounthrel! "

Ezra fell back in his chair. He was outwardly composed, but there was a dangerous glitter in his eye, and his face had turned from a healthy olive to a dull yellow tint.

"You won't do it? " he gasped.

"Do it! D'ye think that a man who's worn Her Majesty's scarlet jacket for twenty years would dirty his hands with such a trick? I tell ye, I wouldn't do it for all the money that iver was coined. Look here, Girdlestone, I know you, but, by the Lord, you don't know me! "

The young merchant sat silently in his chair, with the same livid colour upon his face and savage expression in his eyes. Major Tobias Clutterbuck stood at the end of the table, stooping forward so as to lean his hands upon it, with his eyes protuberant and his scanty grey fringe in a bristle with indignation.

"What right had you to come to me with such a proposal? I don't set up for being a saint, Lord knows, but, be George! I've some morals, such as they are, and I mean to stick to them. One of me rules of life has been niver to know a blackgaird, and so, me young friend, from this day forth you and I go on our own roads. Ged! I'm not particular, but 'you must draw the line somewhere, ' as me frind, Charlie Monteith, of the Indian Horse, used to say when he cut his father-in-law. I draw it at you. "

While the major was solemnly delivering himself of these sentiments, Ezra continued to sit watching him in a particularly venomous manner. His straight, cruel lips were blanched with passion, and the veins stood out upon his forehead. The young man was a famous amateur bruiser, and could fight a round with any professional in London. The old soldier would be a child in his hands. As the latter picked up his hat preparatory to leaving the room, Ezra rose and bolted the door upon the inside. "It's worth five pounds in a police court, " he muttered to himself, and knotting up his great hands, which glittered with rings, he approached his companion with his head sunk upon his breast, his eyes flashing from under his dark brows, and the slow, stealthy step of a beast of prey. There was a characteristic refinement of cruelty about his attack, as though he wished to gloat over the helplessness of his victim, and give him time to realize his position before he set upon him.

If such were his intention he failed signally in producing the desired effect. The instant the major perceived his manoeuvre he pulled himself up to his full height, as he might have done on parade, and slipping his hand beneath the tails of his frock-coat, produced a small glittering implement, which he levelled straight at the young merchant's head.

"A revolver! " Ezra gasped, staggering back.

"No, a derringer, " said the veteran blandly. "I got into the thrick of carrying one when I was in Colorado, and I have stuck to it ever since. You niver know when it may be useful. " As he spoke he continued to hold the black muzzle of his pistol in a dead line with the centre of the young man's forehead, and to follow the latter's movements with a hand which was as steady as a rock. Ezra was no coward, but he ceased his advance and stood irresolute.

"Now, thin, " cried the major, in sharp military accents, "undo that door. "

The young merchant took one look at the threatening apoplectic face of his antagonist, and another at the ugly black spot which covered him. He stooped, and pushed back the bolt.

"Now, open it! Ged, if you don't look alive I'll have to blow a hole in you afther all. You wouldn't be the first man I've killed, nor the last maybe. "

Ezra opened the door precipitately.

"Now walk before me into the strate. "

It struck the waiters at Nelson's well-known restaurant as a somewhat curious thing that their two customers should walk out with such very grave faces and in so unsociable a manner. "C'est la froideur Anglaise! " remarked little Alphonse Lefanue to a fellow exile as they paused in the laying of tables to observe the phenomenon. Neither of them noticed that the stout gentleman behind with his hand placed jauntily in the breast of his coat, was still clutching the brown handle of a pistol.

There was a hansom standing at the door and Major Clutterbuck stepped into it.

"Look ye here, Girdlestone, " he said, as the latter stood looking sulkily up and down the street. "You should learn a lesson from this. Never attack a man unless you're sure that he's unarmed. You may git shot, if you do. "

Ezra continued to stare gloomily into vacancy and took no notice of his late companion's remark.

"Another thing, " said the major. "You must niver take it for granted that every man you mate is as great a blackgaird as yourself. "

The young merchant gave him a malignant glance from his dark eyes and was turning to go, but the gentleman in the cab stretched out his hand to detain him.

"One more lesson, " he said. "Never funk a pistol unless you are sure there's a carthridge inside. Mine hadn't. Drive on, cabby! " With which parting shot the gallant major rattled away down Piccadilly with a fixed determination never again to leave his rooms without a few of Eley's No 4 central fires in his pocket.

CHAPTER XV.

AN ADDITION TO THE HOUSE.

There were rejoicings in Phillimore Gardens over Tom's engagement, for the two old people were both heartily fond of Kate—"our Kate, " as they were wont proudly to call her. The physician chafed at first over the idea of keeping the matter a secret from Girdlestone. A little reflection served to show him, however, that there was nothing to be gained by informing him, while Kate's life, during the time that she was forced to remain under his roof, would be more tolerable as long as he was kept in ignorance of it. In the meanwhile the lovers saw little of each other, and Tom was only consoled by the thought that every day which passed brought him nearer to the time when he could claim his prize without concealment or fear. He went about as happy and as light-hearted a man as any in all London. His mother was delighted at his high spirits, but his bluff old father was not so well satisfied. "Confound the lad! " he said to himself. "He is settling down to a life of idleness. It suits him too well. We must get him to choose one way or the other. "

Accordingly, after breakfast one morning, the doctor asked his son to step with him into the library, where he lit his long cherry-wood pipe, as was his custom after every meal, and smoked for some time in silence.

"You must do something to keep you from mischief, my boy, " he said at last brusquely.

"I'm ready for anything, dad, " replied Tom, "but I don't quite see what I'm fitted for. "

"First of all, what do you think of this? " the doctor asked abruptly, handing a letter over to his son, who opened it and read as follows: —

"DEAR SIR, —

"It has come to my knowledge through my son that your boy has abandoned the study of medicine, and that you are still uncertain as to his future career. I have long had the intention of seeking a young man who might join in our business, and relieve my old shoulders of some of the burden. Ezra urges me to write and propose that your son should become one of us. If he has any taste for business we shall be happy to advance his interest in every way. He would, of course, have to purchase a share in the concern, which would amount to seven thousand pounds, on which he would be paid interest at the rate of five per cent. By allowing this interest to accumulate, and investing also his share of the profits, he might in time absorb a large portion of the business. In case he joined us upon this footing we should have no objection to his name appearing as one of the firm. Should the idea commend itself to you, I should be most happy to talk over details, and to explain to you the advantages which the firm can offer, at my office in Fenchurch Street, any day between ten and four. "

"With kind regards to your family, and hoping that they enjoy the great blessing of health, I remain sincerely yours, "

"JOHN GIRDLESTONE. "

"What d'ye think of that? " the doctor asked, when his son had finished reading it.

"I hardly know, " said Tom; "I should like a little time to think it over. "

"Seven thousand pounds is a good round sum. It is more than half the total capital which I have invested for you. On the other hand, I have heard those who ought to know say there is not a sounder or better managed concern in London. There's no time like the present, Tom. Get your hat, and we'll go down to Fenchurch Street together and look into it. "

While father and son were rattling along in a cab from Kensington to the City, the young man had time to turn the matter over in his mind. He wanted to be at work, and why not take this up as well as anything else. It is true that he disliked what he had seen of both the Girdlestones, but, on the other hand, by becoming a member of the firm he would probably be thrown in the way of meeting the old merchant's ward. This last consideration decided the matter, and long before the cab had pulled up at the long and dirty passage which led to the offices of the great African firm, the party principally interested had fully made up his mind as to the course he should adopt.

They were duly ushered into the small sanctum adorned with the dissected ships, the maps, the charts, the lists of sailing, and the water-colour picture of the barque *Belinda*, where they were received by the head of the firm. With a charming personal modesty, tempered by a becoming pride in the great business which he had himself created, he discoursed upon its transactions and its importance. He took down ledgers and flashed great rows of figures before the eyes of the good doctor, explaining, at the same time, how month after month their receipts increased and their capital grew. Then he spoke touchingly of his own ripe years, and of the quiet and seclusion which he looked forward to after his busy lifetime.

"With my young friend here, " he said, patting Tom affectionately on the shoulder, "and my own boy Ezra, both working together, there will be young blood and life in the concern. They'll bring the energy, and when they want advice they can come to the old man for it. I intend in a year or so, when the new arrangement works smoothly, to have a run over to Palestine. It may seem a weakness to you, but all my life I have hoped some day to stand upon that holy ground, and to look down on those scenes which we have all imagined to ourselves. Your son will start with a good position and a fair income, which he will probably double before he is five years older. The money invested by him is simply to ensure that he shall have a substantial interest in promoting the affairs of the firm. " Thus the old man ran on, and when Tom and his father left the office with the sound of great sums of money, and huge profits, and heavy balances, and safe investments, all jostling each other in their brains, they had both made up their minds as to the future.

Hence in a couple of days there was a stir in the legal house of Jones, Morgan, & Co., with much rustling of parchment, and signing of names, and drinking of inferior sherry. The result of all which was that the firm of Girdlestone & Co. were seven thousand pounds the richer, and Thomas Dimsdale found himself a recognized member of a great commercial house with all the rights and privileges appertaining thereto.

"A good day's work, Tom, " said the old doctor, as they left the lawyer's office together. "You have now taken an irrevocable step in life, my boy. The world is before you. You belong to a first-class firm and you have every chance. May you thrive and prosper. "

"If I don't it won't be my fault, " Tom answered with decision. "I shall work with my whole heart and soul. "

"A good day's work, Ezra, " the African merchant was remarking at that very moment in Fenchurch Street. "The firm is pinched again for working expenses. This will help; " and he threw a little slip of green paper across the table to his son.

"It will help us for a time, " Ezra said, gloomily, glancing at the figures. "It was fortunate that I was able to put you on his track. It is only a drop in the ocean, however. Unless this diamond spec. comes off, nothing can save us. "

"But it shall come off, " his father answered resolutely. He had succeeded in obtaining an agent who appeared to be almost as well fitted for the post as the recalcitrant major. This worthy had started off already for Russia, where the scene of his operations was to lie.

"I hope so, " said Ezra. "We have neglected no precaution. Langworthy should be at Tobolsk by this time. I saw that he had a bag of rough stones with him which would do well enough for his purpose. "

"We have your money ready, too. I can rely upon rather over thirty thousand pounds. Our credit was good for that, but I did not wish to push it too far for fear of setting tongues wagging. "

"I am thinking of starting shortly in the mail boat *Cyprian*, " said Ezra. "I should be at the diamond fields in little more than a month. I dare say Langworthy won't show any signs for some time yet, but I may as well be there as here. It will give me a little while to find my way about. You see, if the tidings and I were to come almost simultaneously, it might arouse suspicions. In the meantime, no one knows our little game. "

"Except your friend Clutterbuck. "

A dark shadow passed over Ezra's handsome face, and his cruel lip tightened in a way which boded little good to the old soldier should he ever lie at his mercy.

CHAPTER XVI.

THE FIRST STEP.

It was a proud day for the ex-medical student when he first entered the counting-house of the African firm and realized that he was one of the governing powers in that busy establishment. Tom Dimsdale's mind was an intensely practical one, and although he had found the study of science an irksome matter, he was able to throw himself into business with uncommon energy and devotion. The clerks soon found that the sunburnt, athletic-looking young man intended to be anything but a sleeping partner, and both they and old Gilray respected him accordingly.

The latter had at first been inclined to resent the new arrangement as far as his gentle down-trodden nature could resent anything. Hitherto he had been the monarch of the counting-house in the absence of the Girdlestones, but now a higher desk had been erected in a more central portion of the room, and this was for the accommodation of the new comer. Gilray, after his thirty years of service, felt this usurpation of his rights very keenly; but there was such a simple kindness about the invader, and he was so grateful for any assistance in his new duties, that the old clerk's resentment soon melted away.

A little incident occurred which strengthened this kindly feeling. It chanced that some few days after Tom's first appearance in the office several of the clerks, who had not yet quite gauged what manner of man this young gentleman might be, took advantage of the absence of the Girdlestones to take a rise out of the manager. One of them, a great rawboned Scotchman, named McCalister, after one or two minor exhibitions of wit concluded by dropping a heavy ruler over the partition of the old man's desk in such a way that it crashed down upon his head as he sat stooping over his writing. Tom, who had been watching the proceedings with a baleful eye, sprang off his stool and made across the office at the offender. McCalister seemed inclined for a moment to brazen it out, but there was a dangerous sling about Tom's shoulders and a flush of honest indignation upon his face. "I didn't mean to hurt him, " said the Scotchman. "Don't hit him, sir! " cried the little manager. "Beg his pardon, " said Tom between his teeth. McCalister stammered out some lame apology, and the matter was ended. It revealed the new partner, however, in an entirely novel light to the inmates of the counting-house. That under such circumstances a complaint should be carried to the senior was only natural, but that the junior should actually take the matter into his own hands and execute lynch law then and there was altogether a new phenomenon. From that day Tom acquired a great ascendancy in the office, and Gilray became his devoted slave. This friendship with the old clerk proved to be very useful, for by means of his shrewd hints and patient teaching the new comer gained a grasp of the business which he could not have attained by any other method.

Girdlestone called him into the office one day and congratulated him upon the progress which he was making. "My dear young man, " he said to him in his patriarchal way, "I am delighted to hear of the way in which you identify yourself with the interests of the firm. If at first you find work allotted to you which may appear to you to be rather menial, you must understand that that is simply due to our desire that you should master the whole business from its very foundations. "

"There is nothing I desire better, " said Tom.

"In addition to the routine of office work, and the superintendence of the clerks, I should wish you to have a thorough grasp of all the details of the shipping, and of the loading and unloading of our vessels, as well as of the storage of goods when landed. When any of our ships are in, I should wish you to go down to the docks and to overlook everything which is done. "

Tom bowed and congratulated himself inwardly upon these new duties, which promised to be interesting.

"As you grow older, " said the senior partner, "you will find it of inestimable value that you have had practical experience of what your subordinates have to do. My whole life has taught me that. When you are in doubt upon any subject you can ask Ezra for assistance and advice. He is a young man whom you might well take as an example, for he has great business capacity. When he has gone to Africa you can come to me if there is anything which you do not understand. " John Girdlestone appeared to be so kindly and benevolent during this and other interviews, that Tom's heart warmed towards him, and he came to the conclusion that his father had judged the old merchant harshly. More than once, so impressed was he by his kindness, that he was on the point of disclosing to him his engagement to his ward, but on each occasion there arose within him a lively recollection of Kate's frightened face when he had suggested such a course, and he felt that without her consent he had no right to divulge the secret.

If the elder Girdlestone improved upon acquaintance it was exactly the reverse with his son Ezra. The dislike with which Tom had originally regarded him deepened as he came in closer contact, and appeared to be reciprocated by the other, so that they held but little intercourse together. Ezra had taken into his own charge all the financial part of the concern, and guarded it the more jealously when he realized that the new partner was so much less simple than he had expected. Thus Tom had no opportunity of ascertaining for himself how the affairs of the firm stood, but believed implicitly, as did Gilray, that every outlay was bringing in a large and remunerative return. Very much astonished would both of them have been had they realized that the working expenses were at present being paid entirely from their own capital until such time as the plot should ripen which was to restore the fortunes of the African company.

In one respect Tom Dimsdale was immeasurably the gainer by his connection with the firm, for without that it is difficult to say how he could have found opportunities for breaking through the barrier which separated him from Kate. The surveillance of the merchant had become stricter of late, and all invitations from Mrs. Dimsdale or other friends who pitied the loneliness of the girl were repulsed by Girdlestone with the curt intimation that his ward's health was not such as to justify him in allowing her to incur any risk of catching a chill. She was practically a prisoner in the great stone cage in Eccleston Square, and even on her walks a warder in the shape of a footman was, as we have seen, told off to guard her. Whatever John Girdlestone's reasons may have been, he had evidently come to the conclusion that it was of the highest importance that she should be kept secluded.

As it was, Tom, thanks to his position as one of the firm, was able occasionally, in spite of every precaution to penetrate through the old man's defensive works. If a question of importance arose at Fenchurch Street during the absence of the senior partner, what more natural than that Mr. Dimsdale should volunteer to walk round to Eccleston Square in order to acquaint him with the fact.

And if it happened that the gentleman was not to be found there, how very natural that the young man should wait half an hour for him, and that Miss Harston should take the opportunity of a chat with an old friend? Precious, precious interviews those, the more so for their rarity. They brightened the dull routine of Kate's weary life and sent Tom back to the office full of spirit and hope. The days were at hand when the memory of them was to shine out like little rifts of light in the dark cloud of existence.

And now the time was coming when it was to be decided whether, by a last bold stroke, the credit of the House of Girdlestone was to be saved, or whether the attempt was to plunge them into deeper and more hopeless ruin. An unscrupulous agent named Langworthy had, as already indicated, been despatched to Russia well primed with instructions as to what to do and how to do it. He had been in the employ of an English corn merchant at Odessa, and had some knowledge of the Russian language which would be invaluable to him in his undertaking. In the character of an English gentleman of scientific tastes he was to establish himself in some convenient village among the Ural Mountains. There he was to remain some little time, so as to arouse confidence in the people before making his pretended discovery. He was then to carry his rough diamonds to Tobolsk, as the nearest large town, and to exhibit them there, backing up his assertion by the evidence of villagers who had seen him dig them up. The Girdlestones knew that that alone would be sufficient when telegraphed to England to produce a panic in the sensitive diamond market. Before any systematic inquiry could be made, Langworthy would have disappeared, and their little speculation would have come off. After that the sooner the people realized that it was a hoax the better for the conspirators. In any case, there seemed to be no possibility that the origin of the rumour could be traced. Meanwhile, Ezra Girdlestone had secured his passage in the Cape mail steamer *Cyprian*. On the night that he left he sat up late in the library at Eccleston Square talking over the matter for the last time with his father.

The old man was pale and nervous. The one weak point in his character was his affection for his son, an affection which he strove to hide under an austere manner, but which was none the less genuine. He had never before parted with him for any length of time, and he felt the wrench keenly. As to Ezra, he was flushed and excited at the thought of the new scenes which lay before him and the daring speculation in which he was about to embark. He flung himself into a chair and stretched his thick, muscular limbs out in front of him.

"I know as much about stones, " he said exultantly, "as any man in London. I was pricing a bag of rough ones at Van Helmer's to-day, and he is reckoned a good judge. He said that no expert could have done it better. Lord bless you! pure or splints, or cracked, or off colour, or spotted, or twin stones, I'm up to them all. I wasn't a pound out in the market value of any one of them. "

"You deserve great credit for your quickness and perseverance, " replied his father. "Your knowledge will be invaluable to you when you are at the fields. Be careful of yourself when you are there, my son, if only for my sake. There are rough fellows at such places, and you must give them soft words. I know that your temper is quick, but remember those wise words, 'He that ruleth his spirit is better than he that taketh a city. '"

"Never fear for me, dad, " said Ezra, with a sinister smile, pointing to a small leather case which lay among his things. "That's the best six-shooter I could get for money. I've taken a tip, you see, from our good friend, the major, and have six answers for any one that wants to argue with me. If I had had that the other day he wouldn't have bounced me so easily. "

"Nay, but Ezra, Ezra, " his father said, in great agitation, "you will promise to be careful and to avoid quarrels and bloodshed. It is against the great law, the new commandment. "

"I won't get into any rows if I can help it, " his son answered. "That's not my game. "

"But if you think that there is no mistake, if your opponent is undoubtedly about to proceed to extremities, shoot him down at once, my dear lad, before he has time to draw. I have heard those who have been out there say that in such cases everything depends upon getting the first shot. I am anxious about you, and shall not be easy until I see you again. "

"Blessed if he hasn't tears in his eyes! " Ezra exclaimed to himself, much astonished at this unprecedented occurrence.

"When do you go? " his father asked.

"My train leaves in an hour or so. I reach the steamer at Southampton about three in the morning, and she starts with the full tide at six. "

"Look after your health, " the old man continued. "Don't get your feet wet, and wear flannel next your skin. Don't forget your religious duties either. It has a good effect upon those among whom you do business. "

Ezra sprang from his chair with an exclamation of disgust and began to pace up and down. "I wish to Heaven you would drop that sort of gammon when we are alone, " he said irritably.

"My dear boy, " said the father, with a mild look of surprise upon his face, "you seem to be under a misapprehension in this matter. You appear to consider that we are embarking upon some unjustifiable undertaking. This is not so. What we are doing is simply a small commercial ruse—a finesse. It is a recognized maxim of trade to endeavour to depreciate the price of whatever you want to buy, and to raise it again when the time comes for selling. "

"It's steering very close to the law, " his son retorted. "No speculating, now, while I am away; whatever comes in must go towards getting us out of this scrape, not to plunging us deeper in the mire. "

"I shall not expend an unnecessary penny. "

"Well, then, good-bye. " said the young man, rising up and holding out his hand. "Keep your eye on Dimsdale and don't trust him. "

"Good-bye, my son, good-bye—God bless you! "

The old merchant was honestly moved, and his voice quivered as he spoke. He stood motionless for a minute or so until the heavy door slammed, and then he threw open the window and gazed sorrowfully down the street at the disappearing cab. His whole attitude expressed such dejection that his ward, who had just entered the room, felt more drawn towards him than she had ever done before. Slipping up to him she placed her warm tender hand upon his sympathetically.

"He will soon be back, dear Mr. Girdlestone, " she said. "You must not be uneasy about him. "

As she stood beside him in her white dress, with a single red ribbon round her neck and a band of the same colour round her waist, she was as fair a specimen of English girl-hood as could have been found in all London. The merchant's features softened as he looked down at her fresh young face, and he put out his hand as though to caress her, but some unpleasant thought must have crossed his mind, for he assumed suddenly a darker look and turned away from her without a word. More than once that night she recalled that strange spasmodic expression of something akin to horror which had passed over her guardian's features as he gazed at her.

CHAPTER XVII.

THE LAND OF DIAMONDS.

The anxious father had not very long to wait before he heard tidings of his son. Upon the first of June the great vessel weighed her anchor in the Southampton Water, and steamed past the Needles into the Channel. On the 5th she was reported from Madeira, and the merchant received telegrams both from the agent of the firm and from his son. Then there was a long interval of silence, for the telegraph did not extend to the Cape at that time, but, at last on the 8th of August, a letter announced Ezra's safe arrival. He wrote again from Wellington, which was the railway terminus, and finally there came a long epistle from Kimberley, the capital of the mining district, in which the young man described his eight hundred miles drive up country and all the adventures which overtook him on the way.

"This place, Kimberley, " he said in his letter, "has grown into a fair-sized town, though a few years ago it was just a camp. Now there are churches, banks, and a club in it. There are a sprinkling of well-dressed people in the streets, but the majority are grimy-looking chaps from the diggings, with slouched hats and coloured shirts, rough fellows to look at, though quiet enough as a rule. Of course, there are blacks everywhere, of all shades, from pure jet up to the lightest yellow. Some of these niggers have money, and are quite independent. You would be surprised at their impertinence. I kicked one of them in the hotel yesterday, and he asked me what the devil I was doing, so I knocked the insolent scoundrel down. He says that he will sue me, but I cannot believe that the law is so servile as to bolster up a black man against a white one.

"Though Kimberley is the capital of the dry diggings, it is not there that all the actual mining is done. It goes on briskly in a lot of little camps, which are dotted along the Vaal River for fifty or sixty miles. The stones are generally bought by licensed agents immediately after they have been found, and are paid for by cheques on banks in Kimberley. I have, therefore, transferred our money to the Standard Bank here, and have taken my licence. I start to-morrow for Hebron, Klipdrift, and other of the mining centres to see for myself how business is done and to make friends with the miners, so as to get myself known. As soon as the news comes I shall buy in all that offers. Keep your eyes on that fellow Dimsdale, and let him know nothing of what is going on. "

He wrote again about a fortnight afterwards, and his letter, as it crossed the Atlantic, passed the outward mail, which bore the news of the wonderful diamond find made by an English geologist among the Ural Mountains.

"I am now on a tour among the camps, " he said. "I have worked right through from Hebron to Klipdrift, Pniel, Cawood's Hope, Waldeck's Plant, Neukirk's Hope, Winterrush, and Bluejacket. To-morrow I push on to Delparte's Hope and Larkin's Flat. I am well received wherever I go, except by the dealers, who are mostly German Jews. They hear that I am a London capitalist, and fear that I may send up the prices. They little know! I bought stones all the way along, but not very valuable ones, for we must husband our resources.

"The process of mining is very simple. The men dig pits in loose gravel lying along the banks of the river, and it is in these pits that the diamonds are found. The black men, or 'boys, ' as they call them, do all the work, and the 'baas, ' or master, superintends. Everything that turns up belongs to the 'baas, ' but the boys have a fixed rate of wages, which never varies, whether the work is paying or not. I was standing at Hebron watching one of the gangs working when the white chap gave a shout, and dived his hand into a heap of stuff he had just turned over, pulling out a dirty looking little lump about the size of a marble. At his shout all the other fellows from every claim within hearing gathered round, until there was quite a crowd.

"'It's a fine stone, ' said the man that turned it up.

"'Fifty carats if it's one, ' cried another, weighing it in the palm of his hand.

"I had my scales with me, so I offered to weigh it. It was sixty-four and a half carats. Then they washed it and examined it. There was a lot of whispering among them and then the one who had found it came forward.

"'You deal, don't you, Mr. Girdlestone? ' he said.

"'Now and then, ' I answered, 'but I'm not very keen about it. I came out here more for pleasure than business.

"'Well, ' he said, 'you may go far before you see a finer stone than this. What will you bid for it? '

"I looked at it. 'It's off-coloured, ' I said.

"'It's white, ' said he and one or two of his chums.

"'Gentlemen, ' I said, 'it is not white. There are two shades of yellow in it. It is worth little or nothing. '

"'Why, if it is yellow it makes it all the more valuable, ' said a big fellow with a black beard and corduroy trousers. 'A yellow stone's as good as a white. '

"'Yes, ' I answered, 'a pure yellow stone is. But this is neither one nor the other. It's off-colour, and you know that as well as I. '

"'Won't you bid for it, then? ' said one of them.

"'I'll bid seventy pounds, ' I said, 'but not a penny more. '

"You should have heard the howl they all set up. 'It's worth five hundred, ' the fellow cried.

"'All right, ' I said, 'keep it and sell it for that; good day, ' and I went off. The stone was sent after me that evening with a request for my cheque, and I sold it for a hundred two days afterwards. [1] You see old Van Harmer's training has come in very handy. I just tell you this little anecdote to let you see that though I'm new in the work I'm not to be done. Nothing in the papers here from Russia. I am ready, come when it may. What would you do if there should be any hitch and the affair did not come off? Would you cut and run, or would you stand by your colours and pay a shilling or so in the pound? The more I think of it the more I curse your insanity in getting us into such a mess. Good-bye. "

"He is right. It was insanity, " said the old merchant leaning his head upon his hands. "It seems unkind of the lad to say so when he is so far away, but he was always plain and blunt. 'If the affair did not come off'—he must have some doubts about the matter, else he would not even suppose such a thing. God knows what I should do then. There are other ways—other ways. " He passed his hand over his eyes as he spoke, as though to shut out some ugly vision. Such a wan, strange expression played over his grim features that he was hardly to be recognized as the revered elder of the Trinitarian Chapel or the esteemed man of business of Fenchurch Street.

He was lost in thought for some little time, and then, rising, he touched the bell upon the table. Gilray trotted in upon the signal so rapidly and noiselessly, that he might have been one of those convenient genii in the Eastern fables, only that the little clerk's appearance, from the tips of his ink-stained fingers to the toes of his seedy boots, was so hopelessly prosaic that it was impossible to picture him as anything but what he was.

"Ah, Gilray! " the merchant began, "is Mr. Dimsdale in the office? "

"Yes, sir. "

"That's all right. He seems to be very regular in his attendance. "

"Very, sir. "

"And seems to take to the business very well. "

"Uncommonly quick, sir, to be sure, " said the head clerk. "What with work among the ships, and work in the office, he's at it late and early. "

"That is very right, " said the old man, playing with the letter weights. "Application in youth, Gilray, leads to leisure in old age. Is the *Maid of Athens* unloading? "

"Mr. Dimsdale has been down to her this morning, sir. They're getting the things out fast. He wants to call attention to the state of the vessel, Mr. Girdlestone. He says that it's making water even in dock, and that some of the hands say that they won't go back in her. "

"Tut! tut! " John Girdlestone said peevishly. "What are the Government inspectors for? There is no use paying them if we are to inspect ourselves. If they insist upon any alterations they shall be made. "

"They were there, sir, at the same time as Mr. Dimsdale, " said Gilray, diffidently.

"Well, what then? " asked his employer.

"He says, sir, that the inspectors went down to the cabin and had some champagne with Captain Spender. They then professed themselves to be very well satisfied with the state of the vessel and came away. "

"There you are! " the senior partner cried triumphantly. "Of course these men can see at a glance how things stand, and if things had really been wrong they would have called attention to it. Let us have no more of these false alarms. You must say a few words on the point to Mr. Dimsdale, as coming from yourself, not from me. Tell him to be more careful before he jumps to conclusions. "

"I will, sir. "

"And bring me ledger No. 33. "

Gilray stretched up his arm and took down a fat little ledger from a high shelf, which he laid respectfully before his employer. Then, seeing that he was no longer wanted, he withdrew.

Ledger No. 33 was secured by a clasp and lock—the latter a patent one which defied all tamperers. John Girdlestone took a small key from his pocket and opened it with a quick snap. A precious volume this, for it was the merchant's private book, which alone contained a true record of the financial state of the firm, all others being made merely for show. Without it he would have been unable to keep his son in the dark for so many months until bitter necessity at last compelled him to show his hand.

He turned the pages over slowly and sadly. Here was a record of the sums sunk in the Lake Tanganyika Gold Company, which was to have paid 33 per cent., and which fell to pieces in the second month of its existence. Here was the money advanced to Durer, Hallett, & Co., on the strength of securities which proved to be the flimsiest of insecurities when tested. Further on was the account of the dealings of the firm with the Levant Petroleum Company, the treasurer of which had levanted with the greater part of the capital. Here, too, was a memorandum of the sums sunk upon the *Evening Star* and the

Providence, whose unfortunate collision had well-nigh proved the death blow of the firm. It was melancholy reading, and perhaps the last page was the most melancholy of all. On it the old man had drawn up in a condensed form an exact account of the present condition of the firm's finances. Here it is exactly word for word as he had written it down himself.

GIRDLESTONE & CO.

Debit.   October 1876
                                      Credit.

Pounds Sterling	Pounds Sterling
Debts incurred previous to disclosure to Ezra 34000	Ezra, in Africa, holds this money with which to speculate. 35000
15000 pounds raised at six months, and 20000 pounds at nine months 35000	Balance in bank, including what remains of Dimsdale's premium. 8400
Interest on said money at 5 per cent. 1125	Profit on the cargo of *Maid of Athens*, now in port. 2000
Working expenses of the firm during the next six months, including cost of ships, at 150 pounds per week 3900	Profit on the cargoes of *Black Eagle*, *Swan* and *Panther*, calculated at the same rate. 6000
Private expenses at Ecclestone Square, say 1000	Deficit 26425
Expenses of Langworthy in Russia, and of my dear son in Africa, say 600	
Insurances 1200	
Total 76825	Total 76825

All this money must be found Within nine months at the outside.

The possibility of the sinking of a ship must not be overlooked—that would bring in from 12000 to 20000 pounds.

"Come, it's not so very bad after all, " the merchant muttered, after he had gone over these figures very slowly and carefully. He leaned back in his chair and looked up at the ceiling with a much more cheerful expression upon his face. "At the worst it is less than thirty thousand pounds. Why, many firms would think little of it. The fact is, that I have so long been accustomed to big balances on the right side that it seems to be a very dreadful thing now that it lies the other way. A dozen things may happen to set all right. I must not forget, however, " he continued, with a darker look, "that I have dipped into my credit so freely that I could not borrow any more without exciting suspicion and having the whole swarm down on us. After all, our hopes lie in the diamonds. Ezra cannot fail. He must succeed. Who can prevent him? "

"Major Tobias Clutterbuck, " cried the sharp, creaky voice of Gilray as if in answer to the question, and the little clerk, who had knocked once or twice unnoticed, opened the door and ushered in the old Campaigner.

[1] It may be well to remark, that this and succeeding incidents occurred in the old Crown Colony days, before the diamond legislation was as strict as it has since become.

CHAPTER XVIII.

MAJOR TOBIAS CLUTTERBUCK COMES IN FOR A THOUSAND POUNDS.

John Girdlestone had frequently heard his son speak of the major in the days when they had been intimate, and had always attributed some of the young man's more obvious vices to the effects of this ungodly companionship. He had also heard from Ezra a mangled version of the interview and quarrel in the private room of Nelson's Restaurant. Hence, as may be imagined, his feelings towards his visitor were far from friendly, and he greeted him as he entered with the coldest of possible bows. The major, however, was by no means abashed by this chilling reception, but stumped forward with beaming face and his pudgy hand outstretched, so that the other had no alternative but to shake it, which he did very gingerly and reluctantly.

"And how are ye? " said the major, stepping back a pace or two, and inspecting the merchant as though he were examining his points with the intention of purchasing him. "Many's the time I've heard talk of ye. It's a real treat to see ye. How are ye? " Pouncing upon the other's unresponsive hand, he wrung it again with effusion.

"I am indebted to Providence for fairly good health, sir, " John Girdlestone answered coldly. "May I request you to take a seat? "

"That was what me friend Fagan was trying to do for twelve years, and ruined himself over it in the ind. He put up at Murphytown in the Conservative interest, and the divil a vote did he get, except one, and that was a blind man who signed the wrong paper be mistake, Ha! ha! " The major laughed boisterously at his own anecdote, and mopped his forehead with his handkerchief.

The two men, as they stood opposite each other, were a strange contrast, the one tall, grave, white, and emotionless, the other noisy and pompous, with protuberant military chest and rubicund features. They had one common characteristic, however. From under the shaggy eyebrows of the merchant and the sparse light-coloured lashes of the major there came the same keen, restless, shifting glance. Both were crafty, and each was keenly on his guard against the other.

"I have heard of you from my son, " the merchant said, motioning his visitor to a chair. "You were, I believe, in the habit of meeting together for the purpose of playing cards, billiards, and other such games, which I by no means countenance myself, but to which my son is unhappily somewhat addicted. "

"You don't play yourself, " said the major, in a sympathetic voice. "Ged, sir, it's never too late to begin, and many a man has put in a very comfortable old age On billiards and whist. Now, if ye feel inclined to make a start, I'll give ye seventy-five points in a hundred for a commincement. "

"Thank you, " said the merchant drily. "It is not one of my ambitions. Was this challenge the business upon which you came? "

The old soldier laughed until his merriment startled the clerks in the counting-house. "Be jabers! " he said, In a wheezy voice, "d'ye think I came five miles to do that? No, sir, I wanted to talk to you about your son. "

"My son! "

"Yes, your son. He's a smart lad—very smart indeed—about as quick as they make 'em. He may be a trifle coarse at times, but that's the spirit of the age, me dear sir. Me friend Tuffleton, of the Blues, says that delicacy went out of fashion with hair powder and beauty patches. he's a demned satirical fellow is Tuffleton. Don't know him, eh? "

"No, sir, I don't, " Girdlestone said angrily; "nor have I any desire to make his acquaintance. Let us proceed to business for my time is valuable. "

The major looked at him with an amiable smile. "That quick temper runs in the family, " he said. "I've noticed It in your son Ezra. As I said before, he's a smart lad; but me friend, he's shockingly rash and extremely indiscrate. Ye musk speak to him about it. "

"What do you mean sir? " asked the merchant, white with anger. "Have you come to insult him in his absence? "

"Absence? " said the soldier, still smiling blandly over his stock. "That's the very point I wanted to get at. He is away in Africa—at the diamond fields. A wonderful interprise, conducted with remarkable energy, but also with remarkable rashness, sir—yes, bedad, inexcusable rashness. "

Old Girdlestone took up his heavy ebony ruler and played with it nervously. He had an overpowering desire to hurl it at the head of his companion.

"What would ye say, now, " the veteran continued, crossing one leg over the other and arguing the matter out in a confidential undertone— "what would you say if a young man came to you, and, on the assumption that you were a dishonest blackgaird, appealed to you to help him in a very shady sort of a scheme? It would argue indiscretion on his part, would it not? "

The merchant sat still, but grew whiter and whiter.

"And if on the top of that he gave you all the details of his schame, without even waiting to see if you favoured it or not, he would be more than indiscrate, wouldn't he? Your own good sinse, me dear sir, will tell you that he would be culpably foolish—culpably so, bedad! "

"Well, sir? " said the old man, in a hoarse voice.

"Well, " continued the major, "I have no doubt that your son told you of the interesting little conversation that we had together. He was good enough to promise that if I went to Russia and pretinded to discover a fictitious mine, I should be liberally rewarded by the firm. I was under the necessity of pointing out to him that certain principles on which me family"—here the major inflated his chest— "on which me family are accustomed to act would prevint me from taking advantage of his offer. He then, I am sorry to say, lost his temper, and some words passed between us, the result of which was that we parted so rapidly that, be jabers! I had hardly time to make him realize how great an indiscretion he had committed. "

The merchant still sat perfectly still, tapping the table with his black ebony ruler.

"Of course, afther hearing a skitch of the plan, " continued the major, "me curiosity was so aroused that I could not help following the details with intherest. I saw the gintleman who departed for

Russia— Langworthy, I believe, was his name. Ged! I knew a chap of that name in the Marines who used to drink raw brandy and cayenne pepper before breakfast every morning. Did ye? Of course you couldn't. What was I talking of at all at all? "

Girdlestone stared gloomily at his visitor. The latter took a pinch of snuff from a tortoise-shell box, and flicked away a few wandering grains which settled upon the front of his coat.

"Yes, " he went on, I saw Langworthy off to Russia. Then I saw your son start for Africa. He's an interprising lad, and sure to do well there. *coelum non animam mutant*, as we used to say at Clongowes. He'll always come to the front, wherever he is, as long as he avoids little slips like this one we're spaking of. About the same time I heard that Girdlestone & Co, had raised riddy money to the extint of five and thirty thousand pounds. That's gone to Africa, too, I presume. It's a lot o' money to invist in such a game, and it might be safe if you were the only people that knew about it, but whin there are others—"

"Others? "

"Why, me, of course, " said the major. "I know about it, and more be token I am not in the swim with you. Sure, I could go this very evening to the diamond merchants about town and give them a tip about the coming fall in prices that would rather astonish 'em. "

"Look here, Major Clutterbuck, " cried the merchant, in a voice which quivered with suppressed passion, "you have come into possession of an important commercial secret. Why beat about the bush any longer? What is the object of your visit to-day? What is it that you want? "

"There now! " the major said, addressing himself and smiling more amicably than ever. "That's business. Bedad, there's where you commercial men have the pull. You go straight to the point and stick there. Ah, when I look at ye, I can't help thinking of your son. The same intelligent eye, the same cheery expression, the same devil-may-care manner and dry humour—"

"Answer my question, will you? " the merchant interrupted savagely.

"And the same hasty timper, " continued the major imperturbably. "I've forgotten, me dear sir, what it was you asked me. "

"What is it you want? "

"Ah, yes, of course. What is it I want? " the old soldier said meditatively. "Some would say more, some less. Some would want half, but that is overdoing it. How does a thousand pound stroike you? Yes, I think we may put it at a thousand pounds. "

"You want a thousand pounds? "

"Ged, I've been wanting it all me life. The difference is that I'm going to git it now. "

"And for what? "

"Sure, for silence—for neutrality. We're all in it now, and there's a fair division of labour. You plan, your son works, I hold me tongue. You make your tens of thousands, I make my modest little thousand. We all git paid for our throuble. "

"And suppose I refuse? "

"Ah! but you wouldn't—you couldn't, " the major said suavely. "Ged, sir, I haven't known ye long, but I have far too high an opinion of ye to suppose ye could do anything so foolish. If you refuse, your speculation is thrown away. There's no help for it. Bedad, it would be painful for me to have to blow the gaff; but you know the old saying, that 'charity begins at home. ' You must sell your knowledge at the best market. "

Girdlestone thought intently for a minute or two, with his great eyebrows drawn down over his little restless eyes.

"You said to my son, " he remarked at last, "that you were too honourable to embark in our undertaking. Do you consider it honourable to make use of knowledge gained in confidence for the purpose of extorting money? "

"Me dear sir, " answered the major, holding up his hand deprecatingly, "you put me in the painful position of having to explain meself in plain words. If I saw a man about to do a murther,

136

I should think nothing of murthering him. If I saw a pickpocket at work, I'd pick his pocket, and think it good fun to do it. Now, this little business of yours is— well, we'll say unusual, and if what I do seems a little unusual too, it's to be excused. Ye can't throw stones at every one, me boy, and then be surprised when some one throws one at you. You bite the diamond holders, d'ye see, and I take a little nibble at you. It's all fair enough. "

The merchant reflected again for some moments. "Suppose we agree to purchasing your silence at this price, " he said, "what guarantee have we that you will not come and extort more money, or that you may not betray our secret after all? "

"The honour of a soldier and a gintleman, " answered the major, rising and tapping his chest with two fingers of his right hand.

A slight sneer played over Girdlestone's pale face, but he made no remark. "We are in your power, " he said, and have no resource but to submit to your terms. You said five hundred pounds? "

"A thousand, " the major answered cheerfully.

"It's a great sum of money. "

"Deuce of a lot! " said the veteran cordially.

"Well, you shall have it. I will communicate with you. " Girdlestone rose as if to terminate the interview.

The major made no remark, but he showed his white teeth again, and tapped Mr. Girdlestone's cheque-book with the silver head of his walking-stick.

"What! Now? "

"Yes, now. "

The two looked at each other for a moment and the merchant sat down again and scribbled out a cheque, which he tossed to his companion. The latter looked it over carefully, took a fat little pocket-book from the depths of his breast pocket, and having placed the precious slip of paper in it, laboriously pushed it back into its receptacle. Then he very slowly and methodically picked up his jaunty curly-brimmed hat and shining kid gloves, and with a cheery nod to his companion, who answered it with a scowl, he swaggered off into the counting-house. There he shook hands with Tom, whom he had known for some months, and having made three successive offers—one to stand immediately an unlimited quantity of champagne, a second to play him five hundred up for anything he would name, and a third to lay a tenner for him at 7 to 4 on Amelia for the Oaks—all of which offers were declined with thanks—he bowed himself out, leaving a vague memory of smiles, shirt collars, and gaiters in the minds of the awe-struck Clerks.

Whatever an impartial judge might think of the means whereby Major Tobias Clutterbuck had successfully screwed a thousand pounds out of the firm of Girdlestone, it is quite certain that that gentleman's seasoned conscience did not reproach him in the least degree. On the contrary, his whole being seemed saturated and impregnated with the wildest hilarity and delight. Twice in less than a hundred yards, he was compelled to stop and lean upon his cane owing to the breathlessness which supervened upon his attempts to smother the delighted chuckles which came surging up from the inmost recesses of his capacious frame. At the second halt he wriggled his hand inside his tight-breasted coat, and after as many contortions as though he were about to shed that garment as a snake does its skin, he produced once more the little fat pocket-book. From it he extracted the cheque and looked it over lovingly. Then he hailed a passing hansom. "Drive to the Capital and Counties Bank, " he said. It had struck him that since the firm was in a shaky state he had better draw the money as soon as possible.

In the bank a gloomy-looking cashier took the cheque and stared at it somewhat longer than the occasion seemed to demand. It was but a few minutes, yet it appeared a very long time to the major.

"How will you have it? " he asked at last, in a mournful voice. It tends to make a man cynical when he spends his days in handling untold riches while his wife and six children are struggling to make both ends meet at home.

"A hunthred in gold and the rest in notes, " said the major, with a sigh of relief.

The cashier counted and handed over a thick packet of crisp rustling paper and a little pile of shining sovereigns. The major stowed away the first in the pocket-book and the latter in his trouser pockets. Then he swaggered out with a great increase of pomposity and importance, and ordered his cabman to drive to Kennedy Place.

Von Baumser was sitting in the major's campaigning chair, smoking his china-bowled pipe and gazing dreamily at the long blue wreaths. Times had been bad with the comrades of late, as the German's seedy appearance sufficiently testified. His friends in Germany had ceased to forward his small remittance, and Endermann's office, in which he had been employed, had given him notice that for a time they could dispense with his services. He had been spending the whole afternoon in perusing the long list of "wanteds" in the *Daily Telegraph*, and his ink-stained forefinger showed the perseverance with which he had been answering every advertisement that could possibly apply to him. A pile of addressed envelopes lay upon the table, and it was only the uncertainty of his finances and the fact that the humble penny stamp mounts into shillings when frequently employed, that prevented him from increasing the number of his applications. He looked up and uttered a word of guttural greeting as his companion came striding in.

"Get out of this, " the major said abruptly. "Get away into the bedroom. "

"Potztausand! Vot is it then? " cried the astonished Teuton.

"Out with you! I want this room to meself. "

Von Baumser shrugged his shoulders and lumbered off like a good-natured plantigrade, closing the door behind him.

When his companion had disappeared the major proceeded to lay out all his notes upon the table, overlapping each other, but still so arranged that every separate one was visible. He then built in the centre ten little golden columns in a circle, each consisting of ten sovereigns, until the whole presented the appearance of a metallic Stonehenge upon a plain of bank notes. This done, he cocked his head on one side, like a fat and very ruddy turkey, and contemplated his little arrangement with much pride and satisfaction.

Solitary delight soon becomes wearisome, however, so the veteran summoned his companion. The Teuton was so dumbfounded by this display of wealth, that he was bereft for a time of all faculty of speech, and could only stare open-mouthed at the table. At last he extended a fore-finger and thumb and rubbed a five pound note between them, as though to convince himself of its reality, after which he began to gyrate round the table in a sort of war dance, never taking his eyes from the heap of influence in front of him. "Mein Gott! " he exclaimed, "Gnadiger Vater! Ach Himmel! Was fur eine Schatze! Donnerwetter! " und a thousand other cacophonous expressions of satisfaction and amazement.

When the old soldier had sufficiently enjoyed the lively emotion which showed itself on every feature of the German's countenance, he picked up the notes and locked them in his desk together with half the gold. The other fifty pounds he returned into his pocket.

"Come on! " he said to his companion abruptly.

"Come vere? Vat is it? "

"Come on! " roared the major irascibly. "What d'ye want to stand asking questions for? Put on your hat and come. "

The major had retained the cab at the door, and the two jumped into it. "Drive to Verdi's Restaurant, " he said to the driver.

When they arrived at that aristocratic and expensive establishment, the soldier ordered the best dinner for two that money could procure. "Have it riddy in two hours sharp, " he said to the manager. "None of your half-and-half wines, mind! We want the rale thing, and, be ged! we can tell the difference! "

Having left the manager much impressed, the two friends set out for a ready-made clothing establishment. "I won't come in, " the major said, slipping ten sovereigns into Von Baumser's hand. "Just you go in and till them ye want the best suit o' clothes they can give you. They've a good seliction there, I know. "

"Gott in Himmel! " cried the amazed German. "But, my dear vriend, you cannot vait in the street. Come in mit me. "

"No, I'll wait, " the old soldier answered. "They might think I was paying for the clothes if I came in. "

"Well, but so you—"

"Eh, would ye? " roared the major, raising his cane, and Von Baumser disappeared precipitately into the shop.

When he emerged once more at the end of twenty minutes, he was attired in an elegant and close-fitting suit of heather tweed. The pair then made successive visits to a shoe-maker, a hatter, and a draper, with the result that Von Baumser developed patent leather boots, a jaunty brown hat, and a pair of light yellow gloves. By the end of their walk there seemed nothing left of the original Von Baumser except a tawny beard, and an expression of hopeless and overpowering astonishment.

Having effected this transformation, the friends retraced their steps to Verdi's and did full justice to the spread awaiting them, after which the old soldier won the heart of the establishment by bestowing largess upon every one who came in his way. As to the further adventures of these two Bohemians, it would be as well perhaps to draw a veil over them. Suffice it that, about two in the morning, the worthy Mrs. Robins was awakened by a stentorian voice in the street below demanding to know "Was ist das Deutsche Vaterland? "—a somewhat vexed question which the owner of the said voice was propounding to the solitary lamp-post of Kennedy Place. On descending the landlady discovered that the author of this disturbance was a fashionably dressed gentleman, who, upon closer inspection, proved to her great surprise to be none other than the usually demure part proprietor of her fourth floor. As to the major, he walked in quietly the next day about twelve o'clock, looking as trim and neat as ever, but minus the balance of the fifty pounds, nor did he think fit ever to make any allusion to this some what heavy deficit.

CHAPTER XIX.

NEWS FROM THE URALS.

Major Tobias Clutterbuck had naturally reckoned that the longer he withheld this trump card of his the greater would be its effect when played. An obstacle appearing at the last moment produces more consternation than when a scheme is still in its infancy. It proved, however, that he had only just levied his blackmail in time, for within a couple of days of his interview with the head of the firm news arrived of the great discovery of diamonds among the Ural Mountains. The first intimation was received through the Central News Agency in the form of the following telegram: —

"Moscow, *August* 22. —It is reported from Tobolsk that an important discovery of diamond fields has been made amongst the spurs of the Ural Mountains, at a point not very far from that city. They are said to have been found by an English geologist, who has exhibited many magnificent gems in proof of his assertion. These stones have been examined at Tobolsk, and are pronounced to be equal, if not superior, in quality to any found elsewhere. A company has been already formed for the purpose of purchasing the land and working the mines. "

Some days afterwards there came a Reuter's telegram giving fuller details. "With regard to the diamond fields near Tobolsk, " it said, "there is every reason to believe that they are of great, and possibly unsurpassed, wealth. There is no question now as to their authenticity, since their discoverer proves to be an English gentleman of high character, and his story is corroborated by villagers from this district who have dug up stones for themselves. The Government contemplate buying out the company and taking over the mines, which might be profitably worked by the forced labour of political prisoners on a system similar to that adopted in the salt mines of Siberia. The discovery is universally regarded as one which has materially increased the internal resources of the country, and there is some talk of the presentation of a substantial testimonial to the energetic and scientific traveller to whom it is due. "

Within a week or ten days of the receipt of these telegrams in London there came letters from the Russian correspondents of the various journals giving fuller details upon a subject of so much general interest. The *Times* directed attention to the matter in a leader.

"It appears, " remarked the great paper, "that a most important addition has been made to the mineral wealth of the Russian Empire. The silver mines of Siberia and the petroleum wells of the Caucasus are to be outrivalled by the new diamond fields of the Ural Mountains. For untold thousands of years these precious fragments of crystallized carbon have been lying unheeded among the gloomy gorges waiting for the hand of man to pick them out. It has fallen to the lot of one of our countrymen to point out to the Russian nation the great wealth which lay untouched and unsuspected in the heart of their realm. The story is a romantic one. It appears that a Mr. Langworthy, a wealthy English gentleman of good extraction, had, in the course of his travels in Russia, continued his journey as far as the great mountain barrier which separates Europe from Asia. Being fond of sport, he was wandering in search of game down one of the Ural valleys, when his attention was attracted by the thick gravel, which was piled up along the track of a dried-up water-course. The appearance and situation of this gravel reminded him forcibly of the South African diamond fields, and so strong was the impression that he at once laid down his gun and proceeded to rake the gravel over and to examine it. His search was rewarded by the discovery of several stones, which he conveyed home with him, and which proved, after being cleaned, to be gems of the first water. Elated at this success, he returned to the spot next day with a spade, and succeeded in obtaining many other specimens, and in convincing himself that the deposit stretched up and down for a long distance on both sides of the torrent. Having satisfied himself upon this point, our compatriot made his way to Tobolsk, where he exhibited his prizes to several of the richest merchants, and proceeded to form a company for the working of the new fields. He was so successful in this that the shares are already far above par, and our correspondent writes that there has been a rush of capitalists, all eager to invest their money in so promising a venture. It is expected that within a few months the necessary plant will have been erected and the concern be in working order. "

The *Daily Telegraph* treated the matter from a jocose and historical point of view.

"It has long been a puzzle to antiquaries and geologists, " it remarked, "as to where those jewels which Solomon brought from the East were originally obtained. There has been much speculation, too, regarding the source of those less apocryphal gems which sparkled in the regalia of the Indian monarchs and adorned the palaces of Delhi and Benares. As a nation we have a personal interest in the question, since the largest and most magnificent of these stones is now in the possession of our most gracious Queen. Mr. Langworthy has thrown a light upon this obscure subject. According to this gentleman's researches these treasures were unearthed amidst that dark and gloomy range of mountains which Providence has interposed between a nascent civilization and a continent of barbarians. Nor is Mr. Langworthy's opinion founded upon theory alone. He lends point to his arguments by presenting to the greedy eyes of the merchants of Tobolsk a bag filled with valuable diamonds, each and every one of which he professes to have discovered in these barren inhospitable valleys. This tweed-suited English tourist, descending like some good spirit among these dreamy Muscovites, points out to them the untold wealth which has lain for so many centuries at their feet, and with the characteristic energy of his race shows them at the same time how to turn the discovery to commercial advantage. If the deposit prove to be as extensive as is supposed, it is possible that our descendants may wear cut diamonds in their eye-glasses, should such accessories be necessary, and marvel at the ignorance of those primitive days when a metamorphosed piece of coal was regarded as the most valuable product of nature. "

The ordinary British paterfamilias, glancing over his morning paper, bestowed probably but few passing thoughts on the incident, but among business men and in the City its significance was at once understood. Not only did it create the deepest consternation amongst all who were connected with the diamond industry, but it reacted upon every other branch of South African commerce. It was the chief subject of conversation upon the Stock Exchange, and many were the surmises as to what the effect of the news would be at the fields. Fugger, the father of the diamond industry, was standing discussing the question, when a little rosy-faced Jew, named Goldschmidt, came bustling up to him. He was much excited, for he speculated in stones, and had just been buying in for a rise.

"Misther Fugger, " he cried, "you're shust the man I want to see. My Gott, vot is to become of us all? Vot is to become of de diamond trade ven one can pick them up like cockles on the sea shore? "

"We must wait for details, " the great financier said phlegmatically. His fortune was so enormous that it mattered little to him whether the report was true or false.

"Details! It is nothing but details, " cried the little Jew. "The papers is full of them. I vish to the Lord that that Langworthy had proke his neck in the Ural Mountains before he got up to any such games. Vat business had he to go examining gravel and peeping about in such places as them. Nobody that's any good would ever go to the Ural Mountains at all. "

"It won't hurt you, " Fugger said; "you'll simply have to pay less for your stones and sell them cheaper after they are cut. It won't make much difference in the long run. "

"Von't it, by Joves! Why, man, I've got over a hundred shtones on my hands now. Vat am I going to do vid 'em. "

"Ah, that's a bad job. You must make up your mind to lose on them. "

"Von't you buy them yourself, Mr. Fugger? " asked the Hebrew, in an insinuating voice. "Maybe this here story will all turn out wrong. S'elp me bob I gave three thousand for the lot, and you shall have them for two. Let's have a deal, my tear Mr. Fugger, do? "

"No more for me, thank you, " Fugger said with decision. "As to the story being wrong, I have telegraphed to Rotterdam, and they have sent on a trusty man. He'll be weeks, however, before we hear from him. "

"Here's Mr. Girdlestone, the great Mr. Girdlestone, " cried Goldschmidt, perceiving our worthy merchant of Fenchurch Street among the crowd. "Oh, Misther Girdlestone, I've got diamonds here what is worth three thousand pounds, and you shall have them for two—you shall, by chingo, and we'll go together now and get them? "

"Don't pester me! " said Girdlestone, brushing the little Jew aside with his long, bony arm. "Can I have a word with you, Fugger? "

"Certainly, " replied the diamond dealer. Girdlestone was a very well-known man upon 'Change, and one who was universally respected and looked up to.

"What do you think about this report? " he asked, in a confidential voice. "Do you imagine that it will affect prices in Africa? "

"Affect prices! My dear sir, if it proves true it will ruin the African fields. The mere report coming in a circumstantial fashion will send prices down fifty per cent. "

"As much as that! " said the merchant, with an excellent affectation of surprise. "I am anxious about it, for my boy is out there. It was a hobby of his, and I let him go. I trust he will not be bitten. "

"He is much more likely to do the biting, " remarked Fugger bluntly. He had met Ezra Girdlestone in business more than once, and had been disagreeably impressed by the young gentleman's sharpness.

"Poor lad! " said his father. "He is young, and has had little experience as yet. I hope all is well with him! " He shook his head despondently, and walked slowly homewards, but his heart beat triumphantly within him, for he was assured now that the report would influence prices as he had foreseen, and the African firm reap the benefit of their daring speculation.

CHAPTER XX.

MR. HECTOR O'FLAHERTY FINDS SOMETHING IN THE PAPER.

Ezra Girdlestone had taken up his quarters in two private rooms at the *Central Hotel*, Kimberley, and had already gained a considerable reputation in the town by the engaging "abandon" of his manners, and by the munificent style in which he entertained the more prominent citizens of the little capital. His personal qualities of strength and beauty had also won him the respect which physical gifts usually command in primitive communities, and the smart young Londoner attracted custom to himself among the diggers in a way which excited the jealousy of the whole tribe of elderly Hebrews who had hitherto enjoyed a monopoly of the trade. Thus, he had already gained his object in making himself known, and his name was a familiar one in every camp from Waldeck's Plant to Cawood's Hope. Keeping his headquarters at Kimberley, he travelled perpetually along the line of the diggings. All the time he was chafing secretly and marvelling within himself how it was that no whisper of the expected news had arrived yet from England.

One sunny day he had returned from a long ride, and, having dined, strolled out into the streets, Panama hat upon head and cigar in mouth. It was the 23rd of October, and he had been nearly ten weeks in the colony. Since his arrival he had taken to growing a beard. Otherwise, he was much as we have seen him in London, save that a ruddier glow of health shone upon his sunburned face. The life of the diggings appeared to agree with him.

As he turned down Stockdale Street, a man passed him leading a pair of horses tired and dusty, with many a strap and buckle hanging down behind them. After him came another leading a second pair, and after him another with a third. They were taking them round to the stables. "Hullo! " cried Ezra, with sudden interest; "what's up? "

"The mail's just in. "

"Mail from Capetown? "

"Yes. "

Ezra quickened his pace and strode down Stockdale Street into the Main Street, which, as the name implies, is the chief thoroughfare of Kimberley. He came out close to the office of the *Vaal River Advertiser and Diamond Field Gazette*. There was a crowd in front of the door. This *Vaal River Advertiser* was a badly conducted newspaper, badly printed upon bad paper, but selling at sixpence a copy, and charging from seven shillings and sixpence to a pound for the insertion of an advertisement. It was edited at present by a certain P. Hector O'Flaherty, who having been successively a dentist, a clerk, a provision merchant, an engineer, and a sign painter, and having failed at each and every one of these employments, had taken to running a newspaper as an easy and profitable occupation. Indeed, as managed by Mr. O'Flaherty, the process was simplicity itself. Having secured by the Monday's mail copies of the London papers of two months before, he spent Tuesday in cutting extracts from them with the greatest impartiality, chopping away everything which might be of value to him. The Wednesday was occupied in cursing at three black boys who helped to put up the type, and on the Thursday a fresh number of the *Vaal River Advertiser and Diamond Field Gazette* was given to the world. The remaining three days were devoted by Mr. O'Flaherty to intoxication, but the Monday brought him back once more to soda water and literature.

It was seldom, indeed, that the *Advertiser* aroused interest enough to cause any one to assemble round the Office. Ezra's heart gave a quick flutter at the sight, and he gathered himself together like a runner who sees his goal in view. Throwing away his cigar, he hurried on ad joined the little crowd.

"What's the row? " he asked.

"There's news come by the mail, " said one or two bystanders. "Big news. "

"What sort of news? "

"Don't know yet. "

"Who said there was news? "

"Driver. "

"Where is he? "

"Don't know. "

"Who will know about it? "

"O'Flaherty. "

Here there was a general shout from the crowd for O'Flaherty, and an irascible-looking man, with a red bloated face and bristling hair came to the office door.

"Now, what the divil d'ye want? " he roared, shaking a quill pen at the crowd. "What are ye after at all? Have ye nothing better to do than to block up the door of a decent office? "

"What's the news? " cried a dozen voices.

"The news, is it? " roared O'Flaherty, more angrily than ever; "and can't ye foind out that by paying your sixpences like men, and taking the *Advertoiser*? It's a paper, though Oi says it as shouldn't, that would cut out some o' these *Telegraphs* and *Chronicles* if it was only in London. Begad, instead of encouraging local talent ye spind your toime standing around in the strate, and trying to suck a man's news out of him for nothing. "

"Look here, boss, " said a rough-looking fellow in the front of the crowd, "you keep your hair on, and don't get slinging words about too freely, or it may be the worse for you and for your office too. We heard as there was big news, an' we come down to hear it, but as to gettin' it without paying, that ain't our sort. I suppose we can call it square if we each hands in sixpence, which is the price o' your paper, and then you can tell us what's on. "

O'Flaherty considered for a moment. "It's worth a shillin' each, " he said, "for it plays the divil with the circulation of a paper whin its news gits out too soon. "

"Well, we won't stick at that, " said the miner. "What say you, boys? "

There was a murmur of assent, and a broad-brimmed straw hat was passed rapidly from hand to band. It was half full of silver when it reached O'Flaherty. The *Advertiser* had never before had such a circulation, for the crowd had rapidly increased during the preceding dialogue, and now numbered some hundreds.

"Thank ye, gintlemen, " said the editor.

"Well, what's the news? " cried the impatient crowd.

"Sure I haven't opened the bag yet, but I soon will. Whativer it is it's bound to be there. Hey there, Billy, ye divil's brat, where's the mail bag? "

Thus apostrophized, a sharp little Kaffir came running out with the brown bag, and Mr. O'Flaherty examined it in a leisurely manner, which elicited many an oath from the eager crowd.

"Here's the *Standard* and the *Times*, " he said, handing the various papers out to his subordinate. "Begad, there's not one of ye knows the expinse of k'aping a great paper loike this going, forebye the brains and no profit at the ind of it. Here's the *Post* and the *News*. If you were men you'd put in an advertisement ivery wake, whether ye needed it or not, just to encourage literature. Here's the *Cape Argus*—it'll be in here whativer it is. "

With great deliberation Mr. Hector O'Flaherty put on a pair of spectacles and folded the paper carefully round, so as to bring the principal page to the front. Then he cleared his throat, with the pomposity which is inseparable with most men from the act of reading aloud.

"Go it, boss! " cried his audience encouragingly.

"'Small-pox at Wellington'—that's not it, is it? 'Germany and the Vatican'—'Custom House Duties at Port Elizabeth'—'Roosian Advances in Cintral Asia' eh? Is that it—'Discovery of great Diamond Moines? '"

"That's it, " roared the crowd; "let's hear about that. " There was an anxious ring in their voices, and their faces were grave and serious as they looked up at the reader upon the steps of the office.

"'Diamond moines have been discovered in Roosia, '" read O'Flaherty, "'which are confidently stated to exceed in riches anything which has existed before. It is ginerally anticipated that this discovery, if confirmed, will have a most prejudicial effect upon the African trade. ' That's an extract from the London news of the *Argus*. "

A buzz of ejaculations and comments arose from the crowd. "Isn't there any more about it? " they cried.

"Here's a later paper, boss, " said the little Kaffir, who had been diligently looking over the dates.

O'Flaherty opened it, and gave a whistle of astonishment. "Here's enough to satisfy you, " he said. "It's in big toipe and takes up noigh the whole of the first page. I can only read ye the headings, for we must get to work and have out a special edition. You'll git details there, an' it'll be out in a few hours. Look here at the fuss they've made about it. " The editor turned the paper as he spoke, and exhibited a series of large black headings in this style: —

RUSSIAN DIAMOND FIELDS.

EXTRAORDINARY DISCOVERY BY AN ENGLISHMAN.
THREATENED EXTINCTION OF THE CAPE INDUSTRY.
GREAT FALL IN PRICES.
OPINIONS OF THE LONDON PRESS.
FULL DETAILS.

"What d'ye think of that? " cried O'Flaherty, triumphantly, as if he had had some hand in the matter. "Now I must git off to me work, and you'll have it all before long in your hands. Ye should bliss your stars that ye have some one among ye to offer ye the convanience of the latest news. Good noight to ye all, " and he trotted back into his office with his hat and its silver contents in his hand.

The crowd broke up into a score of gesticulating chattering groups, and wandered up or down the street. Ezra Girdlestone waited until they had cleared away, and then stepped into the office of the *Advertiser*.

"What's the matter now? " asked O'Flaherty, angrily. He was a man who lived in a state of chronic irritation.

"Have you a duplicate of that paper? "

"Suppose I have? "

"What will you sell it for? "

"What will you give? "

"Half a sovereign. "

"A sovereign. "

"Done! " and so Ezra Girdlestone walked out of the office with full details in his hand, and departed to his hotel, where he read the account through very slowly and deliberately. It appeared to be satisfactory, for he chuckled to himself a good deal as he perused it. Having finished it, he folded the paper up, placed it in his breast pocket, and, having ordered his horse, set off to the neighbouring township of Dutoitspan with the intention of carrying the news with him.

Ezra had two motives in galloping across the veldt that October night. One was to judge with his own ears and eyes what effect the news would have upon practical men. The other was a desire to gratify that sinister pleasure which an ill-natured man has in being the bearer of evil tidings. They had probably heard the report by this time, but it was unlikely that any details had reached them. No one knew better than young Girdlestone that this message from Europe would bring utter ruin and extinction to many a small capitalist, that it would mean the shattering of a thousand hopes, and the advent of poverty and misery to the men with whom he had been associating. In spite of this knowledge, his heart beat high, as his father's had done in London, and as he spurred his horse onwards through the darkness, he was hardly able to refrain from shouting and whooping in his exultation.

The track from Kimberley to Dutoitspan was a rough one, but the moon was up, and the young merchant found no difficulty in following it. When he reached the summit of the low hill over which the road ran, he saw the lights of the little town sparkling in the valley beneath him. It was ten o'clock before he galloped into the main street, and he saw at a glance that the news had, as he expected, arrived before him. In front of the Griqualand Saloon a great crowd of miners had assembled, who were talking excitedly among themselves. The light of the torches shone down upon herculean figures, glaring shirts, and earnest bearded faces. The whole camp appeared to have assembled there to discuss the situation, and it was evident from their anxious countenances and subdued voices, that they took no light view of it.

The instant the young man alighted from his horse he was surrounded by a knot of eager questioners. "You've just come from Kimberley, " they cried. "What is the truth of it, Mr. Girdlestone? Let us know the truth of it. "

"It's a bad business, my friends, " he answered, looking around at the ring of inquiring faces. "I have been reading a full account of it in the *Cape Argus*. They have made a great find in Russia. There seems to be no doubt at all about the matter. "

"D'ye think it will send prices down here as much as they say? "

"I'm afraid it will send them very low. I hold a lot of stones myself, and I should be very glad to get rid of them at any price. I fear it will hardly pay you to work your claims now. "

"And the price of claims will go down? "

"Of course it will. "

"Eh, mister, what's that? " cried a haggard, unkempt little man, pushing his way to the front and catching hold of Ezra's sleeve to ensure his attention. "Did ye say it would send the price o' claims down? You didn't say that, did you? Why, in course, it stands to reason that what happened in Roosia couldn't make no difference over here. That's sense, mates, ain't it? " He looked round him appealingly, and laughed a little nervous laugh.

"You try, " said Ezra coldly. "If you get one-third of what you gave for your claim you'll be lucky. Why, man, you don't suppose we produce diamonds for local consumption. They are for exporting to Europe, and if Europe is already supplied by Russia, where are you to get your market? "

"That's it? " cried several voices.

"If you take my advice, " Ezra continued, "you'll get rid of what you have at any loss, for the time may be coming when you'll get nothing at all. "

"Now, look at that! " cried the little man, throwing out his hands. "They call me Unlucky Jim, and Unlucky Jim I'll be to the end of the chapter. Why, boss, me and Sammy Walker has sunk every damned cent we've got in that claim, the fruit o' nine years' hard work, and here you comes ridin' up as cool as may be, and tells me that it's all gone for nothing. "

"Well, there are others who will suffer as well as you, " said one of the crowd.

"I reckon we're all hit pretty hard if this is true, " remarked another.

"I'm fair sick of it, " said the little man, passing his grimy hand across his eyes and leaving a black smear as he did so. "This ain't the first time—no, nor the second—that my luck has played me this trick. I've a mighty good mind to throw up my hand altogether. "

"Come in and have some whisky, " said a rough sympathizer, and the unlucky one was hustled in through the rude door of the Griqualand Saloon, there to find such comfort as he might from the multitudinous bottles which adorned the interior of that building. Liquor had lost its efficacy that evening, however, and a dead depression rested over the little town. Nor was it confined to Dutoitspan. All along the diggings the dismal tidings spread with a rapidity which was astonishing. At eleven o'clock there was consternation at Klipdrift. At quarter-past one Hebron was up and aghast at the news. At three in the morning a mounted messenger galloped into Bluejacket, and before daybreak a digger committee was sitting at Delporte's Hope discussing the situation. So during that eventful night down the whole long line of the Vaal River there was ruin and heartburning and dismay, while five thousand miles away an old gentleman was sleeping calmly and dreamlessly in his comfortable bed, from whose busy brain had emanated all this misery and misfortune.

Perhaps the said old gentleman might have slumbered a little less profoundly could he have seen the sight which met his son's eyes on the following morning. Ezra had passed the night at Dutoitspan, in the hut of a hospitable miner. Having risen in the morning, he was dressing himself in a leisurely, methodical fashion, when his host, who had been inhaling the morning breeze, thrust his head through the window.

"Come out here, Mr. Girdlestone, " he cried. "There's some fun on. One of the boys is dead drunk, and they are carrying him in. "

Ezra pulled on his coat and ran out. A little group of miners were walking slowly up the main street. He and his host were waiting for the procession to pass them with several jocose remarks appropriate to the occasion ready upon their lips, when their eyes fell upon a horrible splotchy red track which marked the road the party had taken. They both ran forward with exclamations and inquiries.

"It's Jim Stewart, " said one of the bearers. "Him that they used to call Unlucky Jim. "

"What's up with him? "

"He has shot himself through the head. Where d'ye think we found him? Slap in the middle o' his own claim, with his fingers dug into the gravel, as dead as a herring. "

"He's a bad plucked 'un to knock under like that, " Ezra's companion remarked.

"Yes, " said the croupier of the saloon gambling table. "If he'd waited for another deal he might have held every trump. He was always a soft chap, was Jim, and he was saying last night as how this spoiled the last chance he was ever like to have of seeing his wife and childer in England. He's blowed a fine clean hole in himself. Would you like to see it, Mr. Girdlestone? " The fellow was about to remove the blood-stained handkerchief which covered the dead man's face, but Ezra recoiled in horror.

"Mr. Girdlestone looks faint like, " some one observed.

"Yes, " said Ezra, who was white to his very lips. "This has upset me rather. I'll have a drop of brandy. " As he walked back to the hut, he wondered inwardly whether the incident would have discomposed his father.

"I suppose he would call it part of our commercial finesse, " he said bitterly to himself. "However, we have put our hands to the plough, and we must not let homicide stop us. " So saying, he steadied his nerves with a draught of brandy, and prepared for the labours of the day.

CHAPTER XXI.

AN UNEXPECTED BLOW.

The crisis at the African fields was even more acute than had been anticipated by the conspirators. Nothing approaching to it had ever been known in South Africa before. Diamonds went steadily down in value until they were selling at a price which no dealer would have believed possible, and the sale of claims reached such a climax that men were glad to get rid of them for the mere price of the plant and machinery erected at them. The offices of the various dealers at Kimberley were besieged night and day by an importunate crowd of miners, who were willing to sell at any price in order to save something from the general ruin which they imagined was about to come upon the industry. Some, more long-headed or more desperate than their neighbours, continued to work their claims and to keep the stones which they found until prices might be better. As fresh mails came from the Cape, however, each confirming and amplifying the ominous news, these independent workers grew fewer and more faint-hearted, for their boys had to be paid each week, and where was the money to come from with which to pay them? The dealers, too, began to take the alarm, and the most tempting offers would hardly induce them to give hard cash in exchange for stones which might prove to be a drug in the market. Everywhere there was misery and stagnation.

Ezra Girdlestone was not slow to take advantage of this state of things, but he was too cunning to do so in a manner which might call attention to himself or his movements. In his wanderings he had come across an outcast named Farintosh, a man who had once been a clergyman and a master of arts of Trinity College, Dublin, but who was now a broken-down gambler with a slender purse and a still more slender conscience. He still retained a plausible manner and an engaging address, and these qualities first recommended him to the notice of the young merchant. A couple of days after the receipt of the news from Europe, Ezra sent for this fellow and sat with him for some time on the verandah of the hotel, talking over the situation.

"You see, Farintosh, " he remarked, "it might be a false alarm, might it not? "

The ex-clergyman nodded. He was a man of few words.

"If it should be, it would be an excellent thing for those who buy now. "

Farintosh nodded once again.

"Of course, " Ezra continued, "it looks as if the thing was beyond all doubt. My experience has taught me, however, that there is nothing so uncertain as a certainty. That's what makes me think of speculating over this. If I lose it won't hurt me much, and I might win. I came out here more for the sake of seeing a little of the world than anything else, but now that this has turned up I'll have a shy at it. "

"Quite so, " said Farintosh, rubbing his hands.

"You see, " Ezra continued, lighting a cheroot, "I have the name here of having a long purse and of knowing which way the wind blows. If I were to be seen buying others would follow my lead, and prices would soon be as high as ever. Now, what I purpose is to work through you, d'ye see? You can take out a licence and buy in stones on the quiet without attracting much attention. Beat them down as low as you can, and give this hotel as your address. When they call here they shall be paid, which is better than having you carrying the money round with you. "

The clergyman scowled as though he thought it was anything but better. He did not make any remark, however.

"You can get one or two fellows to help you, " said Ezra. "I'll pay for their licences. I can't expect you to work all the camps yourself. Of course, if you offer more for a stone than I care to give, that's your look out, but if you do your work well you shall not be the loser. You shall have a percentage on business done and a weekly salary as well. "

"How much money do you care to invest? " asked Farintosh.

"I'm not particular, " Ezra answered. "If I do a thing I like to do it well. I'll go the length of thirty thousand pounds. "

Farintosh was so astonished at the magnitude of the sum that he sank back in his chair in bewilderment. "Why, sir, " he said, "I think just at present you could buy the country for that. "

Ezra laughed. "We'll make it go as far as we can, " he said. "Of course you may buy claims as well as stones. "

"And I have carte blanche to that amount? "

"Certainly. "

"All right, I'll begin this evening, " said the ex-parson; and picking up his slouched hat, which he still wore somewhat broader in the brim than his comrades, in deference to old associations, he departed upon his mission.

Farintosh was a clever man and soon chose two active subordinates. These were a navvy, named Burt, and Williams, a young Welshman, who had disappeared from home behind a cloud of forged cheques, and having changed his name had made a fresh start in life to the south of the equator. These three worked day and night buying in stones from the more needy and impecunious miners, to whom ready money was a matter of absolute necessity. Farintosh bought in the stock, too, of several small dealers whose nerves had been shaken by the panic. In this way bag after bag was filled with diamonds by Ezra, while he himself was to all appearances doing nothing but smoking cigars and sipping brandy-and-water in front of the *Central Hotel*.

He was becoming somewhat uneasy in his mind as to how long the delusion would be kept up, or how soon news might come from the Cape that the Ural find had been examined into and had proved to be a myth. In any case, he thought that he would be free from suspicion. Still, it might be as well for him by that time to be upon his homeward journey, for he knew that if by any chance the true facts leaked out there would be no hope of mercy from the furious diggers. Hence he incited Farintosh to greater speed, and that worthy divine with his two agents worked so energetically that in less than a week there was little left of five and thirty thousand pounds.

Ezra Girdlestone had shown his power of reading character when he chose the ex-clergyman as his subordinate. It is possible, however, that the young man's judgment had been inferior to his powers of observation. A clever man as a trusty ally is a valuable article, but when the said cleverness may be turned against his employer the advantage becomes a questionable one.

It was perfectly evident to Farintosh that though a stray capitalist might risk a thousand pounds or so on a speculation of this sort, Rothschild himself would hardly care to invest such a sum as had passed through his hands without having some ground on which to go. Having formed this conclusion, and having also turned over in his mind the remarkable coincidence that the news of this discovery in Russia should follow so very rapidly upon the visit of the junior partner of the House of Girdlestone, the astute clergyman began to have some dim perception of the truth. Hence he brooded a good deal as he went about his work, and cogitated deeply in a manner which was once again distinctly undesirable in so very intelligent a subordinate.

These broodings and cogitations culminated in a meeting, which was held by him with his two sub-agents in the private parlour of the Digger's Retreat. It was a low-roofed, smoke-stained room, with a profusion of spittoons scattered over it, which, to judge by the condition of the floor, the patrons of the establishment had taken some pains to avoid. Round a solid, old-fashioned table in the centre of this apartment sat Ezra's staff of assistants, the parson thoughtful but self-satisfied, the others sullen and inquisitive. Farintosh had convened the meeting, and his comrades had an idea that there was something in the wind. They applied themselves steadily, therefore, to the bottle of Hollands upon the table, and waited for him to speak.

"Well, " the ex-clergyman said at last, "the game is nearly over, and we'll not be wanted any more. Girdlestone's off to England in a day or two. "

Burt and Williams groaned sympathetically. Work was scarce in the diggings during the crisis, and their agencies had been paying them well.

"Yes, he's off, " Farintosh went on, glancing keenly at his companions, "and he takes with him five and thirty thousand pounds worth of diamonds that we bought for him. Poor devils like us, Burt, have to do the work, and then are thrown aside as you would throw your pick aside when you are done with it. When he sells out in London and makes his pile, it won't much matter to him that the three men who helped him are starving in Griqualand. "

"Won't he give us somethin' at partin'? " asked Burt, the navvy. He was a savage-looking, hairy man, with a brick-coloured face and over-hanging eyebrows. "Won't he give us nothing to remembrance him by? "

"Give you something! " Farintosh said with a sneer. "Why, man, he says you are too well paid already. "

"Does he, though? " cried the navvy, flushing even redder than nature had made him. "Is that the way he speaks after we makes him? It ain't on the square. I likes to see things honest an' above board betwixt man an' man, and this pitchin' of them as has helped ye over ain't that. "

Farintosh lowered his voice and bent further over the table. His companions involuntarily imitated his movement, until the three cunning, cruel faces were looking closely into one another's eyes.

"Nobody knows that he holds those stones, " said Farintosh. "He's too smart to let it out to any one but ourselves. "

"Where does he keep 'em? " asked the Welshman.

"In a safe in his room. "

"Where is the key? "

"On his watch-chain. "

"Could we get an impression? "

"I have one. "

"Then I can make one, " cried Williams triumphantly.

"It's done, " said Farintosh, taking a small key from his pocket. "This is a duplicate, and will open the safe. I took the moulding from his key while I was speaking to him. "

The navvy laughed hoarsely. "If that don't lick creation for smartness! " he cried. "And how are we to get to this safe? It would serve him right if we collar the lot. It'll teach him that if he ain't honest by nature he's got to be when he deals with the like of us. I like straightness, and by the Lord I'll have it! " He brought his great fist down upon the table to emphasize this commendable sentiment.

"It's not an easy matter, " Farintosh said thoughtfully. "When he goes out he locks his door, and there's no getting in at the window. There's only one chance for us that I can see. His room is a bit cut off from the rest of the hotel. There's a gallery of twenty feet or more that leads to it. Now, I was thinking that if the three of us were to visit him some evening, just to wish him luck on his journey, as it were, and if, while we were in the room something sudden was to happen which would knock him silly for a minute or two, we might walk off with the stones and be clean gone before he could raise an alarm. "

"And what would knock him silly? " asked Williams. He was an unhealthy, scorbutic-looking youth, and his pallid complexion had assumed a greenish tinge of fear as he listened to the clergyman's words. He had the makings in him of a mean and dangerous criminal, but not of a violent one—belonging to the jackal tribe rather than to the tiger.

"What would knock him senseless? " Farintosh asked Burt, with a knowing look.

Burt laughed again in his bushy, red beard. "You can leave that to me, mate, " he said.

Williams glanced from one to the other and he became even more cadaverous. "I'm not in it, " he stammered. "It will be a hanging job. You will kill him as like as not. "

"Not in it, ain't ye? " growled the navvy. "Why, you white-livered hound, you're too deep in it ever to get out again. D'ye think we'll let you spoil a lay of this sort as we might never get a chance of again? "

"You can do it without me, " said the Welshman, trembling in every limb.

"And have you turnin' on us the moment a reward was offered. No, no, chummy, you don't get out of it that way. If you won't stand by us, I'll take care you don't split. "

"Think of the diamonds, " Farintosh put in.

"Think of your own skin, " said the navvy.

"You could go back to England a rich man if you do it. "

"You'll never go back at all if you don't. " Thus worked upon alternately by his hopes and by his fears, Williams showed some signs of yielding. He took a long draught from his glass and filled it up again.

"I ain't afraid, " he said. "Don't imagine that I am afraid. You won't hit him very hard, Mr. Burt? "

"Just enough to curl him up, " the navvy answered. "Lord love ye, it ain't the first man by many a one that I've laid on his back, though I never had the chance before of fingering five and thirty thousand pounds worth of diamonds for my pains. "

"But the hotel-keeper and the servants? "

"That's all right, " said Farintosh. "You leave it to me. If we go up quietly and openly, and come down quietly and openly, who is to suspect anything? Our horses will be outside, in Woodley Street, and we'll be out of their reach in no time. Shall we say to-morrow evening for the job? "

"That's very early, " Williams cried tremulously.

"The sooner the better, " Burt said, with an oath. "And look here, young man, " fixing Williams with his bloodshot eyes, "one sign of drawing back, and by the living jingo I'll let you have more than I'm keeping for him. You hear me, eh? " He grasped the youth's white wrist and squeezed it in his iron grip until he writhed with the pain.

"Oh, I'm with you, heart and soul, " he cried. "I'm sure what you and Mr. Farintosh advise must be for the best. "

"Meet here at eight o'clock to-morrow night then, " said the leader. "We can get it over by nine, and we will have the night for our escape. I'll have the horses ready, and it will be strange if we don't get such a start as will puzzle them. "

So, having arranged all the details of their little plan, these three gentlemen departed in different directions—Farintosh to the *Central Hotel*, to give Ezra his evening report, and the others to the mining-camps, which were the scene of their labours.

The meeting just described took place upon a Tuesday, early in November. On the Saturday Ezra Girdlestone had fully made up his mind to turn his back upon the diggings and begin his homeward journey. He was pining for the pleasures of his old London life, and was weary of the monotonous expanse of the South African veldt. His task was done, too, and it would be well for him to be at a distance before the diggers discovered the manner in which they had been hoaxed. He began to pack his boxes, therefore, and to make every preparation for his departure.

He was busily engaged in this employment upon the Wednesday evening when there was a tap at the door and Farintosh walked in, accompanied by Burt and Williams. Girdlestone glanced up at them, and greeted them briefly. He was not surprised at their visit, for they had come together several times before to report progress or make arrangements. Farintosh bowed as he entered the room, Burt nodded, and Williams rubbed his hands together and looked amiably bilious.

"We looked in, Mr. Girdlestone, " Farintosh began, "to learn if you had any commands for us. "

"I told you before that I had not, " Ezra said curtly. "I am going on Saturday. I have made a mistake in speculating on those diamonds. Prices are sinking lower and lower. "

"I am sorry to hear that, " said Farintosh sympathetically. "Maybe the market will take a turn. "

"Let us hope so, " the merchant answered. "It doesn't look like it. "

"But you are satisfied with us, guv'nor, " Burt struck in, pushing his bulky form in front of Farintosh. "We have done our work all right, haven't we? "

"I have nothing to complain of, " Ezra said coldly.

"Well then, guv'nor, you surely ain't going away without leaving us nothing to remembrance you with, seeing that we've stood by you and never gone back on you. "

"You have been paid every week for what you have done, " the young man said. "You won't get another penny out of me, so you set your mind at rest about that. "

"You won't give us nothing? " cried the navvy angrily.

"No, I won't; and I'll tell you what it is, Burt, big as you are, if you dare to raise your voice in my presence I'll give you the soundest hiding that ever you had in your life. "

Ezra had stood up and showed every indication of being as good as his word.

"Don't let us quarrel the last time we may meet, " Farintosh cried, intervening between the two. "It is not money we expect from you. All we want is a drain of rum to drink success to you with. "

"Oh, if that's all, " said the young merchant—and turned round to pick up the bottle which stood on a table behind him. Quick as a flash Burt sprang upon him and struck him down with a life-preserver. With a gasping cry and a heavy thud Ezra fell face downwards upon the floor, the bottle still clutched in his senseless hand, and the escaping rum forming a horrible mixture with the blood which streamed from a great gash in his head.

"Very neat—very pretty indeed! " cried the ex-parson, in a quiet tone of critical satisfaction, as a connoisseur might speak of a specimen which interested him. He was already busy at the door of the safe.

"Well done, Mr. Burt, well done! " cried Williams, in a quivering voice; and going up to the body he kicked it in the side. "You see I am not afraid, Mr. Burt, am I? "

"Stow your gab! " snarled the navvy. "Here's the rum all gettin' loose. " Picking up the bottle he took a pull of what was left in it. "Here's the bag, parson, " he whispered, pulling a black linen bag from his pocket. "We haven't made much noise over the job. "

"Here are the stones, " said Farintosh, in the same quiet voice. "Hold the mouth open. " He emptied an avalanche of diamonds into the receptacle. "Here are some notes and gold. We may as well have them too. Now, tie it up carefully. That's the way! If we meet any one on the stairs, take it coolly. Turn that lamp out, Williams, so that if any one looks in he'll see nothing. Come along! "

The guilty trio stole out of the room, bearing their plunder with them, and walked down the passage of the hotel unmolested and unharmed.

The moon, as it rose over the veldt that night, shone on three horsemen spurring it along the Capetown road as though their very lives depended upon their speed. Its calm, clear rays streamed over the silent roofs of Kimberley and in through a particular window of the *Central Hotel*, throwing silvery patches upon the carpet, and casting strange shadows from the figure which lay as it had fallen, huddled in an ungainly heap upon the floor.

CHAPTER XXII.

ROBBERS AND ROBBED.

It might perhaps have been as well for the curtailing of this narrative, and for the interests of the world at large if the blow dealt by the sturdy right arm of the navvy had cut short once for all the career of the junior African merchant. Ezra, however, was endowed with a rare vitality, which enabled him not only to shake off the effects of his mishap, but to do so in an extraordinarily short space of time. There was a groan from the prostrate figure, then a feeble movement, then another and a louder groan, and then an oath. Gradually raising himself upon his elbow, he looked around him in a bewildered way, with his other hand pressed to the wound at the back of his head, from which a few narrow little rivulets of blood were still meandering. His glance wandered vaguely over the table and the chairs and the walls, until it rested upon the safe. He could see in the moonlight that it was open, and empty. In a moment the whole circumstances of the case came back to him, and he staggered to the door with a hoarse cry of rage and of despair.

Whatever Ezra's faults may have been, irresolution or want of courage were not among them. In a moment he grasped the situation, and realized that it was absolutely essential that he should act, and at once. The stones must be recovered, or utter and irretrievable ruin stared him in the face. At his cries the landlord and several attendants, white and black, came rushing into the room.

"I've been robbed and assaulted, " Ezra said, steadying himself against the mantelpiece, for he was still weak and giddy. "Don't all start cackling, but do what I ask you. Light the lamp! "

The lamp was lit, and there was a murmur from the little knot of employees, reinforced by some late loungers at the bar, as they saw the disordered room and the great crimson patch upon the carpet.

"The thieves called at nine, " said Ezra, talking rapidly, but collectedly. "Their names were Farintosh, Burt, and Williams. We talked for, some little time, so they probably did not leave the house before a quarter past at the soonest. It is now half-past ten, so they have no very great start. You, Jamieson, and you, Van Muller, run out and find if three men have been seen getting away. Perhaps they

166

took a buggy. Go up and down, and ask all you see. You, Jones, go as hard as you can to Inspector Ainslie. Tell him there has been robbery and attempted murder, and say that I want half a dozen of his best mounted men—not his best men, you understand, but his best horses. I shall see that he is no loser if he is smart. Where's my servant Pete? Pete, you dog, get my horse saddled and bring her round. She ought to be able to catch anything in Griqualand. "

As Ezra gave his orders the men hurried off in different directions to carry them out. He himself commenced to arrange his dress, and tied a handkerchief tightly round his head.

"Surely you are not going, sir? " the landlord said, "You are not fit. "

"Fit or not, I am going, " Ezra said resolutely. "If I have to be strapped to my horse I'll go. Send me up some brandy. Put some in a flask, too. I may feel faint before I get back. "

A great concourse of people had assembled by this time, attracted by the report of the robbery. The whole square in front of the hotel was crowded with diggers and store-keepers and innumerable Kaffirs, all pressing up to the portico in the hope of hearing some fresh details. Mr. Hector O'Flaherty, over the way, was already busy setting up his type in preparation for a special edition, in which the *Vaal River Advertiser* should give its version of the affair. In the office the great man himself, who was just convalescing from an attack of ardent spirits, was busily engaged, with a wet towel round his head, writing a leader upon the event. This production, which was very sonorous and effective, was peppered all over with such phrases as "protection of property, " "outraged majesty of the law, " and "scum of civilization"— expressions which had been used so continuously by Mr. O'Flaherty, that he had come to think that he had a copyright in them, and loudly accused the London papers of plagiarism if he happened to see them in their columns.

There was a buzz of excitement among the crowd when Ezra appeared on the steps of the hotel, looking as white as a sheet, with a handkerchief bound round his head and his collar all crusted with blood. As he mounted his horse one of his emissaries rushed to him.

"If you please, sir, " he said, "they have taken the Capetown road. A dozen people saw them. Their horses were not up to much, for I know the man they got them from. You are sure to catch them. "

A smile played over Ezra's pale face, which boded little good for the fugitives. "Curse those police! " he cried; "are they never going to come? "

"Here they are! " said the landlord; and sure enough, with a jingling of arms and a clatter of hoofs, half a dozen of the Griqualand Mounted Constabulary trotted through the crowd and drew up in front of the steps. They were smart, active young fellows, armed with revolver and sabre, and their horses were tough brutes, uncomely to look at, but with wonderful staying power. Ezra noted the fact with satisfaction as he rode up to the grizzled sergeant in command.

"There's not a moment to be lost, sergeant, " he said. "They have an hour and a half's start, but their cattle are not up to much. Come on! It's the Capetown road. A hundred pounds if we catch them! "

"Threes! " roared the sergeant. "Right half turn—trot! " The crowd split asunder, and the little troop, with Ezra at their head, clove a path through them. "Gallop! " shouted the sergeant, and away they clattered down the High Street of Kimberley, striking fire out of the stone and splashing up the gravel, until the sound of their hoofs died away into a dull, subdued rattle, and finally faded altogether from the ears of the listening crowd.

For the first few miles the party galloped in silence. The moon was still shining brilliantly, and they could see the white line of the road stretching out in front of them and winding away over the undulating veldt. To right and left spread a broad expanse of wiry grass stretching to the horizon, with low bushes and scrub scattered over it in patches. Here and there were groups of long-legged, unhealthy-looking sheep, who crashed through the bushes in wild terror as the riders swept by them. Their plaintive calls were the only sounds which broke the silence of the night, save the occasional dismal hooting of the veldt owl.

Ezra, on his powerful grey, had been riding somewhat ahead of the troopers, but the sergeant managed to get abreast of him. "Beg pardon, sir, " he said, raising his hand to his kepi, "but don't you think this pace is too good to last? The horses will be blown. "

"As long as we catch them, " Ezra answered, "I don't care what becomes of the horses. I would sooner stand you a dozen horses apiece than let them get away. "

The young merchant's words were firm and his seat steady, in spite of the throbbing at his head. The fury in his heart supplied him with strength, and he gnawed his moustache in his impatience and dug his spurs into his horse's flanks until the blood trickled down its glossy coat. Fortune, reputation, above all, revenge, all depended upon the issue of this headlong chase through the darkness.

The sergeant and Ezra galloped along, leather to leather, and rein to rein, while the troop clattered in their rear. "There's Combrink about two miles further on, " said the sergeant; "we will hear news of them there. "

"They can't get off the high road, can they? "

"Not likely, sir. They couldn't get along as fast anywhere else. Indeed, it's hardly safe riding across the veldt. They might be down a pit before they knew of it. "

"As long as they are on the road, we must catch them, " quoth Ezra; "for if it ran straight from here to hell I would follow them there. "

"And we'd stand by you, sir, " said the sergeant, catching something of his companion's enthusiasm. "At this pace, if the horses hold out, we might catch them before morning. There are the lights of the shanty. "

As he spoke they were galloping round a long curve in the road, at the further end of which there was a feeble yellow glimmer. As they came abreast of it they saw that the light came through an open door, in the centre of which a burly Afrikaner was standing with his hands in his breeches pockets and his pipe in his mouth.

"Good evening, " said the sergeant, as his men pulled up their reeking horses. "Has any one passed this way before us? "

"Many a tausand has passed this way before you, " said the Dutchman, taking his pipe out of his mouth to laugh.

"To-night, man, to-night! " the sergeant cried angrily.

"Oh yes; down the Port Elizabeth Road there, not one hour ago. Three men riding fit to kill their horses. "

"That'll do, " Ezra shouted; and away they went once more down the broad white road. They passed Bluewater's Drift at two in the morning, and were at Van Hayden's farm at half-past. At three they left the Modder River far behind them, and at a quarter past four they swept down the main street of the little township of Jacobsdal, their horses weak and weary and all mottled with foam. There was a police patrol in the street.

"Has any one passed? " cried the sergeant.

"Three men, a quarter of an hour ago. "

"Have they gone on? "

"Straight on. Their horses were nearly dead beat, though. "

"Come on! " cried Ezra eagerly. "Come on! "

"Four of the horses are exhausted, sir, " said the sergeant. "They can't move another step. "

"Come on without them then. "

"The patrol could come, " the sergeant suggested.

"I should have to report myself at the office, sir, " said the trooper.

"Jump on to his horse, sergeant, " cried Ezra. "He can take yours to report himself on. Now then you and I at least are bound to come up with them. Forward! gallop! " And they started off once more on their wild career, rousing the quiet burghers of Jacobsdal by the wild turmoil of their hoofs.

Out once more upon the Port Elizabeth Road it was a clear race between the pursuers and the pursued. The former knew that the fugitives, were it daytime, would possibly be within sight of them, and the thought gave them additional ardour. The sergeant having a fresh horse rode in front, his head down and his body forward, getting every possible inch of pace out of the animal. At his heels came Ezra, on his gallant grey, the blood-stained handkerchief fluttering from his head. He was sitting very straight in his saddle with a set stern smile upon his lips. In his right hand he held a cocked revolver. A hundred yards or so behind them the two remaining troopers came toiling along upon their weary nags, working hard with whip and spur to stimulate them to further exertions. Away in the east a long rosy streak lay low upon the horizon, which showed that dawn was approaching, and a grey light stole over the landscape. Suddenly the sergeant pulled his horse up.

"There's some one coming towards us, " he cried.

Ezra and the troopers halted their panting steeds. Through the uncertain light they saw a solitary horseman riding down the road. At first they had thought that it might possibly be one of the fugitives who had turned, but as he came nearer they perceived that it was a stranger. His clothes were so dusty and his horse so foam-flecked and weary that it was evident that he also had left many a long mile of road behind him.

"Have you seen three men on horseback? " cried Ezra as he approached.

"I spoke to them, " the traveller answered. "They are about half a mile ahead. "

"Come on! Come on! " Ezra shouted.

"I am bringing news from Jagersfontein—" the man said.

"Come on! " Ezra interrupted furiously; and the horses stretched their stiff limbs into a feeble lumbering gallop. Ezra and the sergeant shot to the front, and the others followed as best they might. Suddenly in the stillness they heard far away a dull rattling sound like the clatter of distant castanets. "It's their horses' hoofs! " cried Ezra; and the troopers behind raised a cheer to show that they too understood the significance of the sound.

It was a wild, lonely spot, where the plain was bare even of the scanty foliage which usually covered it. Here and there great granite rocks protruded from the brown soil, as though Nature's covering had in bygone days been rent until her gaunt bones protruded through the wound. As Ezra and the sergeant swept round a sharp turn in the road they saw, some little way ahead of them, the three fugitives, enveloped in a cloud of dust. Almost at the same moment they heard a shout and crash behind them, and, looking round, saw a confused heap upon the ground. The horse of the leading trooper had fallen from pure fatigue, and had rolled over upon its rider. The other trooper had dismounted, and was endeavouring to extricate his companion.

"Let us see if he is hurt, " the sergeant cried.

"On! on! " shouted Ezra, whose passion was increased by the sight of the thieves. "Not a foot back. "

"He may have broken his neck, " grumbled the sergeant, drawing his revolver. "Have your pistol ready, sir. We shall be up with them in a few minutes, and they may show fight. "

They were up with them rather sooner than the policeman expected. Farintosh, finding that speed was of no avail, and that the numbers of his pursuers was now reduced to two, had recourse to strategy. There was a sharp turn in the road a hundred yards ahead, and on reaching it the three flung themselves off their horses and lay down behind cover. As Ezra and the sergeant, the grey horse and the bay, came thundering round the curve, there was a fierce splutter of pistol shots from amongst the bushes, and the grey sank down upon its knees with a sobbing moan, struck mortally in the head. Ezra sprang to his feet and rushed at the ambuscade, while the sergeant, who had been grazed on the cheek by the first volley, jumped from his horse and followed him. Burt and Farintosh met them foot to foot with all the Saxon gallantry which underlies the Saxon brutality. Burt stabbed at the sergeant and struck him through the muscle of the neck. Farintosh fired at the policeman, and was himself shot down by Ezra. Burt, seeing his companion fall, sprang past his two assailants with a vicious side blow at the merchant, and throwing himself upon the sergeant's horse, regardless of a bullet from the latter's revolver, he galloped away, and was speedily out of range. As to Williams, from the beginning of the skirmish he had lain face downwards upon the ground, twisting his thin limbs about in an agony of fear, and howling for mercy.

"He's gone! " Ezra said ruefully, gazing after the fugitive. "We have nothing to go after him with. "

"I'm well-nigh gone myself, " said the policeman, mopping up the blood from his stab, which was more painful than dangerous. "He has given me a nasty prod. "

"Never mind, my friend, you shall not be the loser. Get up, you little viper! "—this to Williams, who was still writhing himself into the most extraordinary attitudes.

"Oh, please, Mr. Girdlestone, " he cried, clutching at Ezra's boots with his long thin fingers, "it wasn't me that hit you. It was Mr. Burt. I had nothing to do with robbing you either. That was Mr. Farintosh. I wouldn't have gone with him, only I knew that he was a clergyman, so I expected no harm. I am surprised at you, Mr. Farintosh, I really am. I'm very glad that Mr. Girdlestone has shot you. "

The ex-parson was sitting with his back against a gnarled stump, which gave him some support. He had his hand to his chest, and as he breathed a ghastly whistling sound came from the wound, and spirts of blood rushed from his mouth. His glazed eyes were fixed upon the man who had shot him, and a curious smile played about his thin lips.

"Come here, Mr. Girdlestone, " he croaked; "come here. "

Ezra strode over to him with a face as inexorable as fate.

"You've done for me, " said Farintosh faintly. "It's a queer end for the best man of his year at Trinity—master of arts, sir, and Jacksonian prizeman. Not much worth now, is it? Who'd have thought then that I should have died like a dog in this wilderness? What's the odds how a man dies though. If I'd kept myself straight I should have gone off a few years later in a feather bed as the Dean of St. Patrick's may be. What will that matter? I've enjoyed myself"—the dying man's eyes glistened at the thought of past dissipations. "If I had my time to do over again, " he continued, "I'd enjoy myself the same way. I'm not penitent, sir. No death-bed snivelling about me, or short cuts into heaven. That's not what I wanted to say though. I have a choking in the throat, but I dare say you can hear what I am driving at. You met a man riding towards Jacobsdal, did you not? "

Ezra nodded sullenly.

"You didn't speak to him? Too busy trying to catch yours truly, eh? Will you have your stones back, for they are in the bag by my side, but they'll not be very much good to you. The little spec won't come off this time. You don't know what the news was that the man was bringing? "

A vague feeling of impending misfortune stole over Ezra. He shook his head.

"His news was, " said Farintosh, leaning up upon his hand, "that fresh diamond fields *have* been discovered at Jagersfontein, in the Orange Free State. So Russia, or no Russia, stones will not rise. Ha! ha! will not rise. Look at his face! It's whiter than mine. Ha! ha! ha! " With the laugh upon his lips, a great flow of blood stopped the clergyman's utterance, and he rolled slowly over upon his side, a dead man.

CHAPTER XXIII.

A MOMENTOUS RESOLUTION.

During the months which Ezra Girdlestone had spent in Africa the affairs of the firm in Fenchurch Street had been exceedingly prosperous. Trade upon the coast had been brisker than usual, and three of the company's ships had come in at short intervals with excellent cargoes. Among these was the *Black Eagle* which, to the astonishment of Captain Hamilton Miggs and the disgust of his employer, had weathered a severe gale in the Channel, and had arrived safe and sound once more. This run of luck, supplemented by the business capacity of the old merchant and the indomitable energy of young Dimsdale, made the concern look so flourishing that the former felt more than ever convinced that if he could but stave off the immediate danger things would soon right themselves. Hence he read with delight the letters from Africa, in which his son narrated the success of the conspiracy and the manner in which the miners had been hoodwinked. The old man's figure grew straighter and his step more firm as the conviction grew upon him that the company would soon return once again to its former condition of affluence.

It may be imagined, therefore, that when the rumours of a bona fide diamond find in the Orange Free State came to his ears John Girdlestone was much agitated and distressed. On the same day that he saw the announcement in the papers he received a letter from his son announcing the failure of their enterprise. After narrating the robbery, the pursuit, the death of Farintosh, and the announcement of the new discovery, it gave an account of his subsequent movements.

"There was no doubt about the truth of the scoundrel's words, " he said, "for when we went to the nearest farm to get some food and have the sergeant's wound dressed we found that every one was talking about it. There was a chap there who had just come from the State and knew all about it. After hearing the details from him I saw that there was no doubt of the genuineness of the thing.

"The police rode back to Jacobsdal with Williams, and I promised to come after them; but when I came to think it over it didn't seem good enough. The fact of my having so many diamonds would set every tongue wagging, and, again, the sergeant had heard what Farintosh said to me, so it was very possible that I might have the whole district about my ears. As it was, I had the stones and all my money in the bag. I wrote back to the hotel, therefore, telling the landlord to send on my traps to Cape Town by mail, and promising to settle my bill with him when I received them. I then bought a horse and came straight south. I shall take the first steamer and be with you within a few days of your receiving this.

"As to our speculation, it is, of course, all up. Even when the Russian business proves to be a hoax, the price of stones will remain very low on account of these new fields. It is possible that we may sell our lot at some small profit but it won't be the royal road to a fortune that you prophesied, nor will it help the firm out of the rut into which you have shoved it. My only regret in leaving Africa like this is that that vermin Williams will have no one to prosecute him. My head is almost well now. "

This letter was a rude shock to the African merchant. Within a week of the receipt of it his son Ezra, gloomy and travel-stained, walked into the sanctum at Fenchurch Street and confirmed all the evil tidings by word of mouth. The old man was of too tough a fibre to break down completely, but his bony hands closed convulsively upon the arms of the chair, and a cold perspiration broke out upon his wrinkled forehead as he listened to such details as his son vouchsafed to afford him.

"You have your stones all safe, though? " he stammered out at last.

"They are in my box, at home, " said Ezra, gloomy and morose, leaning against the white marble mantelpiece. "The Lord knows what they are worth! We'll be lucky if we clear as much as they cost and a margin for my expenses and Langworthy's. A broken head is all that I have got from your fine scheme. "

"Who could foresee such a thing? " the old man said plaintively. He might have added Major Clutterbuck's thousand pounds as another item to be cleared, but he thought it as well to keep silent upon the point.

"Any fool could foresee the possibility of it, " quoth Ezra brusquely.

"The fall in prices is sure to be permanent, then? " the old man asked.

"It will last for some years, any way, " Ezra answered. "The Jagersfontein gravel is very rich, and there seems to be plenty of it. "

"And within a few months we must repay both capital and interest. We are ruined! " The old merchant spoke in a broken voice, and his head sank upon his breast. "When that day comes, " he continued, "the firm which has been for thirty years above reproach, and a model to the whole City, will be proclaimed as a bankrupt concern. Worse still, it will be shown to have been kept afloat for years by means which will be deemed fraudulent. I tell you, my dear son, that if any means could be devised which would avert this—*any* means— I should not hesitate to adopt them. I am a frail old man, and I feel that the short balance of my life would be a small thing for me to give in return for the assurance that the work which I have built up should not be altogether thrown away. "

"Your life cannot affect the matter one way or the other unless it were more heavily insured than it is, " Ezra said callously, though somewhat moved by his father's intensity of manner. "Perhaps there is some way out of the wood yet, " he added, in a more cheerful tone.

"It's so paying, so prosperous—that's what goes to my heart. If it had ruined itself it would be easier to bear it, but it is sacrificed to outside speculations—my wretched, wretched speculations. That is what makes it so hard. " He touched the bell, and Gilray answered the summons. "Listen to this, Ezra. What was our turn over last month, Gilray? "

"Fifteen thousand pounds, sir, " said the little clerk, bobbing up and down like a buoy in a gale in his delight at seeing the junior partner once again.

"And the expenses? "

"Nine thousand three hundred. Uncommon brown you look, Mr. Ezra, to be sure, uncommon brown and well. I hopes as you enjoyed yourself in Africa, sir, and was too much for them Hottenpots and Boars. " With this profound ethnological remark Mr. Gilray bobbed himself out of the room and went back radiantly to his ink-stained desk.

"Look at that, " the old man said, when the click of the outer door showed that the clerk was out of ear-shot. "Over five thousand profit in a month. Is it not terrible that such a business should go to ruin? What a fortune it would have been for you! "

"By heavens, it must be saved! " cried Ezra, with meditative brows and hands plunged deep in his trouser pockets. "There is that girl's money. Could we not get the temporary use of it. "

"Impossible! " his father answered with a sigh. "It is so tied up in the will that she cannot sign it away herself until she comes of age. There is no way of touching it except by her marriage—or by her death. "

"Then we must have it by the only means open to us. "

"And that is? "

"I must marry her. "

"You will? "

"I shall. Here is my hand on it. "

"Then we are saved, " cried the old man, throwing up his tremulous hands. "Girdlestone & Son will weather the storm yet. "

"But Girdlestone becomes a sleeping partner, " said Ezra. "It's for my own sake I do it and not for yours, " with which frank remark he drew his hat down over his brows and set off for Eccleston Square.

CHAPTER XXIV.

A DANGEROUS PROMISE.

During Ezra Girdlestone's absence in Africa our heroine's life had been even less eventful than of old. There was a consistency about the merchant's establishment which was characteristic of the man. The house itself was austere and gloomy, and every separate room, in spite of profuse expenditure and gorgeous furniture, had the same air of discomfort. The servants too, were, with one single exception, from the hard-visaged housekeeper to the Calvinistic footman, a depressing and melancholy race. The only departure from this general rule was Kate's own maid, Rebecca Taylforth, a loudly-dressed, dark-eyed, coarse-voiced young woman, who raised up her voice and wept when Ezra departed for Africa. This damsel's presence was most disagreeable to Kate, and, indeed, to John Girdlestone also, who only retained her on account of his son's strong views upon the subject, and out of fear of an explosion which might wreck all his plans.

The old merchant was Kate's only companion during this period, and their conversation was usually limited to a conventional inquiry at breakfast time as to each other's health. On his return from the City in the evening Girdlestone was always in a moody humour, and would eat his dinner hastily and in silence. After dinner he was in the habit of reading methodically the various financial articles in the day's papers, which would occupy him until bedtime. Occasionally his companion would read these aloud to him, and such was the monotony of her uneventful life that she found herself becoming insensibly interested in the fluctuations of Grand Trunk scrip or Ohio and Delaware shares. The papers once exhausted, a bell was rung to summon the domestics, and when all were assembled the merchant, in a hard metallic voice, read through the lesson for the day and the evening prayers. On grand occasions he supplemented this by a short address, in the course of which he would pelt his frightened audience with hard jagged texts until he had reduced them to a fitting state of spiritual misery. No wonder that, under the influence of such an existence, the roses began to fade from his ward's cheeks, and her youthful heart to grow sad and heavy.

One daily tonic there was, however, which never deserted her. Strictly as Girdlestone guarded her, and jealously as he fenced her off from the outer world, he was unable to prevent this one little ray of light penetrating her prison. With an eye to the future he had so placed her that it seemed to him to be impossible that any sympathy could reach her from the outside world. Visits and visitors were alike forbidden to her. On no consideration was she to venture out alone. In spite of all his precautions, however, love has many arts and wiles which defy all opposition, and which can outplot the deepest of plotters.

Eccleston Square was by no means in a direct line between Kensington and the City, yet morning and evening, as sure as the clock pointed to half-past nine and to quarter to six, Tom would stride through the old-fashioned square and past the grim house, whose grimness was softened to his eyes through its association with the bright dream of his life. It was but the momentary glance of a sweet face at the upper window and a single wave of a white hand, but it sent him on with a fresh heart and courage, and it broke the dull monotony of her dreary life.

Occasionally, as we have seen, he even managed to find his way into the interior of this ogre's castle, in which his fair princess was immured. John Girdlestone put an end to this by ordering that business messages should never under any circumstances be conveyed to his private residence. Nothing daunted, however, the lovers soon devised another means of surmounting the barrier which divided them.

The centre of the square was taken up by a garden, rectangular and uninviting, fenced round with high forbidding walls which shut out all intruders and gave the place a resemblance to the exercise ground of a prison. Within the rails were clumps of bushes, and here and there a few despondent trees drooped their heads as though mourning over the uncongenial site in which they had been planted. Among these trees and bushes there were scattered seats, and the whole estate was at the disposal of the inhabitants of Eccleston Square, and was dignified by the name of the Eccleston Gardens. This was the only spot in which Kate was trusted without the surveillance of a footman, and it was therefore a favourite haunt of hers, where she would read or work for hours under the shelter of the scanty foliage.

Hence it came about that one day, as Thomas Dimsdale was making his way Cityward at a rather earlier hour than was customary with him, he missed the usual apparition at the window. Looking round blankly in search of some explanation of this absence, he perceived in the garden a pretty white bonnet which glinted among the leaves, and on closer inspection a pair of bright eyes, which surveyed him merrily from underneath it. The gate was open, and in less time than it takes to tell it the sacrilegious feet of the young man had invaded the sacred domains devoted to the sole use and behoof of the Ecclestonians. It may be imagined that he was somewhat late at the office that morning and on many subsequent mornings, until the clerks began to think that their new employer was losing the enthusiasm for business which had possessed him.

Tom frequently begged permission to inform Mr. Girdlestone of his engagement, but Kate was inflexible upon that point. The fact is, that she knew her guardian's character very much better than her lover did, and remembering his frequent exhortations upon the subject of the vanity and wickedness of such things, she feared the effects of his anger when he learned the truth. In a year or so she would be of age and her own mistress, but at present she was entirely in his power. Why should she subject herself to the certainty of constant harshness and unkindness which would await her? Had her guardian really fulfilled the functions of a father towards her he would have a right to be informed, but as it was she felt that she owed him no such duty. She therefore made up her mind that he should know nothing of the matter; but the fates unfortunately willed otherwise.

It chanced that one morning the interview between the lovers had lasted rather longer than usual, and had been concluded by Kate's returning to the house, while Tom remained sitting upon the garden seat lost in such a reverie as affects men in his position. While thus pleasantly employed, his thoughts were suddenly recalled to earth by the appearance of a dark shadow on the gravel in front of him, and looking up he saw the senior partner standing a short distance away and regarding him with anything but an amiable expression upon his face. He had himself been having a morning stroll in the garden, and had overseen the whole of the recent interview without the preoccupied lovers being aware of his presence.

"Are you coming to the office? " he asked sternly. "If so, we can go together. "

Tom rose and followed him out of the gardens without a word. He knew from the other's expression that all was known to him, and in his heart he was not sorry. His only fear was that the old man's anger might fall upon his ward and this he determined to prevent. They walked side by side as far as the station in complete silence, but on reaching Fenchurch Street Girdlestone asked his young partner to step into his private sanctum.

"Now, sir, " he said, as he closed the door behind him "I think that I have a right to inquire what the meaning may be of the scene of which I was an involuntary witness this morning? "

"It means, " Tom answered firmly but gently, "that I am engaged to Miss Harston, and have been for some time. "

"Oh, indeed, " Girdlestone answered coldly, sitting down at his desk and turning over the pile of letters.

"At my request, " said Tom, "our engagement was kept from your knowledge. I had reason to believe that you objected to early engagements, and I feared that ours might be disagreeable to you. " I trust that the recording angel will not register a very black mark against our friend for this, the one and only falsehood that ever passed his lips.

During the long silent walk the merchant had been revolving in his mind what course he should pursue, and he had come to the conclusion that it was more easy to guide this impetuous stream of youth than to attempt to stem it. He did not realize the strength of the tie that bound these two young people together, and imagined that with judgment and patience it might yet be snapped. It was, therefore, with as good an imitation of geniality as his angular visage would permit of that he answered his companion's confession.

"You can hardly wonder at my being surprised, " he said. "Such a thing never entered my mind for a moment. You would have done better to have confided in me before. "

"I must ask your pardon for not having done so. "

"As far as you are concerned, " said John Girdlestone affably, "I believe you to be hard-working and right-principled. Your conduct since you have joined the firm has been everything which I could desire. "

Tom bowed his acknowledgments, much pleased by this preamble.

"With regard to my ward, " continued the senior partner, speaking very slowly and evidently weighing his words, "I could not wish her to have a better husband. In considering such a question I have, however, as you may imagine, to consult above everything else the wishes of my dead friend, Mr. John Harston, the father of the young lady to whom you say that you are engaged. A trust has been reposed in me, and that trust must, of course, be fulfilled to the letter. "

"Certainly, " said Tom, wondering in his own mind how he could ever have brought himself for one moment to think evil of this kindly and righteous old man.

"It was one of Mr. Harston's most clearly expressed wishes that no words or even thoughts of such matters should be allowed to come in his daughter's way until she had attained maturity, by which he meant the age of one-and-twenty. "

"But he could not foresee the circumstances, " Tom pleaded. "I am sure that a year or so will make no difference in her sentiments in this matter. "

"My duty is to carry out his instructions to the letter. I won't say, however, " continued Mr. Girdlestone, "that circumstances might not arise which might induce me to shorten this probationary period. If my further acquaintance with you confirms the high impression which I now have of your commercial ability, that, of course, would have weight with me; and, again, if I find Miss Harston's mind is made up upon the point, that also would influence my judgment. "

"And what are we to do in the mean time? " asked the junior partner anxiously.

"In the mean time neither you nor your people must write to her, or speak to her, or hold any communication with her whatever. If I find you or them doing so, I shall be compelled in justice to Mr. Harston's last request to send her to some establishment abroad where she shall be entirely out of your way. My mind is irrevocably made up upon that point. It is not a matter of personal inclination, but of conscience. "

"And how long is this to last? " cried Tom.

"It will depend upon yourselves. If you prove yourself to be a man of honour in this matter, I may be inclined to sanction your addresses. In the mean time you must give me your word to let it rest, and neither to attempt to speak to Miss Harston, nor to see her, nor to allow your parents to communicate with her. The last condition may seem to you to be hard, but, in my eyes, it is a very important one. Unless you can bring yourself to promise all this, my duty will compel me to remove my ward entirely out of your reach, a course which would be painful to her and inconvenient to myself. "

"But I must let her know of this arrangement. I must tell her that you hold out hopes to us on condition that we keep apart for a time. "

"It would be cruel not to allow you to do that, " Girdlestone answered. "You may send her *one* letter, but remember there shall be no reply to it. "

"Thank you, sir; thank you! " Tom cried fervently. "I have something to live for now. This separation will but make our hearts grow fonder. What change can time make in either of us? "

"Quite so, " said John Girdlestone, with a smile. "Remember there must be no more walking through the square. You must remain absolutely apart if you wish to gain my consent. "

"It is hard, very, very hard. But I will promise to do it. What would I not promise which would lead to our earlier union? "

"That is settled then. In the mean time, I should be obliged if you would go down to the docks and look after the loading of the transferable corrugated iron houses for New Calabar. "

"All right, sir, and thank you for your kindness, " said Tom, bowing himself out. He hardly knew whether to be pleased or grieved over the result of his interview; but, on the whole, satisfaction prevailed, since at the worst it was but to wait for a year or so, while there seemed to be some hopes of gaining the guardian's consent before that. On the other hand, he had pledged himself to separate from

Kate; but that would, he reflected, only make their re-union the sweeter.

All the morning he was engaged in superintending the stowing of great slabs of iron in the capacious hold of the *Maid of Athens*. When the hour of luncheon arrived no thought of food was in the lad's head, but, burying himself in the back parlour of a little Blackwall public-house, he called for pen, ink, and paper, and proceeded to indite a letter to his sweetheart. Never was so much love and comfort and advice and hope compressed into the limits of four sheets of paper or contained in the narrow boundary of a single envelope. Tom read it over after he had finished, and felt that it feebly expressed his thoughts; but, then, what lover ever yet did succeed in getting his thoughts satisfactorily represented upon paper. Having posted this effusion, in which he had carefully explained the conditions imposed upon him, Tom felt considerably more light-hearted, and returned with renewed vigour to the loading of the corrugated iron. He would hardly have felt so satisfied had he seen John Girdlestone receiving that same letter from the hands of the footman, and reading it afterwards in the privacy of his bedroom with a sardonic smile upon his face. Still less contented would he have been had he beheld the merchant tearing it into small fragments and making a bonfire of it in his capacious grate. Next morning Kate looked in vain out of the accustomed window, and was sore at heart when no tall figure appeared in sight and no friendly hand waved a morning salutation.

CHAPTER XXV.

A CHANGE OF FRONT.

This episode had occurred about a fortnight before Ezra's return from Africa, and was duly retailed to him by his father.

"You need not be discouraged by that, " he said. "I can always keep them apart, and if he is absent and you are present—especially as she has no idea of the cause of his absence—she will end by feeling slighted and preferring you. "

"I cannot understand how you ever came to let the matter go so far, " his son answered sullenly. "What does the young puppy want to come poaching upon our preserves for? The girl belongs to us. She was given to you to look after, and a nice job you seem to have made of it! "

"Never mind, my boy, " replied the merchant. "I'll answer for keeping them apart if you will only push the matter on your own account. "

"I've said that I would do so, and I will, " Ezra returned; and events soon showed that he was as good as his word.

Before his African excursion the relations between young Girdlestone and his father's ward had never been cordial. Kate's nature, however, was so sweet and forgiving, that it was impossible for her to harbour any animosity, and she greeted Ezra kindly on his return from his travels. Within a few days she became conscious that a remarkable change had come over him—a change, as it seemed to her, very much for the better. In the past, weeks had frequently elapsed without his addressing her, but now he went out of his way to make himself agreeable. Sometimes he would sit for a whole evening describing to her all that he had seen in Africa, and really interesting her by his account of men and things. She, poor lass, hailed this new departure with delight, and did all in her power to encourage his better nature and to show that she appreciated the alteration in his bearing. At the same time, she was rather puzzled in her mind, for an occasional flash of coarseness or ferocity showed her that the real nature of the man was unaltered, and that he was putting an unnatural restraint upon himself.

As the days went on, and no word or sign came from Tom, a great fear and perplexity arose within the girl's mind. She had heard nothing of the interview at Fenchurch Street, nor had she any clue at all which could explain the mystery. Could it be that Tom had informed her guardian of their engagement, and had received such a rebuff that he had abandoned her in despair? That was surely impossible; yet why was it that he had ceased to walk through the square? She knew that he was not ill, because she heard her two companions talking of him in connection with business. What could be the matter, then? Her little heart was torn by a thousand conflicting doubts and fears.

In the mean time Ezra gave fresh manifestations of the improvement which travel had wrought upon him. She had remarked one day that she was fond of moss roses. On coming down to breakfast next morning she found a beautiful moss rose upon her plate, and every morning afterwards a fresh flower appeared in the same place. This pretty little piece of courtesy, which she knew could only come from Ezra, surprised and pleased her, for delicacy was the last quality for which she would have given him credit.

On another occasion she had expressed a desire to read Thackeray's works, the books in the library being for the most part of last century. On entering her room that same evening she found, to her astonishment, a handsomely bound edition of the novels in question standing on the centre of her table. For a moment a wild, unreasoning hope awoke in her that perhaps this was Tom's doing— that he had taken this means of showing that she was still dear to him. She soon saw, however, that the books could only have come from the same source as the flowers, and she marvelled more than ever at this fresh proof of the good will of her companion.

One day her guardian took the girl aside. "Your life must be rather dull, " he said. "I have taken a box for you to-night at the opera. I do not care about such spectacles myself, but I have made arrangements for your escort. A change will do you good. "

Poor Kate was too sad at heart to be inclined for amusement. She endeavoured, however, to look pleased and grateful.

"My good friend, Mrs. Wilkinson, is coming for you, " the merchant said, "and Ezra is going too. He has a great liking for music. "

Kate could not help smiling at this last remark, as she thought how very successfully the young man had concealed his taste during the years that she had known him.

She was ready, however, at the appointed hour, and Mrs. Wilkinson, a prim old gentlewoman, who had chaperoned Kate on the rare occasions when she went out, having arrived, the three drove off together.

The opera happened to be "Faust, " and the magnificent scenery and dresses astonished Kate, who had hardly ever before been within the walls of a theatre. She sat as if entranced, with a bright tinge of colour upon her cheeks, which, with her sparkling eyes, made her look surpassingly beautiful. So thought Ezra Girdlestone as he sat in the recesses of the box and watched the varied expressions which flitted across her mobile features. "She is well worth having, money or no, " he muttered to himself, and redoubled his attentions to her during the evening.

An incident occurred between the acts that night which would have pleased the old merchant had he witnessed it. Kate had been looking down from the box, which was upon the third tier, at the sea of heads beneath them. Suddenly she gave a start, and her face grew a trifle paler.

"Isn't that Mr. Dimsdale down there? " she said to her companion.

"Where? " asked Ezra, craning his neck. "Oh yes, there he is, in the second row of the stalls. "

"Do you know who the young lady is that he is talking to? " Kate asked.

"I don't know, " said Ezra. "I have seen him about with her a good deal lately. " The latter was a deliberate falsehood, but Ezra saw his chance of prejudicing his rival, and took prompt advantage of it. "She is very good-looking, " he added presently, keeping his eyes upon his companion.

"Oh, indeed, " said Kate, and turned with some common-place remark to Mrs. Wilkinson. Her heart was sore nevertheless, and she derived little pleasure from the remainder of the performance. As to Ezra, in spite of his great love for music, he dozed peacefully in a corner of the box during the whole of the last act. None of them were sorry when Faust was duly consigned to the nether regions and Marguerite was apotheosed upon a couple of wooden clouds. Ezra narrated the incident of the recognition in the stalls to his father on his return, and the old gentleman rubbed his hands over it.

"Most fortunate! " he exclaimed gleefully. "By working on that idea we might produce great effects. Who was the girl, do you know? "

"Some poor relation, I believe, whom he trots out at times. "

"We will find out her name and all about her. Capital, capital! " cried John Girdlestone; and the two worthies departed to their rooms much pleased at this new card which chance had put into their hands.

During the weary weeks while Tom Dimsdale, in accordance with his promise, avoided Eccleston Square and everything which could remind Kate of his existence, Ezra continued to leave no stone unturned in his endeavours to steal his way into her affections. Poor Tom's sole comfort was the recollection of that last passionate letter which he had written in the Blackwall public-house, and which had, as he imagined, enlightened her as to the reasons of his absence, and had prevented her from feeling any uneasiness or surprise. Had he known the fate that had befallen that epistle, he would hardly have been able to continue his office duties so patiently or to wait with so much resignation for Mr. Girdlestone's sanction to his engagement.

As the days passed and still brought no news, Kate's face grew paler and her heart more weary and desponding. That the young man was well was beyond dispute, since she had seen him with her own eyes at the opera. What explanation could there be, then, for his conduct? Was it possible that he had told Mr. Girdlestone of their engagement, and that her guardian had found some means of dissuading him from continuing his suit—found some appeal to his interest, perhaps, which was too strong for his love. All that she knew of Tom's nature contradicted such a supposition. Again, if Girdlestone had learned anything of their engagement, surely he would have reproached her with it. His manner of late had been kinder rather than harsher. On the other hand, could it have chanced that Tom had met this lady of the opera, and that her charms had proved too much for his constancy? When she thought of the honest grey eyes which had looked down into hers at that last meeting in the garden, she found it hard to imagine the possibility of such things, and yet there was a fact which had to be explained. The more she thought of it the more incomprehensible it grew, but still the pale face grew paler and the sad heart more heavy.

Soon, however, her doubts and fears began to resolve themselves into something more substantial than vague conjecture. The conversation of the Girdlestones used to turn upon their business colleague, and always in the same strain. There were stray remarks about his doings; hints from the father and laughter from the son. "Not much work to be got out of him now, " the old man would say. "When a man's in love he's not over fond of a ledger. "

"A nice-looking girl, too, " said Ezra, in answer to some such remark. "I thought something would come of it. We saw them together at the opera, didn't we, Kate? "

So they would gossip together, and every word a stab to the poor girl. She strove to conceal her feelings, and, indeed, her anger and her pride were stronger even than her grief, for she felt that she had been cruelly used. One day she found Girdlestone alone and unbosomed herself to him.

"Is it really true, " she asked, with a quick pant and a catch of her breath, "that Mr. Dimsdale is engaged to be married? "

"I believe so, my dear, " her guardian answered. "It is commonly reported so. When a young lady and gentleman correspond it is usually a sign of something of the sort. "

"Oh, they correspond? "

"Yes, they certainly correspond. Her letters are sent to him at the office. I don't know that I altogether like that arrangement. It looks as if he were deceiving his parents. " All this was an unmitigated lie, but Girdlestone had gone too far now to stick at trifles.

"Who is the lady? " asked Kate, with a calm set face but a quivering lip.

"A cousin of his. Miss Ossary is her name, I believe. I am not sorry, for it may be a sign that he has sown all his wild oats. Do you know at one time, Kate, I feared that he might take a fancy to you. He has a specious way with him, and I felt my responsibility in the matter. "

"You need not be afraid on that score, " Kate said bitterly. "I think I can gauge Mr. Dimsdale's specious manner at its proper value. " With this valiant speech she marched off, head in air, to her room, and there wept as though her very heart would break.

John Girdlestone told his son of this scene as they walked home from Fenchurch Street that same day. "We must look sharp over it, " he said, "or that young fool may get impatient and upset our plans. "

"It's not such an easy matter, " said his son gloomily. "I get along so far, but no further. It's a more uphill job than I expected. "

"Why, you had a bad enough name among women, " the merchant said, with something approaching to a sneer. "I have been grieved times out of number by your looseness in that respect. I should have thought that you might have made your experience of some use now. "

"There are women and women, " his son remarked. "A girl like this takes as much managing as a skittish horse. "

"Once get her into harness, and I warrant you'll keep her there quiet enough. "

"You bet, " said Ezra, with a loud laugh. "But at present she has the pull. Her mind is still running on that fellow. "

"She spoke bitterly enough of him this morning. "

"So she might, but she thinks of him none the less. If I could once make her thoroughly realize that he had thrown her over I might catch her on the hop. She'd marry for spite if she wouldn't for love. "

"Just so; just so. Wait a bit. That can be managed, I think, if you will leave it to me. "

The old man brooded over the problem all day, for from week to week the necessity for the money was becoming more pressing, and that money could only be hoped for through the success of Ezra's wooing. No wonder that every little detail which might sway the balance one way or the other was anxiously pondered over by the head of the firm, and that even the fluctuations in oil and ivory became secondary to this great object.

Next day, immediately after they had sat down to dinner, some letters were handed in by the footman. "Forwarded on from the office, sir, " said the flunkey. "The clerk says that Mr. Gilray was away and that he did not like to open them. "

"Just like him! " said Girdlestone, peevishly pushing back his plate of soup. "I hate doing business out of hours. " He tore the envelopes off the various letters as he spoke. "What's this? Casks returned as per invoice; that's all right. Note from Rudder & Saxe—that can be answered to-morrow. Memorandum on the Custom duties at Sierra Leone. Hallo! what have we here? 'My darling Tom'—who is this from—Yours ever, Mary Ossary. ' Why, it's one of young Dimsdale's love-letters which has got mixed up with my business papers. Ha! ha! I must really apologize to him for having opened it, but he must take his chance of that, if he has his correspondence sent to the office. I take it for granted that everything there is a business communication. "

Kate's face grew very white as she listened. She ate little dinner that day, poor child, and took the earliest opportunity of retiring to her room.

"You did that uncommonly well, dad, " said Ezra approvingly, after she was gone. "It hit her hard, I could see that. "

"I think it touched her pride. People should not have pride. We are warned against it. Now, that same pride of hers will forbid her ever thinking of that young man again. "

"And you had the letter written? "

"I wrote it myself. I think, in such a case, any stratagem is justifiable. Such large interests are at stake that we must adopt strong measures. I quite agree with the old Churchmen that the end occasionally justifies the means. "

"Capital, dad; very good! " cried Ezra, chewing his toothpick. "I like to hear you argue. It's quite refreshing. "

"I act according to the lights which are vouchsafed me, " said John Girdlestone gravely; on which Ezra leaned back in his chair and laughed heartily.

The very next morning the merchant spoke to Dimsdale on the matter, for he had observed signs of impatience in the young man, and feared that some sudden impulse might lead him to break his promise and so upset everything.

"Take a seat. I should like to have a word with you, " he said graciously, when his junior partner appeared before him to consult with him as to the duties of the day. Tom sat down with hope in his heart.

"It is only fair to you, Mr. Dimsdale, " Girdlestone said, in a kindly voice, "that I should express to you my appreciation of your honourable conduct. You have kept your promise in regard to Miss Harston in the fullest manner. "

"Of course I kept my promise, " said Tom bluntly. "I trust, however, that you will soon see your way to withdrawing your prohibition. It has been a hard trial to me. "

"I have insisted upon it because it seemed to me to be my duty. Every one takes his own view upon such points, and it has always been my custom throughout life to take what some might think a stringent one. It appears to me that I owe it to my deceased friend to prevent his daughter, whom he has confided to me, from making any mistake. As I said before, if you continue to show that you are worthy of her, I may think more favourably of it. Exemplary as your conduct has been since you joined us, I believe that I am not wrong in stating that you were a little wild when you were at Edinburgh. "

"I never did anything that I am ashamed of, " said Tom.

"Very likely not, " Girdlestone answered, with an irrepressible sneer. "The question is, did you do anything that your father was ashamed of? "

"Certainly not, " cried Tom hotly. "I was no milksop or psalm singer, but there is nothing that I ever did there of which I should be ashamed of my father knowing. "

"Don't speak lightly of psalm singing. It is a good practice in its way, and you would have been none the worse had you indulged in it perhaps. However, that is neither here nor there. What I want you clearly to understand is that my ultimate consent to your union depends entirely upon your own conduct. Above all, I insist that you refrain from unsettling the girl's mind at present. "

"I have already promised. Hard as the struggle may be, I shall not break my word. I have the consolation of knowing that if we were separated for twenty years we should still be true to one another. "

"That's very satisfactory, " said the merchant grimly.

"Nevertheless it is a weary, weary time. If I could only write a line—"

"Not a word, " Girdlestone interrupted. "It is only because I trust you that I keep her in London at all. If I thought there was a possibility of your doing such a thing I should remove her at once. "

"I shall do nothing without your permission, " Tom said, taking up his hat to go. He paused with his hand upon the door. "If ever it seems good to me, " he said, "I consider that by giving you due notice I absolve myself from my promise. "

"You would not do anything so foolish. "

"Still I reserve myself the right of doing so, " said Tom, and went off with a heavy heart to his day's work.

"Everything is clear for you now, " the old man said to his son triumphantly. "There's no chance of interference, and the girl is in the very humour to be won. I flatter myself that it has been managed with tact. Remember that all is at stake, and go in and win. "

"I shall go in, " said Ezra "and I think the chances are that I shall win too. "

At which reassuring speech the old man laughed, and slapped his son approvingly upon the shoulder.

CHAPTER XXVI.

BREAKING GROUND.

In spite of John Girdlestone's temporary satisfaction and the stoical face which he presented to the world, it is probable that in the whole of London there was no more unhappy and heart-weary man. The long fight against impending misfortune had shattered his iron constitution and weakened him both in body and in mind. It was remarked upon 'Change how much he had aged of late, and moralists commented upon the vanity and inefficacy of the wealth which could not smooth the wrinkles from the great trader's haggard visage. He was surprised himself when he looked in the glass at the change which had come over him. "Never mind, " he would say in his dogged heart a hundred times a day, "they can't beat me. Do what they will, they can't beat me. " This was the one thought which sustained and consoled him. The preservation of his commercial credit had become the aim and object of his life, to which there was nothing that he was not prepared to sacrifice.

His cunningly devised speculation in diamonds had failed, but this failure had been due to an accident which could neither have been foreseen nor remedied. To carry out this scheme he had, as we have seen, been obliged to borrow money, which had now to be repaid. This he had managed to do, more or less completely, by the sale of the stones which Ezra had brought home, supplemented by the recent profits of the firm. There was still the original deficit to be faced, and John Girdlestone knew that though a settlement might be postponed from month to month, still the day must come, and come soon, when his debts must be met, or his inability to meet them become apparent to the whole world. Should Ezra be successful in his wooing and his ward's forty thousand pounds be thrown into the scale, the firm would shake itself clear from the load which oppressed it. Supposing, however, that Kate were to refuse his son. What was to occur then? The will was so worded that there appeared to be no other way of obtaining the money. A very vulpine look would come over the old man's face as he brooded over that problem.

The strangest of all the phenomena, however, presented by John Girdlestone at this period of his life was his own entire conviction of the righteousness of his actions. When every night and morning he sank upon his knees with his household and prayed for the success of the firm's undertakings, no qualms of conscience ever troubled him as to their intrinsic morality. On Sundays the grey head of the merchant in the first pew was as constant an object as was the pew itself, yet in that head no thought ever rose of the inconsistency of his religion and of his practice. For fifty years he had been persuading himself that he was a righteous man, and the conviction was now so firmly impressed upon his very soul that nothing could ever shake it. Ezra was wrong when he set this down as deliberate hypocrisy. Blind strength of will and self-conceit were at the bottom of his actions, but he would have been astonished and indignant had he been accused of simulating piety or of using it as a tool. To him the firm of Girdlestone was the very representation of religion in the commercial world, and as such must be upheld by every conceivable means.

To his son this state of mind was unintelligible, and he simply gave his father credit for being a consummate and accomplished hypocrite, who found a mantle of piety a very convenient one under which to conceal his real character. He had himself inherited the old man's dogged pertinacity and commercial instincts, and was by nature unscrupulous and impatient of any obstacle placed in his way. He was now keenly alive to the fact that the existence of the firm depended upon the success of his suit, and he knew also how lucrative a concern the African business would prove were it set upon its legs again. He had determined in case he succeeded to put his father aside as a sleeping partner and to take the reins of management entirely into his own hands. His practical mind had already devised countless ways in which the profits might be increased. The first step of all, then, was the gaining possession of the forty thousand pounds, and to that he devoted himself heart and soul. When two such men work together for one end, it is seldom that they fail to achieve it.

It would be a mistake to suppose that Ezra felt himself in any degree in love at this time. He recognized his companion's sweetness and gentleness, but these were not qualities which appealed to his admiration. Kate's amiable, quiet ways seemed insipid to a man who was used to female society of a very different order.

"She has no go or snap about her, " he would complain to his father. "She's not like Polly Lucas at the Pavilion, or Minnie Walker. "

"God forbid! " ejaculated the merchant. "That sort of thing is bad enough out of doors, but worst of all in your own house. "

"It makes courting a good deal easier, " Ezra answered.

"If a girl will answer up and give you an opening now and then, it makes all the difference. "

"You can't write poetry, can you? "

"Not much, " Ezra said with a grin.

"That's a pity. I believe it goes a long way with women. You might get some one to write some, and let her think it is yours. Or you could learn a little off and repeat it. "

"Yes, I might do that. I'm going to buy a collar for that beast of a dog of hers. All the time that I was talking to her yesterday she was so taken up with it that I don't believe she heard half that I said. My fingers itched to catch it up and chuck it through the window. "

"Don't forget yourself, my boy, don't forget yourself! " cried the merchant. "A single false step might ruin every thing. "

"Never fear, " Ezra said confidently, and went off upon the dog-collar mission. While he was in the shop he bought a dog-whip as well, which he locked up in his drawers to use as the occasion served.

During all this time Kate had been entirely unconscious of her companion's intentions and designs. She had been associated with Ezra for so many years, and had met such undeviated want of courtesy from him, that the idea of his presenting himself as a suitor never came into her head. She hailed his charge of demeanour, therefore, as being the result of his larger experience of the world, and often wondered how it was that he had profited so much by his short stay at the Cape. In the cheerless house it was pleasant to have at least one companion who seemed to have kindly feelings towards her. She was only too glad, therefore, to encourage his advances, and to thank him with sweet smiles and eloquent eyes for what appeared to her to be his disinterested kindness.

After a while, however, Ezra's attentions became so marked that it was impossible for her to misunderstand them any longer. Not only did he neglect his usual work in order to hang round her from morning to night, but he paid her many clumsy compliments and gave other similar indications of the state of his affections. As soon as this astounding fact had been fairly realized by the girl, she at once changed her manner and became formal and distant. Ezra, nothing daunted, redoubled his tender words and glances, and once would have kissed her hand had she not rapidly withdrawn it. On this Kate shut herself up in her room, and rarely came out save when the other was away in the City. She was determined that there should be no possibility of any misunderstanding as to her feelings in the matter.

John Girdlestone had been watching these little skirmishes closely and with keen interest. When Kate took to immuring herself in her room he felt that it was time for him to interfere.

"You must go about a little more, and have more fresh air, " he said to her one day, when they were alone after breakfast. "You will lose your roses if you don't. "

"I am sure I don't care whether I lose them or not, " answered his ward listlessly.

"You may not, but there are others who do, " remarked the merchant. "I believe it would break Ezra's heart. "

Kate flushed up at this sudden turn of the conversation. "I don't see what reason your son has to care about it, " she said.

"Care about it! Are you so blind that you don't see that he loves the very ground you walk on. He has grown quite pale and ill these last few days because he has not seen you, and he imagines that he may have offended you. "

"For goodness' sake! " cried Kate earnestly, "persuade him to think of some one else. It will only be painful both to him and to me if he keeps on this way. It cannot possibly lead to anything. "

"And why not? Why should—"

"Oh, don't let us argue about it, " she cried passionately. "The very idea is horrible. It won't bear talking about. "

"But why, my dear, why? You are really too impulsive. Ezra has his faults, but what man has not? He has been a little wild in his youth, but he is settling down now into an excellent man of business. I assure you that, young as he is, there are few names more respected on 'Change. The way in which he managed the business of the firm in Africa was wonderful. He is already a rich man, and will be richer before he dies. I cannot see any cause for this deep-rooted objection of yours. As to looks he is, you must confess, as fine a young fellow as there is in London. "

"I wish you not to speak of it or think of it again, " said Kate. "My mind is entirely made up when I say that I shall never marry any one—him least of all. "

"You will think better of it, I am sure, " her guardian said, patting her chestnut hair kindly as he stood over her. "Since your poor father handed you over to me I have guarded you and cared for you to the best of my ability. Many a sleepless night I have spent thinking of your future and endeavouring to plan it out so as to secure your happiness. I should not be likely to give you bad advice now, or urge you to take a step which would make you unhappy. Have you anything to complain of in my treatment of you? "

"You have been always very just, " Kate said with a sob.

"And this is how you repay me! You are going to break my son's heart, and through his mine. He is my only boy, and if anything went wrong with him I tell you that it would bring my grey hairs in sorrow to the grave. You have it in your power to do this, or, on the other hand, you may make my old age a happy one by the knowledge that the lad is mated with a good woman, and has attained the object on which his whole mind and heart are set. "

"Oh, I can't, I can't. Do let the matter drop. "

"Think it over, " the old man said. "Look at it from every point of view. Remember that the love of an honest man is not to be lightly spurned. I am naturally anxious about it, for my future happiness, as well as his, depends upon your decision. "

John Girdlestone was fairly satisfied with this interview. It seemed to him that his ward was rather less decided in her refusal at the end of it, and that his words had had some effect upon her, which might possibly increase with reflection.

"Give her a little time now, " was his advice to his son. "I think she will come round, but she needs managing. "

"If I could get the money without taking her it would be better for me, " Ezra said with an oath.

"And better for her too, " remarked John Girdlestone grimly.

CHAPTER XXVII.

MRS. SCULLY OF MORRISON'S.

One day Major Tobias Clutterbuck was sitting at the window of his little room smoking his cigarette and sipping his glass of wine, as was his custom if times were reasonably good. While thus agreeably employed he chanced to look across the road and perceived a little fringe of dark hair, and a still darker eye, which surveyed him round the border of one of the curtains which flanked a window opposite. The gallant major was much interested in this apparition, and rose to make a closer inspection of it, but, alas! before he could focus it with his eye-glass it was gone! He bent his gaze resolutely in that direction for a long time, and smoked at least half a dozen cigarettes, besides finishing the bottle of wine; but although he thought he saw certain flittings and whiskings of garments in the dark background of the opposite room, he could not make out anything more definite.

Next day the soldier was on the look-out at the same hour, and was rewarded by the appearance of two eyes, very mischievous and dangerous ones too, which were set in a buxom and by no means unprepossessing face. The lady who owned these charms looked very deliberately up the street, and very deliberately down the street, after which she bethought herself to look across the street, and started to perceive a stout, middle-aged gentleman, with a fiery face, who was looking at her with an expression of intense admiration. So much alarmed was she that she vanished behind the curtains and the major feared that he would see her no more. Fortunately, however, it became evident that the lady's alarm was not very overpowering, for within five minutes she was back at the window, where her eyes again fell upon the beaming face and jaunty figure of the major, who had posed himself in a striking attitude, which was somewhat marred by the fact that he was still enveloped in his purple dressing-gown. This time her eyes lingered a little longer than before and the suspicion of a smile appeared upon her features. On this the major smiled and bowed, and she smiled also, showing a pretty little line of white teeth as she did so. What the veteran's next move might have been no one can tell, for the lady solved the problem by disappearing, and this time permanently. He was very well satisfied, however, and chuckled much to himself while arraying himself in his long frock coat and immaculate collar before setting out for the club. He had been a sly old dog in his day, and had followed Venus almost as much as he had Mars during his chequered career.

All day the recollection of this little episode haunted him. So much pre-occupied was he at the club that he actually played out the thirteenth trump upon his partner's long suit and so sacrificed the game—being the first and only time that he was ever known to throw away a point. He told Von Baumser all about it when he came back.

"She's a demned foine-looking woman, whoever she may be, " he remarked, at they sat together before turning in. "Be George! she's the foinest woman I've seen for a long time. "

"She's a window, " said the German.

"A what? "

"A window—the window of an engineer. "

"Is it a widow you mane? What d'ye know about her? What's her name, and where does she come from? "

"I have heard from the slavey that a win—a widow lives over dere in those rooms. She boards mit Madame Morrison, and that window belongs to her privacy zimmer—dat is, chamber. As to her name, I have not heard it, or else I disremember it. "

"Ged! " said the major, "she'd eyes that looked right through ye, and a figure like Juno. "

"She's vierzig if she's a day—dat is, forty, " Von Baumser remarked.

"Well, if she is, me boy, a woman of forty is just in the proime o' loife. If you'd seen her at the window, she would have taken ye by storm. She stands like this, and she looks up like this, and then down in this way. " The major pursed up his warlike features into what he imagined to be an innocent and captivating expression. Then she looks across and sees me, and down go the lids of her eyes, like the shutting off of a bull's-eye lantern. Then she blushed and stole just one more glance at me round the corner of the curtain. She had two peeps, the divil a doubt of it. "

"Dat is very good, " the German said encouragingly.

"Ah, me boy, twenty years ago, when I was forty inches round the chest and thirty-three round the waist, I was worth looking at twice. Bedad, when a man gets ould and lonely he sees what a fool he was not to make better use of his time when he'd the chance. "

"Mein Gott! " cried Von Baumser. "You don't mean to say that you would marry suppose you had the chance? "

"I don't know, " the major answered reflectively.

"The vomens is not to be trusted, " the German said sadly. "I knew a voman in my own country which was the daughter of a man dat kept a hotel—and she and I was promised to be married to each others. Karl Hagelstein, he was to be vat you call my best man. A very handsome man was Karl, and I sent him often mit little presents of one thing or another to my girl, for there were reasons why I could not go myself. He was nicer than me because my hair was red, and pretty soon she began to like him, and he liked her too. So the day before the vedding she went down the Rhine to Frankfort by the boat, and he went down by train, and there they met and was married the one to the other. "

"And what did you do? " the major asked with interest.

"Ah, dat was the most worst thing of all, for I followed them mit a friend of mine, and when we caught them I did not let her know, but I called him out of his hotel, and I told him that he must fight me. Dat vos a mistake. I should have done him an insult, and then he vould have had to ask me to fight, and I could have chosen my own veapon. As it was he chose swords, for he knew veil that I knew nothing of them, and he had been the best fencer in the whole of his University. Then we met in the morning, and before I had time to do anything he ran me through the left lung. I have shown you the mark of it. After dat I vas in bed for two month and more, and it still hurts me ven de veather is cold. That is vat they call satisfaction, " Baumser added, pulling his long red beard reflectively. "To me it has ever seemed the most dissatisfactory thing that could be imagined. "

"I don't wonder you're afraid of the women after that, " said the major, laughing. "There are plenty of good women in the world, though, if you have the luck to come across them. D'ye know a young fellow called Dimsdale—? Ah, you wouldn't, but I've met him lately at the club. He's got a girl who's the adopted daughter of that same ould Girdlestone that we talk about. I saw the two of them togither one day as happy as a pair of young love birds. Sure, you've only got to look at her face to see that she's as good as gold. I'll bet that that woman over the strate there is another of the right sort. "

"Dat voman is alvays in your head, " the German said, with a smile. "You shall certainly dream about her to-night. I remember a voman in Germany—" And so these two Bohemians rambled on into the small hours, discoursing upon their past experiences and regaling each other with many reminiscences, some of which, perhaps, are just as well omitted and allowed to sink into oblivion. When the major finally retired for the night, his last thought was of the lady at the window and of the means by which he might contrive to learn something of her.

These proved to be more easy than he anticipated, for next morning, on cross-examining the little servant girl from whom Von Baumser had derived his information, the major found out all that he desired to know. According to this authority, the lady was a widow of the name of Scully, the relict of a deceased engineer, and had been staying some little time at Morrison's, which was the rival establishment to that in which the major and Von Baumser resided.

Armed with this information, the major pondered for some time before deciding upon his course of action. He saw no possible means by which he could gain an introduction to his charming neighbour unless he had recourse to some daring strategem. "Audace et toujours audace" had always been the soldier's motto. He rose from his chair, discarded his purple gown, and arrayed himself in his best attire. Never had he paid such attention to his toilet. His face was clean shaven and shining, his sparse hairs were laid out to the best advantage, his collar spotless, his frock coat oppressively respectable, and his *tout ensemble* irreproachable. "Be George! " he said to himself, as he surveyed himself in the small lodging-house glass, "I'd look as young as Baumser if I had some more hair on me head. Bad cess to the helmets and shakoes that wore it all off. "

When his toilet was fully completed and rounded off by the addition of a pair of light gloves and an ebony stick with a silver head, the veteran strode forth with a bold front, but with considerable trepidation at his heart; for when is a man so seasoned as to have no misgivings when he makes the first advances to a woman who really attracts him? Whatever the major's inward feelings may have been, however, he successfully concealed them as he rang the bell of the rival lodging-house and inquired of the servant whether Mrs. Scully was at home.

"Yes, sir, she is, " said the slavey, with a frightened bob, which was a tribute to the major's martial mien and gorgeous attire.

"Would you tell her that I should like to see her, " said the major boldly. "I shan't detain her a moment. Here is my card—Major Tobias Clutterbuck, late of the 119th Light Infantry. "

The servant disappeared with the card, and presently returned with a request that he would step up. The old soldier stumped his way upstairs with the firm footfall of one who has taken a thing in hand and means to carry it through at all hazard. As he ascended, it seemed to him that he heard the sound of feminine laughter in the distance. If so, it could hardly have come from the lady whom he was in quest of, for he was shown into a large and well-furnished room, where she sat looking demure and grave enough, as did another young lady who was crocheting on the ottoman beside her.

The major made his most courtly bow, though he felt very much as the Spaniards may be supposed to have done when they saw their ships blazing behind them. "I trust you will excuse this intrusion on my part, " he began. "I happened to hear that a lady of the name of Scully was stopping here. "

"My name is Scully, sir, " said the lady, whose dark eyes had allured the major to this feat of daring.

"Then perhaps, madam, " the veteran said with another bow, "you will allow me to ask you whether you are any relation to Major-gineral Scully, of the Indian Sappers? "

"Pray take a seat, Major—Major Clutterbuck, " said Mrs. Scully, referring to his card, which she still held in her very well-formed little hand. "Major-general Scully, did you say? Dear me! I know that one of my husband's relations went into the army, but we never heard what became of him. A major-general, is he? Whoever would have thought it! "

"As dashing a souldier, madam, " said the major, warming into eloquence, "as ever hewed a way through the ranks of the enemy, or stormed the snow-clad passes of the Himalayas. "

"Fancy! " ejaculated the young lady with the crochet needle.

"Many a time, " continued the soldier, "he and I after some hard-fought battle have slept togither upon the blood-stained ground wrapped in the same martial cloak. "

"Fancy! " cried both ladies in chorus; and they could not have selected a more appropriate interjection.

"And when at last he died, " the major went on with emotion, "cut in two with a tulwar in a skirmish with hill tribes, he turned to me—"

"After being cut in two? " interrupted the younger lady.

"He turned to me, " said the major inflexibly, "and putting his hand in mine, he said, with his last breath, 'Toby'—that was what he always called me—'Toby, ' he said, 'I have a—' Your husband was his brother, I think you said, ma'am? "

"No, it was Mr. Scully's uncle who went into the army. "

"Ah, quite so. 'I have a nephew in England, ' he said, 'who is very dear to me. He is married to a charming woman. Search out the young couple, Toby. Guard over them. Protict them! ' Those were his last words, madam. Next moment his sowl had fled. When I heard your name casually mintioned I could not feel satisfied in me mind until I had come across and ascertained if you were the lady in question. "

Now, this narrative not only surprised the widow, which was not unnatural, seeing that it was entirely an invention of the old soldier's, but it appealed to her weakest point. The father of the deceased Scully had been of plebeian origin, so that the discovery in the family of a real major-general—albeit he was dead—was a famous windfall, for the widow had social ambitions which hitherto she had never been able to gratify. Hence she smiled sweetly at the veteran in a way which stimulated him to further flights of mendacity.

"Sure he and I were like brothers, " he said. "He was a man that any one might well be proud to know. Commander-in-chief said to me once, 'Clutterbuck, ' says he, 'I don't know what we'd do if we had a European war. I've no one I can rely on, ' says he. 'There's Scully, ' says I. 'Right, ' says he, 'Scully would be our man. ' He was terribly cut up when this occurred. 'Here's a blow to the British army! ' he remarked, as he looked down at him where he lay with a bullet through his head—he did, madam, be Jove! "

"But, major, I understood you to say that he was cut in two? "

"So he was. Cut in two, and shot and mortally wounded in a dozen places besides. Ah, if he could have foreseen that I should have met you he would have died happy. "

"It's strange he never let us know of his existence when he was alive, " the widow remarked.

"Pride, madam, pride! 'Until I reach the top of the tree, Toby, ' he used to say, 'I shall niver reveal myself to me brother. '"

"Nephew, " interpolated the widow.

"Quite so—' I shall niver reveal myself to me nephew. ' He said those very words to me only a few minutes before the fatal shell struck him. "

"A shell, major? You mean a bullet. "

"A shell, madam, a shell, " said the major with decision.

"Dear me! " exclaimed Mrs. Scully, with a somewhat bewildered expression. "How very sad it all is. We must thank you very much, Major Bottletop—"

"Clutterbuck, " said the Major.

"I beg pardon, Major Clutterbuck. It was very kind of you to call upon us in this friendly way and to give us these details. Of course, when a relative dies, even though you don't know much about him, still it is interesting to have a clear account of how it all happened. Just fancy, Clara, " continued the widow, drawing her handkerchief from her reticule and mopping one of her eyes with it. "Just fancy the poor fellow being cut in two with a bullet far away in India and him just speaking about Jack and me a few minutes before. I am sure we must thank Major Bottlenose—"

"Clutterbuck, madam, " cried the major with some indignation.

"I really beg pardon. We must thank him, Clara, for having told us about it and for having called. "

"Do not thank me, me dear Mrs. Scully, " said the major, clearing his throat and waving his stubby hand deprecatingly. "I have already had me reward in having the pleasure and honour of making your acquaintance and of coming nearer to those charums which I had alriddy admired from a distance. "

"Oh, auntie, listen to that! " cried Clara, and both ladies giggled.

"Not forgetting yours, Miss-Miss—"

"Miss Timms, " said Mrs. Scully. "My brother's daughter. "

"Not forgetting your charums, Miss Timms, " continued the major, with a bow and a flourish. "To a lonely man like meself, the very sight of a lady is like dew to a plant. I feel stringthened, madam, vitalized, invigorated. " The major puffed out his chest and looked apoplectically tender over his high white collar.

"The chief object of me visit, " the old soldier said after a pause, "was to learn whether I could be of any assistance to you in any way. Afther your sad bereavement, of which I have heard, it may be that even a comparative stranger may be of service in business matters. "

"I'm sure it's very kind of you, major, " the widow answered. "Since poor Jack died everything has been in disorder. If it wouldn't trouble you, I should very much like your advice on some future occasion. I'll ask your opinion when I have cleared up things a little myself. As to these lawyers, they think of their own interests, not of yours. "

"Quite so, " said the major sympathetically.

"There's the fifteen hundred of poor Jack's insurance. That's not laid out yet. "

"Fifteen hundred! " said the major. "That's seventy-five pounds a year at five per cint. "

"I can get better interest than that, " said the widow gaily. "I've got two thousand laid out at seven per cent. —haven't I, Clara? "

"Safe, too, " said the girl.

"The deuce you have! " thought the major.

"So, when we are making arrangements, I'll ask your assistance and advice, Major Tanglebobs. I know that we poor women are very bad at business. "

"I shall look forward to the day, " said the major gallantly, rising and taking up his hat. He was very well satisfied with his little ruse and his success in breaking the ice.

"Be George! " he remarked to Von Baumser that evening, "she's got money as well as her looks. It's a lucky man that gits her. "

"I vill bet dat you ask her for to marry you, " Von Baumser said with a smile.

"I'll bet that she refuses me if I do, " answered the major despondently, in spite of which he retired that night feeling considerably more elated than on the preceding evening.

CHAPTER XXVIII.

BACK IN BOHEMIA.

Fortune had been smiling upon the Bohemians of late. Ever since the major's successful visit to Fenchurch Street he had been able to live in a state of luxury to which he had long been unaccustomed. His uncle, the earl, too, had condescended to think of his humble relative, and had made a small provision for him, which, with his other resources, removed all anxiety as to the future. Von Baumser had his fair share in this sudden accession of prosperity. The German had resumed his situation as commercial clerk and foreign correspondent to Eckermann & Co., so that his circumstances had also improved. The pair had even had some conversation as to the expediency of migrating into larger and more expensive lodgings, but the major's increasing intimacy with his fair neighbour opposite stood in the way of a change. In any case, they were loth to leave their fourth floor, and to have the trouble of moving their effects.

These same effects were the pride of Major Clutterbuck's heart. Small as their sanctum was, it was a very museum of curious objects brought from every part of the world, most of them of little intrinsic value, but all possessing a charm of association to their owner. They were his trophies of travel, battle, and the chase. From the bison rug and tiger skin upon the floor to the great Sumatran bat which hung head downwards, as in the days of its earthly existence, from the ceiling, there was not an object but had its own special history. In one corner was an Afghan matchlock, and a bundle of spears from the southern seas; in another a carved Indian paddle, a Kaffir assegai, and an American blowpipe, with its little sheaf of poisoned arrows. Here was a hookah, richly mounted, and with all due accessories, just as it was presented to the major twenty years before by a Mahommedan chieftain, and there was a high Mexican saddle on which he had ridden through the land of the Aztecs. There was not a square foot of the walls which was not adorned by knives, javelins, Malay kreeses, Chinese opium pipes, and such other trifles as old travellers gather round them. By the side of the fire rested the campaigner's straight regulation sword in its dim sheath—all the dimmer because the companions occasionally used it as a poker when that instrument happened to be missing.

"It's not the value of thim, " the major remarked, glancing round the apartment, "but, bedad, there's not one of the lot that has not got a story tacked on to it. Look at that bear's head now, that's grinning at ye from over the door. That's a Thibet bear, not much bigger than a Newfoundland dog, but as fierce as a grizzly. That's the very one that clawed Charley Travers, of the 49th. Ged, he'd have been done for if I hadn't got me Westley Richards to bear on him. 'Duck man I duck! ' I cried, for they were so mixed that I couldn't tell one from the other. He put his head down, and I caught the brute right between the eyes. Ye can see the track of the bullet on the bone. "

The major paused, and the pair smoked meditatively, for Baumser had returned from the City, and the twilight was falling and everything conduced to tobacco and reverie.

"See that necklace of cowrie shells hanging beside it, " continued the veteran, waving his cigarette in that direction; "that came from the neck of a Hottentot woman—a black Vanus, be Jove! We were trekking up country before the second Kaffir war. Made an appintment—could not go—orderly duty—so sent a trusty man to tell her. He was found next day with twenty assegais in his body. She was a decoy duck, bedad, and the whole thing a plant. "

"Mein Gott! " Von Baumser ejaculated. "What a life you have led! I have lived with you now many months and heard you tell many tales, but ever there are fresh ones. "

"Yes, a strange life, " answered the major, stretching out his gaitered legs and gazing up at the ceiling. I niver thought to be stranded in me ould age. If I hadn't commuted I'd have had a fair pinsion, but I drew me money in a lump sum, and went to Monte Carlo to break the bank. Instead o' that the bank broke me, and yet I believe me system was correct enough, and I must have won if I had had more capital. "

"There is many says dat, " grunted Von Baumser doubtfully.

"I believe it for all that, " the major continued. "Why, man, I was always the luckiest chap at cards. I depinded on me skill principally, but still I had luck as well. I remimber once being becalmed for a fortnight in the Bay of Biscay in a small transport. Skipper and I tried to kill time by playing nap, and we had the stakes low enough at first, but they soon grew higher, for he kept trying to cover his losses. Before the ind of the two weeks I cleared out of him nearly all he had in the world. 'Look here, Clutterbuck, ' he said at last, looking mighty white about the gills, 'this ship that we are in is more than half mine. I am chief owner. I'll stake me share of the ship on the next game against all that I have lost. ' 'Done! ' said I, and shuffled, cut, and dealt. He went four on three highest trumps, and an ace, and I held four small trumps. 'It's a bad job for my creditors, ' he said, as he threw his hand down. Ged! I started on that vyage a poor captain, and I came into port very fairly well off, and sailing in me own ship, too! What d'ye think of that? "

"Wunderbar! " ejaculated the German. "And the captain? "

"Brandy, and delirium tremens, " the major said, between the puffs of his cigarette. "Jumped overboard off Finisterre, on the homeward vyage. Shocking thing, gamblin'—when you lose. "

"Ach Gott! And those two knives upon the wall, the straight one and the one with the crook; is there a history about them? "

"An incident, " the major answered languidly. "Curious, but true. Saw it meself. In the Afghan war I was convoying supplies through the passes, when we were set upon by Afreedees, hillmen, and robbers. I had fifty men of the 27th Native Infantry under me, with a sergeant. Among the Afreedees was a thumping big chief, who stood among the rocks with that very knife in his hand, the long one, shouting insults at our fellows. Our sergeant was a smart little nigger, and this cheek set his blood up. Be jabers! he chucked his gun down, pulled out that curved dagger—a Ghoorkha knife it is—and made for the big hillman. Both sides stopped firing to see the two chaps fight. As our fellow came scrambling up over the rocks, the chief ran at him and thrust with all his stringth. Be jabers! I thought I saw the pint of the blade come out through the sergeant's back. He managed to twist round though, so as to dodge it. At the same time he hit up from below, and the hillman sprang into the air, looking for all the world like one o' those open sheep you see outside a butcher's shop. He was ripped up from stomach to throat. The sight knocked all the fight out of the other spalpeens, and they took to their heels as hard as they could run. I took the dead man's knife away, and the sergeant sold me his for a few rupees, so there they are. Not much to make a story of, but it was intheresting to see. I'd have bet five to three on the chief. "

"Bad discipline, very bad, " Baumser remarked. "To break the ranks and run mit knives would make my old Unter-offizier Kritzer very mad indeed. " The German had served his time in the Prussian Army, and was still mindful of his training.

"Your stiff-backed Pickelhaubes would have had a poor chance in the passes, " answered the major. "It was ivery man for himself there. You might lie, or stand, or do what you liked as long as you didn't run. Discipline goes to pieces in a war of that sort. "

"Dat is what you call gorilla warfare, " said Von Baumser, with a proud consciousness of having mastered an English idiom. "For all dat, discipline is a very fine thing—very good indeed. I vell remember in the great krieg—the war with Austria—we had made a mine and were about to fire it. A sentry had been placed just over this, and after the match was lit it was forgotten to withdraw the man. He knew well that the powder beneath him would presently him into the air lift, but since he had not been dismissed in right form he remained until the ausbruch had exploded. He was never seen no more, and, indeed, dat he had ever been dere might well have been forgotten, had it not been dat his nadelgewehr was dere found. Dat was a proper soldier, I think, to be placed in command had he lived. "

"To be placed in a lunatic asylum if he lived, " said the Irishman testily. "Hullo, what's this? "

The "this" was the appearance of the boarding-house slavey with a very neat pink envelope upon a tray, addressed, in the most elegant of female hands, to "Major Tobias Clutterbuck, late of Her Majesty's Hundred and Nineteenth. "

"Ah! " cried Von Baumser, laughing in his red beard, "it is from a woman. You are what the English call a sly hog, a very sly hog—or, I should say, dog, though it is much the same. "

"It's for you as well as for me. See here. 'Mrs. Lavinia Scully presints her compliments to Major Tobias Clutterbuck and to his friend, Mr. Sigismund von Baumser, and trusts that they may be able to favour her with their company on Tuesday evening at eight, to meet a few frinds. ' It's a dance, " said the major. "That accounts for the harp and the tables and binches and wine cases I saw going in this morning. "

"Will you go? "

"Yes, of course I will, and so shall you. We'd better answer it. "

So in due course an acceptance was sent across to Mrs. Scully's hospitable invitation.

Never was there such a brushing and scrubbing in the bedroom of a couple of quiet bachelors as occurred some two evenings afterwards in the top story of Mrs. Robins' establishment. The major's suit had been pursued unremittingly since his first daring advance upon the widow, but under many difficulties and discouragements. In the occasional chance interviews which he had with his attractive neighbour he became more and more enamoured, but he had no opportunity of ascertaining whether the feeling was mutual. This invitation appeared to promise him the very chance which he desired, and many were the stern resolutions which he formed as he stood in front of his toilet-table and arranged his tie and his shirt front to his satisfaction. Von Baumser, who was arrayed in a dress coat of antiquated shape, and very shiny about the joints, sat on the side of the bed, eyeing his companion's irreproachable get-up with envy and admiration.

"It fits you beautiful, " he said, alluding to the coat.

"It came from Poole's, " answered the major carelessly.

"As for me, " said Von Baumser, "I have never used mine in England at all. Truly, as you know, I hate all dances and dinners. I come with you, however, very willingly, for I would not for nothing in the world give offence to the liebchen of my comrade. Since I go, I shall go as a gentleman should. " He looked down as he spoke with much satisfaction at his withered suit of black.

"But, me good fellow, " cried the major, who had now completed his toilet, "you've got your tie under your lift ear. It looks very quaint and ornamintal there, but still it's not quite the place for it. You look as if you were ticketed for sale. "

"They von't see it unless I puts it out sideways from under my beard, " the German said apologetically. "However, if you think it should be hidden, it shall be so. How are my stud-buttons? You have them of gold, I see, but mine are of mother-of-oysters. "

"Mother-of-pearl, " said the major, laughing. "They will do very well. There's the divil of a lot of cabs at their door, " he continued, peering round the corner of the blind. "The rooms are all lighted up, and I can hear them tuning the instruments. Maybe we'd better go across. "

"Vorvarts, then! " said Von Baumser resolutely; and the two set off, the major with a fixed determination that he should know his fate before the evening was over.

CHAPTER XXIX.

THE GREAT DANCE AT MORRISON'S.

Never in the whole history of Morrison's boarding establishment had such festive preparations been known. The landlady herself had entered heart and soul into the business, and as all the boarders had received invitations for themselves and their friends, they co-operated in every possible manner to make the evening a success. The large drawing-room had been cleared and the floor waxed. This process left it in a very glassy and orthodox condition, as the cook discovered when, on bustling in, the back of her cranium came in violent contact with the boards, while her body described a half-circle with a velocity which completely eclipsed any subsequent feats of agility shown by the dancers in the evening. The saloon had been very tastefully laid out as a supper-room, and numerous other little chambers were thrown open and brightened up to serve as lounging places for those who were fatigued. In the parlour there were two card-tables, and every other convenience for any who preferred sedentary amusements. Altogether both Mrs. Morrison and the boarders, in solemn conclave assembled, agreed that the thing looked very promising, and that it would be a credit to the establishment.

The guests were as varied as the wines, though hardly as select. Mrs. Scully's exuberant hospitality included, as already intimated, not only her own friends, but those of her fellow-boarders, so that from an early hour the rooms began to fill, and by nine o'clock there was hardly space for the dancers. Hansoms and growlers rattled up in a continuous stream and discharged their burdens. There was a carpet down from the kerb to the head of the lodging-house steps, "like r'yalty, " as the cook expressed it, and the greengrocer's man in the hall looked so pompous and inflated in his gorgeous attire that his own cabbages would hardly have recognized him. His main defect as a footman was that he was somewhat hard of hearing, and had a marvellous faculty of misinterpreting whatever was said to him, which occasionally led to remarkable results. Thus, when he announced the sporting Captain Livingstone Tuck under the title of Captain Lives-on-his-luck, it was felt that he was rather too near the truth to be pleasant. Indeed, the company had hardly recovered from the confusion produced by this small incident when the two Bohemians made their appearance.

Mrs. Scully, who was tastefully arrayed in black satin and lace, stood near the door of the drawing-room, and looked very charming and captivating as she fulfilled her duties as hostess. So thought the major as he approached her and shook her hand, with some well turned compliment upon his lips.

"Let me inthroduce me friend, Herr von Baumser, " he added.

Mrs. Scully smiled upon the German in a way that won his Teutonic heart. "You will find programmes over there, " she explained. "I think the first is a round dance. No, thank you, major; I shall stand out, or there will be no one to receive the people. " She hurried away to greet a party of new arrivals, while the major and Baumser wandered off in search of partners.

There was no want of spirit or of variety in the dancing at Morrison's. From Mr. Snodder, the exciseman, who danced the original old-fashioned trois-temps, to young Bucklebury, of the Bank, who stationed himself immediately underneath the central chandelier, and spun rapidly round with his partner upon his own axis, like a couple of beetles impaled upon a single pin, every possible variation of the art of waltzing was to be observed. There was Mr. Smith, of the Medical College, rotating round with Miss Clara Timms, their faces wearing that pained and anxious expression which the British countenance naturally assumes when dancing, giving the impression that the legs have suddenly burst forth in a festive mood, and have dragged the rest of the body into it very much against its will. There was the major too, who had succeeded in obtaining Mrs. Scully as a partner, and was dancing as old soldiers can dance, threading his way through the crowded room with the ease begotten by the experience of a lifetime. Meanwhile Von Baumser, at the other end, was floundering about with a broad smile upon his face and an elderly lady tucked under his right arm, while he held her disengaged hand straight out at right angles, as if she had been a banjo. In short, the fun was fast and furious, and waltz followed polka and mazurka followed waltz with a rapidity which weeded out the weaker vessels among the dancers and tested the stamina of the musicians.

Then there was the card-room, whither the Widow Scully and the major and many others of the elders repaired when they found the pace too fast for them. Very snug and comfortable it was, with its square tables, each with a fringe of chairs, and the clean shining cards spread out over their green baize surfaces. The major and his hostess played against Captain Livingstone Tuck and an old gentleman who came from Lambeth, with the result that the gallant captain and his partner rose up poorer and sadder men, which was rather a blow to the former, who reckoned upon clearing a little on such occasions, and had not expected to find himself opposed by such a past master of the art as the major. Then the veteran and another played the hostess and another lady, and the cunning old dog managed to lose in such a natural manner, and to pay up with such a good grace, and with so many pretty speeches and compliments, that the widow's partner was visibly impressed, a fact which, curiously enough, seemed to be anything but agreeable to the widow. After that they all filed off to supper, where they found the dancers already in possession, and there was much crushing and crowding, which tended to do away with ceremony and to promote the harmony of the evening.

If the major had contrived to win favour from Mrs. Lavinia Scully in the early part of the evening, he managed now to increase any advantage he had gained. In the first place he inquired in a very loud voice of Captain Tuck, at the other end of the table, whether that gentleman had ever met the deceased Major-General Scully, and being answered in the negative, he descanted fluently upon the merits of that imaginary warrior. After this unscrupulous manoeuvre the major proceeded to do justice to the wine and to indulge in sporting reminiscences, and military reminiscences, and travelling reminiscences, and social reminiscences, all of which he treated in a manner which called forth the admiration of his audience. Then, when supper had at last been finished, and the last cork drawn and the last glass filled, the dancers went back to their dance and the card-players to their cards, and the major addressed himself more assiduously than ever to the pursuit of the widow.

"I am afraid that you find the rooms very hot, major, " she remarked.

"They are rather hot, " he answered candidly.

"There is a room here, " she said, "where you might be cooler. You might have a cigarette, too. I meant these rooms as smoking-rooms. "

"Then you must come, too. "

"No, no, major. You must remember that I am the hostess. "

"But there is no one to entertain. They are all entertaining each other. You are too unselfish. "

"But really, major—"

"Sure you are tired out and need a little rest. "

He held the door open so persuasively that she yielded. It was a snug little room, somewhat retired from the bustle, with two or three chintz-covered chairs scattered round it, and a sofa of the same material at one side. The widow sat down at one end of this sofa, and the major perched himself at the other, looking even redder than usual, and puffing out his chest and frowning, as was his custom upon critical occasions.

"Do light a cigarette? " said Mrs. Scully.

"But the smell? "

"I like it. "

The major extracted one from his flat silver case. His companion rolled a spill and lit it at the gas.

"To one who is as lonely as I am, " she remarked, "it Is a pleasure to feel that one has friends near one, and to serve them even in trifles. "

"Lonely! " said the major, shuffling along the sofa, "I might talk with authority on that point. If I were to turn me toes up to-morrow there's not a human being would care a thraneen about the mather, unless it were old Von Baumser. "

"Oh, don't talk so, " cried Mrs. Scully, with emotion.

"It is a fact. I've kicked against me fate at times, though. I've had fancies of late of something happier and cheerier. They have come on me as I sat over yonder at the window, and, do what I will, I have not been able to git them from me heart. Yit I know how rash I have been to treasure them, for if they fail me I shall feel me loneliness as I niver did before. "

The major paused and cleared his throat huskily, while the widow remained silent, with her head bent and her eyes intent upon the pattern of the carpet.

"These hopes are, " said the major, in a low voice, leaning forward and taking his companion's little ring-covered hand in his thick, pudgy fingers, "that you will have pity upon me; that you will—"

"Ach, my very goot vriend! " cried Von Baumser heartily, suddenly protruding his hairy head into the room and smiling benignantly.

"Go to the divil! " roared the major, springing furiously to his feet, while the German's head disappeared like a Jack-in-the-box. "Forgive the warmth of me language, " the veteran continued, apologetically, "but me feelings overcame me. Will you be mine, Lavinia? I am a plain ould soldier, and have little to offer you save a faithful heart, and that is yours, and always will be. Will you make the remainder of me life happy by becoming me wife? " He endeavoured to pass his arm round her waist, but she sprang up from the sofa and stood upon the rug, facing him with an amused and somewhat triumphant smile upon her buxom features.

"Look here, major, " she said, "I am a plain-spoken woman, as my poor Tom that's dead was a plain-spoken man. Out with it straight, now—have you come after me, or have you come after my money? "

The major was so astonished at this point-blank question, that for a moment he sat speechless upon the sofa. Being a man of ready resource, however, and one who was accustomed to sudden emergencies, he soon recovered himself.

"Yoursilf, of course" cried he. "If you hadn't a stiver I would do the same. "

"Take care! take care! " said the lady, with a warning finger uplifted. "You heard of the breaking of the Agra Bank? "

"What of that? "

"Every penny that I had in the world was in it. "

This was facer number two for the campaigner. He recovered himself more quickly from this one, however, and inflated his chest with even more than his usual pomposity.

"Lavinia, " said he, "you have been straight with me, and, bedad, I'll be so with you? When I first thought of you I was down in the world, and, much as I admired you, I own that your money was an inducement as well as yoursilf. I was so placed that it was impossible for me to think of any woman who had not enough to keep up her own end of the game. Since that time I've done bether. How I got it is neither here nor there, but I have a little nist-egg in the bank and see me way to increasing it. You tell me your money's gone, and I tell you I've enough for two; so say the word, acushla, and it's done. "

"What! without the money? "

"Damn the money? " exclaimed Major Tobias Clutterbuck, and put his arm for the second time around his companion. This time it remained there. What happened after that is neither my business nor the reader's. Couples who have left their youth behind them have their own little romance quite as much as their juniors, and it is occasionally the more heartfelt of the two.

"What a naughty boy to swear! " exclaimed the widow at last. "Now I must give you a lecture since I have the chance. "

"Bless her mischievous eyes! " cried the major, with delight in every feature of his face. "You shall give me as many lectures as you plase. "

"You must be good, then, Toby, if you are to be my husband. You must not play billiards for money any more. "

"No billiards! Why, pool is worth three or four pound a wake to me. "

"It doesn't matter. No billiards and no cards, and no racing and no betting. Toby must be very good and behave as a distinguished soldier should do. "

"What are you afther at all? " the major cried. "Sure if I am to give up me pool and whist, how is a distinguished soldier, and, above all, a distinguished soldier's wife, going to live? "

"We'll manage, dear, " she said, looking roguishly up into his face. "I told you that my money was all in the Agra Bank that broke. "

"You did, worse luck! "

"But I didn't tell you that I had drawn it all out before it broke, Toby dear. It was too bad to put you to such a trial, wasn't it? but really I couldn't resist the temptation. Toby shall have money enough without betting, and he shall settle down and tell his stories, and do what he likes without anything to bother him. "

"Bless her heart! " cried the major fervently; and the battered old Bohemian, as he stooped over and kissed her, felt a tear spring to his eyes as he knew that he had come into harbour after life's stormy tossings.

"No billiards or cards for three months, then, " said the little woman firmly, with her hands round his arm. "None at all mind! I am going into Hampshire on a visit to my cousins in the country, and you shall not see me for that time, though you may write. If you can give me your word of honour when I come back that you've given up your naughty ways, why then—"

"What then? "

"Wait till then and you'll see, " she said, with a merry laugh. "No, really, I won't stay another moment. Whatever will the guests say? I must, Toby; I really must—" Away she tripped, while the major remained standing where she had left him, feeling a better man than he had done since he was a young ensign and kissed his mother for the last time at the Portsmouth jetty before the great transport carried him off to India.

Everything in the world must have an end, and Mrs. Scully's dance was no exception to the rule. The day was breaking, however, before the last guests had muffled themselves up and the last hansom dashed away from the door. The major lingered behind to bid farewell, and then rejoined his German friend, who had been compelled to wait at the door for the latchkey.

"Look here, major, " the latter said, when they came into their room, "is it well to tell a Brussian gentleman to go to the devil? You have much offended me. Truly I was surprised that you should have so spoken! "

"Me dear friend, " the old soldier answered, shaking his hand, "I would not hurt your feelings for the world. Bedad, if I come into the room while you are proposing to a lady, you are welcome to use the strongest German verb to me that you can lay your tongue to. "

"You have probosed, then? " cried the good-natured German, forgetting all about his grievance in an instant.

"Yes. "

"And been took—received by her? "

"Yes. "

"Dat Is gloriful! " Von Baumser cried, clapping his hands. "Three hochs for Frau Scully, and another one for Frau Clutterbuck. We must drink a drink on it; we truly must. "

"So we shall, me boy, but it's time we turned in now. She's a good woman, and she plays a good hand at whist. Ged! she cleared the trumps and made her long suit to-night as well as ever I saw it done in me life! " With which characteristic piece of eulogy the major bade his comrade good night and retired to his room.

CHAPTER XXX.

AT THE "COCK AND COWSLIP. "

Tom Dimsdale's duties were far from light. Not only was he expected to supervise the clerks' accounts and to treat with the wholesale dealers, but he was also supposed to spend a great part of his time in the docks, overlooking the loading of the outgoing ships and checking the cargo of the incoming ones. This latter portion of his work was welcome as taking him some hours a day from the close counting-house, and allowing him to get a sniff of the sea air— if, indeed, a sniff is to be had on the inland side of Woolwich. There was a pleasing life and bustle, too, in the broad, brown river, with its never-ending panorama of vessels of every size and shape which ebb and flow in the great artery of national life.

So interesting was this liquid highway to Tom's practical mind, that he would often stand at the head of the wharf when his work was done and smoke a meditative pipe. It was a quiet spot, which had once been busy enough, but was now superseded by new quays and more convenient landing-places. All over it were scattered great rusty anchors, colossal iron chains, deserted melancholy boilers, and other debris which are found in such places, and which might seem to the fanciful to be the shells and skeletons of strange monsters washed up there by the tide. To whom do these things belong? Who has an interest in them? Of what use are they? It appeared to Tom sometimes as if the original owners and their heirs must have all died away, and left these grim relics behind them to any one who might have the charity to remove them.

From this coign of vantage a long reach of the river was visible, and Tom sitting there would watch the fleets of passing vessels, and let his imagination wander away to the broad oceans which they had traversed, and the fair lands under bluer skies and warmer suns from which they had sailed. Here is a tiny steam-tug panting and toiling in front of a majestic three-master with her great black hulk towering out of the water and her masts shooting up until the topmast rigging looks like the delicate web of some Titanic spider. She is from Canton, with tea, and coffee, and spices, and all good things from the land of small feet and almond eyes. Here, too, is a Messagerie boat, the French ensign drooping daintily over her stern, and her steam whistle screeching a warning to some obstinate lighters, crawling with their burden of coal to a grimy collier whose steam-winch is whizzing away like a corncrake of the deep. That floating palace is an Orient boat from Australia. See how, as the darkness falls, a long row of yellow eyes glimmer out from her sides as the light streams through her countless portholes. And there is the Rotterdam packet-boat coming slowly up, very glad to get back into safe waters again, for she has had a wildish time in the North Sea. A coasting brig has evidently had a wilder time still, for her main-topmast is cracked across, and her rigging is full of the little human mites who crawl about, and reef, and splice, and mend.

An old acquaintance of ours was out in that same gale, and is even now making his way into the shelter of the Albert docks. This was none other than the redoubtable Captain Hamilton Miggs, whose ship will persistently keep afloat, to the astonishment of the gallant captain himself, and of every one else who knows anything of her sea-going qualities. Again and again she had been on the point of foundering; and again and again some change in the weather or the steady pumping of the crew had prevented her from fulfilling her destiny. So surprised was the skipper at these repeated interpositions of Providence that he had quite made up his superstitious mind that the ship never would go down, and now devoted himself with a whole heart to his old occupation of drinking himself into delirium tremens and physicking himself out of it again.

The *Black Eagle* had a fair cargo aboard, and Miggs was proportionately jubilant. The drunken old sea-dog had taken a fancy to Tom's frank face and honest eyes, and greeted him with effusion when he came aboard next morning.

"Knock me asunder, but you look rosy, man! " he cried. "It's easy to see that you have not been lying off Fernando Po, or getting the land mist into your lungs in the Gaboon. "

"You look well yourself, captain, " said Tom.

"Tolerable, tolerable. Just a touch of the jumps at times. "

"We can begin getting our cargo out, I suppose? I have a list here to check it. Will you have the hatches off at once? "

"No work for me, " said Captain Hamilton Miggs with decision. "Here, Sandy—Sandy McPherson, start the cargo, will ye, and stir your great Scotch bones. I've done enough in bringing this sieve of a ship all the way from Africa, without working when I am in dock. "

McPherson was the first mate, a tall, yellow-bearded Aberdonian. "I'll see t'it, " he said shortly. "You can gang ashore or where you wull. "

"The *Cock and Cowslip*, " said the captain, "I say, you—Master Dimsdale—when you're done come up an' have a glass o' wine with me. I'm only a plain sailor man, but I'm damned if my heart ain't in the right place. You too, McPherson—you'll come up and show Mr. Dimsdale the way. *Cock and Cowslip*, corner o' Sextant Court. " The two having accepted his invitation, the captain shuffled off across the gangway and on to terra firma.

All day Tom stood at the hatchway of the *Black Eagle*, checking the cargo as it was hoisted out of her, while McPherson and his motley assistants, dock labourers, seamen, and black Kroomen from the coast, worked and toiled in the depths below. The engine rattled and snorted, and the great chain clanked as it was lowered into the hold.

"Make fast there! " cries the mate.

"Aye, aye, sir! "

"All right? "

"All right, sir. "

"Hoist away! "

And clank, clank went the chain again, and whir-r-r the engine, and up would come a pair of oil casks, as though the crane were some giant forceps which was plucking out the great wooden teeth of the vessel. It seemed to Tom, as he stood looking down, note-book in hand, that some of the actual malarious air of the coast had been carried home in the hold, so foul and close were the smells evolved from it. Great cockchafers crawled about over the packages, and occasionally a rat would scamper over the barrels, such a rat as is only to be found in ships which hail from the tropics. On one occasion too, as a tusk of ivory was being hoisted out, there was a sudden cry of alarm among the workers, and a long, yellow snake crawled out of the cavity of the trunk and writhed away into the darkness. It is no uncommon thing to find the deadly creatures hibernating in the hollow of the tusks until the cold English air arouses them from their torpor, to the cost occasionally of some unhappy stevedore or labourer.

All day Tom stood amid grease and steam, bustle and blasphemy, checking off the cargo, and looking to its conveyance to the warehouses. At one o'clock there was a break of an hour for dinner, and then the work went on until six, when all hands struck and went off to their homes or to the public-house according to inclination. Tom and the mate, both fairly tired by their day's work, prepared to accept the captain's invitation, and to meet him up in his quarters. The mate dived down into his cabin, and soon reappeared with his face shining and his long hair combed into some sort of order.

"I've been performing my ablutions, " he said, rolling out the last word with great emphasis and pomposity, for, like many Scotchmen, he had the greatest possible reverence for a sonorous polysyllable. Indeed, in McPherson, this national foible was pushed to excess, for, however inappropriate the word, he never hesitated to drag it into his conversation if he thought it would aid in the general effect.

"The captain, " he continued, "has been far from salubrious this voyage. He's aye complainin' o' his bodily infirmities. "

"Hypochondriacal, perhaps, " Tom remarked.

The Scotchman looked at his companion with a great accession of respect. "My certie! " he cried. "That's the best I've heard since a word that Jimmy M'Gee, of the *Corisco*, said the voyage afore last. Would you kindly arteeculate it again. "

"Hypochondriacal, " said Tom laughing heartily.

"Hypo-chon-driacal, " the mate repeated slowly. "I shouldn't think Jimmy M'Gee kens that, or he'd ha' communicated it to me. I shall certainly utilize it, and am obleeged to you for namin' it. "

"Don't mention it, " said Tom. "I'll let you have as many long words as you like, if you are a collector of them. But what is the matter with the captain? "

"It's aye the drink, " the mate said gravely. "I can tak' my modicum mysel' and enjoy it, but that's no the same as for a man to lock himself up in his cabin, and drink rum steady on from four bells in the mornin' watch to eight bells in the evenin'. And then the cussin', and prayin', and swearin' as he sets up is just awfu'. It's what might weel be described as pandemoniacal. "

"Is he often like that, then? " Tom asked.

"Often! Why, he's never anything else, sir. And yet he's a good seaman too, and however fu' he may be, he keeps some form o' reckoning, and never vera far oot either. He's an ambeequosity to me, sir, for if I took a tithe o' the amount I'd be clean daft. "

"He must be dangerous when he is like that? " Tom remarked.

"He is that. He emptied a sax-shooter down the deck last bout he had, and nigh perforated the carpenter. Another time he scoots after the cook—chased him with a handspike in his hand right up the rigging to the cross-trees. If the cook hadn't slid down the backstay of the mast, he'd ha' been obeetuarised. "

Tom could not refrain from laughing at the last expression. "That's a new word, " he said.

"Ha! " his companion cried with great satisfaction, "it is, is it? Then we are quits now on the hypochondriacal. " He was so pleased that he chuckled to himself for some minutes in the depths of his tawny beard. "Yes, " he continued at last, "he is dangerous to us at times, and he is dangerous to you. This is atween oorsels, as man to man, and is said withoot prejudice, but he do go on when he is in they fits aboot the firm, and aboot insurances, and rotten ships, and ither such things, which is all vera well when sequestrated amang gentlemen like oorsels, but sounds awfu' bad when it fa's on the ignorant tympanums of common seamen. "

"It's scandalous, " Tom said gravely, "that he should spread such reports about his employer. Our ships are old, and some of them, in my opinion, hardly safe, but that's a very different thing from implying, as you hint, that Mr. Girdlestone wishes them to go down. "

"We'll no argue aboot that, " said the canny Scot. "Muster Girdlestone kens on which side his bread is buttered. He may wish 'em to sink or he may wish 'em to swim. That's no for us to judge. You'll hear him speak o't to-night as like as not, for he's aye on it when he's half over. Here we are, sir. The corner edifice wi' the red blinds in the window. "

During this conversation the two had been threading their way through the intricate and dirty lanes which lead up from the water side to the outskirts of Stepney. It was quite dark by the time that they reached a long thoroughfare, lined by numerous shops, with great gas flares outside them. Many of these belonged to dealers in marine stores, and the numerous suits of oil-skin, hung up for exhibition, swung to and fro in the uncertain light, like rows of attenuated pirates. At every corner was a great public-house with glittering windows, and a crowd of slatternly women and jersey-clad men elbowing each other at the door. At the largest and most imposing of these gin-palaces the mate and Dimsdale now pulled up.

"Come in this way, " said McPherson, who had evidently paid many a visit there before. Pushing open a swinging door, he made his way into the crowded bar, where the reek of bad spirits and the smell of squalid humanity seemed to Tom to be even more horrible than the effluvium of the grease-laden hold.

"Captain Miggs in? " asked McPherson of a rubicund, white-aproned personage behind the bar.

"Yes, sir. He's in his room, sir, and expectin' you. There's a gent with him, sir, but he told me to send you up. This way, sir. "

They were pushing their way through the crowd to reach the door which led behind the bar, when Tom's attention was arrested by the conversation of a very seedy-looking individual who was leaning with his elbows upon the zinc-covered counter.

"You take my tip, " he said to an elderly man beside him. "You stick to the beer. The sperits in here is clean poison, and it's a sin and a shame as they should be let sell such stuff to Christian men. See here—see my sleeve! " He showed the threadbare cuff of his coat, which was corroded away in one part, as by a powerful acid. "I give ye my word I done that by wiping my lips wi' it two or three times

229

after drinkin' at this bar. That was afore I found out that the whisky was solid vitriol. If thread and cotton can't stand it, how's the linin' of a poor cove's stomach, I'd like to know? "

"I wonder, " thought Tom to himself, "if one of these poor devils goes home and murders his wife, who ought to be hung for it? Is it he, or that smug-faced villain behind the bar, who, for the sake of the gain of a few greasy coppers, gives him the poison that maddens him? " He was still pondering over this knotty point when they were ushered into the captain's room.

That worthy was leaning back in a rocking-chair with his feet perched upon the mantelpiece and a large glass of rum arid water within reach of his great leathery hand. Opposite him, in a similar chair and with a similar glass, was no less an individual than our old acquaintance, Von Baumser. As a mercantile clerk in the London office of a Hamburg firm the German was thrown into contact with the shippers of the African fleet, and had contracted a special alliance with the bibulous Miggs, who was a social soul in his hours of relaxation.

"Come in, my hearties, come in! " he cried huskily. "Take a seat, Mr. Dimsdale. And you, Sandy, can't you bring yourself to your berth without being asked? You should know your moorings by this time. This is my friend, Mr. Von Baumser from Eckermann's office. "

"And dis, I think, is Mr. Dimsdale, " said the German, shaking hands with Tom. "I have heard my very goot vriend, Major Clutterbuck, speak of your name, sir. "

"Ah, the old major, " Tom answered. "Of course, I remember him well. "

"He is not so very old either, " said Von Baumser, in a somewhat surly voice. "He has been took by a very charming and entirely pleasant woman, and they are about to be married before three months, the one to the other. Let me tell you, sir, I, who have lived with him so long, dat I have met no man for whom I have greater respect than for the major, however much they give him pills at a club or other such snobberies. "

"Fill your glasses, " Miggs broke in, pushing over the bottle of rum. "There are weeds in that box—never paid duty, either the one or the other. By the Lord, Sandy, a couple of days ago we hardly hoped ever to be yarning here. "

"It was rather beyond our prognostication, sir, " said the mate, taking a pull at his rum.

"It was that! A nasty sea on, Mr. Dimsdale, sir, and the old ship so full o' water that she could not rise to it. They were making a clean breach over us, and we lost nigh everything we could lose. "

"I suppose you'll have her thoroughly repaired now? " Tom remarked.

Both the skipper and the mate laughed heartily at the observation. "That wouldn't do, Sandy, would it? " said Miggs, shaking his head. "We couldn't afford to have our screw cut down like that. "

"Cut down! You don't mean to say you are paid in proportion to the rottenness of the ships? "

"There ain't no use makin' a secret of it among friends, " said Miggs. "That's just how the land lies with us. A voyage or two back I spoke to Mr. Girdlestone, and I says to him, says I, 'Give the ship an overhauling, ' says I. 'Well and good, ' says he, 'but it will mean so much off your wage, ' says he, 'and the mate's wage as well. ' I put it to him straight and strong, but he stuck at that. So Sandy and me, we put our heads together, and we 'greed It was better to take fifteen pound and the risk, than come down to twelve pound and safety. "

"It is scandalous! " cried Tom Dimsdale hotly. "I could not have believed it. "

"God bless ye! it's done every day, and will be while there is insurance money to be gained, " said Miggs, blowing a blue cloud up to the ceiling. "It's an easy thing to turn a few thousands a year while there are old ships to be bought, and offices which will insure them above their value. There was D'Arcy Campbell, of the *Silvertown*—what a trade that man did! He was smart—tarnation smart! Collisions was his line, and he worked 'em well. There warn't a skipper out of Liverpool as could get run down as nat'ral as he could. "

"Get run down? "

"Aye. He'd go lolloping about in the Channel if there was any fog on, steering for the lights o' any steamers or headin' round for all the fog whistles if it was too thick to see. Sooner or later, as sure as fate, he'd get cut down to the water's edge. Lor', it was a fine game! Half a 'yard o' print about his noble conduc' in the newspapers, and maybe a leader about the British tar and unexpected emergencies. It once went the length o' a subscription. Ha! ha! " Miggs laughed until he choked.

"And what became of this British star? " asked the German.

"He's still about. He's in the passenger trade now. "

"Potztausand! " Von Baumser ejaculated. "I would not go as a passenger with him for something. "

"There's many a way that it's done, sir, " the mate added, filling up his glass again, and passing the bottle to the captain. "There's loadin' a cranky vessel wi' grain in bulk without usin' partition boards. If you get a little water in, as you are bound to do with a ship o' that kind, the grain will swell and swell until it bursts the seams open, and down ye go. Then there's ignition o' coal gas aboard o' steamers. That's a safe game, for nobody can deny it. And there are accidents to propellers. If the shaft o' a propeller breaks in heavy weather it's a bad look-out. I've known ships leave the docks with their propellers half sawn through all round. Lor', there's no end o' the tricks o' the trade. "

"I cannot believe, however, " said Tom stoutly, "that Mr. Girdlestone connives at such things. "

"He's on the waitin' lay, " the seaman answered. "He doesn't send 'em down, but he just hangs on, and keeps his insurances up, and trusts in Providence. He's had some good hauls that way, though not o' late. There was the *Belinda* at Cape Palmas. That was five thousand, clear, if it was a penny. And the *Sockatoo*—that was a bad business! She was never heard of, nor her crew. Went down at sea, and left no trace. "

"The crew too! " Tom cried with horror. "But how about yourselves, if what you say is true? "

"We are paid for the risk, " said both the seamen, shrugging their shoulders.

"But there are Government inspectors? "

"Ha! ha! I dare say you've seen the way some o' them do their work! " said Miggs.

Tom's mind was filled with consternation at what he had heard. If the African merchant were capable of this, what might he not be capable of? Was his word to be depended on under any circumstances? And what sort of firm must this be, which turned so fair a side to the world and in which he had embarked his fortune? All these thoughts flashed through his mind as he listened to the gossip of the garrulous old sea dogs. A greater shock still, however, was in store for him.

Von Baumser had been listening to the conversation with an amused look upon his good-humoured face. "Ah! " said he, suddenly striking in, "I vill tell you something of your own firm which perhaps you do not know. Have you heard dat Mr. Ezra Girdlestone is about to be married? "

"To be married! "

"Oh yes; I have heard It dis morning at Eckermann's office. I think it is the talk of the City. "

"Who's the gal? " Miggs asked, with languid interest.

"I disremember her name, " Von Baumser answered. "It is a girl the major has met—the young lady who has lived in the same house, and is vat they call a warder. "

"Not—not his ward? " cried Tom, springing to his feet and turning as white as a sheet. "Not Miss Harston? You don't tell me that he is going to marry Miss Harston? "

"Dat is the name. Miss Harston it is, sure enough. "

"It is a lie—an infamous lie! " Tom cried hotly.

"So it may be, " Von Baumser answered serenely. "I do but say vat I have heard, and heard more than once on good authority. "

"If it is true there is villainy in it, " cried Tom, with wild eyes, "the blackest villainy that ever was done upon earth. I'll go—I'll see him to-night. By heavens, I shall know the truth! " He rushed furiously downstairs and through the bar. There was a cab near the door. "Drive into London! " he cried; "69, Eccleston Square. I am on fire to be there! " The cabman sprang on the box, and they rattled away as fast as the horse would go.

This sudden exit caused, as may be imagined, considerable surprise in the parlour of the *Cock and Cowslip*.

"He's a vera tumultuous young man, " the mate remarked. "He was off like a clipper in a hurricane. "

"I perceive, " said Von Baumser, "dat he has left his hat behind him. I do now remember dat I have heard his name spoken with dat of dis very young lady by my good vriend, the major. "

"Then he's jealous belike, " said Hamilton Miggs, with a knowing shake of the head. "I've felt that way myself before now. I rounded on Billy Barlow, o' the *Flying Scud*, over that very thing, twelve months ago come Christmas. But I don't think it was the thing for this young chap to cut away and never say 'With your leave, ' or 'By your leave, ' or as much as 'Good night, gentlemen all. ' It ain't what you call straight up an' down. "

"It's transcendental, " said the mate severely; "that is what I call it. "

"Ah, my vriends, " the German put in, "when a man is in love you must make excuses for him. I am very sure dat he did mean no offence. "

In spite of this assurance Captain Hamilton Miggs continued to be very sore upon the point. It was only by dint of many replenishings of his glass and many arguments that his companions could restore him to his pristine good humour. Meanwhile, the truant was speeding through the night with a fixed determination in his heart that he should have before morning such an understanding, one way or the other, as would never again leave room for a doubt.

CHAPTER XXXI.

A CRISIS AT ECCLESTON SQUARE.

His father's encouraging words had given Ezra Girdlestone fresh heart, and he had renewed his importunities with greater energy than ever. Never surely did any man devote every moment of his time more completely to the winning of a woman's heart. From morning until night the one idea was ever before his mind and every little want of Kate's was forestalled with a care and foresight which astonished her. The richest fruit and flowers found their way unexpectedly into her room; her table was littered with the latest books from Mudie's, and the newest pieces lay upon her music-stand. Nothing which attention and thoughtfulness could do was left undone either by the father or the son.

In spite of these attentions, however, and the frequent solicitations of her guardian, Kate stood firmly to her colours. If the Tom of the present were false, she at least would be true to the memory of the Tom of other days, the lad who had first whispered words of love into her ears. Her ideal should remain with her whatever might befall. No other man could ever take the place of that.

That Tom was from some unexplained and unaccountable reason false to her appeared to be beyond all question. Her trusting and innocent heart could not dream of the subtle network which was being wound round her. Her secluded life had left her very ignorant of the ways of the world, and the possibility of an elaborate deceit being practised upon her had never occurred to her. From the day that she heard the extract of the letter read by her guardian she never doubted but that such letters were received at the office by the man who professed to love her. How could she hesitate to believe it when it was confirmed by his avoidance of Eccleston Square and of herself? The cause of it all was a mystery which no amount of speculation could clear up. Sometimes the poor girl would blame herself, as is the way of women in such cases. "I have not seen enough of the world, " she would say to herself. "I have none of the charms of these women whom I read of in the novels. No doubt I seemed dull and insipid in his eyes. And yet—and yet—" There always remained at the end of her cogitations the same vague sense of bewilderment and mystery.

She endeavoured as far as possible to avoid Ezra Girdlestone, and stay in her room for the most part on the days when he was at home. He had, however, on the advice of his father, ceased pressing his suit except in the silent manner aforementioned, so that she gradually took courage, and ended by resuming her old habits. In her heart she pitied the young merchant very sincerely, for he was looking haggard and pale. "Poor fellow, " she thought as she watched him, "he certainly loves me. Ah, Tom, Tom! had you only been as constant, how happy we should be! " She was even prompted sometimes to cheer Ezra up by some kind word or look. This he naturally took to be an encouragement to renew his advances. Perhaps he was not far wrong, for if love be wanting pity is occasionally an excellent substitute.

One morning after breakfast the elder Girdlestone called his son aside into the library. "I've had a notice, " he said, "as to paying up dividends. Our time is short, Ezra. You must bring matters to a head. If you don't it will be too late. "

"You mustn't pick fruit before it is ripe, " the other answered moodily.

"You can try if it is ripe, though. If not, you can try again. I think that your chance is a good one. She is alone in the breakfast-room, and the table has been cleared. You cannot have a better opening. Go, my son, and may Heaven prosper you! "

"Very well. Do you wait in here, and I shall let you know how things go. "

The young man buttoned up his coat, pulled down his cuffs, and walked back into the breakfast-room with a sullen look of resolution upon his dark face.

Kate was sitting in a wicker chair by the window, arranging flowers in a vase. The morning sunlight streaming in upon her gave a colour to her pale face and glittered in her heavy coils of chestnut hair. She wore a light pink morning dress which added to the ethereal effect of her lithe beautiful figure. As Ezra entered she looked round and started at sight of his face. Instinctively she knew on what errand he had come.

"You will be late at Fenchurch Street, " she said, with a constrained smile. "It is nearly eleven now. "

"I am not going to the office to-day, " he answered gravely. "I am come in here, Kate, to know my fate. You know very well, and must have known for some time back, that I love you. If you'll marry me you'll make me a happy man, and I'll make you a happy woman. I'm not very eloquent and that sort of thing, but what I say I mean. What have you to say in answer? " He leaned his broad hands on the back of a chair as he spoke, and drummed nervously with his fingers.

Kate had drooped her head over the flowers, but she looked up at him now with frank, pitying eyes.

"Put this idea out of your head, Ezra, " she said, in a low but firm voice. "Believe me, I shall always be grateful to you for the kindness which you have shown me of late. I will be a sister to you, if you will let me, but I can never be more. "

"And why not? " asked Ezra, still leaning over the chair, with an angry light beginning to sparkle in his dark eyes. "Why can you never be my wife? "

"It is so, Ezra. You must not think of it. I am so sorry to grieve you. "

"You can't love me, then, " cried the young merchant hoarsely. "Other women before now would have given their eyes to have had me. Do you know that? "

"For goodness' sake, then go back to the others, " said Kate, half amused and half angry.

That suspicion of a smile upon her face was the one thing needed to set Ezra's temper in a blaze. "You won't have me, " he cried savagely. "I haven't got the airs and graces of that fellow, I suppose. You haven't got him out of your head, though he is off with another girl. "

"How dare you speak to me so? " Kate cried, springing to her feet in honest anger.

"It's the truth, and you know it, " returned Ezra, with a sneer. "Aren't you too proud to be hanging on to a man who doesn't want you— a man that is a smooth-tongued sneak, with the heart of a rabbit? "

"If he were here you would not dare to say so! " Kate retorted hotly.

"Wouldn't I? " he snarled fiercely.

"No, you wouldn't. I don't believe that he has ever been untrue to me. I believe that you and your father have planned to make me believe it and to keep us apart. "

Heaven knows what it was that suddenly brought this idea most clearly before Kate's mind. Perhaps it was that Ezra's face, distorted with passion, gave her some dim perception of the wickedness of which such a nature might be capable. The dark face turned so much darker at her words that she felt a great throb of joy at her heart, and knew that this strange new thought which had flashed upon her was the truth.

"You can't deny it, " she cried, with shining eyes and clenched hands. "You know that it is true. I shall see him and hear from his own lips what he has to say. He loves me still, and I love him, and have never ceased to love him. "

"Oh, you do, do you? " snarled Ezra, taking a step forward, with a devilish gleam in his eyes. "Your love may do him very little good. We shall see which of us gets the best of it in the long run. We'll—" His passion was so furious that he stopped, fairly unable to articulate another word.

With a threatening motion of his hands he turned upon his heel and rushed from the room. As he passed it chanced that Flo, Kate's little Skye terrier, ran across his path. All the brutality of the man's soul rose up in the instant. He raised his heavy boot, and sent the poor little creature howling and writhing under the sofa, whence it piteously emerged upon three legs, trailing the fourth one behind it.

"The brute! " Kate cried, as she fondled the injured animal and poured indignant tears over it. Her gentle soul was so stirred by the cowardly deed that she felt that she could have flown at her late suitor were he still in the room. "Poor little Flo! That kick was meant for me in reality, my little pet. Never mind, dear, there are bright days coming, and he has not forgotten me, Flo. I know it! I know it! "

The little dog whined sympathetically, and licked its mistress's hand as though it were looking into its canine future, and could also discern better days ahead.

Ezra Girdlestone, fierce and lowering, tramped into the library, and told his father brusquely of the result of his wooing. What occurred in that interview was never known to any third person. The servants, who had some idea that something was afoot, have recorded that at the beginning of the conversation the bass voice of the son and the high raucous tones of the father were heard in loud recrimination and reproach. Then they suddenly sunk into tones so low that there might have been complete silence in the room for all that any one could tell from the passage outside. This whispered conversation may have lasted the greater part of an hour. At the end of it the young merchant departed for the City. It has been remarked that from that time there came a change over both the father and the son—a change so subtle that It could hardly be described, though it left its mark upon them both. It was not that the grey, wolfish face of the old man looked even greyer and fiercer, or that the hard, arrogant expression of Ezra deepened into something even more sinister. It was that a shadow hung over both their brows—a vague indefinable shadow—as of men who carry a thought in their minds on which it is not good to dwell.

During that long hour Kate had remained in the breakfast-room, still nursing her injured companion, and very busy with her own thoughts. She was as convinced now that Tom had been true to her as if she had had the assurance from his own lips. Still there was much that was unaccountable—much which she was unable to fathom. A vague sense of the wickedness around her depressed and weighed her down. What deep scheme could these men have invented to keep him away from her during these long weeks? Was he, too, under some delusion, or the victim of some conspiracy? Whatever had been done was certainly connived at by her guardian. For the first time a true estimate of the character of the elder Girdlestone broke upon her, and she dimly realized that the pious, soft-spoken merchant was more to be dreaded than his brutal son. A shudder ran through her whole frame as, looking up, she saw him standing before her.

His appearance was far from reassuring. His hands were clasped behind his back, his head bent forward, and he surveyed her with a most malignant expression upon his face.

"Well done! " he said, with a bitter smile. "Well done! This is a good morning's work, Miss Harston. You have repaid your father's friend for the care he has bestowed upon you. "

"My only wish is to leave your house, " cried Kate, with an angry flash in her deep blue eyes. "You are a cruel, wicked, hypocritical old man. You have deceived me about Mr. Dimsdale. I read it in your son's face, and now I read it in your own. How could you do it—oh, how could you have the heart? "

John Girdlestone was fairly staggered by this blaze of feminine anger in his demure and obedient ward. "God knows, " he said, "whatever my faults may have been, neglect of you has not been among them. I am not immaculate. Even the just man falleth. If I have endeavoured to wean you from this foolish love affair of yours, it has been entirely because I saw that it was against your own interests. "

"You have told lies in order to turn me away from the only man who ever loved me. You and your odious son have conspired to ruin my happiness and break my heart. What have you told him that keeps him away? I shall see him and learn the truth. " Kate's face was unnaturally calm and rigid as she faced her guardian's angry gaze.

"Silence! " the old man cried hoarsely. "You forget your position in this house. You are presuming too much upon my kindness. As to this girl's fancy of yours, you may put all thought of it out of your head. I am still your guardian, and I should be culpably remiss if I ever allowed you to see this man again. This afternoon you shall come with me to Hampshire. "

"To Hampshire? "

"Yes. I have taken a small country seat there, where we intend to spend some months of the winter. You shall leave it when you have reconciled yourself to forget these romantic ideas of yours—but not till then. "

"Then I shall never leave it, " said Kate, with a sigh.

"That will depend upon yourself. You shall at least be guarded there from the advances of designing persons. When you come of age you may follow your own fancies. Until then my conscience demands, and the law allows, that I should spare no pains to protect you from your own folly. We start from Waterloo at four. " Girdlestone turned for the door, but looked round as he was leaving the room. "May God forgive you, " he said solemnly, raising his lean hands towards the ceiling, "for what you have done this day! "

Poor Kate, left to herself, was much concerned by this fresh misfortune. She knew that her guardian had power to carry out his plan, and that there was no appeal from his decision. What could she do? She had not a friend in the wide world to whom she could turn for advice or assistance. It occurred to her to fly to the Dimsdales at Kensington, and throw herself upon their compassion. It was only the thought of Tom which prevented her. In her heart she had fully exonerated him, yet there was much to be explained before they could be to each other as of old. She might write to Mrs. Dimsdale, but then her guardian had not told her what part of Hampshire they were going to. She finally came to the conclusion that it would be better to wait, and to write when she had reached her destination. In the meantime, she went drearily to her room and began packing, aided by the ruddy-cheeked maid, Rebecca.

At half-past three a cab drove up to the door, and the old merchant stepped out of it. The boxes were thrown upon the top, and the young lady curtly ordered to get in. Girdlestone took his seat beside her, and gave a sign to the cabman to drive on. As they rattled out of the square, Kate looked back at the great gloomy mansion in which she had spent the last three years of her life. Had she known what the future was to bring, it is possible that she would have clung even to that sombre and melancholy old house as to an ark of safety.

Another cab passed through Eccleston Square that evening—a cab which bore a pale-faced and wild-eyed young man, who looked ever and anon impatiently out of the window to see if he were nearing his destination. Long before reaching No. 69 he had opened the door, and was standing upon the step. The instant that the cab pulled up he sprang off, and rang loudly at the great brass bell which flanked the heavy door.

"Is Mr. Girdlestone in? " he asked, as Rebecca appeared at the door.

"No, sir. "

"Miss Harston, is she at home? " he said excitedly.

"No, sir. They have both gone away. "

"Gone away! "

"Yes. Gone into the country, sir. And Mr. Ezra, too, sir. "

"And when are they coming back? " he asked, in bewilderment.

"They are not coming back. "

"Impossible! " Tom cried in despair. "What is their address, then? "

"They have left no address. I am sorry I can't help you. Good night, sir. " Rebecca closed the door, laughing maliciously at the visitor's bewildered looks. She knew the facts of the case well, and having long been jealous of her young mistress, she was not sorry to find things going wrong with her.

Tom Dimsdale stood upon the doorstep looking blankly into the night. He felt dazed and bewildered. What fresh villainy was this? Was it a confirmation of the German's report, or was it a contradiction of it? Cold beads stood upon his forehead as he thought of the possibility of such a thing. "I must find her, " he cried, with clenched hands, and turned away heartsick into the turmoil and bustle of the London streets.

CHAPTER XXXII.

A CONVERSATION IN THE ECCLESTON SQUARE LIBRARY.

Rebecca, the fresh-complexioned waiting-maid, was still standing behind the ponderous hall door, listening, with a smile upon her face, to young Dimsdale's retreating footsteps, when another and a brisker tread caught her ear coming from the opposite direction. The smile died away as she heard it, and her features assumed a peculiar expression, in which it would be hard to say whether fear or pleasure predominated. She passed her hands up over her face and smoothed her hair with a quick nervous gesture, glancing down at the same time at her snowy apron and the bright ribbons which set it off. Whatever her intentions may have been, she had no time to improve upon her toilet before a key turned in the door and Ezra Girdlestone stepped into the hall. As he saw her shadowy figure, for the gas was low, he uttered a hoarse cry of surprise and fear, and staggered backwards against the door-post.

"Don't be afeared, Mister Ezra, " she said in a whisper; "it's only me. "

"The devil take you! " cried Ezra furiously. "What makes you stand about like that? You gave me quite a turn. "

"I didn't mean for to do it. I've only just been answering of the door. Why, surely you've come in before now and found me in the hall without making much account of it. "

"Ah, lass, " answered Ezra, "my nerves have had a shake of late. I've felt queer all day. Look how my hand shakes. "

"Well, I'm blessed! " said the girl, with a titter, turning up the gas. "I never thought to see you afeared of anything. Why, you looks as white as a sheet! "

"There, that's enough! " he answered roughly. "Where are the others? "

"Jane is out. Cook and William and the boy are downstairs. "

"Come into the library here. They will think that you are up in the bedrooms. I want to have a quiet word or two with you. Turn up that reading lamp. Well, are they gone? "

"Yes, they are gone, " she answered, standing by the side of the couch on which he had thrown himself. "Your father came about three with a cab, and took her away. "

"She didn't make a fuss? "

"Make a fuss? No; why should she? There's fuss enough made about her, in all conscience. Oh, Ezra, before she got between us you was kind to me at times. I could stand harsh words from you six days a week, if there was a chance of a kind one on the seventh. But now— now what notice do you take of me? " She began to whimper and to wipe her eyes with a little discoloured pocket-handkerchief.

"Drop it, woman, drop it! " cried her companion testily. "I want information, not snivelling. She seemed reconciled to go? "

"Yes, she went quiet enough, " the girl said, with a furtive sob.

"Just give me a drop of brandy out of that bottle over there—the one with the cork half out. I've not got over my start yet. Did you hear my father say anything as to where they were going? "

"I heard him tell the cabman to drive to Waterloo Station. "

"Nothing more? "

"No. "

"Well, if he won't tell you, I will. They have gone down to Hampshire, my lass. Bedsworth is the name of the place, and it is a pleasant little corner near the sea. I want you to go down there as well to-morrow. "

"Want me to go? "

"Yes; they need some one who is smart and handy to keep house for them. There is some old woman already, I believe, but she is old and useless. I'll warrant you wouldn't take long getting things shipshape.

My father intends to stay down there some little time with Miss Harston. "

"And how about you? " the girl asked, with a quick flash of suspicion in her dark eyes.

"Don't trouble about me. I shall stay behind and mind the business. Some one must be on the spot. I think cook and Jane and William ought to be able to look after me among them. "

"And I won't see you at all? " the girl cried, with a quiver in her voice.

"Oh yes, you shall. I'll be down from Saturday to Monday every week, and perhaps oftener. If business goes well I may come down and stay for some time. Whether I do or not may depend upon you. "

Rebecca Taylforth started and uttered an exclamation of surprise. "How can it depend upon me? " she asked eagerly.

"Well, " said Ezra, in a hesitating way, "it may depend upon whether you are a good girl, and do what you are told or not. I am sure that you would do anything to serve me, would you not? "

"You know very well that I would, Mister Ezra. When you want anything done you remember it, but if you have no use for me, then there is never a kind look on your face or a kind word from your lips. If I was a dog you could not use me worse. I could stand your harshness. I could stand the blow you gave me, and forgive you for it, from my heart; but, oh! it cut me to the very soul to be standing by and waiting while you were making up to another woman. It was more than I can bear. "

"Never mind, my girl, " said Ezra in a soothing voice; "that's all over and done with. See what I've brought you. " He rummaged in his pocket and produced a little parcel of tissue paper, which he handed to her.

It was only a small silver anchor, with Scotch pebbles inlaid in it. The woman's eyes, however, flashed as she looked at it, and she raised it to her lips and kissed it passionately.

"God bless it and you too! " she said. "I've heard tell as the anchor's the emblem of hope, and so it shall be with me. Oh, Ezra, you may travel far and meet them as can play and can sing and do many a thing as I can't do, but you'll never get one who will love you as dearly and well. "

"I know it, my lass, I know it, " said Ezra, smoothing down her dark hair, for she had dropped upon her knees beside the couch. "I've never met your equal yet. That's why I want you down at Bedsworth. I must have some one there that I can trust.

"What am I to do down at Bedsworth? " she asked.

"I want you to be Miss Harston's companion. She'll be lonely, and will need some other woman in the house to look after her. "

"Curse her! " cried Rebecca, springing to her feet with flashing eyes. "You are still thinking of her, then! She must have this; she must have that! Everything else is as dirt before her. I'll not serve her—so there! You can knock me down if you like. "

"Rebecca, " said Ezra slowly, "do you hate Kate Harston? "

"From the bottom of my soul, " she answered.

"Well, if you hate her, I tell you that I hate her a thousand times more. You thought that I was fond of her. All that is over now, and you may set your mind at ease. "

"Why do you want her so well cared for, then? " asked the girl suspiciously.

"I want some one who feels towards her as I do to be by her side. If she were never to come back from Bedsworth it would be nothing to me. "

"What makes you look at me so strangely? " she said, shrinking away from his intense gaze.

"Never mind. You go. You will understand many things in time which seem strange to you now. At present if you will do what I ask you will oblige me greatly. Will you go? "

"Yes, I will go. "

"There's a good lass. Give us a kiss, my girl. You have the right spirit in you. I'll let you know when the train goes to-morrow, and I will write to my father to expect you. Now, off with you, or you'll have them gossiping downstairs. Good night. "

"Good night, Mister Ezra, " said the girl, with her hand upon the handle of the library door. "You've made my heart glad this night. I live in hope—ever in hope. "

"I wonder what the deuce she hopes about, " the young merchant said to himself as she closed the door behind her. "Hopes I'll marry her, I suppose. She must be of a very sanguine disposition. A girl like that might be invaluable down at Bedsworth. If we had no other need for her, she would be an excellent spy. " He lay for some little time on the couch with bent brow and pursed lips, musing over the possibilities of the future.

While this dialogue had been going on in the library of Eccleston Square, Tom Dimsdale was still wending his way homewards with a feeling of weight in his mind and a presentiment of misfortune which overshadowed his whole soul. In vain he assured himself that this disappearance of Kate's was but temporary, and that the rumour of an engagement between her and Ezra was too ridiculous to be believed for a moment. Argue it as he would, the same dread, horrible feeling of impending trouble weighed upon him. Impossible as it was to imagine that Kate was false to him, it was strange that on the very day that this rumour reached his ears she should disappear from London. How bitterly he regretted now that he had allowed himself to be persuaded by John Girdlestone into ceasing to communicate with her. He began to realize that he had been duped, and that all these specious promises as to a future consent to their union had been so many baits to amuse him while the valuable present was slipping away. What could he do now to repair the past? His only course was to wait for the morrow and see whether the senior partner would appear at the offices. If he did so, the young man was determined that he should have an understanding with him.

So downcast was Tom that, on arriving at Phillimore Gardens, he would have slipped off to his room at once had he not met his burly father upon the stairs. "Bed! " roared the old man upon hearing his son's proposition. "Nothing of the sort, sir. Come down into the parlour and smoke a pipe with me. Your mother has been waiting for you all the evening. "

"I am sorry to be late, mother, " the lad said, kissing the old lady. "I have been down at the docks all day and have been busy and worried. "

Mrs. Dimsdale was sitting in her chair beside the fire, knitting, when her son came in. At the sound of his voice she glanced anxiously up at his face, with all her motherly instincts on the alert.

"What is it, my boy? " she said. "You don't look yourself. Something has gone wrong with you. Surely you're not keeping anything secret from your old mother? "

"Don't be so foolish as that, my boy, " said the doctor earnestly. "If you have anything on your mind, out with it. There's nothing so far wrong but that it can't be set right, I'll be bound. "

Thus pressed, their son told them all that had happened, the rumour which he had heard from Von Baumser at the *Cock and Cowslip*, and the subsequent visit to Eccleston Square. "I can hardly realize it all yet, " he said in conclusion. "My head seems to be in a whirl, and I can't reason about it. "

The old couple listened very attentively to his narrative, and were silent some little time after he had finished. His mother first broke the silence. "I was always sure, " she said, "that we were wrong to stop our correspondence at the request of Mr. Girdlestone. "

"It's easy enough to say that now, " said Tom ruefully. "At the time it seemed as if we had no alternative. "

"There's no use crying over spilt milk, " remarked the old physician, who had been very grave during his son's narrative. "We must set to work and get things right again. There is one thing very certain, Tom, and that is that Kate Harston is a girl who never did or could do a dishonourable thing. If she said that she would wait for you, my boy, you may feel perfectly safe; and if you doubt her for one moment you ought to be deuced well ashamed of yourself. "

"Well said, governor! " cried Tom, with beaming face. "Now, that is exactly my own feeling, but there is so much to be explained. Why have they left London, and where have they gone to? "

"No doubt that old scoundrel Girdlestone thought that your patience would soon come to an end, so he got the start of you by carrying the girl off into the country. "

"And if he has done this, what can I do? "

"Nothing. It is entirely within his right to do it. "

"And have her stowed away in some little cottage in the country, with that brute Ezra Girdlestone hanging round her all the time. It is the thought of that that drives me wild. "

"You trust in her, my boy, " said the old doctor. "We'll try our best in the meantime to find out where she has gone to. If she is unhappy or needs a friend you may be sure that she will write to your mother. "

"Yes, there is always that hope, " exclaimed Tom, in a more cheerful voice. "To-morrow I may learn something at the office. "

"Don't make the mistake of quarrelling with the Girdlestones. After all, they are within their rights in doing what they appear to have done. "

"They may be within their legal rights, " Tom cried indignantly; "but the old man made a deliberate compact with me, which he has broken. "

"Never mind. Don't give them an advantage by losing your temper. " The doctor chatted away over the matter for some time, and his words, together with those of his mother, cheered the young fellow's heart. Nevertheless, after they had retired to their rooms, Dr. Dimsdale continued to be very thoughtful and very grave. "I don't like it, " he said, more than once. "I don't like the idea of the poor girl being left entirely in the hands of that pair of beauties. God grant that no harm come of it, Matilda! " a prayer which his good wife echoed with all the strength of her kindly nature.

CHAPTER XXXIII.

THE JOURNEY TO THE PRIORY.

It was already dusk when John Girdlestone and his ward reached Waterloo Station. He gave orders to the guard that the luggage should be stamped, but took care that she should not hear the name of their destination. Hurrying her rapidly down the platform amid the confused heaps of luggage and currents of eager passengers, he pushed her into a first-class carriage, and sprang after her just as the bell rang and the wheels began to revolve.

They were alone. Kate crouched up into the corner among the cushions, and wrapped her rug round her, for it was bitterly cold. The merchant pulled a note-book from his pocket and proceeded by the light of the lamp above him to add up columns of figures. He sat very upright in his seat, and appeared to be as absorbed in his work as though he were among his papers in Fenchurch Street. He neither glanced at his companion nor made any inquiry as to her comfort.

As she sat opposite to him she could not keep her eyes from his hard angular face, every rugged feature of which was exaggerated by the flickering yellow light above him. Those deep-set eyes and sunken cheeks had been familiar to her for years. How was it that they now, for the first time, struck her as being terrible? Was it that new expression which had appeared upon them, that hard inexorable set about the mouth, which gave a more sinister character to his whole face? As she gazed at him an ineffable loathing and dread rose in her soul, and she could have shrieked out of pure terror. She put her hand up to her throat with a gasp to keep down the sudden inclination to cry out. As she did so her guardian glanced over the top of the note-book with his piercing light grey eyes.

"Don't get hysterical! " he cried. "You have given us trouble enough without that. "

"Oh, why are you so harsh? " she cried, throwing out her arms towards him in eloquent entreaty, while the tears coursed down her cheeks. "What have I done that is so dreadful? I *could* not love your son, and I do love another. I am so grieved to have offended you. You used to be kind and like a father to me. "

"And a nice return you have made me! 'Honour your father, ' says the good old Book. What honour did you give me save to disobey every command which I have ever given you. I have to blame myself to some extent for having allowed you to go on that most pernicious trip to Scotland, where you were thrown into the company of this young adventurer by his scheming old fool of a father. "

It would have been a study for a Rembrandt to depict the craggy, strongly lined face of the old merchant, and the beautiful pleading one which looked across at him, with the light throwing strange shadows over both. As he spoke she brushed the tears from her eyes and an angry flush sprang to her cheeks.

"You may say what you like of me, " she said bitterly. "I suppose that is one of your privileges as my guardian. You have no right, however, to speak evil of my friends. 'He who calleth his brother a fool, ' I think the good old Book says something of that. "

Girdlestone was staggered for a moment by this unexpected counter. Then he took off his broad-brimmed hat and bowed his head with drooping lids.

"Out of the mouths of babes and of sucklings! " he cried. "You are right. I spoke too warmly. It is my zeal for you which betrays me. "

"The same zeal which made you tell me so many things which I now know to be untrue about Mr. Dimsdale, " said Kate, waxing more fearless as her mind turned to her wrongs.

"You are becoming impertinent, " he answered, and resumed his calculations in his note-book.

Kate cowered back into her corner again, while the train thundered and screeched and rattled through the darkness. Looking through the steamy window, nothing was to be seen save the twinkle here and there of the lights of the scattered country cottages. Occasionally a red signal lamp would glare down upon her like the bloodshot eye of some demon who presided over this kingdom of iron and steam. Far behind a lurid trail of smoke marked the way that they had come. To Kate's mind it was all as weird and gloomy and cheerless even as the thoughts within her.

And they were gloomy enough. Where was she going? How long was she going for? What was she to do when there? On all these points she was absolutely ignorant. What was the object of this sudden flight from London? Her guardian could have separated her from the Dimsdales in many less elaborate ways than this. Could it be that he intended some system of pressure and terrorism by which she should be forced to accept Ezra as a suitor. She clenched her little white teeth as she thought of it, and registered a vow that nothing in this world would ever bring her to give in upon that point. There was only one bright spot in her outlook. When she reached her destination she would at once write to Mrs. Dimsdale, tell her where she was, and ask her frankly for an explanation of their sudden silence. How much wiser if she had done so before. Only a foolish pride had withheld her from it.

The train had already stopped at one large junction. Looking out through the window she saw by the lamps that it was Guildford. After another interminable interval of clattering and tossing and plunging through the darkness, they came to a second station of importance, Petersfield. "We are nearing our destination, " Girdlestone remarked, shutting up his book.

This proved to be a small wayside station, illuminated by a single lamp, which gave no information as to the name. They were the only passengers who alighted, and the train rolled on for Portsmouth, leaving them with their trunks upon the dark and narrow platform. It was a black night with a bitter wind which carried with it a suspicion of dampness, which might have been rain, or might have been the drift of the neighbouring ocean. Kate was numb with the cold, and even her gaunt companion stamped his feet and shivered as he looked about him.

"I telegraphed for a trap, " said he to the guard. "Is there not one waiting? "

"Yes, sir; if you be Mister Girdlestone, there's a trap from the *Flyin' Bull*. Here, Carker, here's your gentleman. "

At this summons a rough-looking ostler emerged into the circle of light thrown by the single lamp and, touching his hat, announced in a surly voice that he was the individual In question. The guard and he then proceeded to drag the trunks to the vehicle. It was a small wagonette, with a high seat for the driver in front.

"Where to, sir? " asked the driver, when the travellers had taken their seats.

"To Hampton Priory. Do you know where that is? "

"Better'n two mile from here, and close to the railway line, " said the man. "There hain't been no one livin' there for two year at the least. "

"We are expected and all will be ready for us, " said Girdlestone. "Go as fast as you can, for we are cold. "

The driver cracked his whip, and the horse started at a brisk trot down the dark country road.

Looking round her, Kate saw that they were passing through a large country village, consisting of a broad main street, with a few insignificant offshoots branching away on either side. A church stood on one side, and on the other the village inn. The door was open and the light shining through the red curtains of the bar parlour looked warm and cosy. The clink of glasses and the murmur of cheerful voices sounded from within. Kate, as she looked across, felt doubly cheerless and lonely by the contrast. Girdlestone looked too, but with different emotions.

"Another plague spot, " he cried, jerking his head in that direction. "In town or country it is the same. These poison-sellers are scattered over the whole face of the land, and every one of them is a focus of disease and misery. "

"Beg your pardon, sir, " the surly driver observed, screwing round in his seat. "That 'ere's the *Flyin' Bull*, sir, where I be in sarvice, and it ain't no poison-seller, but a real right down good house. "

"All liquor is poison, and every house devoted to the sale of it is a sinful house, " Girdlestone said curtly.

"Don't you say that to my maister, " remarked the driver. "He be a big man wi' a ter'bly bad temper and a hand like a leg o' mutton. Hold up, will ye! "

The last remark was addressed to the horse, which had stumbled in going down a sharp incline. They were out of the village by this time, and the road was lined on either side by high hedges, which threw a dense shadow over everything. The feeble lamps of the wagonette bored two little yellow tunnels of light on either side. The man let the reins lie loose upon the horse's back, and the animal picked out the roadway for itself. As they swung round from the narrow lane on to a broader road Kate broke out into a little cry of pleasure.

"There's the sea! " she exclaimed joyfully. The moon had broken from behind the clouds and glittered on the vast silvery expanse.

"Yes, that's the sea, " the driver said, "and them lights down yonder is at Lea Claxton, where the fisher-folk live; and over there, " pointing with his whip to a long dark shadow on the waters, "is the Oilywoite. "

"The what? "

"The Isle of Wight, he means, " said Girdlestone. The driver looked at him reproachfully. "Of course, " said he, "if you Lunnon folks knows more about it than we who are born an' bred in the place, it's no manner o' use our tryin' to teach you. " With this sarcastic comment he withdrew into himself, and refused to utter another word until the end of their journey.

It was not long before this was attained. Passing down a deeply rutted lane, they came to a high stone wall which extended for a couple of hundred yards. It had a crumbling, decaying appearance, as far as could be judged in the uncertain light. This wall was broken by a single iron gate, flanked by two high pillars, each of which was surmounted by some weather-beaten heraldic device. Passing through they turned up a winding avenue, with lines of trees on either side, which shot their branches so thickly above them that they might have been driving through some sombre tunnel. This avenue terminated in an open space, in the midst of which towered a great irregular whitewashed building, which was the old Priory. All below it was swathed in darkness, but the upper windows caught the glint of the moon and emitted a pallid and sickly glimmer. The whole effect was so weird and gloomy that Kate felt her heart sink within her. The wagonette pulled up in front of the door, and Girdlestone assisted her to alight.

There had been no lights or any symptoms of welcome, but as they pulled down the trunks the door opened and a little old woman appeared with a candle in her hand, which she carefully shaded from the wind while she peered out into the darkness.

"Is that Mr. Girdlestone? " she cried.

"Of course it is, " the merchant said impatiently. "Did I not telegraph and tell you that I was coming? "

"Yes, yes, " she answered, hobbling forward with the light. "And this is the young lady? Come in, my dear, come in. We have not got things very smart yet, but they will soon come right. "

She led the way through a lofty hall into a large sitting-room, which, no doubt, had been the monkish refectory in bygone days. It looked very bleak and cold now, although a small fire sputtered and sparkled in the corner of the great iron grate. There was a pan upon the fire, and the deal table in the centre of the room was laid out roughly as for a meal. The candle which the old woman had carried in was the only light, though the flickering fire cast strange fantastic shadows in the further corners and among the great oaken rafters which formed the ceiling.

"Come up to the fire, my dear, " said the old woman. "Take off your cloak and warm yourself. " She held her own shrivelled arms towards the blaze, as though her short exposure to the night air had chilled her. Glancing at her, Kate saw that her face was sharp-featured and cunning, with a loose lower lip which exposed a line of yellow teeth, and a chin which bristled with a tuft of long grey hairs.

From without there came the crunching of gravel as the wagonette turned and rattled down the avenue. Kate listened to the sound of the wheels until they died away in the distance. They seemed somehow to be the last link which bound her to the human race. Her heart failed her completely, and she burst into tears.

"What's the matter then? " the old woman asked, looking up at her. "What are ye crying about? "

"Oh, I am so miserable and so lonely, " she cried. "What have I done that I should be so unhappy? Why should I be taken to this horrible, horrible place? "

"What's the matter with the place? " asked her withered companion. "I don't see nought amiss with it. Here's Mr. Girdlestone a-comin'. He don't grumble at the place, I'll warr'nt. "

The merchant was not in the best of tempers, for he had had an altercation with the driver about the fare, and was cold into the bargain. "At it again? " he said roughly, as he entered. "It is I who ought to weep, I think, who have been put to all this trouble and inconvenience by your disobedience and weakness of mind. "

Kate did not answer, but sat upon a coarse deal chair beside the fire, and buried her face in her hands. All manner of vague fears and fancies filled her mind. What was Tom doing now? How quickly he would fly to her rescue did he but know how strangely she was situated! She determined that her very first action next morning should be to write to Mrs. Dimsdale and to tell her, not only where she was, but all that had occurred. The reflection that she could do this cheered her heart, and she managed to eat a little of the supper which the old woman had now placed upon the table. It was a rough stew of some sort, but the long journey had given an edge to their appetites, and the merchant, though usually epicurean in his tastes, ate a hearty meal.

When supper was over the crone, who was addressed by Girdlestone as Jorrocks, led the way upstairs and showed Kate to her room. If the furniture of the dining-room had been Spartan in its simplicity, this was even more so, for there was nothing in it save a small iron bedstead, much rusted from want of use, and a high wooden box on which stood the simplest toilet requisites. In spite of the poverty of the apartment Kate had never been more glad to enter her luxurious chamber at home. The little carpetless room was a haven of rest where she would be left, for one night at least, to her own thoughts. As she lay in bed, however, she could hear far away the subdued murmur of Girdlestone's voice and the shrill tones of the old woman. They were in deep and animated converse. Though they were too far distant for her to distinguish a word, something told her that their talk was about herself, and the same instinct assured her that it boded her little good.

CHAPTER XXXIV.

THE MAN WITH THE CAMP-STOOL.

When she awoke in the morning it was some little time before she could realize where she was or recall the events which had made such a sudden change in her life. The bare, cold room, with the whitewashed walls, and the narrow bed upon which she lay, brought back to her the recollection of a hospital ward which she had seen in Edinburgh, and her first thought was that she had had some accident and had been conveyed to some such establishment. The delusion was only momentary, however, for her true situation came back to her at once with all its vague horror. Of the two, she would have preferred that her first impression had been correct.

The small window of her apartment was covered by a dirty muslin blind. She rose and, drawing it aside, looked eagerly out. From what she had seen the night before she had hoped that this prison to which she had been conveyed might make amends for its loneliness by some degree of natural beauty. The scene which now met her eyes soon dispelled any expectations of the sort. The avenue with its trees lay on the other side of the house. From her window nothing was visible but a dreary expanse of bog-land and mudbanks stretching down to the sea. At high tide this enormous waste of dreariness and filth was covered by the water, but at present it lay before her in all its naked hideousness, the very type of dullness and desolation. Here and there a few scattered reeds, or an unhealthy greenish scum upon the mud, gave a touch of colour to the scene; but for the most part the great plain was all of the same sombre mud tint, with its monotony broken only by the white flecks where the swarms of gulls and kittiwakes had settled in the hope of picking up whatever had been left by the receding tide. Away across the broad surface a line of sparkling foam marked the fringe of the ocean, which stretched away to the horizon.

A mile or two to the eastward of her Kate saw some sign of houses, and a blue smoke which flickered up into the air. This she guessed to be the fishing village of Lea Claxton, which the driver had mentioned the night before. She felt, as she gazed at the little hamlet and the masts of the boats in front of it, that she was not alone in the world, and that even in this strange and desolate place there were honest hearts to whom as a last resource she could appeal.

She was still standing at the window when there came a knocking at the door, and she heard the voice of the old woman asking if she were awake. "Breakfast is ready, " she said, "and the master is a-wondering why you bean't down. "

On this summons Kate hastened her toilet and made her way down the old winding stair to the room in which they had supped the night before. Surely Girdlestone must have had a heart of flint not to be melted by the sight of that fair, fresh face. His features set as hard as adamant as she entered the room, and he looked at her with eyes which were puckered and angry.

"You are late, " he said coldly. "You must remember that you are not in Eccleston Square. 'An idle soul shall suffer hunger, ' says the prophet. You are here to be disciplined, and disciplined you shall be. "

"I am sorry, " she answered. "I think that I must have been tired by our journey. "

The vast room looked even more comfortless and bleak than on the preceding evening. On the table was a plate of ham and eggs. John Girdlestone served out a portion, and pushed it in her direction. She sat down on one of the rough wooden chairs and ate listlessly, wondering how all this was going to end.

After breakfast Girdlestone ordered the old woman out of the room, and, standing in front of the fire with his long legs apart and his hands behind his back, he told her in harsh concise language what his intentions were.

"I had long determined, " he said, "that if you ran counter to my wishes, and persisted in your infatuated affection for that scapegrace, I should remove you to some secluded spot, where you might reconsider your conduct and form better resolutions for the future. This country house answered the purpose admirably, and as an old servant of mine, Mrs. Jorrocks, chanced to reside in the neighbourhood, I have warned her that at any time I might come down and should expect to find things ready. Your rash and heartless conduct has, however, precipitated matters, and we have arrived before her preparations were complete. Our future arrangements will therefore be less primitive than they are at present. Here you shall remain, young lady, until you show signs of repentance, and of a willingness to undo the harm which you have done. "

"If you mean until I consent to marry your son, then I shall live and die here, " the girl said bravely.

"That rests with yourself. As I said before, you are under discipline here, and you may not find existence such a bed of roses as it was in Eccleston Square. "

"Can I have my maid? " Kate asked. "I can hardly stay here with no one but the old woman in the house. "

"Rebecca is coming down. I had a telegram from Ezra to that effect, and he will himself join us for a day or two in each week. "

"Ezra here! " Kate cried in horror. Her chief consolation through all her troubles had been that there seemed to be some chance of getting rid of her terrible suitor.

"And why not? " the old man asked angrily. "Are you so bitter against the lad as to grudge him the society of his own father? "

Kate was saved from further reproaches by the entrance of the old woman to clear the table. The last item of intelligence, however, had given her a terrible shock, and at the same time had filled her with astonishment. What could the fast-living, comfort-seeking man about town want in this dreary abode? She knew Ezra well, and was sure that he was not a man to alter his ways of life or suffer discomfort of any kind without some very definite object. It seemed to her that this was a new mesh in the net which was being drawn round her.

When her guardian had left the room Kate asked Mrs. Jorrocks for a sheet of paper. The crone shook her head and wagged her pendulous lip in derision.

"Mister Girdlestone thought as you would be after that, " she said. "There ain't no paper here, nor pens neither, nor ink neither. "

"What, none! Dear Mrs. Jorrocks, do have pity on me, and get me a sheet, however old and soiled. See, here is some silver! You are very welcome to it if you will give me the materials for writing one letter. "

Mrs. Jorrocks looked longingly with her bleared eyes at the few shillings which the girl held out to her, but she shook her head. "I dursn't do it, " she said. "It's as much as my place is worth. "

"Then I shall walk down to Bedsworth myself, " said Kate angrily. "I have no doubt that the people in the post office will let me sit there and write it. "

The old hag laughed hoarsely to herself until the scraggy sinews of her withered neck stood out like whipcord. She was still chuckling and coughing when the merchant came back into the room.

"What then? " he asked sternly, looking from one to the other. He was himself constitutionally averse to merriment, and he was irritated by it in others. "Why are you laughing, Mrs. Jorrocks? "

"I was a-laughing at her, " the woman wheezed, pointing with tremulous fingers. "She was askin' me for paper, and sayin' as she would go and write a letter at the Bedsworth Post Office. "

"You must understand once for all, " Girdlestone roared, turning savagely upon the girl, "that you are cut off entirely from the outer world. I shall give you no loophole which you may utilize to continue your intimacy with undesirable people. I have given orders that you should not be provided with either paper or ink. "

Poor Kate's last hope seemed to be fading away. Her heart sank within her, but she kept a brave face, for she did not wish him to see how his words had stricken her. She had a desperate plan in her head, which would be more likely to be successful could she but put him off his guard.

She spent the morning in her own little room. She had been provided with a ponderous brown Bible, out of which the fly leaves had been carefully cut, and this she read, though her thoughts often wandered away from the sacred pages. About one o'clock she heard the clatter of hoofs and the sound of wheels on the drive. Going down, she found that it was a cart which had come from Bedsworth with furniture. There were carpets, a chest of drawers, tables, and several other articles, which the driver proceeded to carry upstairs, helped by John Girdlestone. The old woman was in the upper room. It seemed to Kate that she might never again have such an opportunity of carrying out the resolve which she had formed. She put on her bonnet, and began to stroll listlessly about in front of the door, picking a few straggling leaves from the neglected lawn. Gradually she sauntered away in this manner to the head of the avenue, and then, taking one swift timid glance around, she slipped in among the trees, and made the best of her way, half walking, half running, down the dark winding drive.

Oh, the joy of the moment when the great white house which had already become so hateful to her was obscured among the trees behind her! She had some idea of the road which she had traversed the night before. Behind her were all her troubles. In front the avenue gate, Bedsworth, and freedom. She would send both a telegram and a letter to Dr. Dimsdale, and explain to him her exact situation. If the kind-hearted and energetic physician once knew of it, he would take care that no harm befell her. She could return then, and face with a light heart the worst which her guardian could do to her. Here was the avenue entrance now, the high lichen-eaten stone pillars, with the battered device upon the top. The iron gate between was open. With a glad cry she quickened her pace, and in another moment would have been in the high-road, when—

"Now then, where are you a-comin' to? " cried a gruff voice from among the bushes which flanked the gate.

The girl stopped, all in a tremble. In the shadow of the trees there was a camp-stool, and on the camp-stool sat a savage-looking man, dressed in a dark corduroy suit, with a blackened clay pipe stuck in the corner of his mouth. His weather-beaten mahogany face was plentifully covered with small-pox marks, and one of his eyes was sightless and white from the effects of the same disease. He rose now, and interposed himself between her and the gate.

"Sink me, if it ain't her, " he said slowly, surveying her from head to foot. "I were given to understand that she was a spanker, an' a spanker she be. " With this oracular remark he took a step back and surveyed Kate again with his one eye.

"My good man, " she said, in a trembling voice, for his appearance was far from reassuring, "I wish to go past and to get to Bedsworth. Here is a shilling, and I beg that you will not detain me. "

Her companion stretched out a very dirty hand, took the coin, spun it up in the air, caught it, bit it, and finally plunged it into the depths of his trouser pockets. "No road this way, missy, " he said; "I've given my word to the guv'nor, and I can't go back from it. "

"You have no right to detain me, " Kate cried angrily. "I have good friends in London who will make you suffer for this. "

"She's a-goin' to flare up, " said the one-eyed man; "knock me helpless, if she ain't! "

"I shall come through! " the girl cried in desperation. She was only a dozen yards from the lane which led to freedom, so she made a quick little feminine rush in the hope of avoiding this dreadful sentinel who barred her passage. He caught her round the waist, however, and hurled her back with such violence that she staggered across the path, and would have fallen had she not struck violently against a tree. As it was, she was badly bruised and the breath shaken out of her body.

"She *has* flared up, " said the one-eyed man, removing his pipe from his lips. "Blow me asunder if she bean't a rustler! " He brought his camp-stool from the side of the pillar and, planting it right in the centre of the gateway, sat down upon it again. "You see, missy, " he remarked, "it's no manner o' use. If you did get out it would only be to be put in a reg'lar 'sylum. "

"An asylum! " gasped Kate, sobbing with pain and anger. "Do you think I am mad, then? "

"I don't think nowt about it, " the man remarked calmly. "I knows it. "

This was a new light to Kate. She was so bewildered that she could hardly realize the significance of the remark.

"Who are you? " she said. "Why is it that you treat me in this cruel way? "

"Ah, now we come to business, " he said, in a satisfied way, crossing his legs, and blowing great wreaths from his pipe. "This is more like reason. Who am I? says you. Well, my name's Stevens—Bill Stevens, hesquire, o' Claxton, in the county o' Hants. I've been an A. B. in the navy, and I've got my pension to show it. I've been in the loon'cy business, too—was second warder in the suicide ward at Portsmouth for more'n two year. I've been out of a billet for some time, and

Muster Girdlestone he came to me and he says, 'You're William Stevens, hesquire? ' says he. 'I am, ' says I. 'You've had experience o' loonies? ' says he. 'I have, ' says I. 'Then you're the man I want, ' says he. 'You shall have a pound a week an' nothing to do. ' 'The very crib for me, ' says I. 'You've got to sit at the gate, ' says he, 'and prevent a patient from gettin' out! ' That was all as he said. Then you comes down from Lunnon, an' I comes up from Claxton, and here we be, all snug an' comfort'ble. So, you see, missy, it ain't no use at all, and you'll never get out this way. "

"But if you let me past he will think that I ran by so quickly that you could not stop me. He could not be very angry then, and I shall give you more money than you would lose. "

"No, no, " said the man, shaking his head energetically, "I'm true to my colours, sink me, but I am! I never was bribed yet, and never will be unless you can offer cash down instead o' promises. You can't lay them by to live on in your old age. "

"Alas! " Kate cried, "I have no money except these few shillings. "

"Give them over here, then. " He put them in his trouser pocket beside the other one. "That's all right, missy, " he said, in a beery whisper. "I won't say anything now to Muster Girdlestone about this job. He'd be wild if he knew, but mum's the word with William Stevens, hesquire. Lor', if this ain't my wife a-comin' out wi' my dinner! Away with ye, away! If she seed me a-speakin' to you she'd tear your hair for you as like as not. She's jealous, that's what's the matter wi' her. If she sees a woman makin' much o' me, it's just pisen to her, and she goes for 'em straight. She's the one to make the fur fly! Away with you, I say! "

Poor Kate, appalled by the possibility of making a new enemy, turned and retraced her steps slowly and sadly up the avenue. As she glanced back she saw a gaunt, hard-featured woman trudging up the lane with a tin can in her hand. Lonely and forlorn, but not yet quite destitute of hope, she turned to the right among the trees, and pushed her way through bushes and brambles to the boundary of the Priory grounds. It was a lofty wall, at least nine feet in height, with a coping which bristled with jagged pieces of glass. Kate walked along the base Of it, her fair skin all torn and bleeding with scratches from the briars, until she satisfied herself that there was no break in it. There was one small wooden door on the side which was skirted by the railway line, but it was locked and impassable. The only opening through which a human being could pass was that which was guarded in the manner she had seen. The sickening conviction took possession of her mind that without wings it was an utter impossibility either to get away or to give the least information to any one in the world as to where she was or what might befall her.

When she came back to the house, tired and dishevelled after her journey of exploration, Girdlestone was standing by the door to receive her with a sardonic smile upon his thin lips. "How do you like the grounds, then? " he asked, with, the nearest approach to hilarity which she had ever heard from him. "And the ornamental fencing? and the lodge-keeper? How did you like them all? "

Kate tried for a moment to make some brave retort, but it was a useless attempt. Her lips trembled, her eyes filled, and, with a cry of grief and despair which might have moved a wild beast, she fled to her room, and, throwing herself upon her bed, burst into such scalding bitter tears as few women are ever called upon to shed.

CHAPTER XXXV.

A TALK ON THE LAWN.

That same evening Rebecca came down from London. Her presence was a comfort to Kate, for though she had never liked or trusted the girl, yet the mere fact of having some one of her own age near her, gave her a sense of security and of companionship. Her room, too, had been altered for the better, and the maid was given the one next door, so that by knocking on the wall she could always communicate with her. This was an unspeakable consolation, for at night the old house was so full of the sudden crackings of warped timber and the scampering of rats that entire loneliness was unendurable.

Apart from these uncanny sounds there were other circumstances which gave the Priory a sinister reputation. The very aspect of the building was enough to suggest weird impressions. Its high white walls were blotched with patches of mildew, and in some parts there were long greenish stains from roof to ground, like tear streaks on the crumbling plaster. Indoors there was a dank graveyard smell in the low corridors and narrow stair-cases. Floors and ceilings were equally worm-eaten and rotten. Broad flakes of plaster from the walls lay littered about in the passages. The wind, too, penetrated the building through many cracks and crannies, so that there was a constant sighing and soughing in the big dreary rooms, which had a most eerie and melancholy effect.

Kate soon learned, however, that, besides these vague terrors, all predisposing the mind to alarm and exciting the imagination, there was a general belief that another more definite cause for fear existed in the old monastery. With cruel minuteness of detail her guardian had told her the legend which haunted those gloomy corridors.

It appears that in olden times the Priory had been inhabited by Dominicans, and that in the course of years these monks had fallen away from their original state of sanctity. They preserved a name for piety among the country folk by their austere demeanour, but in secret, within the walls of their own monastery, they practised every sort of dissipation and crime.

While the community was in this state of demoralization, each, from the abbot downwards, vying with the other in the number and enormity of their sins, there came a pious-minded youth from a neighbouring village, who begged that he might be permitted to join the order. He had been attracted, he said, by the fame of their sanctity. He was received amongst them, and at first was not admitted to their revels, but gradually, as his conscience was supposed to become more hardened, he was duly initiated into all their mysteries. Horrified by what he saw, the good youth concealed his indignation until he had mastered all the abominations of the establishment, and then, rising up on the altar steps, he denounced them in fiery, scathing words. He would leave them that night, he said, and he would tell his experiences through the length and breadth of the country. Incensed and alarmed, the friars held a hasty meeting, and then, seizing the young novice, they dragged him down the cellar steps and locked him up there. This same cellar had long been celebrated for the size and ferocity of the rats which inhabited it which were so fierce and strong that even during the day they had been known to attack those who entered. It is said that long into the weary hours of the night, the fearful shrieks and terrible struggles of the captive, as he fought with his innumerable assailants, resounded through the long corridors.

"They do say that he walks about the house at times, " Girdlestone said, in conclusion. "No one has ever been found who would live here very long since then. But, of course, such a strong-minded young woman as you, who cannot even obey your own guardian, would never be frightened by such a childish idea as that. "

"I do not believe in ghosts, and I don't think I shall be frightened, " Kate answered; but, for all that, the horrible story stuck in her mind, and added another to the many terrors which surrounded her.

Mr. Girdlestone's room was immediately above hers. On the second day of her imprisonment she went up on to this landing, for, having nothing to read save the Bible, and no materials for writing, she had little to do but to wander over the old house, and through the grounds. The door of Girdlestone's room was ajar, and she could not help observing as she passed that the apartment was most elegantly and comfortably furnished. So was the next room, the door of which was also open. The solid furniture and rich carpet contrasted strangely with her own bare, whitewashed chamber. All this pointed to the fact that her removal to the Priory had not been a sudden impulse on the part of the old merchant, but that he had planned and arranged every detail beforehand. Her refusal of Ezra was only the excuse for setting the machinery in motion. What was the object, then, and what was to be the end of this subtle scheming? That was the question which occurred to her every hour of the day, and every hour the answer seemed more grim and menacing.

There was one link in the chain which was ever hidden from her. It had never occurred to the girl that her fortune could be of moment to the firm. She had been so accustomed to hear Ezra and his father talk glibly of millions, that she depreciated her own little capital and failed to realize how important it might be in a commercial crisis. Indeed, the possibility of such a crisis never entered her head, for one of her earliest impressions was hearing her father talk of the great resources of the firm and of its stability. That this firm was now in the direst straits, and that her money was absolutely essential to its existence, were things which never for one instant entered her thoughts.

Yet that necessity was becoming more pressing every day. Ezra, in London, was doing all that indomitable energy and extraordinary business capacity could do to prolong the struggle. As debts became due, he would still stave off each creditor with such skill and plausibility as allayed every suspicion. Day by day, however, the work became more severe, and he felt that he was propping up an edifice which was so rotten that it must, sooner or later, come crumbling about his ears. When he came down to the Priory upon the Saturday, the young man's haggard and anxious face showed the severe ordeal which he had undergone.

Kate had already retired to her room when he arrived. She heard the sound of the trap, however, and guessed who it was, even before his deep bass voice sounded in the room beneath. Looking out of her window a little later she saw him walking to and fro in the moonlight, talking earnestly to his father. It was a bitter night, and she wondered what they could have to talk about which might not be said beside the warm fire in the dining-room. They flickered up and down among the shadows for more than an hour, and then the girl heard the door slam, and shortly afterwards the heavy tread of the two men passed her chamber, and ascended to the rooms above.

It was a momentous conversation which she had witnessed. In it Ezra had shown his father how impossible it was to keep up appearances, and how infallible was their ruin unless help came speedily.

"I don't think any of them smell a rat, " he said. "Mortimer and Johnson pressed for their bill in rather an ugly manner, but I talked them over completely. I took out my cheque-book. 'Look here, gentlemen, ' said I, 'if you wish I shall write a cheque for the amount. If I do, it will be the last piece of business which we shall do together. A great house like ours can't afford to be disturbed in the routine of their business. ' They curled up at once, and said no more about it. It was an anxious moment though, for if they had taken my offer, the whole murder would have been out. "

The old man started at the word his son had used, and rubbed his hands together as though a sudden chill had struck through him.

"Don't you think, Ezra, " he said, clutching his son's arm, "that is a very foolish saying about 'murder will out'? I remember Pilkington, the detective, who was a member of our church when I used to worship at Durham Street, speaking on this subject. He said that it was his opinion that people are being continually made away with, and that not more than one in ten are ever accounted for. Nine chances to one, Ezra, and then those which are found out are very vulgar affairs. If a man of intellect gave his mind to it, there would be little chance of detection. How very cold the night is! "

"Yes, " returned his son. "It is best to talk of such things in the open air, though. How has all gone since you have been down here? "

"Very well. She was restive the first day, and wanted to get to Bedsworth. I think that she has given it up now as a bad job. Stevens, the gatekeeper, is a very worthy fellow. "

"What steps have you taken? " asked Ezra, striking a fusee and lighting a cigar.

"I have taken care that they should know that she is an invalid, both at Bedsworth and at Claxton. They have all heard of the poor sick young lady at the Priory. I have let them know also that her mind is a little strange, which accounts, of course, for her being kept in solitude. When it happens—"

"For God's sake, be quiet! " the young man cried, with a shudder. "It's an awful job; it won't bear thinking of. "

"Yes, it is a sad business; but what else is there? "

"And how would you do it? " Ezra asked, in a hoarse whisper. "No violence, I hope. "

"It may come to that. I have other plans in my head, however, which may be tried first. I think that I see one way out of it which would simplify matters. "

"If there is no alternative I have a man who is ripe for any job of the sort. "

"Ah, who is that? "

"A fellow who can hit a good downright blow, as I can testify to my cost. His name is Burt. He is the man who cut my head open in Africa. I met him in London the other day, and spotted him at once. He is a half-starved, poor devil, and as desperate as a man could be. He is just in the key for any business of the sort. I've got the whip-hand of him now, and he knows it, so that I could put him up to anything. I believe that such a job would be a positive pleasure to him, for the fellow is more like a wild beast than a man. "

"Sad, sad! " Girdlestone exclaimed. "If a man once falls away, what is there to separate him from the beasts? How can I find this man? "

"Wire to me. Put 'Send a doctor; ' that will do as well as anything else, and will sound well at the post-office. I'll see that he comes down by the next train. You'd best meet him at the station, for the chances are that he will be drunk. "

"Bring him down, " said Girdlestone. "You must be here yourself. "

"Surely you can do without me? "

"No, no. We must stand or fall together. "

"I've a good mind to throw the thing over, " said Ezra, stopping in his walk. "It sickens me. "

"What! Go back now! " the old man cried vehemently. "No, no, that would be too craven. We have everything in our favour, and all that we want is a stout heart. Oh, my boy, my boy, on the one side of you are ruin, dishonour, a sordid existence, and the scorn of your old companions; on the other are success and riches and fame and all that can make life pleasant. You know as well as I do that the girl's money would turn the scale, and that all would then be well. Your whole future depends upon her death. We have given her every chance. She laughed at your love. It is time now to show her your hate. "

"That is true enough, " Ezra said, walking on. "There is no reason why I should pity her. I've put my hand to the plough, and I shall go on. I seem to be getting into your infernal knack of scripture quoting. "

"There is a brave, good lad, " cried his father. "It would not do to draw back now. "

"You will find Rebecca useful, " the young man said, "You may trust her entirely. "

"You did well to send her. Have they asked for me much? "

"Yes. I have told them all the same story—nervous exhaustion, and doctor's orders that you were not to be disturbed by any business letters. The only man who seemed to smell a rat was that young Dimsdale. "

"Ah! " cried the old man, with a chuckle; "of course he would be surprised at our disappearance. "

"He looks like a madman; asked me where you had gone, and when I answered him as I had the others, stormed out that he had a right to know, and that he would know. His blood was up, and there was nearly being a pretty scene before the clerks. He follows me home every evening to Eccleston Square, and waits outside half the night through to see that I do not leave the house. "

"Does he, though? "

"Yes; he came after me to the station to-day. He had a cravat round his mouth and an ulster, but I could see that it was he. I took a ticket for Colchester. He took one also, and made for the Colchester train. I gave him the slip, got the right ticket, and came on. I've no doubt he is at Colchester at this moment. "

"Remember, my boy, " the merchant said, as they turned from the door, "this is the last of our trials. If we succeed in this, all is well for the future. "

"We have tried diamonds, and we have tried marriage. The third time is the charm, " said Ezra, as he threw away his cigar and followed his father.

CHAPTER XXXVI.

THE INCIDENT OF THE CORRIDOR.

Ezra Girdlestone hardly went through the formality of greeting Kate next morning when she came down to breakfast. He was evidently ill at ease, and turned away his eyes when she looked at him, though he glanced at her furtively from time to time. His father chatted with him upon City matters, but the young man's answers were brusque and monosyllabic. His sleep had been troubled and broken, for the conversation of the night before had obtruded unpleasantly on his dreams.

Kate slipped away from them as soon as she could and, putting on her bonnet, went for a long walk through the grounds, partly for the sake of exercise, and partly in the hope of finding some egress. The one-eyed gate-keeper was at his post, and set up a hideous shout of laughter when he saw her; so she branched off among the trees to avoid him, and walked once more very carefully round the boundary wall. It was no easy matter to follow it continuously, for the briars and brambles grew in a confused tangle up to its very base. By perseverance, however, she succeeded in tracing every foot of it, and so satisfying herself finally that there was no diminution anywhere in its height, no break in its continuity, save the one small wooden door which was securely fastened.

There was one spot, however, where a gleam of hope presented itself. At an angle of the wall there stood a deserted wooden shed, which had been used for the protection of gardeners' tools in the days when the grounds had been kept in better order. It was not buttressed up against the wall, but stood some eight or ten feet from it. Beside the shed was an empty barrel which had once been a water-butt. The girl managed to climb to the top of the barrel, and from this she was easily able to gain the sloping roof of the shed. Up this she clambered until she stood upon the summit, a considerable height above the ground. From it she was able to look down over the wall on to the country-road and the railway line which lay on the other side of it. True that an impassable chasm lay between her and the wall, but it would be surely possible for her to hail passers-by from here, and to persuade some of them to carry a letter to Bedsworth or to bring paper from there. Fresh hope gushed into her heart at the thought.

It was not a very secure footing, for the planks of, which the shed was composed were worm-eaten and rotten. They cracked and crumbled beneath her feet, but what would she not dare to see a friendly human face? As she stood there a couple of country louts, young lads about sixteen, came strolling down the road, the one whistling and the other munching at a raw turnip. They lounged along until they came opposite to Kate's point of observation, when one of them looking up saw her pale face surmounting the wall.

"Hey, Bill, " he cried to his companion, "blowed if the mad wench bean't up on the shed over yander! "

"So she be! " said the other eagerly. "Give me your turnip. Jimmy, an' I'll shy it at her. "

"Noa, I'll shy it mysel', " said the gallant Jimmy; and at the word whizz came the half of a turnip within art inch of Kate's ear.

"You've missed her! " shrieked the other savage. "'Ere, quick, where be a stone? " But before he could find one the poor girl, sick at heart, clambered down from her exposed situation.

"There is no hope for me anywhere, " she sobbed to herself. "Every man's hand is against me. I have only one true friend, and he is far away. " She went back to her room utterly disheartened and dispirited.

Her guardian knocked at her door before dinner time. "I trust, " he said, "that you have read over the service. It is as well to do so when you cannot go to church. "

"And why should you prevent me from going to church? " she asked.

"Ah, my lady, " he said with a sneer, "you are reaping what you have sown. You are tasting now, the bitter fruits of your disobedience. Repent before it is too late! "

"I have done no wrong, " she said, turning on him with flashing eyes. "It is for *you* to repent, you violent and hypocritical man. It is for you to answer for your godly words and your ungodly and wicked actions. There is a power which will judge between us some day, and will exact atonement for your broken oath to your dead

friend and for your cruel treatment of one who was left to your care.
" She spoke with burning cheeks and with such fearless energy that
the hard City man fairly cowered away from her.

"We will leave that to the future, " he said. "I came up to do you a
kindness, and you abuse me. I hear that there are insects about the
house, beetles and the like. A few drops from this bottle scattered
about the room would keep them away. Take care, for it is a violent
though painless poison if taken by a human being. " He handed her
a phial, with a brownish turbid liquid in it, and a large red poison
label, which she took without comment and placed upon the
mantelpiece. Girdlestone gave a quick, keen glance at her as he
retired. In truth he was astonished at the alteration which the last
few days had made in her appearance. Her cheeks were colourless
and sunken, save for the single hectic spot, which announced the
fever within. Her eyes were unnaturally bright. A strange and new
expression had settled upon her whole countenance. It seemed to
Girdlestone that there was every chance that his story might become
a reality, and her reason be permanently deranged. She had,
however, more vitality than her guardian gave her credit for. Indeed,
at the very time when he set her down in his mind as a broken
woman, she had formed a fresh plan for escape, which it would
require both energy and determination to put into execution.

During the last few days she had endeavoured to make friends with
the maid Rebecca, but the invincible aversion which the latter had
entertained for her, ever since Ezra had visited her with his
unwelcome attentions, was not to be overcome by any advances
which she could make. She performed her offices with a heart full of
malice, and an eye which triumphed in her mistress's misfortunes.

Kate had bethought herself that Stevens, the gatekeeper, only
mounted guard during the day. She had observed, too, at the time of
her conversation with him, that the iron gate was in such a state of
disrepair that, even if it were locked, it would not be a difficult
matter to scramble through or over it. If she could only gain the open
air during the night there would be nothing to prevent her from
making her way to Bedsworth, whence she could travel on to
Portsmouth, which was only seven miles away. Surely there she
would find some charitable people who would communicate with
her friends and give her a temporary shelter.

The front door of the house was locked every night, but there was a nail behind it, on which she hoped to find the key. There was another door at the back. Then there were the windows of the ground-floor, which might be tried in case the doors were too securely fastened. If only she could avoid waking any one there was no reason why she should not succeed. If the worst came to the worst and she was detected, they could not treat her more cruelly than they had already done.

Ezra had gone back to London, so that she had only three enemies to contend against, Girdlestone, Rebecca, and old Mrs. Jorrocks. Of these, Girdlestone slept upon the floor above, and Mrs. Jorrocks, who might have been the most dangerous of all, as her room was on the ground-floor, was fortunately so deaf that there was little risk of disturbing her. The problem resolved itself, therefore, into being able to pass Rebecca's room without arousing her, and, as she knew the maid to be a sound sleeper, there seemed to be every chance of success.

She sat at her window all that afternoon steeling her mind to the ordeal before her. She was weak, poor girl, and shaken, little fit for anything which required courage and resolution. Her mind ran much upon her father, and upon the mother whom she had never known, but whose miniature was among her most precious treasures. The thought of them helped to dispel the dreadful feeling of utter loneliness, which was the most unendurable of all her troubles.

It was a cold, bright day, and the tide was in, covering the mudbanks and lapping up against the walls of the Priory grounds. So clear was it that she could distinguish the houses at the east end of the Isle of Wight. When she opened her window and looked out she could perceive that the sea upon her right formed a great inlet, dreary and dry at low tide, but looking now like a broad, reed-girt lake. This was Langston Harbour, and far away at its mouth she could make out a clump of buildings which marked the watering-place of Hayling.

There were other signs, however, of the presence of man. From her window she could see the great men-of-war steaming up the Channel, to and from the anchorage at Spithead. Some were low in the water and venomous looking, with bulbous turrets and tiny masts. Others were long and stately, with great lowering hulks and broad expanse of canvas. Occasionally a foreign service gunboat would pass, white and ghostly, like some tired seabird flapping its way home. It was one of Kate's few amusements to watch the passing and repassing of the vessels, and to speculate upon whence they had come and whither they were bound.

On that eventful evening Rebecca went to bed rather earlier than usual. Kate retired to her room, and having made her final preparations and stuffed her few articles of jewelry into her pockets, to serve in place of money, she lay down upon her bed, and trembled at the thought of what was in front of her. Down below she could hear her guardian's shuffling step as he moved about the refectory. Then came the creaking of the rusty lock as he secured the door, and shortly afterwards he passed upstairs to his room. Mrs. Jorrocks had also gone to bed, and all was quiet in the house.

Kate knew that some hours must elapse before she could venture to make the attempt. She remembered to have read in some book that the sleep of a human being was usually deepest about two in the morning, so she had chosen that hour for her enterprise. She had put on her strongest dress and her thickest shoes, but had muffled the latter in cloth, so that they should make no sound. No precaution which she could think of had been neglected. There was now nothing to be done but to spend the time as best she might until the hour of action should arrive.

She rose and looked out of the window again. The tide was out now, and the moon glittered upon the distant ocean. A mist was creeping up, however, and even as she looked it drew its veil over the water. It was bitterly cold. She shivered and her teeth began to chatter. Stretching herself upon the bed once more, she wrapped the blankets round her, and, worn out with anxiety and fatigue, dropped into a troubled sleep.

She slumbered some hours before she awoke.

Looking at her watch she found that it was after two. She must not delay any longer. With the little bundle of her more valuable possessions in her hand, she gave such a gasp as a diver gives before he makes his spring, and slipping past Rebecca's half-opened door she felt her way down the wooden stair, picking her steps very carefully.

Even in the daytime she had often noticed how those old planks creaked and cracked beneath her weight. Now, in the dead silence of the night, they emitted such sounds that her heart sank within her. She stopped several times, convinced that she must be discovered, but all was hushed and still. It was a relief when at last she reached the ground-floor, and was able to feel her way along the passage to the door.

Shaking in every limb from cold and fear, she put her hand to the lock; the key was not there. She tried the nail; there was nothing there. Her wary gaoler had evidently carried it away with him to his room. Would it occur to him to do the same in the case of the back door? It was very possible that he might have overlooked it. She retraced her steps down the passage, passed Mrs. Jorrocks' room, where the old woman was snoring peacefully, and began to make her way as best she could through the great rambling building.

Running along the basement floor from front to back there was a long corridor, one side of which was pierced for windows. At the end of this corridor was the door which she wished to reach. The moon had broken through the fog, and pouring its light through each opening cast a succession of silvery flickering spots upon the floor. Between each of these bars of uncertain light was an interval of darkness. Kate stood at the head of this corridor with her hand against the wall, awed by the sudden sight of the moonlight and by the weird effect which was produced by the alternate patches of shadow and brightness. As she stood there, suddenly, with eyes distended with horror, she became aware that something was approaching her down the corridor.

She saw it moving as a dark formless mass at the further end. It passed through the bar of light, vanished, appeared once more, lost itself in the darkness, emerged again. It was half-way down the passage and still coming on. Petrified with terror, she could only wait and watch. Nearer it came and nearer. It was gliding into the last bar of light Immediately in front of her! It was on her! God of mercy, it was a Dominican friar! The moon shone clear and cold upon his gaunt figure and his sombre robes. The poor girl threw up her hands, gave one terrible scream of horror, which rang through the old house, and sank senseless to the ground.

CHAPTER XXXVII.

A CHASE AND A BRAWL.

It would be impossible to describe the suspense in which Tom Dimsdale lived during these weeks. In vain he tried in every manner to find some way of tracing the fugitives. He wandered aimlessly about London from one inquiry office to another, telling his story and appealing for assistance. He advertised in papers and cross-questioned every one who might know anything of the matter. There were none, however, who could help him or throw any light upon the mystery.

No one at the office knew anything of the movements of the senior partner. To all inquiries Ezra replied that he had been ordered by the doctors to seek complete repose in the country. Dimsdale dogged Ezra's footsteps night after night in the hope of gaining some clue, but in vain. On the Saturday he followed him to the railway station, but Ezra, as we have seen, succeeded in giving him the slip.

His father became seriously anxious about the young fellow's health. He ate nothing and his sleep was much broken. Both the old people tried to inculcate patience and moderation.

"That fellow, Ezra Girdlestone, knows where they are, " Tom would cry, striding wildly up and down the room with unkempt hair and clenched hands. "I will have his secret, if I have to tear it out of him. "

"Steady, lad, steady! " the doctor replied to one of these outbursts. "There is nothing to be gained by violence. They are on the right side of the law at present, and you will be on the wrong if you do anything rash. The girl could have written if she were uncomfortable. "

"Ah, so she could. She must have forgotten us. How could she, after all that has passed! "

"Let us hope for the best, let us hope for the best, " the doctor would say soothingly. Yet it must be confessed that he was considerably staggered by the turn which things had taken. He had seen so much of the world in his professional capacity that he had become a very reliable judge of character. All his instincts told him that Kate Harston was a true-hearted and well-principled girl. It was not in her nature to leave London and never to send a single line to her friends to tell them where or why she had gone. There must, he was sure, be some good reason for her silence, and this reason resolved itself into one or two things—either she was ill and unable to hold a pen, or she had lost her freedom and was restrained from writing to them. The last supposition seemed to the doctor to be the more serious of the two.

Had he known the instability of the Girdlestone firm, and the necessity they were under of getting ready money, he would at once have held the key to the enigma. He had no idea of that, but in spite of his ignorance he was deeply distrustful of both father and son. He knew and had often deplored the clause in John Harston's will by which the ward's money reverted to the guardian. Forty thousand pounds were a bait which might tempt even a wealthy man into crooked paths.

It was Saturday—the third Saturday since Girdlestone and his ward had disappeared. Dimsdale had fully made up his mind that, go where he would, Ezra should not escape him this time. On two consecutive Saturdays the young merchant had managed to get away from him, and had been absent each time until the Monday morning. Tom knew, and the thought was a bitter one, that these days were spent in some unknown retreat in the company of Kate and of her guardian. This time at least he should not get away without revealing his destination.

The two young men remained in the office until two o'clock. Then Ezra put on his hat and overcoat, buttoning it up close, for the weather was bitterly cold. Tom at once picked up his wide-awake and followed him out into Fenchurch Street, so close to his heels that the swinging door had not shut on the one before the other passed through. Ezra glanced round at him when he heard the footsteps, and gave a snarl like an angry dog. There was no longer any pretence of civility between the two, and whenever their eyes met it was only to exchange glances of hatred and defiance.

A hansom was passing down the street, and Ezra, with a few muttered words to the driver, sprang in. Fortunately another had just discharged its fare, and was still waiting by the curb. Tom ran up to it. "Keep that red cab in sight, " he said. "Whatever you do, don't let it get away from you. " The driver, who was a man of few words, nodded and whipped up his horse.

It chanced that this same horse was either a faster or a fresher one than that which bore the young merchant. The red cab rattled down Fleet Street, then doubled on its tracks, and coming back by St. Paul's plunged into a labyrinth of side streets, from which it eventually emerged upon the Thames Embankment. In spite of all its efforts, however, it was unable to shake off its pursuer. The red cab journeyed on down the Embankment and across one of the bridges, Tom's able charioteer still keeping only a few yards behind it. Among the narrow streets on the Surrey side Ezra's vehicle pulled up at a low beer-shop. Tom's drove on a hundred yards or so, and then stopped where he could have a good view of whatever occurred. Ezra had jumped out and entered the public-house. Tom waited patiently outside until he should reappear. His movements hitherto had puzzled him completely. For a moment the wild hope came into his head that Kate might be concealed in this strange hiding-place, but a little reflection showed him the absurdity and impossibility of the idea.

He had not long to wait. In a very few minutes young Girdlestone came out again, accompanied by a tall, burly man, with a bushy red beard, who was miserably dressed, and appeared to be somewhat the worse for drink. He was helped into the cab by Ezra, and the pair drove off together. Tom was more bewildered than ever. Who was this fellow, and what connexion had he with the matter on hand? Like a sleuth-hound the pursuing hansom threaded its way through the torrent of vehicles which pour down the London streets, never for one moment losing sight of its quarry. Presently they wheeled into the Waterloo Road, close to the Waterloo Station. The red cab turned sharp round and rattled up the incline which leads to the main line. Tom sprang out, tossed a sovereign to the driver, and followed on foot at the top of his speed.

As he ran into the station Ezra Girdlestone and the red-bearded stranger were immediately in front of him. There was a great swarm of people all around, for, as it was Saturday, there were special trains to the country. Tom was afraid of losing sight of the two men in the crowd, so he elbowed his way through as quickly as he could, and got immediately behind them—so close that he could have touched them with his hand. They were approaching the booking-office, when Ezra glanced round and saw his rival standing behind him. He gave a bitter curse, and whispered something to his half-drunken companion. The latter turned, and with an inarticulate cry, like a wild beast, rushed at the young man and seized him by the throat with his brawny hands.

It is one thing, however, to catch a man by the throat, and another to retain that grip, especially when your antagonist happens to be an International football player. To Tom this red-bearded rough, who charged him so furiously, was nothing more than the thousands of bull-headed forwards who had come upon him like thunder-bolts in the days of old. With the ease begotten by practice he circled his assailant with his long muscular arms, and gave a quick convulsive jerk in which every sinew of his body participated. The red-bearded man's stumpy legs described a half-circle in the air, and he came down on the stone pavement with a sounding crash which shook every particle of breath from his enormous body.

Tom's fighting blood was all aflame now, and his grey eyes glittered with a Berserk joy as he made at Ezra. All the cautions of his father and the exhortations of his mother were cast to the winds as he saw his enemy standing before him. To do him justice, Ezra was nothing loth, but sprang forward to meet him, hitting with both hands. They were well matched, for both were trained boxers and exceptionally powerful men. Ezra was perhaps the stronger, but Tom was in better condition. There was a short eager rally—blow and guard and counter so quick and hard that the eye could hardly follow it. Then a rush of railway servants and bystanders tore them asunder. Tom had a red flush on his forehead where a blow had fallen, Ezra was spitting out the fragments of a broken tooth, and bleeding profusely. Each struggled furiously to get at the other, with the result that they were dragged farther apart. Eventually a burly policeman seized Tom by the collar, and held him as in a vice.

"Where is he? " Tom cried, craning his neck to catch a glimpse of his enemy. "He'll get away after all. "

"Can't 'elp that, " said the guardian of the peace phlegmatically. "A gen'elman like you ought to be ashamed. Keep quiet now! Would yer, then! " This last at some specially energetic effort on the part of the prisoner to recover his freedom.

"They'll get away! I know they will! " Tom cried in despair, for both Ezra and his companion, who was none other than Burt, of African notoriety, had disappeared from his sight. His fears proved to be only too well founded, for when at last he succeeded in wresting himself from the constable's clutches he could find no trace of his enemies. A dozen bystanders gave a dozen different accounts of their movements. He rushed from one platform to another over all the great station. He could have torn his hair at the thought of the way in which he had allowed them to slip through his fingers. It was fully an hour before he finally abandoned the search, and acknowledged to himself that he had been hoodwinked for the third time, and that a long week would elapse before he could have another chance of solving the mystery.

He turned at last sadly and reluctantly away from the station, and walked across to Waterloo Bridge, brooding over all that had occurred, and cursing himself for his stupidity in allowing himself to be drawn into a vulgar brawl, when he might have attained his end so much better by quiet observation. It was some consolation, however, that he had had one fair crack at Ezra Girdlestone. He glanced down at his knuckles, which were raw and bleeding, with a mixture of satisfaction and disgust. With half a smile he put his injured hand in his pocket, and looking up once more became aware that a red-faced gentleman was approaching him in a highly excited manner.

It could not be said that the red-faced gentleman walked, neither could it be said that the red-faced gentleman ran. His mode of progression might best be described as a succession of short and unwieldy jumps, which, as he was a rather stout gentleman, appeared to indicate some very urgent and pressing need for hurry. His face was bathed in perspiration, and his collar had become flaccid and shapeless from the same cause. It appeared to Tom, as he gazed at those rubicund, though anxious, features, that they should be well known to him. That glossy hat, those speckless gaiters, and the long frock-coat, surely they could belong to none other than the gallant Major Tobias Clutterbuck, late of her Majesty's 119th of the Line?

As the old soldier approached Tom, he quickened his pace, so that when he eventually came up with him he could only puff and pant and hold out a soiled letter.

"Read! " he managed to ejaculate.

Tom opened the letter and glanced his eye over the contents, with a face which had turned as pale as the major's was red. When he finished it he turned without a word, and began to run in the direction from which he had come, the major following as quickly as his breath would permit.

CHAPTER XXXVIII.

GIRDLESTONE SENDS FOR THE DOCTOR.

When Kate came to herself after the terrible incident which frustrated her attempt at escape, she found herself in bed in her own little room. By the light which shone in through the window she knew that it must be well on in the day. Her head was throbbing violently, and she was so weak that she could hardly raise herself in bed. When she looked round she found that Rebecca had brought a chair in from her room and was sitting by the fire. At the sound of her movement the maid glanced up and perceived that her mistress had recovered consciousness.

"Lor' bless me! " she cried, "you've given us a pretty fright. We thought you wasn't coming back to your senses no more. You've been a-lyin' there since the middle of the night, and now it's close on to twelve o'clock. "

Kate lay silent for some little time, putting together all that had occurred. "Oh, Rebecca, " she said at last, shivering at the recollection, "I have seen the most dreadful sight. Either I am going mad, or I have seen a ghost. "

"We thought you were a ghost yourself, " said the girl reproachfully. "What with the screechin' and you lying so white in the middle of the passage, it was enough to make any one's 'air turn grey. Mr. Girdlestone, he lifted you up, an' carried you back into your room. He was cut to the heart, the good gentleman, when he saw what you'd been after, a-tryin' to give him the slip. "

"Oh, this dreadful house will kill me—it will kill me! " Kate moaned. "I cannot stay in it any longer. What shall I do? Oh, Rebecca, Rebecca, what shall I do? "

The fresh-coloured maid came across with a simper upon her pretty, vulgar face, and sat on the side of the bed. "What's the matter, then? " she asked. "What is it that you have seen? "

"I have seen—oh, Rebecca, it is too dreadful to talk of. I have seen that poor monk who was killed in the cellars. It was not fancy. I saw him as plainly as I see you now, with his tall thin figure, and long loose gown, and the brown cowl drawn over his face. "

"God preserve us! " cried Rebecca nervously, glancing over her shoulder. "It is enough to give one the creeps. "

"I pray that I may never see such a sight again. Oh, Rebecca, if you have the heart of a woman, help me to get away from this place. They mean that I should never go from it alive. I have read it in my guardian's eyes. He longs for my death. Do, do tell me what I should do for the best. "

"I'm surprised at you! " the maid said with dignity. "When Mr. Girdlestone and Mr. Ezra is so good to you, and provides you with a country-house and every convenience as 'eart could wish, all you can find to do is to go screamin' about at night, and then talk as if you was a-goin' to be murdered in the day. I really am surprised. There's Mr. Girdlestone a-callin. ' He'd be shocked, poor gentleman, if he knew how you was abusin' of him. " Rebecca's face assumed an expression of virtuous indignation as she swept out of the room, but her black eyes shone with the unholy light of cruelty and revenge.

Left to herself, Kate rose and dressed as well as her weakness would permit. Her nerves were so shaken that she started at the least sound, and she could hardly recognize the poor pale face which she saw in the glass as her own. She had scarcely finished her toilet before her guardian came up into her room.

"You are better, then? " he said.

"I am very ill, " she answered gently.

"No wonder, after rushing about the corridors in that absurd fashion in the dead of the night. Rebecca tells me that you imagine you met with some apparition. You are crying. Are you so unhappy, then? "

"Very, very miserable, " Kate answered, sinking her face upon her hands.

"Ah, " said Girdlestone softly, "it is only in some higher life that we shall find entire peace and contentment. " His voice had altered, so that a little warm spring of hope began to rise in the girl's heart, that perhaps the sight of her many miseries was beginning to melt this iron man.

"Beyond the grave is rest, " he continued, in the same gentle tones. "It has seemed to me sometimes that if it were not for the duties which I have to perform in this world, and the many who are dependent upon me, I should be tempted to shorten my existence in order to attain the peace which is to come. Some precisians have pronounced it to be sinful to cut the thread of life. For my part I have never thought it so, and yet my view of morals has been a strict one. I hold that of all things in this world one's life is the thing which belongs most entirely to one's self, and may therefore most freely be terminated when it seems good to us. " He picked up the phial from the mantelpiece and gazed thoughtfully at it. "How strange, " he said, "to think that within the compass of this tiny bottle lies a cure for every earthly evil! One draught and the body slips off like a garment, while the soul walks forth in all its beauty and freedom. Trouble is over. One draught, and—Ah, let go, I say! What have you done? "

Kate had snatched the bottle from him, and with a quick feminine gesture had hurled it against the wall, where it splintered to pieces, sending a strong turpentiney odour through the apartment. Her strength was so impaired that she staggered back after this feat, and sat down on the side of the bed, while her guardian, grim and threatening, stood over her with his long, bony fingers opening and shutting, as though he found it difficult to keep them from her throat.

"I will not help you in it, " she said, in a low but firm voice. "You would kill my soul as well. "

The mask had fairly dropped from Girdlestone. No gaunt old wolf could have glared down with fiercer eyes or a more cruel mouth. "You fool! " he hissed.

"I am not afraid to die, " she said, looking up at him with brave, steadfast eyes.

Girdlestone recovered his self-possession by an effort. "It is clear to me, " he said calmly, "that your reason is unhinged. What is all this nonsense about death? There is nothing that will harm you except your own evil actions. " He turned abruptly and strode out of the room with the firm and decided step of a man who has taken an irrevocable resolution.

With a set and rigid face he ascended the steps which led to his bedroom, and, rummaging in his desk, produced a telegram form. This he filled up and took with him downstairs. There he put on his hat and started off to the Bedsworth Post-office at full speed.

At the avenue gate he met his sentinel, who was sitting on his camp stool as grim as ever.

"She is very bad, Stevens, " Girdlestone said, stopping and jerking his head in the direction of the house. "She is going downhill. I am afraid that she can't last long. If any one asks you about her, you can say that she was despaired of. I am just sending off a telegram to a doctor in London, so that she may have the best advice. "

Stevens touched his greasy-peaked cap as a token of respect. "She was down here behavin' outrageous the other day, " said he. "'Let me pass, ' says she, 'and you shall have ten golden guineas. ' Them's her very words. 'Not for ten hundred golden guineas, ' I answers, 'would William Stevens, hesquire, do what he didn't ought to. '"

"Very proper, very proper indeed, " said Girdlestone approvingly. "Every man in his own station has his own duties to fulfil, and he will be judged as he has fulfilled them, well or ill. I shall see that you are no loser by your staunchness. "

"Thank ye, guv'nor. "

"She is wild and delirious, and can get about in spite of her low state of health. It is possible that she may make some effort to get away, so be vigilant. Good day to you. "

"Good day, sir. " William Stevens stood at the gate, looking pensively after his employer; then he reseated himself upon his camp-stool, and, lighting his pipe, resumed his meditations. "I can't make nought of it, " he muttered, scratching his head, "It do seem uncommon queer, to be sure. The boss he says, 'She's very low, ' says he, and then next minute he says, 'She may be comin' down and tryin' to escape. 'I've seen diers o' all shapes and sizes, but I've never seed one as went a galivantin' about like this—at least, not among them as died a nat'ral death. It do seem uncommon strange. Then, again, he's off telegrayphin' for a doctor to Lunnon, when there's Doctor Corbett, o' Claxton, or Doctor Hutton, o' Bedsworth, would come quick enough if he wanted them. I can't make no sense of it. Why, bust my buttons! " he continued, taking his pipe out of his mouth in a paroxysm of astonishment, "if here hain't the dier herself! "

It was, indeed, Kate, who, learning that her guardian was gone, had come out with some vague idea of making a last struggle for her life and freedom. With the courage of despair, she came straight down the avenue to the sole spot where escape seemed possible.

"Good mornin', missy, " cried Stevens, as she approached. "You don't look extra bright this mornin', but you ain't as bad as your good guardian made me think. You don't seem to feel no difficulty in gettin' about. "

"There is nothing the matter with me, " the girl answered earnestly. "I assure you there is not. My mind is as sound as yours. "

"That's what they all says, " said the ex-warder with a chuckle.

"But it is so. I cannot stay in that house longer. I cannot, Mr. Stevens, I cannot! It is haunted, and my guardian will murder me. He means to. I read it in his eyes. He as good as tried this morning. To die without one word to those I love—without any explanation of what has passed—that would give a sting to death. "

"Well, if this ain't outragis! " cried the one-eyed man; "perfectly outragis! Going to murder you, says you! What's he a-goin' to do that for? "

"God knows! He hates me for some reason. I have never gone against his wishes, save in one respect, and in that I can never obey him, for it is a matter in which he has no right to command. "

"Quite so! " said Stevens, winking his one eye. "I knows the feeling myself, cuss me, but I do! 'Thine for once and thine for never, ' as the song says. "

"Why won't you let me pass? " pleaded Kate. "You may have had daughters of your own. What would you do if they were treated as I have been? If I had money you should have it, but I have none. Do, do let me go! God will reward you for it. Perhaps when you are on your last bed of sickness the memory of this one good deed may outweigh all the evil that you have done. "

"Lor', don't she speak! " said Stevens, appealing confidentially to the nearest tree. "It's like a dictionary. "

"And you won't lose by it in this life, " the girl added eagerly. "See, here is my watch and my chain. You shall have that if you will let me through? "

"Let's see it. " He opened it and examined it critically. "Eighteen carat—it's only a Geneva, though. What can you expect for a Geneva? "

"And you shall have fifty pounds when I get back to my friends. Do let me pass, good Mr. Stevens, for my guardian may return at any moment. "

"See here, miss, " Stevens said solemnly; "dooty is dooty, and if every hair of your 'ead was tagged wi' a jewel, and you offered to make me your barber, I wouldn't let you through that gate. As to this 'ere watch, if so be as you would like to write a line to your friends, I'll post it for you at Bedsworth in exchange for it, though it be only a Geneva. "

"You good, kind man! " cried Kate, all excitement and delight. "I have a pencil in my pocket. What shall I do for paper? " She looked eagerly round and spied a small piece which lay among the brushwood. With a cry of joy she picked it out. It was very coarse and very dirty, but she managed to scrawl a few lines upon it, describing her situation and asking for aid. "I will write the address upon the back, " she said. "When you get to Bedsworth you must buy an envelope and ask the post-office people to copy the address on to it. "

"I bargained to post it for the Geneva, " he said. "I didn't bargain to buy envelopes and copy addresses. That's a nice pencil-case of yourn. Now I'll make a clean job of it if you'll throw that in. "

Kate handed it over without a murmur. At last a small ray of light seemed to be finding its way through the darkness which had so long surrounded her. Stevens put the watch and pencil-case in his pocket, and took the little scrap of paper on which so much depended. As Kate handed it to him she saw over his shoulder that coming up the lane was a small pony-carriage, in which sat a buxom lady and a very small page. The sleek little brown pony which drew it ambled along at a methodical pace which showed that it was entirely master of the situation, while the whole turnout had an indescribable air of comfort and good nature. Poor Kate had been so separated from her kind that the sight of people who, if not friendly, were at least not hostile to her, sent a thrill of pleasure into her heart. There was something wholesome and prosaic too about this homely equipage, which was inexpressibly soothing to a mind so worn by successive terrors.

"Here's some one a-comin', " cried Stevens. "Clear out from here—it's the governor's orders. "

"Oh, do let me stay and say one word to the lady! " Stevens seized his great stick savagely. "Clear out! " he cried in a hoarse, angry voice, and made a step towards her as if he would strike her. She shrank away from him, and then, a sudden thought seizing her, she turned and ran through the woods as fast as her feeble strength would allow. The instant that she was out of sight, Stevens very deliberately and carefully tore up the little slip of paper with which she had entrusted him, and scattered the pieces to the wind.

CHAPTER XXXIX.

A GLEAM OF LIGHT.

Kate Harston fled as quickly as she could through the wood, stumbling over the brambles and crashing through the briars, regardless of pain or scratches or anything else which could stand between her and the possibility of safety. She soon gained the shed and managed to mount on to the top of it by the aid of the barrel. Craning her neck, she could see the long dusty lane, with the bare withered hedges upon either side, and the dreary line of the railway embankment beyond. There was no pony-carriage in sight.

She hardly expected that there would be, for she had taken a short cut, and the carriage would have to go some distance round. The road along which it was travelling ran at right angles to the one which she was now overlooking, and the chances were equal as to whether the lady would turn round or go straight on. In the latter case, it would not be possible for her to attract her attention. Her heart seemed to stand still with anxiety as she peered over the high wall at the spot where the two roads crossed.

Presently she heard the rattle of wheels, and the brown pony trotted round the corner. The carriage drew up at the end of the lane, and the driver seemed to be uncertain how to proceed. Then she shook the reins, and the pony lumbered on along the road. Kate gave a cry of despair and the last ray of hope died away from her heart.

It chanced, however, that the page in the carriage was just at that happy age when the senses are keen and on the alert. He heard the cry, and glancing round he saw through a break in the hedge that a lady was looking over the wall which skirted the lane they had passed. He mentioned the fact to his mistress.

"Maybe we'd better go back, ma'am, " he said.

"Maybe we'd better not, John, " said the buxom lady. "People can look over their garden walls without our interfering with them, can't they? "

"Yes, ma'am, but she was a-hollerin' at us. "

"No, John, was she though? Maybe this is a private road and we have no right to be on it. "

"She gave a holler as if some one was a-hurtin' of her, " said John with decision.

"Then we'll go back, " said the lady, and turned the pony round.

Hence it came about that just as Kate was descending with a sad heart from her post of observation, she was electrified to see the brown pony reappear and come trotting round the curve of the lane, with a rapidity which was altogether foreign to that quadruped's usual habits. Indeed, the girl turned so very white at the sight, and her face assumed such an expression of relief and delight, that the lady who was approaching saw at once that it was no common matter which had caused her to summon them.

"What is it, my dear? " she cried, pulling up when she came abreast of the place. Her good, kind heart was touched already by the pleading expression upon the girl's sweet face.

"Oh, madam, whoever you may be, " said Kate, in a low, rapid voice, "I believe God has sent you here this day. I am shut up in these grounds, and shall be murdered unless help comes. "

"Be murdered! " cried the lady in the pony-carriage, dropping back in her seat and raising her hands in astonishment.

"It is only too true, " Kate said, trying to speak concisely and clearly so as to enforce conviction, but feeling a choking sensation about her throat, as though an hysterical attack were impending. "My guardian has shut me up here for some weeks, and I firmly believe that he will never let me out alive. Oh, don't, pray don't think me mad! I am as sane as you are, though, God knows, what I have gone through has been enough to shake my reason. "

This last appeal of Kate's was in answer to an expression of incredulity and doubt which had passed over the face of the lady below. It was successful in its object, for the ring of truth with which she spoke and the look of anxiety and terror upon her face were too genuine to be mistaken. The lady drew her rein so as to bring the carriage as near the wall as was possible without losing sight of Kate's face.

"My dear, " she said, "you may safely tell me everything. Whatever I can do to help you shall be done, and where I am powerless there are others who are my friends and may be of assistance. Scully is my name— Mrs. Lavinia Scully, of London. Don't cry, my poor girl, but tell me all about it, and let us see how we can put matters right. "

Thus encouraged, Kate wiped away the tears which had been brought to her eyes by the unwonted sound of a friendly voice. Leaning forward as far as she could, and preventing herself from falling by passing her arm round a great branch which shot across the top of the shed, she gave in as few words as she could a detailed account of all that had befallen her. She described her guardian's anxiety that she should marry his son, her refusal, their sudden departure from London, their life at the Priory, the manner in which she was cut off from all human aid, and the reasons which made her believe that an attempt would be made upon her life. In conclusion, she narrated the scene which had occurred that very morning, when her guardian had tempted her to commit suicide. The only incident which she omitted from her story was that which had occurred the night before, for she felt that it might put too severe a tax upon Mrs. Scully's credulity. Indeed, looking back at it, she almost persuaded herself that the sight which she had seen might be some phantom conjured up by her own imagination, weakened as she was in mind and in body.

Having concluded her narrative, she wound up by imploring her new-found friend to assist her by letting her friends in London know what had become of her and where she was. Mrs. Scully listened with a face which expressed alternately the most profound pity and the most burning indignation. When Kate had finished, she sat silent for a minute or more entirely absorbed in her own thoughts. She switched her whip up and down viciously, and her usually placid countenance assumed an expression so fierce that Kate, looking down at her, feared that she had given her offence. When she looked up at last, however, she smiled so pleasantly that the poor girl was reassured, and felt instinctively that she had really found a true and effective friend at last.

"We must act promptly, " she said, "for we don't know what they may be about, or what their plans are for the future. Who did you say your friends were? "

"Dr. Dimsdale, of Phillimore Gardens, Kensington. "

"Hasn't he got a grown-up son? "

"Yes, " said Kate, with a slight flush on her pale cheeks.

"Ah! " cried the good lady, with a very roguish smile. "I see how the land lies. Of course, of course, why shouldn't it? I remember hearing about that young man. I have heard about the Girdlestones also. African merchants they were in the City. You see I know all about you. "

"You know Tom? " Kate cried in astonishment.

"Oh, don't let us get talking of Tom, " said Mrs. Scully good-humouredly. "When girls get on a subject of that sort there's an end to everything. What I want now is business. In the first place I shall drive down to Bedsworth, and I shall send to London. "

"God bless you! " ejaculated Kate.

"But not to Phillimore Gardens. Hot-headed young men do foolish things under such circumstances as these. This is a case that wants careful management. I know a gentleman in London who is just the man, and who I know would be only too proud to help a lady in distress. He is a retired officer, and his name is Major Clutterbuck—Major Tobias Clutterbuck. "

"Oh, I know him very well, and I have heard of you, too, " said Kate, with a smile. "I remember your name now in connection with his. "

It was Mrs. Scully's turn to blush now. "Never mind that, " she said. "I can trust the major, and I know he will be down here at a word from me. I shall let him have the facts, and he can tell the Dimsdales if he thinks it best. Good-bye, dear; don't be unhappy any more, but remember that you have friends outside who will very quickly set all right. Good-bye! " and waving her hand in encouragement, the good widow woke up the pony, which had fallen fast asleep, and rattled away down the lane in the direction from which she had come.

CHAPTER XL.

THE MAJOR HAS A LETTER.

At four o'clock Mr. Girdlestone stepped into the Bedsworth telegraph office and wired his short message. It ran thus: "Case hopeless. Come on to-morrow with a doctor. " On receipt of this he knew by their agreement that his son would come down, bringing with him the man of violence whom he had spoken of at their last interview. There was nothing for it now but that his ward should die. If he delayed longer, the crash might come before her money was available, and then how vain all regrets would be.

It seemed to him that there was very little risk in the matter. The girl had had no communication with any one. Even of those around her, Mrs. Jorrocks was in her dotage, Rebecca Taylforth was staunch and true, and Stevens knew nothing. Every one on the country side had heard of the invalid young lady at the Priory. Who would be surprised to hear that she had passed away? He dare not call in any local medical man, but his inventive brain had overcome the difficulty, and had hit upon a device by which he might defy both doctors and coroner. If all went as he had planned it, it was difficult to see any chance of detection. In the case of a poorer man the fact that the girl's money reverted to him might arouse suspicion, but he rightly argued that with his great reputation no one would ever dream that such a consideration could have weight with him.

Having sent the telegram off, and so taken a final step, John Girdlestone felt more at his ease. He was proud of his own energy and decision. As he walked very pompously and gravely down the village street, his heart glowed within him at the thought of the long struggle which he had maintained against misfortune. He passed over in his mind all the successive borrowings and speculations and makeshifts and ruses which the firm had resorted to. Yet, in spite of every danger and difficulty, it still held up its head with the best, and would weather the storm at last. He reflected proudly that there was no other man in the City who would have had the dogged tenacity and the grim resolution which he had displayed during the last twelve months. "If ever any one should put it all in a book, " he said to himself, "there are few who would believe it possible. It is not by my own strength that I have done it. "

The man had no consciousness of blasphemy in him as he revolved this thought in his mind. He was as thoroughly in earnest as were any of those religious fanatics who, throughout history, have burned, sacked, and destroyed, committing every sin under heaven in the name of a God of peace and of mercy.

When he was half-way to the Priory he met a small pony-carriage, which was rattling towards Bedsworth at a great pace, driven by a good-looking middle-aged lady with a small page by her side. The merchant encountered this equipage in a narrow country lane without a footpath, and as it approached him he could not help observing that the lady wore an indignant and gloomy look upon her features which was out of keeping with their general contour. Her forehead was contracted into a very decided frown, and her lips were gathered into what might be described as a negative smile. Girdlestone stood aside to let her pass, but the lady, by a sudden twitch of her right-hand rein, brought the wheels across in so sudden a manner that they were within an ace of going over his toes. He only saved himself by springing back into a gap of the hedge. As it was, he found on looking down that his pearl grey trousers were covered with flakes of wet mud. What made the incident more perplexing was that both the middle-aged lady and the page laughed very heartily as they rattled away to the village. The merchant proceeded on his way marvelling in his heart at the uncharitableness and innate wickedness of unregenerated human nature.

Good Mrs. Scully little dreamed of the urgency of the case. Had she seen the telegram which John Girdlestone had just despatched, it is conceivable that she might have read between the words, and by acting more promptly have prevented a terrible crime. As a matter of fact, with all her sympathy the worthy woman had taken a large part of Kate's story with the proverbial grain of salt. It seemed to her to be incredible and impossible that in this nineteenth century such a thing as deliberate and carefully planned murder should occur in Christian England. That these things occur in the abstract we are ready to admit, but we find it very difficult to realize that they may come within the horizon of our own experience. Hence Mrs. Scully set no importance upon Kate's fears for her life, and put them down to the excited state of the girl's imagination. She did consider it, however, to be a very iniquitous and unjustifiable thing that a young girl should be cooped up and separated from all the world in such a very dreary place of seclusion as the Priory. This consideration and nothing more serious had set that look of wrath upon her pleasant face, and had stirred her up to frustrate Girdlestone and to communicate with Kate's friends.

Her intention had been to telegraph to London, but as she drove to Bedsworth she bethought her how impossible it would be for her within the limits of a telegram to explain to her satisfaction all that she wanted to express. A letter, she reflected, would, if posted now, reach the major by the first post on Saturday morning. It would simply mean a few hours' delay in the taking of steps to relieve Kate, and what difference could a few hours more or less make to the girl. She determined, therefore, that she would write to the major, explaining all the circumstances, and leave it to him what course of action should be pursued.

Mrs. Scully was well known at the post office, and they quickly accommodated her with the requisites for correspondence. Within a quarter of an hour she had written, sealed, stamped, and posted the following epistle: —

"DEAREST TOBY,

"I am afraid you must find your period of probation very slow. Poor boy! what does he do? No billiards, no cards, no betting— how does he manage to get through the day at all? Smokes, I suppose, and looks out of the window, and tells all his grievances to Mr. Von Baumser. Aren't you sorry that ever you made the acquaintance of Morrison's second floor front? Poor Toby!

"Who do you think I have come across down here? No less a person than that Miss Harston who was Girdlestone's ward. You used to talk about her, I remember, and indeed you were a great admirer of hers. You would be surprised if you saw her now, so thin and worn and pale. Still her face is very sweet and pretty, so I won't deny your good taste—how could I after you have paid your addresses to me?

"Her guardian has brought her down here and has locked her up in a great bleak house called the Priory. She has no one to speak to, and is not allowed to write letters. She seemed to be heart-broken because none of her friends know where she is, and she fears that they may imagine that she has willingly deserted them. Of course, by her friends she means that curly-headed Mr. Dimsdale that you spoke of. The poor girl is in a very low nervous state, and told me over the wall of the park that she feared her guardian had designs on her life. I can hardly believe that, but I do think that she is far from well, and that it is enough to drive her mad to coop her up like that. We must get her out somehow or another. I suppose that her guardian is within his rights, and that it is not a police matter. You must consider what must be done, and let young Dimsdale know if you think best. He will want to come down to see her, no doubt, and if Toby were to come too I should not be sorry.

"I should have telegraphed about it, but I could not explain myself sufficiently. I assure you that the poor girl is in a very bad way, and we can't be too energetic in what we do. It was very sad to hear the positive manner in which she declared that her guardian would murder her, though she did not attempt to give any reason why he should commit such a terrible crime. We saw a horrid one-eyed man at the gate, who appeared to be on guard to prevent any one from coming out or in. On our way to Bedsworth we met no less a person than the great Mr. Girdlestone himself, and we actually drove so clumsily that we splashed him all over with mud. Wasn't that a very sad and unaccountable thing? I fancy I see Toby smiling over that.

"Good-bye, my dear lad. Be as good as you can. I know you've got rather out of the way of it, but practice works wonders.

"Ever yours,

"LAVINIA SCULLY. "

It happened that on the morning on which this missive came to Kennedy Place, Von Baumser had not gone to the City. The major had just performed his toilet and was marching up and down with a cigarette in his mouth and the *United Service Gazette* in his hand, descanting fluently, as is the habit of old soldiers, on the favouritism of the Horse Guards and the deterioration of the service.

"Look at this fellow Carmoichael! " he cried excitedly, slapping the paper with one, hand, while he crumpled it up with the other.

"They've made him lieutinant-gineral! The demndest booby in the regiment, sir! A fellow who's seen no service and never heard a shot fired in anger. They promoted him on the stringth of a sham fight, bedad! He commanded a definding force operating along the Thames and opposing an invading army that was advancing from Guildford. Did iver ye hear such infernal nonsense in your life? And there's Stares, and Knight, and Underwood, and a dozen more I could mintion, that have volunteered for everything since the Sikh war of '46, all neglicted, sir—neglicted! The British Army is going straight to the divil. "

"Dat's a very bad look-out for the devil, " said Von Baumser, filling up a cup of coffee.

The major continued to stride angrily about the room. "That's why we niver have a satisfactory campaign with a European foe, " he broke out. "Our success is always half and half, and leads to nothing. Yet we have the finest raw material and the greatest individual fighting power and divilment of any army in the world. "

"Always, of course, not counting de army of his most graceworthy majesty de Emperor William, " said Von Baumser, with his mouth full of toast. "Here is de girl mit a letter. Let us hope dat it is my Frankfort money. "

"Two to one it's for me. "

"Ah, he must not bet! " cried Von Baumser, with upraised finger. "You have right, though. It is for you, and from de proper quarter too, I think. "

It was the letter which we have already quoted. The major broke the seal and read it over very carefully, after which he read it again. Von Baumser, watching him across the table, saw a very anxious and troubled look upon his ruddy face.

"I hope dere is nothing wrong mit my good vriend, Madame Scully? " he remarked at last.

"No, nothing wrong with her. There is with some one else, though; " and with that he read to his companion all that part of his letter which referred to Miss Harston.

"Dat is no joke at all, " the German remarked; and the two sat for some little time lost in thought, the major with the letter still lying open upon his knee.

"What d'ye think of it? " he asked at last.

"I think dat it is a more bad thing than the good madame seems to think. I think dat if Miss Harston says dat Herr Girdlestone intends to kill her, it is very likely dat he has dat intention"

"Ged, he's not a man to stick at troifles, " the major said, rubbing his chin reflectively. "Here's a nice kettle of fish! What the deuce could cause him to do such a thing? "

"Money, of course. I have told you, my good vriend, dat since a year de firm has been in a very bad way indeed. It is not generally known, but I know it, and so do others. Dis girl, I have heard, has money which would come to de old man in case of her death. It is as plain as de vingers on my hand. "

"Be George, the thing looks very ugly! " said the major, pacing up and down the room. "I believe that fellow and his beauty of a son are game for anything. Lavinia takes the mather too lightly. Fancy any one being such a scounthrel as to lay a hand on that dear girl, though. Ged, Baumser, it makes ivery drop of blood in me body tingle in me veins! "

"My dear vriend, " Von Baumser answered, "it is very good of your blood for to tingle, but I do not see how dat will help the mees. Let us be practical, and make up our brains what we should do. "

"I must find young Dimsdale at once. He has a right to know. "

"Yes, I should find him. Dere is no doubt that you and he should at once start off for dis place. I know dat young man. Dere vill be no holding him at all when he has heard of it. You must go too, to prevent him from doing dummheiten, and also because good Madame Scully has said so in her letter. "

"Certainly. We shall go down togither. One of us will manage to see the young lady and find out if she requoires assistance. Bedad, if she does, she shall have it, guardian or no guardian. If we don't whip her out in a brace of shakes me name's not Clutterbuck. "

"You must remember, " remarked Baumser, "dat dese people are desperate. If dey intend to murder a voman dey vould certainly not stick at a man or two men. You have no knowledge of how many dere may be. Dere is certainly Herr Girdlestone and his son and de man mit de eye, but madame knows not how many may be at de house. Remember also dat de police are not on your side, but rather against you, for as yet dere is no evidence dat any crime is intentioned. Ven you think of all dis I am sure dat you vill agree with me dat it would be vell to take mit you two or tree men dat would stick by you through thin and broad. "

The major was so busy in making his preparations for departure that he could only signify by a nod that he agreed with his friend's remarks. "What men could I git? " he asked.

"Dere is I myself, " said the German, counting upon his big red fingers, "and dere are some of our society who would very gladly come on such an errand, and are men who are altogether to be relied upon. Dere is little Fritz Bulow, of Kiel, and a Russian man whose name I disremember, but he is a good man. He vas a Nihilist at Odessa, and is sentenced to death suppose they could him catch. Dere are others as good, but it might take me time to find dem. Dese two I can very easily get. Dey are living together, and have neither of dem nothing to do. "

"Bring them, then, " said the major. "Git a cab and run them down to Waterloo Station. That's the one for Bedsworth. I'll bring Dimsdale down with me and mate you there. In me opinion there's no time to be lost. "

The major was ready to start, so Von Baumser threw on his coat and hat, and picked out a thick stick from a rack in the corner. "We may need something of de sort, " he said.

"I have me derringer, " the soldier answered. They left the house together, and Von Baumser drove off to the East End, where his political friends resided. The major called a cab and rattled away to Phillimore Gardens and thence to the office, without being able to find the man of whom he was in search. He then rushed down the Strand as quickly as he could, intending to catch the next train and go alone, but on his way to Waterloo Station he fell in with Tom Dimsdale, as recorded in a preceding chapter.

The letter was a thunderbolt to Tom, In his worst dreams he had never imagined anything so dark as this. He hurried back to the station at such a pace that the poor major was reduced to a most asthmatical and wheezy condition. He trotted along pluckily, however, and as he went heard the account of Tom's adventures in the morning and of the departure of Ezra Girdlestone and of his red-bearded companion. The major's face grew more anxious still when he heard of it. "Pray God we may not be too late! " he panted.

CHAPTER XLI.

THE CLOUDS GROW DARKER.

When Kate had made a clean breast of all her troubles to the widow Scully, and had secured that good woman's co-operation, a great weight seemed to have been lifted from her heart, and she sprang from the shed a different woman. It would soon be like a dream, all these dreary weeks in the grim old house. Within a day she was sure that either Tom or the major would find means of communicating with her. The thought made her so happy that the colour stole back into her cheeks, and she sang for very lightness of heart as she made her way back to the Priory.

Mrs. Jorrocks and Rebecca observed the change which had come over her and marvelled at it. Kate attempted to aid the former in her household work, but the old crone refused her assistance and repulsed her harshly. Her maid too answered her curtly when she addressed her, and eyed her in anything but a friendly manner.

"You don't seem much the worse, " she remarked, "for all the wonderful things you seed in the night. "

"Oh, don't speak of it, " said Kate. "I am afraid that I have given you a great fright. I was feeling far from well, and I suppose that I must have imagined all about that dreadful monk. Yet, at the time, I assure you that I saw it as plainly as I see you now. "

"What's that she says? " asked Mrs. Jorrocks, with her hand to her ear.

"She says that she saw a ghost last night as plain as she sees you now. "

"Pack of nonsense! " cried the old woman, rattling the poker in the grate. "I've been here afore she came—all alone in the house, too—and I hain't seen nothing of the sort. When she's got nothing else to grumble about she pretends as she has seen a ghost. "

"No, no, " the girl said cheerily. "I am not grumbling—indeed I am not. "

"It's like her contrariness to say so, " old Mrs. Jorrocks cried hoarsely. "She's always a-contradictin'. "

"You're not in a good temper to-day, " Kate remarked, and went off to her room, going up the steps two at a time with her old springy footstep.

Rebecca followed her, and noticing the change, interpreted it in her own narrow fashion.

"You seems cheerful enough now, " she said, standing at Kate's door and looking into her room, with a bitter smile on her lips. "To-morrow is Saturday. That's what's the matter with you. "

"To-morrow Saturday! " Kate repeated in astonishment.

"Yes; you know what I mean well enough. It's no use pretending that you don't. "

The girl's manner was so aggressive that Kate was astonished. "I haven't the least idea of what you mean, " she said.

"Oh no, " cried Rebecca, with her arms akimbo and a sneer on her face. "She doesn't know what I mean. She doesn't know that her young man is coming down on the Saturday. She does not know that Mr. Ezra comes all the way from London on that day just for to see her. It isn't that that makes you cheerful, is it? Oh, you double face! " The girl's pretty features were all distorted with malice as she spoke, and her two hands were clenched passionately.

"Rebecca! " cried Kate energetically, "I really think that you are the most complete fool that ever I met in my life. I will trouble you to remember that I am your mistress and you are my servant. How dare you speak to me in such a way? Leave my room this instant! "

The girl stood her ground as though she intended to brazen it out, but Kate swept towards her with so much honest anger in her voice, and such natural dignity in her bearing, that she sank her bold gaze, and with a few muttered words slunk away into her own room. Kate closed the door behind her, and then, her sense of the ludicrous overpowering her anger, she laughed for the first time since she had been in the Priory. It was so intensely ridiculous that even the most foolish of mortals should imagine that she could, under any circumstances, be desirous of seeing Ezra Girdlestone. The very thought of him brought her amusement to an end, for the maid was right, and to-morrow would bring him down once more. Perhaps her friends might arrive before he did. God grant it!

It was a cold but a bright day. From her window she could see the snow-white sails of the Hampshire fishing-boats dipping and rising against the deep blue sea. A single barque rode amongst them, like a swan among ducklings, beating up against the wind for Portsmouth or Southampton. Away on the right was the long line of white foam which marked the Winner Sands. The tide was in and the great mudbanks had disappeared, save that here and there their dun-coloured convexity rose above the surface like the back of a sleeping leviathan. Overhead a great flock of wild geese were flapping their way southward, like a broad arrow against the sky. It was an exhilarating, bracing scene, and accorded well with her own humour. She felt so full of life and hope that she could hardly believe that she was the same girl who that very morning had hurled away the poison bottle, knowing in her heart that unless she destroyed it she might be tempted to follow her guardian's sinister suggestions. Yet the incident was real enough, for there were the fragments of glass scattered over the bare planks of her floor, and the insidious odour of the drug was still so strong that she opened the window in order to dissipate it. Looking back at it now, it all seemed like some hideous nightmare.

She had no very clear idea as to what she expected her friends to do. That she would be saved, and that speedily, she never for one instant doubted. She had only to wait patiently and all would be well. By to-morrow night, at the latest, her troubles would be over.

So thought Girdlestone too, as he sat down below, with his head bent upon his breast and his eyes looking moodily from under his shaggy brows at the glowing coals. To-morrow evening would settle the matter once and for ever. Burt and Ezra would be down by five o'clock, and that would be the beginning of the end. As to Burt's future there was no difficulty about that. He was a broken man. If well supplied with unlimited liquor he would not live long to trouble them. He had nothing to gain, and everything to lose by denouncing them. Should the worst come to the worst, the ravings of a dipsomaniac could do little harm to a man as respected as the African merchant. Every event had been foreseen and provided for by the old schemer. Above all, he had devised a method by which even a coroner's inquiry could be faced with impunity, and which would do away with all necessity for elaborate concealment.

He beckoned Mrs. Jorrocks over to him, for he had been sitting in the large room, which was used both as a dining-room and as a kitchen.

"What is the latest train to-morrow? " he asked.

"There be one that reaches Bedsworth at a quarter to ten. "

"It passes the grounds at about twenty to ten, then? "

"That reg'lar that I could set my clock by it. "

"That'll do. Where is Miss Harston? "

"Upstairs, sir. She came back a-laughin' and a-jumpin' and as sassy as you please to them as was old before she was born. "

"Laughing! " said Girdlestone, raising his eyebrows. "She did not seem in a laughing mood this morning. You don't think she has gone out of her mind, do you? "

"I don't know nought about that. There was Rebecca came down here a-cryin' 'cause she'd ordered her out of her room. Oh, she's mistress of the house—there's no doubt about that. She'll be a-givin' of us all the sack presently. "

Girdlestone relapsed into silence, but his face showed that he was puzzled by what he had heard.

Kate slept a sound and dreamless sleep that night. At her age trouble is shaken from the young mind like water from the feathers of a duck. It had been all very gloomy and terrible while it lasted, but now the dawn of better days had come. She woke cheerful and light-hearted. She felt that when once she was free she could forgive her guardian and Rebecca and all of them—even Ezra. She would bury the whole hideous incident, and never think of it or refer to it again.

She amused herself that morning by reckoning up in her mind what the sequence of events would be in London, and how long it would be before she heard from her friends. If Mrs. Scully had telegraphed, news would have reached them last night. Probably she would write as well, giving all the particulars about her. The post came in about nine o'clock, she thought. Then some time would elapse before the major could find Tom. After that, no doubt they would have to consider what had best be done, and perhaps would go and consult with Dr. Dimsdale. That would occupy the morning and part of the afternoon. They could hardly reach the Priory before nightfall.

Ezra would be down by that time. On the Saturday before he had arrived between five and six. A great dread filled her soul at the thought of meeting the young merchant again. It was merely the natural instinct of a lady shrinking from whatever is rough and coarse and antagonistic. She had no conception of the impending danger, or of what his coming might mean to her.

Mr. Girdlestone was more gracious to her than usual that morning at breakfast. He seemed anxious to efface the remembrance of his fierce and threatening words the day before. Rebecca, who waited upon them, was astonished to hear the way in which he spoke. His whole manner was less heavy and ungainly than usual, for now that the time for action was at hand he felt braced and invigorated, as energetic men do.

"You should study botany while you are down here, " he said blandly. "Depend upon it, one cannot learn too many things in one's youth. Besides, a knowledge of natural science teaches us the marvellous harmony which prevails throughout the universe, and so enlarges our minds. "

"I should very much like to know something of it, " answered Kate. "My only fear is that I should not be clever enough to learn it. "

"The wood here is full of wonders. The tiniest mushroom is as extraordinary and as worthy of study as the largest oak. Your father was fond of plants and animals. "

"Yes, I can remember that, " said Kate, her face growing sad as her mind travelled back to years gone by. What would that same father have thought, she wondered, had he known how this man opposite to her had treated her! What did it matter now, though, when she would so soon be out of his power!

"I remember, " said Girdlestone, stirring his tea thoughtfully, "when we lived in the City as 'prentice lads together, we shared a room above the shop. He used to have a dormouse that he was very fond of. All his leisure time was spent in nursing the creature and cleaning its cage. It seemed to be his only pleasure in life. One night it was running across the floor, and I put my foot upon it. "

"Oh, poor papa! " cried Kate.

"I did it upon principle. 'You have devoted too much time to the creature, ' I said. 'Raise up your thoughts higher! ' He was grieved and angry, but in time he came to thank me. It was a useful lesson. "

Kate was so startled by this anecdote that she remained silent for some little time. "How old were you then? " she asked at last.

"I was about sixteen. "

"Then you were always—inclined that way? " She found some difficulty in conveying her meaning in polite tones.

"Yes; I received a call when I was very young. I became one of the elect at an early age. "

"And which are the elect? " his ward asked demurely.

"The members of the Community of the Primitive Trinitarians—or, at least those of them who frequent Purbrook Street Chapel. I hold that the ministers in the other chapels that I have attended do not preach the unadulterated Word, and have therefore missed the narrow path. "

"Then, " said Kate, "you think that no one will be saved except those who frequent the Purbrook Street Chapel? "

"And not all of them—no, nor one in ten, " the merchant said confidently, and with some approach to satisfaction. "Heaven must be a very small place, " Kate remarked, as she rose from the table.

"Are you going out? "

"I was thinking of having a stroll in the wood. "

"Think over a text as you walk. It is an excellent commencement of the day. "

"What text should I think of? " she asked, standing smiling in the doorway, with the bright sunshine bursting in behind her.

"'In the midst of life we are in death, '" he said solemnly. His voice was so hollow and stern that it struck a chill into the girl's heart. The effect was only momentary, however. The day was so fine, and the breeze so fresh, that sadness was out of the question. Besides, was not her deliverance at hand! On this of all mornings she should be free from vague presentiments and dim forebodings. The change in her guardian's manner was an additional cause for cheerfulness. She almost persuaded herself that she had misconstrued his words and his intentions upon the preceding day.

She went down the avenue and had a few words with the sentry there. She felt no bitterness against him now—on the contrary, she could afford to laugh at his peculiarities. He was in a very bad humour on account of some domestic difficulties. His wife had been abusing him, and had ended by assaulting him. "She used to argey first, and then fetch the poker, " he said ruefully; "but now it's the poker first, and there ain't no argeyment at all. "

Kate looked at his savage face and burly figure, and thought what a very courageous woman his wife must be.

"It's all 'cause the fisher lasses won't lemme alone, " he explained with a leer. "She don't like it, knock me sideways if she do! It ain't my fault, though. I allers had a kind o' a fetchin' way wi' women. "

"Did you post my note? " asked Kate.

"Yes, in course I did, " he answered. "It'll be in Lunnon now, most like. " His one eye moved about in such a very shifty way as he spoke that she was convinced that he was telling a lie. She could not be sufficiently thankful that she had something else to rely upon besides the old scoundrel's assurances.

There was nothing to be seen down the lane except a single cart with a loutish young man walking at the horse's head. She had a horror of the country folk since her encounter with the two bumpkins upon the Sunday. She therefore slipped away from the gate, and went through the wood to the shed, which she mounted. On the other side of the wall there was standing a little boy in buttons, so rigid and motionless that he might have been one of Madame Tussaud's figures, were it not for his eyes, which were rolling about in every direction, and which finally fixed themselves on Kate's face.

"Good morning, miss, " said this apparition.

"Good morning, " she answered. "I think I saw you with Mrs. Scully yesterday? "

"Yes, miss. Missus, she told me to wait here and never to move until I seed you. She said as you would be sure to come. I've been waitin' here for nigh on an hour. "

"Your mistress is an angel, " Kate said enthusiastically, "and you are a very good little boy. "

"Indeed, you've hit it about the missus, " said the youth, in a hoarse whisper, nodding his head to emphasize his remarks. "She's got a heart as is big enough for three. "

Kate could not help smiling at the enthusiasm with which the little fellow spoke.

"You seem fond of her, " she said.

"I'd be a bad 'un if I wasn't. She took me out of the work'us without character or nothing, and now she's a-educatin' of me. She sent me 'ere with a message? "

"What was it? "

"She said as how she had written instead o' electro-telegraphing, 'cause she had so much to say she couldn't fit it all on a telegraph. "

"I thought that would be so, " Kate said.

"She wrote to Major—Major—him as is a-follerin' of her. She said as she had no doubt as he'd be down to-day, and you was to keep up your sperrits and let her know by me if any one was a-wexin' you. "

"No, no. Not at all, " Kate answered, smiling again. "You can tell her that my guardian has been much kinder to-day. I am full of hope now. Give her my warmest thanks for her kindness. "

"All right, miss. Say, that chap at the gate hasn't been giving you no cheek has he—him with the game eye? "

"No, no, John. "

John looked at her suspiciously. "If he hasn't, it's all right, " he said; "but I think as you're one of them as don't complain if you can 'elp it. " He opened his hand and showed a great jagged flint which he carried. "I'd ha' knocked his other peeper out with this, " he said, "blowed if I wouldn't! "

"Don't do anything of the sort, John, but run home like a good little boy. "

"All right, miss. Good-bye to ye! "

Kate watched him stroll down the lane. He paused at the bottom as if irresolute, and then she was relieved to see him throw the stone over into a turnip field, and walk rapidly off in the opposite direction to the Priory gates.

CHAPTER XLII.

THE THREE FACES AT THE WINDOW.

Late in the afternoon Ezra arrived at the Priory. From one of the passage windows Kate saw him driving up the avenue in a high dog-cart. There was a broad-shouldered, red-bearded man sitting beside him, and the ostler from the *Flying Bull* was perched behind. Kate had rushed to the window on hearing the sound of wheels, with some dim expectation that her friends had come sooner than she anticipated. A glance, however, showed her that the hope was vain. From behind a curtain she watched them alight and come into the house, while the trap wheeled round and rattled off for Bedsworth again.

She went slowly back to her room, wondering what friend this could be whom Ezra had brought with him. She had noticed that he was roughly clad, presenting a contrast to the young merchant, who was vulgarly spruce in his attire. Evidently he intended to pass the night at the Priory, since they had let the trap go back to the village. She was glad that he had come, for his presence would act as a restraint upon the Girdlestones. In spite of her guardian's amiability at breakfast, she could not forget the words which he had used the morning before or the incident of the poison bottle. She was as convinced as ever that he meant mischief to her, but she had ceased to fear him. It never for one moment occurred to her that her guardian's machinations might come to a head before her rescuers could arrive.

As the long afternoon stole away she became more and more impatient and expectant. She had been sewing in her room, but she found that she could no longer keep her attention on the stitches. She paced nervously up and down the little apartment. In the room beneath she could hear the dull muffled sound of men's voices in a long continuous monotone, broken only by the interposition now and again of one voice which was so deep and loud that it reminded her of the growl of a beast of prey. This must belong to the red-bearded stranger. Kate wondered what it could be that they were talking over so earnestly. City affairs, no doubt, or other business matters of importance. She remembered having once heard it remarked that many of the richest men on 'Change were eccentric and slovenly in their dress, so the new-comer might be a more important person than he seemed.

She had determined to remain in her room all the afternoon to avoid Ezra, but her restlessness was so great that she felt feverish and hot. The fresh air, she thought, would have a reviving effect upon her. She slipped down the staircase, treading as lightly as possible not to disturb the gentlemen in the refectory. They appeared to hear her however, for the hum of conversation died away, and there was a dead silence until after she had passed.

She went out on to the little lawn which lay in front of the old house. There were some flower-beds scattered about on it, but they were overgrown with weeds and in the last stage of neglect. She amused herself by attempting to improve the condition of one of them and kneeling down beside it she pulled up a number of the weeds which covered it. There was a withered rose-bush in the centre, so she pulled up that also, and succeeded in imparting some degree of order among the few plants which remained. She worked with unnatural energy, pausing every now and again to glance down the dark avenue, or to listen intently to any chance sound which might catch her ear.

In the course of her work she chanced to look up at the Priory. The refectory faced the lawn, and at the window of it there stood the three men looking out at her. The Girdlestones were nodding their heads, as though they were pointing her out to the third man, who stood between them. He was looking at her with an expression of interest. Kate thought as she returned his gaze that she had never seen a more savage and brutal face. He was flushed and laughing, while Ezra beside him appeared to be pale and anxious. They all, when they saw that she noticed them, stepped precipitately back from the window. She had only a momentary glance at them, and yet the three faces—the strange fierce red one, and the two hard familiar pale ones which flanked it—remained vividly impressed upon her memory.

Girdlestone had been so pleased at the early appearance of his allies, and the prospect of settling the matter once for all, that he received them with a cordiality which was foreign to his nature.

"Always punctual, my dear son, and always to be relied upon, " he said. "You are a model to our young business men. As to you, Mr.

Burt, " he continued, grasping the navvy's horny hand, "I am delighted to see you at the Priory, much as I regret the sad necessity which has brought you down. "

"Talk it over afterwards, " said Ezra shortly. "Burt and I have had no luncheon yet. "

"I am cursed near starved, " the other growled, throwing himself into a chair. Ezra had been careful to keep him from drink on the way down, and he was now sober, or as nearly sober as a brain saturated with liquor could ever be.

Girdlestone called for Mrs. Jorrocks, who laid the cloth and put a piece of cold corned beef and a jug of beer upon the table. Ezra appeared to have a poor appetite, but Burt ate voraciously, and filled his glass again and again from the jug. When the meal was finished and the ale all consumed, he rose with a grunt of repletion, and, pulling a roll of black tobacco from his pocket, proceeded to cut it into slices, and to cram it into his pipe. Ezra drew a chair up to the fire, and his father did the same, after ordering the old woman out of the room and carefully closing the door behind her.

"You have spoken to our friend here about the business? " Girdlestone asked, nodding his head in the direction of Burt.

"Yes. I have made it all clear. "

"Five hundred pounds down, and a free passage to Africa, " said Burt.

"An energetic man like you can do a great deal in the colonies with five hundred pounds, " Girdlestone remarked.

"What I do with it is nothin' to you, guv'nor, " Burt remarked surlily. "I does the job, you pays the money, and there's an end as far as you are concerned. "

"Quite so, " the merchant said in a conciliatory voice. "You are free to do what you like with the money. "

"Without axin' your leave, " growled Burt. He was a man of such a turbulent and quarrelsome disposition that he was always ready to go out of his way to make himself disagreeable.

"The question is how it is to be done, " interposed Ezra. He was looking very nervous and uneasy. Hard as he was, he had neither the pseudo-religious monomania of his father, nor the callous brutality of Burt, and he shuddered at the thought of what was to come. His eyes were red and bleared, and he sat with one arm thrown over the back of his chair, while he drummed nervously with the fingers of his other hand upon his knee. "You've got some plan in your head, I suppose, " he said to his father. "It's high time the thing was carried through, or we shall have to put up the shutters in Fenchurch Street. "

His father shivered at the very thought. "Anything rather than that, " he said.

"It will precious soon come to that. It was the devil of a fight to keep things straight last week. "

"What's the matter with your lip? It seems to be swollen. "

"I had a turn with that fellow Dimsdale, " Ezra answered, putting his hand up to his mouth to hide the disfigurement. "He followed us to the station, and we had to beat him off; but I think I left my marks upon him. "

"He played some damned hokey-pokey business on me, " said Burt. "He tripped me in some new-fangled way, and nigh knocked the breath out of me. I don't fall as light as I used. "

"He did not succeed in tracing you? " Girdlestone asked uneasily. "There is no chance of his turning up here and spoiling the whole business? "

"Not the least, " said Ezra confidently. "He was in the hands of a policeman when I saw him last. "

"That is well. Now I should like, before we go further, to say a few words to Mr. Burt as to what has led up to this. "

"You haven't got a drop to drink, boss? "

"Yes, yes, of course. What is that in the bottle over there? Ginger wine. How will that do? "

"Here's something better, " Ezra said, rummaging in the cupboard. "Here is a bottle of Hollands. It is Mrs. Jorrocks' private store, I fancy. "

Burt poured himself out half a tumblerful, and filled it up with water. "Drive along, " he said; "I am lisnin'. "

Girdlestone rose and stood with his back to the fire, and his hands under his coat-tails. "I wish you to understand, " he said, "that this is no sudden determination of ours, but that events have led up to it in such a way that it was impossible to avoid it. Our commercial honour and integrity are more precious to us than anything else, and we have both agreed that we are ready to sacrifice anything rather than lose it. Unfortunately, our affairs have become somewhat involved, and it was absolutely necessary that the firm should have a sum of money promptly in order to extricate itself from its difficulties. This sum we endeavoured to get through a daring speculation in diamonds, which was, though I say it, ingeniously planned and cleverly carried out, and which would have succeeded admirably had it not been for an unfortunate chance. "

"I remember, " said Burt.

"Of course. You were there at the time. We were able to struggle along for some time after this on money which we borrowed and on the profits of our African trade. The time came, however, when the borrowed money was to be repaid, and once again the firm was in danger. It was then that we first thought of the fortune of my ward. It was enough to turn the scale in our favour, could we lay our hands upon it. It was securely tied up, however, in such a way that there were only two means by which we could touch a penny of it. One was by marrying her to my son; the other was by the young lady's death. Do you follow me? "

Burt nodded his shaggy head.

"This being so, we did all that we could to arrange a marriage. Without flattery I may say that no girl was ever approached in a more delicate and honourable way than she was by my son Ezra. I, for my part, brought all my influence to bear upon her in order to induce her to meet his advances in a proper spirit. In spite of our efforts, she rejected him in the most decided way, and gave us to understand that it was hopeless to attempt to make her change her mind. "

"Some one else, maybe, " suggested Burt.

"The man who put you on your back at the station, " said Ezra.

"Ha! I'll pay him for that, " the navvy growled viciously.

"A human life, Mr. Burt, " continued Girdlestone, "is a sacred thing, but a human life, when weighed against the existence of a great firm from which hundreds derive their means of livelihood, is a small consideration indeed. When the fate of Miss Harston is put against the fate of the great commercial house of Girdlestone, it is evident which must go to the wall. "

Burt nodded, and poured some more Hollands from the square bottle.

"Having seen, " Girdlestone continued, "that this sad necessity might arise, I had made every arrangement some time before. This building is, as you may have observed in your drive, situated in a lonely and secluded part of the country. It is walled round too in such a manner that any one residing here is practically a prisoner. I removed the lady so suddenly that no one can possibly know where she has gone to, and I have spread such reports as to her condition that no one down here would be surprised to hear of her decease. "

"But there is bound to be an inquiry. How about a medical certificate? " asked Ezra.

"I shall insist upon a coroner's inquest, " his father answered.

"An inquest! Are you mad? "

"When you have heard me I think that you will come to just the opposite conclusion. I think that I have hit upon a scheme which is really neat—neat in its simplicity. " He rubbed his hands together, and showed his long yellow fangs in his enjoyment of his own astuteness.

Burt and Ezra leaned forward to listen, while the old man sank his voice to a whisper.

"They think that she is insane, " he said.

"Yes. "

"There's a small door in the boundary wall which leads out to the railway line. "

"Well, what of that? "

"Suppose that door to be left open, would it be an impossible thing for a crazy woman to slip out through it, and to be run over by the ten o'clock express? "

"If she would only get in the way of it. "

"You don't quite catch my idea yet. Suppose that the express ran over the dead body of a woman, would there be anything to prove afterwards that she *was* dead, and not alive at the time of the accident? Do you think that it would ever occur to any one's mind that the express ran over a dead body? "

"I see your meaning, " said his son thoughtfully. "You would settle her, and then put her there. "

"Of course. What could be more delightfully simple. Friend Burt here does his work; we carry her through the garden gate, and lay her on the darkest part of the rails. Then we miss her at the house. There is an alarm and a search. The gate is found open. We naturally go through with lanterns, and find her on the line. I don't think we need fear the coroner, or any one else then? "

"He's a sharp 'un, is the guv'nor, " cried Burt, slapping his thigh enthusiastically. "It's the downiest lay I have heard this many a day. "

"I believe you are the devil incarnate, " said Ezra, looking at his father with a mixture of horror and of admiration. "But how about Jorrocks and Stevens and Rebecca? Would you trust them? "

"Certainly not! " Girdlestone answered. "It is not necessary. Mr. Burt can do his part of the business out of doors. We can entice her out upon some excuse. There is no reason why any one should have a suspicion of the truth. "

"But they know that she is not mad. "

"They will think that she did it on purpose. The secret will be locked up in our three breasts. After one night's work our friend here goes to the colonies a prosperous man, and the firm of Girdlestone holds up its head once more, stainless and irreproachable. "

"Speak low! " said Ezra, in a whisper. "I hear her coming downstairs. " They listened to her light springy footstep as it passed the door. "Come here, Burt, " he said, after a pause. "She is at work on the lawn. Come and have a look at her. "

They all went over to the window, and looked out. It was then that Kate, glancing up, saw the three cruel faces surveying her.

"She's a rare well-built 'un, " said Burt, as he stepped back from the window. "It is the ugliest job as ever I was on. "

"But we can rely upon you? " Girdlestone asked, looking at him with puckered eyes.

"You bet—as long as you pay me, " the navvy answered phlegmatically, and went back to his pipe and to Mrs. Jorrocks' bottle of Hollands.

CHAPTER XLIII.

THE BAIT ON THE HOOK.

The grey winter evening was beginning to steal in before the details had all been arranged by the conspirators. It had grown so chill that Kate had abandoned her attempt at gardening, and had gone back to her room. Ezra left his father and Burt by the fire and came out to the open hall-door. The grim old trees looked gaunt and eerie as they waved their naked arms about in the cutting wind. A slight fog had come up from the sea and lay in light wreaths over the upper branches, like a thin veil of gauze. Ezra was shivering as he surveyed the dreary scene, when he felt a hand on his arm, and looking round saw that the maid Rebecca was standing beside him.

"Haven't you got one word for me? " she said sadly, looking up into his face. "It's but once a week, and then never a word of greeting. "

"I didn't see you, my lass, " Ezra answered. "How does the Priory suit you? "

"One place is the same as another to me, " she said drearily. "You asked me to come here, and I have come. You said once that you would let me know how I could serve you down here. When am I to know? "

"Why, there's no secret about that. You do serve me when you look after my father as you have done these weeks back. That old woman isn't fit to manage the whole place by herself. "

"That wasn't what you meant, though, " said the girl, looking at him with questioning eyes. "I remember your face now as you spoke the words. You have something on your mind, and have now, only you keep it to yourself. Why won't you trust me with it? "

"Don't be a fool! " answered Ezra curtly. "I have a great deal to worry me in business matters. Much good it would do telling you about them! "

"It's more than that, " said Rebecca doggedly. "Who is that man who has come down? "

"A business man from London. He has come to consult my father about money matters. Any more questions you would like to ask? "

"I should like to know how long we are to be kept down here, and what the meaning of it all may be. "

"We are going back before the end of the winter, and the meaning of it is that Miss Harston was not well and needed a change of air. Now are you satisfied? " He was determined to allay as far as possible any suspicions that the girl might have previously formed.

"And what brings *you* down here? " she asked, with the same searching look. "You don't come down into this hole without some good reason. I did think at first that you might come down in order to see me, but you soon showed me that it wasn't that. There was a time when you was fond of me. "

"So I am now, lass. "

"Ay, very fond! Not a word nor a look from you last time you came. You must have some reason, though, that brings you here. "

"There's nothing wonderful in a man coming to see his own father, "

"Much you cared for him in London, " she cried, with a shrill laugh. "If he was under the sod you would not be the sadder. It's my belief as you come down after that doll-faced missy upstairs. "

"Dry up, now! " said Ezra roughly. "I've had enough of your confounded nonsense. "

"You don't talk in that style to her, " she said excitedly. "You scorn me, but I know this, that if I can't have your love no one else shall. I've got a dash of the gipsy in me, as you know. Rather than that girl should have you, I would knife her and you, too! " She shook her clenched right hand as she spoke, and her face was so full of vindictive passion that Ezra was astonished.

"I always knew that you were a spitfire, " he said, "but you never came it quite so strong as this before. "

The reaction had already come upon her, however, and tears were running down her cheeks. "You'll never leave me entirely? " she cried, clasping his arm. "I could bear to share your love with another, but I wouldn't have you turn altogether against me. "

"You'll have my father out presently with your damned noise! " said Ezra. "Get away, and wash your face. "

His word was law to her, and she turned away, still weeping bitterly. In her poor, dim, eventless life the sole bright spot had been the attention which the young merchant had occasionally shown her. To her distorted fancy he was a man among men, a hero, all that was admirable and magnificent. What was there which she would not do for him? She had the faithfulness of a dog, but like a dog she would snarl fiercely at any one who came between her master's affection and herself. Deep down in her heart rankled the one suspicion which no assurances could remove, that an understanding existed between the man she loved and the woman she hated. As she withdrew to her room she determined that during this visit of Ezra's she would manage in such a way that no communication could pass between them without her knowledge. She knew that it was a dangerous thing to play the spy upon the young man, for he had shown her before now that her sex was no precaution against his brutality. Nevertheless, she set herself to do it, with all the cunning and perseverance of a jealous woman.

As the light faded and the greys of evening deepened into darkness, Kate sat patiently in her bare little room. A coal fire sputtered and sparkled in the rusty grate, and there was a tin bucket full of coals beside the fender from which to replenish it. She was very cold, so she drew her single chair up to the blaze and held her hands over it. It was a lonesome and melancholy vigil, while the wind whistled through the branches of the trees and moaned drearily in the cracks and crannies of the old house. When were her friends coming? Perhaps something had occurred to detain them to-day. This morning such a thing would have appeared to her to be an impossibility, but now that the time had come when she had expected them, it appeared probable enough that something might have delayed them. To-morrow at latest they could not fail to come. She wondered what they would do if they did arrive. Would they come boldly up the avenue and claim her from the Girdlestones, or would they endeavour to communicate with her first? Whatever they decided upon would be sure to be for the best.

She went to the window once and looked out. It promised to be a wild night. Far away in the south-west lay a great cumulus of rugged clouds from which dark streamers radiated over the sky, like the advance guard of an army. Here and there a pale star twinkled dimly out through the rifts, but the greater part of the heavens was black and threatening. It was so dark that she could no longer see the sea, but the crashing, booming sound of the great waves filled the air and the salt spray came driving in through the open window. She shut it and resumed her seat by the fire, shivering partly from cold and partly from some vague presentiment of evil.

An hour or more had passed when she heard a step upon the stairs and a knock came to her door. It was Rebecca, with a cup of tea upon a tray and some bread-and-butter. Kate was grateful at this attention, for it saved her from having to go down to the dining-room and face Ezra and his unpleasant-looking companion. Rebecca laid down the tray, and then, to her mistress's surprise, turned back and shut the door. The girl's face was very pale, and her manner was wild and excited.

"Here's a note for you, " she said. "It was given Mrs. Jorrocks to give you, but I am better at climbing stairs than she is, so I brought it up. " She handed Kate a little slip of paper as she spoke.

A note for her! Could it be that her friends had arrived and had managed to send a message to her? It must be so. She took it from the maid. As she did so she noticed that the other's hands were shaking as though she had the ague. "You are not well, Rebecca, " said Kate kindly. "Oh yes, I am. You read your note and don't mind me, " the girl answered, in her usual surly fashion. Instead of leaving the room, she was bustling about the bed as though putting things in order.

Kate's impatience was too great to allow her to wait, so she untwisted the paper, which had no seal or fastening. She had hoped in her heart to see the name of her lover at the end of it. Instead of that, her eye fell upon the signature of Ezra Girdlestone. What could he have to say to her? She moved the solitary candle on to the mantelpiece, and read the following note, roughly scribbled upon a coarse piece of paper: —

"MY DEAR MISS HARSTON. "

"I am afraid your confinement here has been very irksome to you. I have repeatedly requested my father to alleviate or modify it, but he has invariably refused. As he still persists in his refusal, I wish to offer you my aid, and, to show you that I am your sincere friend in spite of all that has passed, it you could slip out to-night at nine o'clock and meet me by the withered oak at the head of the avenue, I shall see you safe to Bedsworth, and you can, if you wish, go on to Portsmouth by the next train. I shall manage so that you may find the door open by that time. I shall not, of course, go to Portsmouth with you, but shall return here after dropping you at the station. I do this small thing to show you that, hopeless as it may be, the affection which I bear you is still as deep as ever. "

"Yours, "

"E. GIRDLESTONE. "

Our heroine was so surprised at this epistle that she sat for some time dangling the slip of paper between her fingers and lost in thought. When she glanced round, Rebecca had left the room. She rolled the paper up and threw it into the fire. Ezra, then, was not so hard-hearted as she had thought him. He had used his influence to soften his father. Should she accept this chance of escape, or should she wait some word from her friends? Perhaps they were already in Bedsworth, but did not know how to communicate with her. If so, this offer of Ezra's was just what was needed. In any case, she could go on to Portsmouth and telegraph from there to the Dimsdales. It was too good an offer to be refused. She made up her mind that she would accept it. It was past eight now, and nine was the hour. She stood up with the intention of putting on her cloak and her bonnet.

CHAPTER XLIV.

THE SHADOW OF DEATH.

This conversation with Rebecca had suggested to Ezra that he might still have influence enough with his father's ward to induce her to come out of doors, and so put herself within the reach of Burt. He had proposed the plan to his father, who approved of it heartily. The only weak point in his scheme had been the difficulty which might arise in inducing the girl to venture out of the Priory on that tempestuous winter's night. There was evidently only one incentive strong enough to bring it about, and that was the hope of escape. By harping skilfully upon this string they might lure her into the trap. Ezra and his father composed the letter together, and the former handed it to Mrs. Jorrocks, with a request that she should deliver it.

It chanced, however, that Rebecca, keenly alive to any attempt at communication between the young merchant and her mistress, saw the crone hobbling down the passage with the note in her hand.

"What's that, mother? " she asked.

"It's a letter for her, " wheezed the old woman, nodding her tremulous head in the direction of Kate's room.

"I'll take it up, " said Rebecca eagerly. "I am just going up there with her tea. "

"Thank ye. Them stairs tries my rheumatiz something cruel. "

The maid took the note and carried it upstairs. Instead of taking it straight to her mistress she slipped into her own room and read every word of it. It appeared to confirm her worst suspicions. Here was Ezra asking an interview with the woman whom he had assured her that he hated. It was true that the request was made in measured words and on a plausible pretext. No doubt that was merely to deceive any other eye which might rest upon it. There was an understanding between them, and this was an assignation. The girl walked swiftly up and down the room like a caged tigress, striking her head with her clenched hands in her anger and biting her lip until the blood came. It was some time before she could overcome her agitation sufficiently to deliver the note, and when she did so her mistress, as we have seen, noticed that her manner was nervous and wild. She little dreamed of the struggle which was going on in the dark-eyed girl's mind against the impulse which urged her to seize her imagined rival by the white throat and choke the life out of her.

"It's eight o'clock now, " Ezra was saying downstairs. "I wonder whether she will come? "

"She is sure to come, " his father said briefly.

"Suppose she didn't? "

"In that case we should find other means to bring her out. We have not gone so far, to break down over a trifle at the last moment. "

"I must have something to drink, " Ezra said, after a pause, helping himself from the bottle. "I feel as cold as ice and as nervous as a cat. I can't understand how you look so unconcerned. If you were going to sign an invoice or audit an account or anything else in the way of business you could not take it more calmly. I wish the time would come. This waiting is terrible. "

"Let us pass the time to advantage, " said John Girdlestone; and drawing a little fat Bible from his pocket he began to read it aloud in a solemn and sonorous voice. The yellow light illuminated the old merchant's massive features as he stooped forwards towards the candle. His strongly marked nose and his hollow cheeks gave him a vulture-like aspect, which was increased by the effect of his deep-set glittering eyes.

Ezra, leaning back in his chair with the firelight flickering over his haggard but still handsome face, looked across at his father with a puzzled expression. He had never yet been able to determine whether the old man was a consummate hypocrite or a religious monomaniac. Burt lay with his feet in the light of the fire and his head sunk back across the arm of the chair, fast asleep and snoring loudly.

"Isn't it time to wake him up? " Ezra asked, interrupting the reading.

"Yes, I think it is, " his father answered, closing the sacred volume reverently and replacing it in his bosom.

Ezra took up the candle and held it over the sleeping man. "What a brute he looks! " he said. "Did ever you see such an animal in your life? "

The navvy was certainly not a pretty sight. His muscular arms and legs were all a-sprawl and his head hung back at a strange angle to his body, so that his fiery red beard pointed upwards, exposing all the thick sinewy throat beneath it. His eyes were half open and looked bleared and unhealthy, while his thick lips puffed out with a whistling sound at every expiration. His dirty brown coat was thrown open, and out of one of the pockets protruded a short thick cudgel with a leaden head.

John Girdlestone picked it out and tried it in the air. "I think I could kill an ox with this, " he said.

"Don't wave it about *my* head, " cried Ezra. "As you stand in the firelight brandishing that stick in your long arms you are less attractive than usual. "

John Girdlestone smiled and replaced the cudgel in the sleeper's pocket. "Wake up, Burt, " he cried, shaking him by the arm. "It's half-past eight. "

The navvy started to his feet with an oath and then fell back into his chair, staring round him vacantly, at a loss as to where he might be. His eye fell upon the bottle of Hollands, which was now nearly empty, and he held out his hand to it with an exclamation of recognition.

"I've been asleep, guv'nor, " he said hoarsely. "Must have a dram to set me straight. Did you say it was time for the job. "

"We have made arrangements by which she will be out by the withered oak at nine o'clock. "

"That's not for half an hour, " cried Burt, in a surly voice. "You need not have woke me yet. "

"We'd better go out there now. She may come rather before the time"

"Come on, then! " said the navvy, buttoning up his coat and rolling a ragged cravat round his throat. "Who is a-comin' with me? "

"We shall both come, " answered John Girdlestone firmly. "You will need help to carry her to the railway line. "

"Surely Burt can do that himself, " Ezra remarked. "She's not so very heavy. "

Girdlestone drew his son aside. "Don't be so foolish, Ezra, " he said. "We can't trust the half-drunken fellow. It must be done with the greatest carefulness and precision, and no traces left. Our old business watchword was to overlook everything ourselves, and we shall certainly do so now. "

"It's a horrible affair! " Ezra said, with a shudder. "I wish I was out of it. "

"You won't think that to-morrow morning when you realize that the firm is saved and no one the wiser. He has gone on. Don't lose sight of him. "

They both hurried out, and found Burt standing in front of the door. It was blowing half a gale now, and the wind was bitterly cold. There came a melancholy rasping and rustling from the leafless wood, and every now and again a sharp crackling sound would announce that some rotten branch had come crashing down. The clouds drove across the face of the moon, so that at times the cold, clear light silvered the dark wood and the old monastery, while at others all was plunged in darkness. From the open door a broad golden bar was shot across the lawn from the lamp in the hall. The three dark figures with their long fantastic shadows looked eerie and unnatural in the yellow glare.

"Are we to have a lantern? " asked Burt.

"No, no, " cried Ezra. "We shall see quite enough as it is. We don't want a light. "

"I have one, " said the father. "We can use it if it is necessary. I think we had better take our places now. She may come sooner than we expect. It will be well to leave the door as it is. She will see that there is no obstacle in the way. "

"You're not half sharp enough, " said Ezra. "If the door was left like that it might suggest a trap to her. Better close the dining-room door and then leave the hall door just a little ajar. That would look more natural. She would conclude that Burt and you were in there. "

"Where are Jorrocks and Rebecca? " Girdlestone asked, closing the door as suggested.

"Jorrocks is in her room. Rebecca, I have no doubt, is in hers also. "

"Things look safe enough. Come along, Burt. This way. "

The three tramped their way across the gravelled drive and over the slushy grass to the border of the wood.

"This is the withered oak, " said Girdlestone, as a dark mass loomed in front of them. It stood somewhat apart from the other trees, and the base of it was free from the brambles which formed a thick undergrowth elsewhere.

Burt walked round the great trunk and made as careful an examination of the ground as he could in the dark.

"Would the lantern be of any use to you? " Girdlestone asked.

"No, It's all serene. I think I know how to fix it now. You two can get behind those trees, or where you like, as long as you're not in the way. I don't want no 'sistance. When Jem Burt takes a job in hand he carries it through in a workmanlike manner. I don't want nobody else foolin' around. "

"We would not dream of interfering with your arrangements, " said Girdlestone.

"You'd better not! " Burt growled. "I'll lay down behind this oak, d'ye see. When she comes, she'll think as he's not arrived yet, and she'll get standin' around and waitin'. When I see my chance, I'll get behind her, and she'll never know that she has not been struck by lightnin'. "

"Excellent! " cried John Girdlestone; "excellent! We had best get into our places. "

"Mind you do it all in one crack, " Ezra said. "Don't let us have any crying out afterwards. I could stand a good deal, but not that. "

"You should know how I hits, " Burt remarked with a malicious grin, which was hidden from his companion. "If your head wasn't well nigh solid you wouldn't be here now. "

Ezra's hand involuntarily went up to the old scar. "I think such a one as that would settle her! " he said, as he withdrew with his father. The two took up their position under the shadow of some trees fifty yards off or more. Burt crouched down behind the withered oak with his weapon in his hand and waited for the coming of his victim.

Ezra, though usually resolute and daring, had completely lost his nerve, and his teeth were chattering in his head. His father, on the other hand, was emotionless and impassive as ever.

"It's close upon nine o'clock, " Ezra whispered.

"Ten minutes to, " said the other, peering at his great golden chronometer through the darkness.

"What if she fails to come? "

"We must devise other means of bringing her out. "

From the spot where they stood they had a view of the whole of the Priory. She could not come out without being seen. Above the door was a long narrow window which opened upon the staircase. On this Girdlestone and his son fixed their eyes, for they knew that on her way down she would be visible at it. As they looked, the dim light which shone through it was obscured and then reappeared.

"She has passed! "

"Hush! "

Another moment and the door was stealthily opened. Once again the broad golden bar shot out across the lawn almost to the spot where the confederates were crouching. In the centre of the zone of light there stood a figure—the figure of the girl. Even at that distance they could distinguish the pearl-grey mantle which she usually wore and the close-fitting bonnet. She had wrapped a shawl round the lower part of her face to protect her from the boisterous wind. For a minute or more she stood peering out into the darkness of the night, as though uncertain whether to proceed or to go back. Then, with a quick, sudden gesture she closed the door behind her. The light was no longer there, but they knew that she was outside the house, and that the appointment would be kept.

What an age it seemed before they heard her footsteps. She came very slowly, putting one foot gingerly before the other, as if afraid of falling over something in the darkness. Once or twice she stopped altogether, looking round, no doubt, to make sure of her whereabouts. At that instant the moon shone out from behind a cloud, and they saw her dark figure a short distance on. The light enabled her to see the withered oak, for she came rapidly towards it. As she approached, she satisfied herself apparently that she was the first on the ground, for she slackened her pace once more and walked in the listless way that people assume when they are waiting. The clouds were overtaking the moon again, and the light was getting dimmer.

"I can see her still, " said Ezra in a whisper, grasping his father's wrist in his excitement.

The old man said nothing, but he peered through the darkness with eager, straining eyes.

"There she is, standing out a little from the oak, " the young merchant said, pointing with a quivering finger. "She's not near enough for him to reach her. "

"He's coming out from the shadow now, " the other said huskily. "Don't you see him crawling along the ground? "

"I see him, " returned the other in the same subdued, awestruck voice. "Now he has stopped; now he goes on again! My God, he's close behind her! She is looking the other way. "

A thin ray of light shot down between the clouds. In its silvery radiance two figures stood out hard and black, that of the unconscious girl and of the man who crouched like a beast of prey behind her. He made a step forward, which brought him within a yard of her. She may have heard the heavy footfall above the shriek of the storm, for she turned suddenly and faced him. At the same instance she was struck down with a crashing blow. There was no time for a prayer, no time for a scream. One moment had seen her a magnificent woman in all the pride of her youthful beauty, the next left her a poor battered, senseless wreck. The navvy had earned his blood-money.

At the sound of the blow and the sight of the fall both the old man and the young ran out from their place of concealment. Burt was standing over the body, his bludgeon in his hand.

"Not even a groan! " he said. "What d'ye think of that? "

Girdlestone wrung his hand and congratulated him warmly. "Shall I light the lantern? " he asked.

"For God's sake, don't! " Ezra said earnestly.

"I had no idea that you were so faint-hearted, my son, " the merchant remarked. "However, I know the way to the gate well enough to go there blindfold. What a comfort it is to know that there is no blood about! That's the advantage of a stick over a knife. "

"You're correct there, guv'nor, " Burt said approvingly.

"Will you kindly carry one end and I'll take the other. I'll go first, if you don't mind, because I know the way best. The train will pass in less than half an hour, so we have not long to wait. Within that time every chance of detection will have gone. "

Girdlestone raised up the head of the murdered girl, and Burt took her feet. Ezra walked behind as though he were in some dreadful dream. He had fully recognized the necessity for the murder, but he had never before realized how ghastly the details would be. Already he had begun to repent that he had ever acquiesced in it. Then came thoughts of the splendid possibilities of the African business, which could only be saved from destruction by this woman's death. How could he, with his luxurious tastes, bear the squalor and poverty which would be his lot were the firm to fail? Better a rope and a long drop than such a life as that! All these considerations thronged into his mind as he plodded along the slippery footpath which led through the forest to the wooden gate.

CHAPTER XLV.

THE INVASION OF HAMPSHIRE.

When Tom and the major arrived at Waterloo Station, the latter in the breathless condition described in a preceding chapter, they found the German waiting for them with his two fellow-exiles. The gentleman of Nihilistic proclivities was somewhat tall and thin, with a long frock-coat buttoned almost up to his throat, which showed signs of giving at the seams every here and there. His grizzly hair fell over his collar behind, and he had a short bristling beard. He stood with one hand stuck into the front of his coat and the other upon his hip, as though rehearsing the position in which his statue might be some day erected in the streets of his native Russia, when the people had their own, and despotism was no more. In spite of his worn attire there was something noble and striking about the man. His bow, when Baumser introduced him to the major and Tom, would have graced any Court in Europe. Round his neck he had a coarse string from which hung a pair of double eye-glasses. These he fixed upon his aquiline nose, and took a good look at the gentlemen whom he had come to serve.

Bulow, of Kiel, was a small, dark-eyed, clean-shaven fellow, quick and energetic in his movements, having more the appearance of a Celt than of a Teuton. He seemed to be full of amiability, and assured the major in execrable English how very happy he was to be able to do a service to one who had shown kindness to their esteemed colleague and persecuted patriot, Von Baumser. Indeed both of the men showed great deference to the German, and the major began to perceive that his friend was a very exalted individual in Socialistic circles. He liked the look of the two foreigners, and congratulated himself upon having their co-operation in the matter on hand.

Ill luck was in store for the expedition, however. On inquiry at the ticket-office they found that there was no train for upwards of two hours, and then it was a slow one which would not land them until eight o'clock at Bedsworth. At this piece of information Tom Dimsdale fairly broke down, and stamped about the station, raving and beseeching the officials to run a special, be the cost what it might. This, however, could by no means be done, owing to the press of Saturday traffic. There was nothing for it but to wait. The three foreigners went off in search of something to eat, and having found a convenient cookshop they disappeared therein and feasted royally at Von Baumser's expense. Major Tobias Clutterbuck remained with the young man, who resolutely refused to leave the platform. The major knew of a snug little corner not far off where he could have put in the time very comfortably, but he could not bring himself to desert his companion even for a minute. I have no doubt that that wait of two hours in the draughty station is marked up somewhere to the old sinner's credit account.

Indeed, it was well that day that young Dimsdale had good friends at his back. His appearance was so strange and wild that the passers-by turned back to have another look at him, His eyes were open and staring, giving a fear-inspiring character to his expression. He could not sit still for an instant, but paced up and down and backwards and forwards under the influence of the fierce energy which consumed him, while the major plodded along manfully at his side, suggesting every consideration which might cheer him up, and narrating many tales, true and apocryphal, most of which fell upon heedless ears.

Ezra Girdlestone had four hours' start of them. That was the thought which rankled in Tom's heart and outweighed every other consideration. He knew Kate's nature so well that he was convinced that she would never have expressed such fears to Mrs. Scully unless she had very assured reasons for them. In fact, apart from her own words, what could this secrecy and seclusion mean except foul play. After what he had learned about the insurance of the ships and the manner in which the elder Girdlestone had induced him to cease corresponding with Kate, he could believe anything of his partners. He knew, also, that in case of Kate's death the money reverted to her guardian. There was not a single link missing in the chain of evidence which showed that a crime was in contemplation. Then, who was that butcher-like man whom Ezra was taking down with him? Tom could have torn his hair as he thought of his present impotence and of his folly in losing sight of young Girdlestone.

The major has put it on record that those two hours appeared to him the longest that ever he passed in his life, and Tom, no doubt, would endorse the sentiment. Everything must have an end, however, and the station clock, the hands of which seemed several times to have stopped altogether, began at last to approach the hour at which the Portsmouth train was timed to depart. Baumser and his two friends had come back, all three smoking cigarettes, and looking the better for their visit to the cookshop. The five got into a first-class railway carriage and waited. Would they never have done examining tickets and stamping luggage and going through all sorts of tedious formalities? At last, thank God! comes the shrill whistle of the guard, the answering snort from the engine, and they are fairly started upon their mission of rescue.

There was much to be arranged as to their plan of action. Tom, Von Baumser, and the major talked it over in a low voice, while the two Socialists chatted together in German and consumed eternal cigarettes. Tom was for marching straight up to the Priory and demanding that Girdlestone should deliver his ward up to them. To the major and the German this seemed an unwise proceeding. It was to put themselves hopelessly wrong from a legal point of view. Girdlestone had only to say, as he assuredly would, that the whole story was a ridiculous mare's nest, and then what proof could they adduce, or what excuse give for their interference. However plausible their suspicions might be, they were, after all, only suspicions, which other people might not view in as grave a light.

"What would you advise, then? " Tom asked, passing his hand over his heated forehead.

"Bedad! I'll tell you the plan, " the old soldier answered, "and I think me friend Von Baumser will agray with me. I understand that this place is surrounded by a wall to which there is only one gate. Sure, we shall wait outside this wall, and one of us can go in as a skirmisher and find out how the land lies. Let him ascertain from the young lady herself if she requires immadiate help, and what she would wish done. If he can't make his way to her, let him hang about the house, and see and hear all that he can. We shall then have something solid to work on. I have a dog whistle here on me watch-chain, given me by Charley Gill, of the Inniskillens. Our skirmisher could take that with him, and if he wants immadiate help one blow of it would be enough to bring the four of us over to him. Though how the divil I am to git over a wall, " concluded the major ruefully, looking down at his own proportions, "is more than I can tell. "

"I hope, my vriends, " said Von Baumser, "dat you vill allow me the honour of going first, for ven I vas in the Swabian Jager I vas always counted a very good spion. "

"That is my place, " said Tom with decision.

"You have the best claim, " the major answered. "What a train this is! Ged, it's as slow as the one which Jimmy Travers, of the Commissariat, travelled in in America. They were staming along, according to Jimmy, when they saw a cow walking along the loine in front of them. They all thought that they were going to run into her, but it was all right, for they never overtook her, and she soon walked clane out of sight. Here we are at a station! How far to Bedsworth, guard? "

"Next station, sir. "

"Thank the Lord! It's twinty to eight. We are rather behind our time. You always are if you are in a particular hurry. "

It was nearly eight o'clock by the time they reached their destination. The station-master directed them to the *Flying Bull*, where they secured the very vehicle in which Kate and her guardian had been originally driven up. By the time that the horse was put in it was close upon the half-hour.

"Drive as hard as you can go to the Proiory, me man, " said the major.

The sulky ostler made no remark, but a look of surprise passed over his phlegmatic countenance. For years back so little had been heard of the old monastery that its very existence had been almost forgotten in Bedsworth. Now whole troops of Londoners were coming down in succession, demanding to be driven there. He pondered over the strange fact as he drove through the darkness, but the only conclusion to which his bucolic mind could come was that it was high time to raise the fare to that particular point.

It was a miserable night, stormy and wet and bitterly cold. None of the five men had a thought to spare for the weather, however. The two foreigners had been so infected by the suppressed excitement of their companions, or had so identified themselves with their comrades' cause, that they were as eager as the others.

"Are we near? " the major asked.

"The gate is just at the end o' the lane, sir. "

"Don't pull up at the gate, but take us a little past it. "

"There ain't no way in except the gate, " the driver remarked.

"Do what you're ordered, " said the major sternly. Once again the ostler's face betrayed unbounded astonishment. He slewed half-way round in his seat and took as good a look as was possible in the uncertain light at the faces of his passengers. It had occurred to him that it was more than likely that he would have to swear to them at some future date in a police-court. "I'd know that thick 'un wi' the red face, " he muttered to himself, "and him wi' the yeller beard and the stick. "

They passed the stone pillars with the weather-beaten heraldic devices, and drove along by the high park wall. When they had gone a hundred yards or so the major ordered the driver to pull up, and they all got down. The increased fare was paid without remonstrance, and the ostler rattled away homewards, with the intention of pulling up at the county police-station and lodging information as to the suspicious visitors whom he had brought down.

"It is loikely that they have a watch at the gate, " said the major. "We must kape away from there. This wall is a great hoight. We'd best kape on until we find the aisiest place to scale it. "

"I could get over it here, " Tom said eagerly.

"Wait a bit. A few minutes can make no difference one way or the other. Ould Sir Colin used to say that there were more battles lost by over-haste than by slowness. What's the high bank running along on the right here? "

"Dat's a railway bankment, " said Von Baumser. "See de posts and de little red lights over yonder. "

"So it is. The wall seems to me to be lower here. What's this dark thing? Hullo, here's a door lading into the grounds. "

"It is locked though. "

"Give me a hoist here, " Tom said imploringly. "Don't throw a minute away. You can't tell what may be going on inside. At this very moment for all we know they may be plotting her murder. "

"He has right, " said Von Baumser. "We shall await here until we hear from you. Help him, my vriends—shove him up! "

Tom caught the coping of the wall, although the broken glass cut deeply into his hands. With a great heave he swung himself up, and was soon astride upon the top.

"Here's the whistle, " said the major, standing on tiptoe to reach a downstretched hand. "If you want us, give a good blow at it. We'll be with you in a brace of shakes. If we can't get over the wall we'll have the door down. Divil a fear but we'll be there! "

Tom was in the act of letting himself drop into the wood, when suddenly the watchers below saw him crouch down upon the wall, and lie motionless, as though listening intently.

"Hush! " he whispered, leaning over. "Some one is coming through the wood. "

The wind had died away and the storm subsided. Even from the lane they could hear the sound of feet, and of muffled voices inside the grounds. They all crouched down in the shadow of the wall. Tom lay flat upon the glass-studded coping, and no one looking from below could distinguish him from the wall itself.

The voices and the footsteps sounded louder and louder, until they were just at the other side of the boundary. They seemed to come from several people walking slowly and heavily. There was the shrill rasping of a key, and the wooden door swung back on its rusty hinges, while three dark figures passed out who appeared to bear some burden between them. The party in the shadow crouched closer still, and peered through the darkness with eager, anxious eyes. They could discern little save the vague outlines of the moving men, and yet as they gazed at them an unaccountable and overpowering horror crept into the hearts of every one of them. They breathed the atmosphere of death.

The new-comers tramped across the road, and, pushing through the thin hedge, ascended the railway embankment upon the other side.

It was evident that their burden was a heavy one, for they stopped more than once while ascending the steep grassy slope, and once, when near the top, one of the party slipped, and there was a sound as though he had fallen upon his knees, together with a stifled oath. They reached the top, however, and their figures, which had disappeared from view, came into sight again, standing out dimly against the murky sky. They bent down over the railway line, and placed the indistinguishable mass which they bore carefully upon it.

"We must have the light, " said a voice.

"No, no; there's no need, " another expostulated.

"We can't work in the dark, " said a third, loudly and harshly. "Where's your lantern, guv'nor? I've got a lucifer. "

"We must manage that the train passes over right, " the first voice remarked. "Here, Burt, you light it? "

There was the sharp sound of the striking of a match, and a feeble glimmer appeared, in the darkness. It flickered and waned, as though the wind would extinguish it, but next instant the wick of the lantern had caught, and threw a strong yellow glare upon the scene. The light fell upon the major and his comrades, who had sprung into the road, and it lit up the group on the railway line. Yet it was not upon the rescuing party that the murderers fixed their terror-stricken eyes, and the major and his friends had lost all thought of the miscreants above them—for there, standing in the centre of the roadway, there with the light flickering over her pale sweet face, like a spirit from the tomb, stood none other than the much-enduring, cruelly-treated girl for whom Burt's murderous blow had been intended.

For a few moments she stood there without either party moving a foot or uttering a sound. Then there came from the railway line a cry so wild that it will ring for ever in the ears of those who heard it. Burt dropped upon his knees and put his band over his eyes to keep out the sight. John Girdlestone caught his son by the wrist and dashed away into the darkness, flying wildly, madly, with white faces and staring eyes, as men who have looked upon that which is not of this world. In the meantime, Tom had sprung down from his perch, and had clasped Kate in his arms, and there she lay, sobbing and laughing, with many pretty feminine ejaculations and exclamations and questions, saved at last from the net of death which had been closing upon her so long.

CHAPTER XLVI.

A MIDNIGHT CRUISE.

If ever two men were completely cowed and broken down those two were the African merchants and his son. Wet, torn, and soiled, they still struggled on in their aimless flight, crashing through hedges and clambering over obstacles, with the one idea in their frenzied minds of leaving miles between them and that fair accusing face. Exhausted and panting they still battled through the darkness and the storm, until they saw the gleam of the surge and heard the crash of the great waves upon the beach. Then they stopped amid the sand and the shingle. The moon was shining down now in all its calm splendour, illuminating the great tossing ocean and the long dark sweep of the Hampshire coast. By its light the two men looked at one another, such a look as two lost souls might have exchanged when they heard the gates of hell first clang behind them.

Who could have recognized them now as the respected trader of Fenchurch Street and his fastidious son. Their clothes were tattered, their faces splashed with mud and scarred by brambles and thorns, the elder man had lost his hat, and his silvery hair blew out in a confused tangle behind him. Even more noticeable, however, than the change in their attire was the alteration in their expression. Both had the same startled, furtive look of apprehension, like beasts of prey who hear the baying of the hounds in the distance. Their quivering hands and gasping breath betrayed their exhaustion, yet they glanced around them nervously, as though the least sound would send them off once more upon their wild career.

"You devil! " Ezra cried at last, in a harsh, choking voice, taking a step towards his father with a gesture as though he would have struck him. "You have brought us to this with your canting and scheming and plotting. What are we to do now—eh? Answer me that! " He caught the old man by the coat and shook him violently.

Girdlestone's face was all drawn, as though he were threatened with a fit, and his eyes were glassy and vacant. The moonlight glittered in them and played over his contorted features. "Did you see her? " he whispered with trembling lips. "Did you see her? "

"Yes, I saw her, " the other answered brusquely; "and I saw that infernal fellow from London, and the major, and God knows how many more behind her. A nice hornets' nest to bring about one's ears. "

"It was her spirit, " said his father in the same awe-struck voice. "The spirit of John Harston's murdered daughter. "

"It was the girl herself, " said Ezra. He had been panic-stricken at the moment, but had had time during their flight to realize the situation. "We have made a pretty botch of the whole thing. "

"The girl herself! " cried Girdlestone in bewilderment. "For Heaven's sake, don't mock me! Who was it that we carried through the wood and laid upon the rails? "

"Who was it? Why that jealous jade, Rebecca Taylforth, of course, who must have read my note and come out in the other's cloak and hat to hear what I had to say to her. The cursed fool! "

"The wrong woman! " Girdlestone muttered with the same vacant look upon his face. "All for nothing, then—for nothing! "

"Don't stand mumbling to yourself there, " cried Ezra, catching his father's arm and half dragging him along the beach. "Don't you understand that there's a hue and cry out after you, and that we'll be hung if we are taken. Wake up and exert yourself. The gallows would be a nice end to all your preaching and praying, wouldn't it? "

They hurried along together down the beach, ploughing their way through the loose shingle and tripping over the great mats of seaweed which had been cast up in the recent gale. The wind was still so great that they had to lower their heads and to put their shoulders against it, while the salt spray caused their eyes to smart and tingled on their lips.

"Where are you taking me, my son? " asked the old man once.

"To the only chance we have of safety. Come on, and ask no questions. "

Through the murkiness of the night they saw a single light flickering dimly ahead of them. This was evidently the goal at which Ezra was aiming. As they toiled on it grew larger and brighter, until it resolved itself into the glare of a lamp shining through a small diamond-paned window. Girdlestone recognized the place now. It was the hut of a fisherman named Sampson, who lived a mile or more from Claxton. He remembered having his attention attracted to the place by the curious nature of the building, which was constructed out of the remnants of a Norwegian barque stranded some years before. The thatch which covered it and the windows and door cut in the sides gave it a curiously hybrid appearance, and made it an object of interest to sightseers in those parts. Sampson was the owner of a fair-sized fishing-boat, which he worked with his eldest son, and which was said to yield him a decent livelihood.

"What are you going to do? " asked Girdlestone, as his son made his way to the door.

"Don't look like a ghost, " Ezra answered in an angry whisper. "We're all safe, if we are only cool. "

"I am better now. You can trust me. "

"Keep a smiling face, then, " said Ezra, and knocked loudly at the door of the hut. The occupants had not heard their approach owing to the storm, but the instant that the young merchant struck the door there was a buzz of conversation and the sharp barking of a dog. Then came a dull thud and the barking ceased, from which Ezra concluded that some one had hurled a boot at the animal.

"We hain't no bait, " cried a gruff voice.

"Can I see Mr. Sampson? " asked Ezra.

"I tell 'ee we hain't no bait, " roared the voice in a more irritable tone.

"We don't want bait. We want a word of talk, " said Ezra.

As he spoke, the door flew open, and a burly middle-aged man, in a red shirt, appeared, with a face which was almost the same colour as his garment. "We hain't got no—" he was beginning, when he suddenly recognized his visitors and broke short off, staring at them with as much surprise as it is possible for human features to express.

"Well, if it ain't the genelman from the Priory! " he exclaimed at last, with a whistle, which seemed to be his way of letting off the astonishment which would otherwise remain bottled up in his system.

"We want a minute's talk with you, Mr. Sampson, " said Ezra.

"Surely, sir—sure-ly! " the fisherman cried, bustling indoors and rubbing the top of two stools with his sleeve. "Coom in! 'Ere, Jarge, pull the seats up for the genelmen. "

At this summons, a lanky, big-boned hobbledehoy, in sea boots, pushed the stools up towards the fire, on which a log of wood was blazing cheerily. The two Girdlestones sat warming themselves, while the fisherman and his son surveyed them silently with open eyes and mouth, as though they were a pair of strange zoological curiosities cast up by the gale.

"Keep doon, Sammy! " the fisherman said hoarsely to a great collie dog who was licking at Girdlestone's hands. "What be he a suckin' at? Why, sure, sir, there be blood on your hands. "

"My father scratched himself, " said Ezra promptly.

"His hat has blown away too, and we lost our way in the dark, so we're rather in a mess. "

"Why, so you be! " Sampson cried, eyeing them up and down. "I thought, when I heard you, as it was they folk from Claxton as comes 'ere for bait whenever they be short. That's nigh about the only visitors we ever gets here; bean't it, Jarge? "

George, thus appealed to, made no articulate reply, but he opened his great mouth and laughed vociferously.

"We've come for something which will pay you better than that, " said Ezra. "You remember my meeting you two or three Saturdays ago, and speaking to you about your house and your boat and one thing or another? "

The fisherman nodded.

"You said something then about your boat being a good sea-going craft, and that it was as roomy as many a yacht. I think I told you that I might give it a try some day. "

The fisherman nodded again. His wondering eyes were still surveying his visitors, dwelling on every rent in their clothes or stain on their persons.

"My father and I want to get down the coast as far as the Downs. Now we thought that we might just as well give your boat a turn and have your son and yourself to work it. I suppose she is fit to go that distance? "

"Fit! whoy she be fit to go to 'Meriky! The Downs ain't more'n hunder and twenty mile. With a good breeze she would do it in a day. By to-morrow afternoon we'd be ready to make a start if the wind slackens. "

"To-morrow afternoon! We must be there by that time. We want you to start to-night. "

The seaman looked round at his son, and the boy burst out laughing once again.

"It 'ud be a rum start for a vyage at this time o' night, with half a gale from the sou'-west. I never heard tell o' sich a thing! "

"Look here, " said Ezra, bending forward and emphasizing his words with his uplifted hand, "we've set our minds on going, and we don't mind paying for the fancy. The sooner we start the better pleased we shall be. Name your price. If you won't take us, there are many in Claxton that will. "

"Well, it be a cruel bad night to be sure, " the fisherman answered. "Like as not we'd get the boat knocked about, an' maybe have her riggin' damaged. We've been a-fresh paintin' of her too, and that would be spoiled. It's a powerful long way, and then there's the gettin' back. It means the loss of two or three days' work, and there's plenty of fish on the coast now, and a good market for them. "

"Would thirty pounds pay you? " asked Ezra.

The sum was considerably more than the fisherman would have ventured to ask. The very magnificence of it, however, encouraged him to hope that more might be forthcoming.

"Five-and-thirty wouldn't pay me for the loss and trouble, " he said; "forbye the damage to the boat. "

"Say forty, then, " said Ezra. "It's rather much to pay for a freak of this sort, but we won't haggle over a pound or two. "

The old seaman scratched his head as though uncertain whether to take this blessing which the gods had sent or to hold out for more.

Ezra solved the matter by springing to his feet. "Come on to Claxton, father, " he cried. "We'll get what we want there. "

"Steady, sir, steady! " the fisherman said hastily. "I didn't say as I wasn't good for the job. I'm ready to start for the sum you names. Hurry up, Jarge, and get the tackle ready. "

The sea-booted youth began to bustle about at this summons, bearing things out into the darkness and running back for more with an alacrity which one would hardly have suspected from his uncouth appearance.

"Can I wash my hands? " asked Girdlestone. There were several crimson stains where he had held the body of the murdered girl. It appeared that Burt's bludgeon was not such a bloodless weapon after all.

"There's water, sir, in that bucket. Maybe you would like a bit o' plaster to bind up the cut? "

"It's not bad enough for that, " said the merchant hastily.

"I'll leave you here, " the fisherman remarked. "There's much to be done down theer. You'll have poor feedin' I'm afraid; biscuits and water and bully beef. "

"Never mind that. Hurry up all you can. " The man tramped away down to the beach, and Ezra remained with his father in the hut. The old man washed his hands very carefully, and poured the stained water away outside the door.

"How are you going to pay this man? " he asked.

"I have some money sewed up in my waistcoat, " Ezra answered. "I wasn't such a fool as not to know that a crash might come at any moment. I was determined that all should not go to the creditors. "

"How much have you? "

"What's that to you? " Ezra asked angrily. "You mind your own affairs. The money's mine, since I have saved it. It's quite enough if I spend part of it in helping you away. "

"I don't dispute it, my boy, " the old merchant said meekly. "It's a blessing that you had the foresight to secure it. Are you thinking of making for France now? "

"France! Pshaw, man, the telegraph would have set every gendarme on the coast on the look-out. No, no, that would be a poor hope of safety! "

"Where then? "

"Where is the fisherman? " asked Ezra suspiciously, peering out from the door into the darkness. "No one must know our destination. We'll pick up Migg's ship, the *Black Eagle*, in the Downs. She was to have gone down the Thames to-day, and to lie at Gravesend, and then to work round to the Downs, where she will be to-morrow. It will be a Sunday, so no news can get about. If we get away with him they will lose all trace of us. We'll get him to land up upon the Spanish coast. I think it will fairly puzzle the police. No doubt they are watching every station on the line by this time. I wonder what has become of Burt? "

"I trust that they will hang him, " John Girdlestone cried, with a gleam of his old energy. "If he had taken the ordinary precaution of making sure who the girl was, this would never have occurred. "

"Don't throw the blame on him, " said Ezra bitterly. "Who was it who kept us all up to it whenever we wished to back out? If it had not been for you, who would have thought of it? "

"I acted for the best, " cried the old man, throwing his hands up with a piteous gesture. "You should be the last to upbraid me. It was the dream of leaving you rich and honoured which drove me on. I was prepared to do anything for that end. "

"You have always excellent intentions, " his son said callously. "They have a queer way of showing themselves, however. Look out, here's Sampson! "

As he spoke they heard the crunching of the fisherman's heavy boots on the shingle, and he looked in, with his ruddy face all shining with the salt water.

"We're all ready now, sirs, " he said. "Jarge and I will get into our oil duds, and then we can lock up the shop. It'll have to take care of itself until we come back. "

The two gentlemen walked down to the edge of the sea. There was a little dinghy there, and the boat was anchored a couple of hundred yards off. They could just make out the loom of her through the darkness, and see her shadowy spars, dipping, rising, and falling with the wash of the waves. To right and left spread the long white line of thundering foam, as though the ocean were some great beast of prey which was gnashing its glistening teeth at them. The gale had partially died away, but there still came fitful gusts from the south-west, and the thick clouds overhead were sweeping in a majestic procession across the sky, and falling like a dark cataract over the horizon, showing that up there at least there was no lull in the tempest. It was bitterly cold, and both men buttoned up their coats and slapped their hands against each other to preserve their warmth.

After some little delay, Sampson and his son came down from the hut with a lantern in each of their hands. They had locked the door behind them, which showed that they were ready for a final start. By the lights which they carried it could be seen that they were dressed in yellow suits of oilskin and sou'wester hats, as if prepared for a wet night.

"You ain't half dressed for a cruise of this kind, " Sampson said. "You'll be nigh soaked through, I fear. "

"That's our look-out, " answered Ezra. "Let us get off. "

"Step in, sir, and we'll get in after. "

The dinghy was shoved off into the surf, and the two seamen clambered in after. Ezra and his father sat in the sheets, while the others rowed. The sea was running very high—so high that when the dinghy lay in the trough of a wave they could see neither the boat for which they were steering nor the shore which they had left—nothing indeed but the black line of hissing water above their heads. At times they would go up until they hung on the crest of a great roller and saw the dark valleys gaping beyond into which they were forthwith precipitated. Sometimes, when they were high upon a wave, the fishing-boat would be between the seas, and then there would be nothing of her visible except the upper portion of her mast. It was only a couple of hundred yards, but seemed a long journey to the shivering fugitives.

"Stand by with the boat-hook! " Sampson cried at last. The dark outline of the boat was looming immediately above them.

"All right, father. "

The dinghy was held alongside, and the two gentlemen scrambled aboard as best they could, followed by their companions.

"Have you the painter, Jarge? "

"Ay, ay. "

"Make it fast aft then! "

The lad fastened the rope which held the dinghy to a stanchion beside the tiller. Then he and his father proceeded to hoist the foresail so as to get the boat's head round.

"She'll do now, " Sampson cried. "Give us a hand here, sir, if you don't mind. "

Ezra caught hold of the rope which was handed him and pulled for some time. It was a relief to him to have something, however small, which would distract his mind from the events of the night.

"That will do, sir, " the skipper cried, and, leaning over the bows, he seized the anchor which Ezra had hauled up, and tumbled it with a crash on the deck.

"Now, Jarge, with three reefs in her we might give her the mains'le. "

With much pulling at ropes and with many strange nautical cries the father and the son, aided by their passengers, succeeded in raising the great brown sail. The little vessel lay over under the pressure of the wind until her lee bulwark was flush with the water, and the deck lay at such an angle that it was only by holding on to the weather rigging that the two gentlemen could retain their footing. The wild waves swirled and foamed round her bows, and beat at her quarter and beneath her counter, but the little boat rose gallantly to them, and shot away through the storm, running due eastward.

"It ain't much of a cabin, " Sampson said apologetically. "Such as it is, you'll find it down there. "

"Thank you, " answered Ezra; "we'll stay on deck at present. When ought we to get to the Downs? "

"At this rate we'll be there by to-morrow afternoon. "

"Thank you. "

The fisherman and his boy took turn and turn, one steering and the other keeping a look-out forward and trimming the sails. The two passengers crouched huddled together against the weather rail. They were each too occupied with thought to have time for speech. Suddenly, after passing Claxton and rounding the point, they came in full sight of the Priory, every window of which was blazing with light. They could see dark figures passing to and fro against the glare.

"Look there, " Girdlestone whispered.

"Ay, the police have not taken long, " his son answered. John Girdlestone was silent for some time. Then he suddenly dropped his face upon his hands, and sobbed hoarsely for the first and last time in his career.

"I am thinking of Monday in Fenchurch Street, " he said. "My God! is this the end of a life of hard work! Oh, my business, my business, that I built up myself! It will break my heart! "

And so through the long cold winter's night they sat together while the boat ploughed its way down the English Channel. Who shall say what their thoughts were as they stared with pale, rigid faces into the darkness, while their minds, perhaps, peered even more cheerlessly into the dismal obscurity which lay over their future. Better be the lifeless wreck whom they have carried up to the Priory, than be torn as these men are torn, by the demons of fear and remorse and grief, and crushed down by the weight of a sin-stained and irrevocable past.

CHAPTER XLVII.

LAW AND ORDER.

The ruffian Burt was so horror-stricken at the sight of the girl whom he imagined that he had murdered, that he lay grovelling on the railway lines by the side of his victim, moaning with terror, and incapable of any resistance. He was promptly seized by the major's party, and the Nihilist secured his hands with a handkerchief so quickly and effectively that it was clearly not the first time that he had performed the feat. He then calmly drew a very long and bright knife from the recesses of his frock-coat, and having pressed it against Burt's nose to ensure his attention, he brandished it in front of him in a menacing way, as a hint that an attempt at escape might be dangerous.

"And who is dis? " asked Baumser, lifting up the dead woman's head, and resting it upon his knee.

"Poor girl! She will niver spake again, whoever she may have been, " the major said, holding the lantern to her cold pale face. "Here's where the cowards struck her. Death must have been instantaneous and painless. I could have sworn it was the young lady we came afther, if it were not that we have her safe down there, thank the Lord! "

"Vere are those oders? " asked Von Baumser, peering about through the darkness. "If dere is justice in de country, dey vill hang for the work of dis night. "

"They are off, " the major answered, laying the girl's head reverently down again. "It's hopeless to follow them, as we know nothing of the counthry, nor which direction they took. They ran like madmen. Hullo! What the divil can this be? "

The sight which had attracted the veteran's attention was nothing less than the appearance at the end of the lane of three brilliant luminous discs moving along abreast of one another. They came rapidly nearer, increasing in brilliancy as they approached. Then a voice rang out of the darkness, "There they are, officers! Close with them! Don't let 'em get away! " And before the major and his party could quite grasp the situation they were valiantly charged by three of those much-enduring, stout-hearted mortals known as the British police force.

It takes courage to plunge into the boiling surf and to carry the rope to the breaking vessel. It takes courage to spring from the ship's side and support the struggling swimmer, never knowing the moment at which a flickering shadow may appear in the deep green water, and the tiger of the deep turn its white belly upwards as it dashes on its prey. There is courage too in the infantryman who takes a sturdy grip of his rifle and plants his feet firmly as he sees the Lancers sweeping down on his comrades and himself. But of all these types of bravery there is none that can compare with that of our homely constable when he finds on the dark November nights that a door on his beat is ajar, and, listening below, learns that the time has come to show the manhood that is in him. He must fight odds in the dark. He must, single-handed, cage up desperate men like rats in a hole. He must oppose his simple weapon to the six-shooter and the life-preserver. All these thoughts, and the remembrance of his wife and children at home, and of how easy it would be not to observe the open door, come upon him, and then what does he do? Why, with the thought of duty in his heart, and his little cudgel in his hand, he goes to what is too often his death, like a valiant high-minded Englishman, who fears the reproach of his own conscience more than pistol bullet, or bludgeon stroke.

Which digression may serve to emphasize the fact that these three burly Hampshire policemen, having been placed upon our friends' track by the ostler of the *Flying Bull*, and having themselves observed manoeuvres which could only be characterized as suspicious, charged down with such vehemence, that in less time than it takes to tell it, both Tom and the major and Von Baumser were in safe custody. The Nihilist, who had an unextinguishable hatred of the law, and who could never be brought to understand that it might under any circumstances be on his side, pulled himself very straight and held his knife down at his hip as though he meant to use it, while Bulow, of Kiel, likewise assumed an aggressive attitude. Fortunately, however, the appearance of their prisoners and a few hurried words from the major made the inspector in charge understand how the land lay, and he transferred his attention to Burt, on whose wrists he placed the handcuffs. He then listened to a more detailed account of the circumstances from the lips of the major.

"Who is this young lady? " he asked, pointing to Kate.

"This is the Miss Harston whom we came to rescue, and for whom no doubt the blow was intended which killed this unhappy girl. "

"Perhaps, sir, " said the inspector to Tom, "you had better take her up to the house. "

"Thank you, " said Tom, and went off through the wood with Kate upon his arm. On their way, she told him how, being unable to find her bonnet and cloak, which Rebecca had abstracted, she had determined to keep her appointment without them. Her delay rendered her a little late, however; but on reaching the withered oak she heard voices and steps in front of her, which she had followed. These had led her to the open gate, and the lighting of the lantern had revealed her to friends and foes. Ere she concluded her story Tom noticed that she leaned more and more heavily upon him, until by the time that they reached the Priory he was obliged to lift her up and carry her to prevent her from falling. The hardships of the last few weeks, and this final terrible and yet most joyful incident of all, had broken down her strength. He bore her into the house, and laying her by the fire in the dining-room, watched tenderly over her, and exhausted his humble stock of medical knowledge in devising remedies for her condition.

In the meantime the inspector, having thoroughly grasped the major's lucid narrative, was taking prompt and energetic measures.

"You go down to the station, Constable Jones, " he ordered. "Wire to London, 'John Girdlestone, aged sixty-one, and his son, aged twenty-eight, wanted for murder. Address, Eccleston Square and Fenchurch Street, City. ' Send a description of them. 'Father, six feet one inch in height, hatchet-faced, grey hair and whiskers, deep-set eyes, heavy brows, round shoulders. Son, five feet ten, dark-faced, black eyes, black curly hair, strongly made, legs rather bandy, well dressed, usually wears a dog's head scarf-pin. ' That ought to do! "

"Yes, that's near enough, " observed the major.

"Wire to every station along the line to be on the look-out. Send a description to the chief constable of Portsmouth, and have a watch kept on the shipping. That should catch them! "

"It vill, " cried Von Baumser confidentially. "I'll bet money dat it vill. " It was as well that the German's sporting offer found no takers, otherwise our good friend would have been a poorer man.

"Let us carry the poor soul up to the house, " the inspector continued, after making careful examination of the ground all round the body.

The party assisted in raising the girl up, and in carrying her back along the path by which she had been brought.

Burt tramped stolidly along behind with the remaining policeman beside him. The Nihilist brought up the rear with his keen eye fixed upon the navvy, and his knife still ready for use. When they reached the Priory the prisoner was safely locked away in one of the numerous empty rooms, while Rebecca was carried upstairs and laid upon the very bed which had been hers.

"We must search the house, " the inspector said; and Mrs. Jorrocks having been brought out of her room, and having forthwith fainted and been revived again, was ordered to accompany the police in their investigation, which she did in a very dazed and stupefied manner. Indeed, not a word could be got from her until, entering the dining-room, she perceived her bottle of Hollands upon the table, on which she raised up her voice and cursed the whole company, from the inspector downwards, with the shrillest volubility of invective. Having satisfied her soul in this manner, she wound up by a perfect shriek of profanity, and breaking away from her guardians, she regained the shelter of her room and locked herself up there, after which they could hear by the drumming of her heels that she went into a violent hysterical attack upon the floor.

Kate had, however, recovered sufficiently to be able to show the police the different rooms, and to explain to them which was which. The inspector examined the scanty furniture of Kate's apartment with great interest.

"You say you have been living here for three weeks? " he said.

"Nearly a month, " Kate answered.

"God help you! No wonder you look pale and ill. You have a fine prospect from the window. " He drew the blind aside and looked out into the darkness. A gleam of moonlight lay upon the heaving ocean, and in the centre of this silver streak was a single brown-sailed fishing-boat running to the eastward before the wind. The inspector's keen eye rested upon it for an instant, and then he dropped the blind and turned away. It never flashed across his mind that the men whom he was hunting down could have chosen that means of escape, and were already beyond his reach.

He examined very carefully the rooms of Ezra and of his father. Both had been furnished comfortably, if not solidly, with spring mattresses to their beds and carpets upon the floor. The young man's room had little in it beyond the mere furniture, which was natural, as his visits were so short. In the merchant's chamber, however, were many books and papers. On the little square table was a long slip of foolscap covered with complex figures. It appeared to be a statement of his affairs, in which he had been computing the liabilities of the firm. By the side of it was a small calf-bound diary. The inspector glanced over one of the pages and uttered an exclamation of disgust. "Here are some pretty entries, " he cried. "'Feel the workings of grace within me! ' 'Prayed that I might be given a livelier interest in the Holy Scriptures! ' The book's full of that sort of thing! " he added, turning over the leaves. "The fellow seems to have played the hypocrite even with himself, for he could never have known that other eyes would rest upon this. "

"Dere'll be some queer company among de elect if he is dere! " Von Baumser remarked.

"What's all this? " asked the inspector, tumbling a heap of clothes out of the corner with his foot. "Why, here's a monk's dress! "

Kate sprang forward at the words. "Then I did see him! " she cried. "I had almost persuaded myself that it was a dream. "

"What was that? "

Kate told her story as well as she could, and the inspector made notes of it.

"The crafty old dog! " he cried. "No doubt he could reconcile it with his conscience more easily to frighten you to death than to actually kill you. He told you that cock-and-a-bull story to excite your imagination, and then, feeling sure that you would sooner or later try and escape by night, he kept guard in this rig. The only wonder is that he didn't succeed in either killing you or driving you mad with fright. "

"Never mind now, dear, " Tom whispered, as he saw the look of fear spring into her eyes at the recollection of what had passed. "Don't think of these terrible things. You will soon be safe in Phillimore Gardens in my mother's arms. In the meanwhile, I think you would be the better for some sleep. "

"I think I should, Tom. "

"Are you afraid to sleep in your own room? "

"No; I am afraid of nothing, now that I know you are near me. I knew so well that you would come. I have been expecting you all the evening. "

"I can never thank my good friends here enough for the help which they have given me! " Tom exclaimed, turning to his companions.

"It is I who should thank them, " said Kate earnestly, "I have found friends, indeed. Who can say now that the days of chivalry are past? "

"Me dear young lady, " the major answered, bowing with all the innate grace of an Irish gentleman, "ye have warmed us by what ye say. I personally was, as ye know, under orders which left me no choice but to come. I hope, however, that ye will believe that had Mrs. Scully not occupied the place in me affections which she does, I should still be as prompt as me friends here to hasten to the rescue of a lady. Tobias Clutterbuck may be ould, Miss Harston, but his heart will niver grow so hardened but that it will milt at the thought of beauty in distriss. " With this beautiful sentiment the major placed his fat hand over his heart, and bowed again, even more gracefully than before. The three foreigners behind made no remark, but they all stood in a line grinning in a most amicable fashion, and nodding their heads as if to intimate that the major was expressing their united sentiments to a nicety. Kate's last recollection of that eventful evening was the smiling visages of Von Baumser, Bulow, and the nameless Russian as they beamed their good night at her.

CHAPTER XLVIII.

CAPTAIN HAMILTON MIGGS SEES A VISION.

Ezra Girdlestone had given many indications during his life, both in Africa and elsewhere, of being possessed of the power of grasping a situation and of acting for the best at the shortest notice. He never showed this quality more conclusively than at that terrible moment, when he realized not only that the crime in which he bad participated had failed, but that all was discovered, and that his father and he were hunted criminals. With the same intuitive quickness which made him a brilliant man of business, he saw instantly what were the only available means of escape, and proceeded at once to adopt them. If they could but reach the vessel of Captain Hamilton Miggs they might defy the pursuit of the law.

The *Black Eagle* had dropped down the Thames on the very Saturday which was so fruitful of eventful episodes. Miggs would lie at Gravesend, and intended afterwards to beat round to the Downs, there to await the final instructions of the firm. If they could catch him before he left, there was very little chance that he would know anything of what had occurred. It was a fortunate chance that the next day was Sunday, and there would be no morning paper to enlighten him as to the doings in Hampshire. They had only to invent some plausible excuse for their wish to accompany him, and get him to drop them upon the Spanish coast. Once out of sight of England and on the broad ocean, what detective could follow their track?

Of course upon Sampson's return all would come out. Ezra reckoned, however, that it would be some time before the fisherman got back from his journey. What was a favourable wind going would be dead in his teeth coming back. It might take him a week's tacking and beating about before he got home. By that time Ezra hoped to be beyond the reach of all danger. He had a thousand five pound Bank of England notes sewn into the back of his waistcoat, for knowing that a crash might come at any moment, he had long made provision against it. With this he felt that he could begin life again in the new world, and with his youth and energy he might hope to attain success. As to his father, he was fully determined to abandon him completely at the first opportunity.

Through the whole of that wintry night the fishing-boat scudded away to the eastward, and the two fugitives remained upon deck, drenched through with rain and with spray, but feeling that the wild turmoil around them was welcome as a relief to their own thoughts. Better the cutting wind and the angry sea than the thought of the dead girl upon the rails and of the bloodhounds of the law.

Ezra pointed up once at the moon, on whose face two storm wreaths had marked a rectangular device.

"Look at that! " he cried. "It looks like a gallows. "

"What is there to live for? " said his father, looking up with the cold light glittering on his deep-set eyes.

"Not much for you, perhaps, " his son retorted. "You've had your fling, but I am young and have not yet had a fair show. I have no fancy to be scragged yet. "

"Poor lad! " the father muttered; "poor lad! "

"They haven't caught me yet, " said Ezra. "If they did I question whether they could do much. They couldn't hang three for the death of one. You would have to swing, and that's about all. "

About two in the morning they saw a line of lights, which the fisherman informed them was from the town of Worthing. Again before daybreak they scudded past another and far brighter and larger area of twinkling points, which marked the position of Brighton. They were nearly half-way upon their journey already. As the dawn approached the dark storm-clouds gathered away to the northern horizon and lay in a great shadow over the coast. On all other points the sky was clear, save that here and there a single puff of white vapour sailed along like the feather of some gigantic bird floating in the ocean of air. These isolated clouds, which had been pearly grey in the dim light of early day, gradually took a lilac tint, which deepened into pink, and then blushed suddenly to a fiery scarlet as the red rim of the sun rose majestically over the horizon. All the heaven was filled with colour from the palest, lightest blue at the zenith to the most brilliant crimson in the east, as though it were nature's palette on which she had dashed every tint that she possessed. The sea reflected the rich glow, and the tossing waves were gashed with scarlet streaks. "It looks like a sea of blood, " the merchant remarked with a shudder, as he gazed at the wonderful spectacle.

By the returning light the two fugitives were able to notice each other's appearance. Both were pale, haggard, dishevelled, with bloodshot, dark-rimmed eyes and anxious, weary faces.

"This won't do! " remarked Ezra. "If Miggs sees us like this he'll smell a rat. "

He dipped a bucket overboard, and after some search a small piece of soap and a broken comb were extracted from one of the lockers. With these materials they managed to perform their toilets. They re-arranged and cleaned each other's clothing too, and Ezra purchased a yachting-cap from Sampson for his father, the jaunty nature of which contrasted strangely with the old man's grim angular visage.

"There's a fine view! " Sampson observed, pointing towards the land, just as his two passengers had finished their toilet.

They were passing a high range of cliffs which ran along for a great distance. Some were of chalk and others were brownish, as though consisting of some sort of earth. There was one which terminated the line towering up above the rest, and as remarkable for the boldness of its outline as for its height. A lighthouse stood upon the summit, and the whole showed up so clearly in the bright morning air that the fugitives could see the green grass round the house and the coastguardsman at the signal station, who was strolling leisurely about and looking down from his elevation at their little craft. To the eastward of this chalk promontory was a large fine-looking town, which stretched in a wide semicircle round the shores of a curving bay.

"That's Beachy Head, " said Sampson, pointing at the cliff. "It's the hoiest p'int down Channel, and they have a look-out place up there to report ships as pass. It was a Muster Lloyd as put it up. I doan't know who he be, that same Muster Lloyd, but he do seem to take a powerful deal of interest in everythink which has to do wi' shipping. He's an admiral belike, or something o' the sort. "

Neither of the Girdlestones appeared inclined to enlighten him upon the point.

"What's the town? " asked Ezra.

"Eastbourne, " the fisherman answered shortly, and lounged away into the bows, while his son remained at the tiller.

The two fugitives had their breakfast; but as it consisted of nothing more appetising than tinned corned-beef and ships' biscuits, and as neither of them had much inclination for food, it was not a very lengthy meal. Then they sat in the sheets once more, watching the grand panorama of green woodland and swelling down and towering cliff, which passed before them on the one side while on the other the great ocean highway was dotted with every variety of vessel, from the Portland ketch or the Sunderland brig, with its cargo of coals, to the majestic four-masted liner which swept past, with the green waves swirling round her forefoot and breaking away into a fork of eddying waters in her wake.

Ezra cautioned his father to sit down, for he observed a row of curious faces gazing at them over the quarter of one great vessel.

"Our dress isn't quite what you would expect to see in a fishing-boat, " he said. "There is no use setting tongues wagging. " There was still a fresh breeze, and the little boat continued to fly before it at the rate of six or eight knots. "This wind is a lucky chance, " Ezra remarked, rather to himself than to his companion.

"It is the working of Providence, " answered John Girdlestone, with an earnestness which showed that his mind still retained its habitual peculiarity.

By ten o'clock they were abreast of the long stone terraces of Hastings; at half-past eleven they saw the masts of the fishing-smacks of Winchelsea. By one they were rounding the sharp bold promontory of Dungeness. They kept further to sea after that, so that the long white wall and the spires of Folkestone and of Dover lay far on the horizon. On the other side a dim haze upon the blue water marked the position of the French coast. It was nearly five, and the sun was beginning to sink down again in the west, when the fisherman, after gazing steadily ahead for some time, with his horny hand shading his eyes, touched Ezra on the sleeve.

"See them breakers over there, " he said, pointing over the starboard bow. Far away Ezra could see a long roll of foam breaking the monotony of the broad stretch of ocean. "Them's the Goodwins, " he went on; "and them craft ahead is at anchor in the Downs. "

The vessels in question were miles away, but Ezra brightened up at the sight of their destination, and he once again arranged his toilet and that of his father.

"Thank goodness! " he muttered, with a long sigh of relief as he peered at the ships, which were growing clearer and larger every moment. "That outer one is the *Black Eagle*, or I am much mistaken. He's not gone yet! "

"That is the *Black Eagle*, " his father said with confidence. "I know her by the cut of her stern and the rake of her masts. "

As they came nearer still, any lingering doubt was finally dispelled.

"There's the white paint line, " said Ezra. "It's certainly her. Take us alongside that ship which is lying to the outside there, Sampson. "

The fisherman looked ahead once more. "To the barque which has just got her anchor up? " he said. "Why, we won't be in time to catch her. "

"Her anchor up! " screamed Ezra. "You don't mean to tell me she's off! "

"Look at that! " the man answered.

As he spoke they saw first one great square of canvas appear above the vessel, and then another, until she had spread her white wings to their fullest extent.

"Don't say we can't catch her! " cried Ezra, with a furious oath. "I tell you, man, that we must catch her. Everything depends on that. "

"She must take three short tacks before she's out from the Goodwins. If we run right on as we are going, we may get near her before she's free. "

"For God's sake! clap on all the sail you can! Get these reefs out! " With trembling fingers Ezra let out the sail, and the boat lay over further under the increased pressure. "Is there no other sail that we could put up? "

"If we were running, we could rig up a spinnaker, " the fisherman answered; "but the wind has come round three points. We can do no more. "

"I think we are catching her, " John Girdlestone cried, keeping his eyes fixed upon the barque, which was about a mile and a half ahead.

"Yes, we are now, but she hain't got her way on yet. She'll draw ahead presently; won't she, Jarge? "

The fisherman's son nodded, and burst into hoarse merriment. "It's better'n a race, " he cried.

"With our necks for a prize, " Ezra muttered to himself.

"It's a little too exciting to be pleasant. We are still gaining. "

They had a clear view of the dark hull and towering canvas of the barque as she swept along in front of them, intending evidently to take advantage of the wind in order to get outside the Goodwins before beating up Channel.

"She's going about, " Sampson remarked. As he spoke the snow-white pile lay over in the opposite direction, and the whole broadside of the vessel became visible to them, every sail standing out as though carved from ivory against the cold blue sky. "If we don't catch her on this tack we won't get her at all, " the fisherman observed. "When they put about next they'll reach right out into the Channel. "

"Where's something white? " said Ezra excitedly. He dived into the cabin and reappeared with a dirty table-cloth. "Stand up here, father! Now keep on waving it! They may see you. "

"I think as we are overhaulin' of them, " remarked the boy.

"We're doing that, " his father answered. "The question is, will we get near enough to stop 'em afore they gets off on the next tack? "

The old merchant was standing in the bows waving the signal in the air. His son sprang up beside him and flourished his handkerchief. "They don't look more than half a mile off. Let us shout together. " The two blended their voices in a hoarse roar, which was taken up by the boatman and his son. "Once again! " cried Ezra; and again their shout resounded over the sea—a long-drawn cry it was, with a ring of despair and of sorrow. Still the barque kept steadily on her way.

"If they don't go about we shall catch them, " the fisherman said. "If they keep on another five minutes we are right. "

"Do you hear that? " Ezra cried to his father; and they both shouted with new energy and waved their signals.

"They're goin' about, " George burst in. "It's all up. " Girdlestone groaned as he saw the mainyard swing back. They all strained their eyes, waiting for the other to follow. It remained stationary.

"They have seen us! " cried the fisherman. "They are waitin' to pick us up! "

"Then we are saved! " said Ezra, stepping down and wiping the perspiration which poured from his forehead. "Go down into the cabin, father, and put yourself straight. You look like a ghost. "

Captain Hamilton Miggs had found the liquor of the *Cock and Cowslip* so very much to his taste, in spite of its vitriolic peculiarities recorded in a preceding chapter, that he rejoined his ship in a very shaky and demoralized condition. He was a devout believer in the homoeopathic revelation that like may be cured by like, so he forthwith proceeded to set himself straight by the consumption of an unlimited quantity of ship's rum. "What's the good of having a pilot aboard if I am to keep sober? " he hiccoughed to his mate McPherson. After which piece of logic he shut himself up in his cabin and roared comic songs all the way from London to Gravesend. He was so exhausted by his performance that he fell fast asleep, and snored stertorously for fifteen hours, at the end of which time he came on deck and found that the *Black Eagle* was lying off Deal, and that her anchor was just being hoisted for a start up Channel.

Captain Hamilton Miggs watched the sail-setting with his hands in his pockets, and swore promiscuously at every one, from the mate downwards, in a hearty comprehensive way, which showed a mind that was superior to petty distinctions. Having run over all the oaths that he could think of, he dived below and helped himself from the rum bottle, a process which appeared to aid his memory or his invention, for he reappeared upon deck and evolved a new many-jointed expletive at the man at the wheel. He then strode in gloomy majesty up and down the quarter-deck, casting his eyes at the sails and at the clouds in a critical way calculated to impress the crew generally with a sense of their captain's extraordinary sagacity.

The *Blank Eagle* had gone about for the second time, and was just about to free herself from the Goodwins and reach out into the Channel, when Miggs' eye happened to fall upon the fishing boat in pursuit and the white flutter in her bows. He examined her with his glass, steadying it as well as he could by leaning it across the rail, as his hand was very shaky. After a short inspection, a look of astonishment, followed by one of resignation, stole over his features.

"I've got them again, Mac, " he remarked to the mate.

"Got what, sir? "

"The diddleums, the jumps, the visions. It's the change of air as has done it. "

"You look all right, " remarked the mate in a sympathetic voice.

"So I may; but I've got 'em. It's usually rats—rats, and sometimes cockroaches; but it's worse than that this time. As I'm a livin' man, I looked through the glass at that fishing-boat astern of us, and I saw young Muster Ezra Girdlestone in it, and the old boss standin' up wi' a yachtin'-cap at the side of his head and waving a towel. This is the smartest bout that ever I have had. I'll take some of the medicine left from my last touch and I'll turn in. " He vanished down the companion, and having taken a strong dose of bromide of potassium, tumbled into his bunk, cursing loudly at his ill luck.

The astonishment of McPherson upon deck was as great as that of Captain Miggs, when, on looking through the glass, he ascertained beyond all doubt that both of his employers were in the fishing-boat. He at once ordered the mainyard to be hauled back and awaited their arrival. In a few minutes the boat was alongside, a ladder thrown down, and the two Girdlestones were on the deck of their own ship.

"Where's the captain? " asked the head of the firm.

"He's below, sir. He's no very salubrious. " The mate's love of long words rose superior to any personal emotion.

"You can square the yard, " said Ezra. "We are going with you. "

"Ay, ay, sir. Square away that yard there! " It swung round into position, and the *Black Eagle* resumed her voyage.

"There is some business to be looked after in Spain, " Girdlestone remarked to McPherson. "It came up suddenly or we should have given you notice. It was absolutely necessary that we should be there personally. It was more convenient to go in our own vessel than to wait for a passenger ship. "

"Where will you sleep, sir? " asked the mate. "I doubt the accommodation's no very munificent. "

"There are two settees in the cabin. We can do on them very well. I think we can't do better than go down there at once, for we have had a long and tiring journey. "

After they had disappeared into the cabin, McPherson trod the deck for the remainder of his watch with a grave and a thoughtful face. Like most of his countrymen he was shrewd and long-headed. It struck him that it was a very strange thing for the two partners to be absent at the same time from their business. Again, where was their luggage? Grave misgivings arose in his mind as to the reason of it all. He kept them to himself, however, and contented himself with remarking to the carpenter that in all his experience he had never met with a more "monumentous episode. "

CHAPTER XLIX.

A VOYAGE IN A COFFIN SHIP.

The early part of the voyage of the *Black Eagle* was extremely fortunate. The wind came round to the eastward, and wafted them steadily down Channel, until on the third day they saw the Isle of Ushant lying low upon the sky-line. No inquisitive gunboat or lurking police launch came within sight of them, though whenever any vessel's course brought her in their direction the heart of Ezra Girdlestone sank within him. On one occasion a small brig signalled to them, and the wretched fugitives, when they saw the flags run up, thought that all was lost. It proved, however, to be merely some trivial message, and the two owners breathed again.

The wind fell away on the day that they cleared the Channel, and the whole surface of the sea was like a great expanse of quicksilver, which shimmered in the rays of the wintry sun. There was still a considerable swell after the recent gale, and the *Black Eagle* lay rolling about as though she had learned habits of inebriation from her skipper. The sky was very clear above, but all round the horizon a low haze lay upon the water. So silent was it that the creaking of the boats as they swung at the davits, and the straining of the shrouds as the ship rolled, sounded loud and clear, as did the raucous cries of a couple of gulls which hovered round the poop. Every now and then a rumbling noise ending in a thud down below showed that the swing of the ship had caused something to come down with a run. Underlying all other sounds, however, was a muffled clank, clank, which might almost make one forget that this was a sailing ship, it sounded so like the chipping of a propeller.

"What is that noise, Captain Miggs? " asked John Girdlestone as he stood leaning over the quarter rail, while the old sea-dog, sextant in hand, was taking his midday observations. The captain had been on his good behaviour since the unexpected advent of his employers, and he was now in a wonderful and unprecedented state of sobriety.

"Them's the pumps a-goin', " Miggs answered, packing his sextant away in its case.

"The pumps! I thought they were only used when a ship was in danger? "

Ezra came along the deck at this moment, and listened with interest to the conversation.

"This ship is in danger, " Miggs remarked calmly.

"In danger! " cried Ezra, looking round the clear sky and placid sea. "Where is the danger? I did not think you were such an old woman, Miggs. "

"We will see about that, " the seaman answered angrily. "If a ship's got no bottom in her she's bound to be in danger, be the weather fair or foul. "

"Do you mean to tell me this ship has no bottom? "

"I mean to tell you that there are places where you could put your fingers through her seams. It's only the pumpin' that keeps her afloat. "

"This is a pretty state of things, " said Girdlestone. "How is it that I have not been informed of it before! It is most dangerous. "

"Informed! " cried Miggs. "Informed of it! Has there been a v'yage yet that I haven't come to ye, Muster Girdlestone, and told ye I was surprised ever to find myself back in Lunnon? A year agone I told ye how this ship was, and ye laughed at me, ye did. It's only when ye find yourselves on her in the middle o' the broad sea that ye understan' what it is that sailor folk have to put up wi'. "

Girdlestone was about to make some angry reply to this address, but his son put his hand on his arm to restrain him. It would never do to quarrel with Hamilton Miggs before they reached their port of refuge. They were too completely in his power.

"What the captain says has a great deal of truth in it, " he remarked, with a laugh. "You don't realize a thing until you've had to experience it. The *Black Eagle* shall certainly have an overhauling next time, and we'll see if we can't give her captain an increase at the same time. "

Miggs gave a grunt which, might be taken as expressing thanks or as signifying doubt. Perhaps there was a mixture of both in his mind.

"I presume, " Girdlestone said, in a conciliatory voice, "that there would be no real danger as long as the weather was fine? "

"It won't be fine long, " the captain answered gruffly. "The glass was well under thirty when I come up, and it is fallin' fast. I've been about here before at this time o' year in a calm, with a ground swell and a sinkin' glass. No good ever came of it. Look there at the norrard. What d'ye make o' that, Sandy? "

"In conjunction wi' the descending glass, it has an ominous appairance, " the Scotchman answered, with much stress on the first syllable of the adjective.

The phenomenon which had attracted their professional attention did not appear to either of the Girdlestones to be a very important one. The haze on the horizon to the north was rather thicker than elsewhere, and a few thin streaky clouds straggled upwards across the clear cold heaven, like the feelers of some giant octopus which lay behind the fog bank. At the same time the sea changed in places from the appearance of quicksilver to that of grained glass.

"There's the wind, " Miggs said confidently. "I'd furl the top-gallant sails and get her stay-sails down, Mr. McPherson. " Whenever he gave an order he was careful to give the mate his full title, though at other times he called him indiscriminately Sandy or Mac.

The mate gave the necessary commands, while Miggs dived down into the cabin. He came up again looking even graver than when he left the deck.

"The glass is nearly down to twenty-eight, " he said. "I never seed it as low since I've been at sea. Take in the mains'l, Mr. McPherson, and have the topsails reefed down! "

"Ay, ay, sir. "

There was no lack of noise now as the men hauled at the halliards with their shrill strange cries, which sounded like the piping of innumerable sea-birds. Half a dozen lay out on the yard above, tucking away the great sail and making all snug.

"Take a reef in the fores'l! " the mate roared, "and look alive about it! "

"Hurry up, ye swabs! " Miggs bellowed. "You'll be blown away, every mother's son of ye, if you don't stir yourselves! "

Even the two landsmen could see now that the danger was no imaginary one, and that a storm was about to burst over them. The long black lines of vapour had lengthened and coalesced, until now the whole northern heaven was one great rolling black cloud, with an angry, ragged fringe which bespoke the violence of the wind that drove it. Here and there against the deep black background a small whitish or sulphur-coloured wreath stood clearly out, looking livid and dangerous. The whole great mass was sweeping onwards with prodigious and majestic rapidity, darkening the ocean beneath it, and emitting a dull, moaning, muttering sound, which was indescribably menacing and mournful.

"This may be the same gale as was on some days ago, " Miggs remarked. "They travel in circles very often, and come back to where they start from. "

"We are all snug aloft, but this ship won't stand much knocking about, an' that's a fact, " observed the mate gloomily.

It was blowing now in short frequent puffs, which ruffled the surface of the water, and caused the *Black Eagle* to surge slowly forward over the rollers. A few drops of rain came pattering down upon the deck. The great bank of cloud was above the ship, still hurrying wildly across the heavens.

"Look out! " cried an old quartermaster. "Here she comes! "

As he spoke the storm burst with a shriek, as though all the demons of the air had been suddenly unchained and were rejoicing in their freedom. The force of the blast was so great that Girdlestone could almost have believed that he had been struck by some solid object. The barque heeled over until her lee rail touched the water, and lay so for a minute or more in a smother of foam. Her deck was at such an angle that it seemed as though she never could right herself. Gradually, however, she rose a little, staggered and trembled like a living thing, and then plunged away through the storm, as a piece of paper is whirled before the wind.

By evening the gale was at its height. The *Black Eagle* was running under maintopsail and foretopmast staysail. The sea had risen very quickly, as it will when wind comes upon a swell. As far as the eye could see from the summit of a wave there was a vista of dark towering ridges with their threatening crests of foam. When the barque sank in the hollow these gleaming summits rose as high as her mainyard, and the two fugitives, clinging to the weather-shrouds, looked up in terror and amazement at the masses of water which hung above them. Once or twice waves actually broke over the vessel, crashing and roaring down the deck, and washing hither and thither until gradually absorbed between the planks or drained away through the scupper-holes. On each of these occasions the poor rotten vessel would lurch and shiver in every plank, as if with a foreknowledge of her fate.

It was a dreary night for all on board. As long as there was light they could at least see what danger was to be faced, but now the barque was plunging and tossing through an inky obscurity. With a wild scooping motion she was hurled up on the summit of a great wave, and thence she shot down into the black gulf beyond with such force that when checked by meeting the next billow her whole fabric jarred from truck to keelson. There were two seamen at the wheel and two at the relieving tackles, yet it was all that they could do among the wild commotion to keep her steady.

No one thought of going below. It was better to see and know the worst than to be shut up in a coffin where one could not stretch out a hand to help one's self. Once Captain Hamilton Miggs clawed his way along the rail to where the Girdlestones were standing.

"Look there! " he roared, pointing to windward.

It was difficult to turn one's face straight to the wild rush of wind and spray and hail. Shading their eyes, they peered into the storm. Right in the heart of it, and apparently not more than a couple of hundred yards from the barque, was a lurid glare of ruddy light, rising and falling with the sea, but advancing rapidly through it. There was a bright central glowing spot, with smaller lights glimmering above and beside it. The effect of the single glare of light against the inky darkness of the sea and sky would have made a study for a Turner.

"What's that? "

"It's a steamer, " the captain shouted. It was only by great exertions that he could make himself audible above the shrieking of the wind and the dash of the waves.

"What do you think of it all? " Ezra asked.

"Very bad, " Miggs answered. "Couldn't be worse; " and with that he clawed his way aft again, grasping every stanchion or shroud on his way, like a parroquet in a cage.

The clouds above broke somewhat towards morning, but there was no sign of abatement in the tempest. Here and there through the rifts the glimmer of the stars might be seen, and once the pale moon gleamed through the storm wreath. The dawn broke cheerless and dreary, disclosing the great turmoil of endless slate-coloured waves and the solitary little barque, with her rag of canvas, like a broken-winged seabird, staggering to the south.

Even the Girdlestones had noticed that, whereas towards the commencement of the storm it had been a rare occurrence for a wave to break over the ship, the decks were now continually knee-deep in water, and there was a constant splashing and crashing as the seas curled over the weather bulwark. Miggs had already observed it, and conferred gravely with his mate on the point.

"I don't like the looks of her, Mac, " he shouted. "She don't rise to them. "

"She's near water-logged, I'm thinkin', " the mate responded gravely.

He knew the danger, and his thoughts were wandering away to a little slate-tiled cottage near Peterhead. It is true that there was not much in it save a wife, who was said to give Sandy the rough side of her tongue, and occasionally something rougher still. Affection is a capricious emotion, however, and will cling to the most unlikely objects; so the big Scotchman's eyes were damp with something else beside the sea spray as he realized that he might never look upon cottage or occupant again.

"No wonder, " said Miggs, "when she's takin' in water above and below too. The men are weary wi' pumpin', and it still gains. "

"I doot it's our last v'yage thgither, " the mate remarked, his Scottish accent waxing broader under the influence of emotion.

"What d'ye say to heavin' her to? "

"I'd let her run on. She would na rise tae the waves, I'm fearin'. We canna be vera fa' frae the Spanish coast, accordin' to my surmisation. That wud gie us a chance o' savin' oorsels, though I'm a feared na boat would live in siccan a sea. "

"You're right. We have a better chance so than if we let her ride. She'd founder as sure as eggs are eggs. Damn it, Mac, I could almost be glad this has happened now we've got them two aboard. We'll teach 'em what coffin ships is like in a gale o' wind. " The rough seaman laughed hoarsely as he spoke.

The carpenter came aft at this moment, balancing himself as best he could, for the deck was only a few degrees off the perpendicular.

"The leak is gaining fast, " he said. "The hands are clean done up. There's land on the port bow. "

The mate and the captain peered out through the dense wrack and haze. A great dark cliff loomed out upon the left, jagged, inhospitable, and menacing.

"We'd best run towards it, " the mate said. "We've na chance o' saving the ship, but we might run her ashore. "

"The ship will go down before you reach it, " the carpenter remarked gloomily.

"Keep your heart up! " Miggs shouted, and then crawled along to the Girdlestones. "There is no hope for the ship but we may save ourselves, " he said. "You'll have to take your turn at the pumps. "

They followed him forward without a word. The crew, listless and weary, were grouped about the pumps. The feeble clanking sounded like the ticking of a watch amid the horrible uproar which filled the air.

"Buckle to again, boys! " cried Miggs. "These two will help you and the carpenter and mate. "

Ezra and his father, the old man's grizzled locks flying wildly from his head, seized the rope and worked with the crew, hardly able to retain their foothold upon the slippery sloping decks. Miggs went down into the cabin. His behaviour during the gale had been most exemplary, but he recognized now that there was nothing more to be done, and, having thrown off his public responsibilities, he renewed his private peculiarities. He filled out nearly a tumblerful of raw rum and took it off at a gulp. Then he began to sing and made his way on deck in a very hilarious and reckless mood.

The vessel was still flying towards the rugged line of cliffs, which were now visible along the whole horizon, the great projection on the left being their culminating point. She was obviously sinking lower in the water, and she plunged in a heavy, sulky manner through the waves, instead of rising to them as she did before. The water was steadily gaining in her interior, and it was clear that she would not float long. The straining of the gale had increased the long-neglected rifts between her timbers, and no amount of pumping could save her. On the other hand, the sky had broken above them, and the wind was by no means so violent as before. The sun broke through between two great hurrying clouds, and turned all the waves to the brightest emerald green, with sparkling snow-white crests of foam. This sudden change and the brightness of the scene made their fate seem all the harder to the seamen aboard the sinking vessel.

"The gale is clearin', " remarked McPherson. "If we'd had a ship that wasna rotten to the hairt, like her owners, we'd ha pu'ed through. "

"Right you are, old Sandy! But we're all goin' together, captain and owners and the whole bilin', " yelled Miggs recklessly.

The mate looked at him half in surprise and half in contempt. "You've been at the bottle, " he said. "Eh mun, mun, if we are a' drooned, as seems likely, it's an awfu' thing to appear before your Maker wi' your meeserable soul a' steeped in drink. "

"You go down and have a drink yourself, " Miggs cried huskily.

"Na, na. If I am to dee, I'll dee sober. "

"You'll die a fool, " the skipper shouted wrathfully.

"Well, old preacher, you've brought us into a nice hole with your damned insurance cheating, cheese-paring business. What d'ye think of it now, when the ship's settlin' down under our feet, eh? Would you repair her if you had her back in the Albert Dock, eh? "

This speech was addressed to the old merchant, who had ceased pumping, and was leaning against the cuddy and looking up hopelessly at the long line of brown cliffs which were now only half a mile away. They could hear the roar of the surf, and saw the white breakers where the Atlantic stormed in all its fury against nature's break-water.

"He's not fit to command, " said Ezra to the mate. "What would you advise? "

"We'll bring her round and lower the boats on the lee side. They may live or no, but it's the only chance for us. Them twa boats will hold us a' easy. "

The ship was settling down in the water so fast that it was no difficult matter to let the boats down. They only hung a few feet above the surface. The majority of the crew got safely into the long boat, and the Girdlestones, with Miggs and four seamen, occupied the gig. It was no easy thing to prevent the boats from being stove, as the waves alternately drove them from the ship's side or brought the two together with a force which seemed irresistible. By skilful management, however, they both succeeded in casting off and getting clear without accident.

It was only when they emerged from under the shelter of the vessel that they felt the full power of the sea. If it had appeared stupendous when they trod the deck of the barque, how much more so now, when, by leaning the arm over the side, they could touch the surface. The great glassy green billows hurled them up and down, and tossed them and buffeted them as though the two boats were their playthings, and they were trying what antics they could perform with them without destroying them. Girdlestone sat very grim and pale, with Ezra at his side. The young fellow's expression was that of a daring man who realizes his danger, but is determined to throw no chance of safety away. His mouth was set firm and hard, and his dark eyebrows were drawn down over his keen eyes, which glanced swiftly to right and left, like a rat in a trap. Miggs held the tiller, and laughed from time to time in a drunken fashion, while the four seamen, quiet and subdued, steadied the boat as long as they could with their oars, and looked occasionally over their shoulders at the breakers behind them. The sun was shining on the rugged precipices, showing out the green turf upon their summit and a little dark group of peasants, who were watching the scene from above, but making no effort to assist the castaways. There was no alternative but to row straight in for the nearest point of land, for the boats were filling, and might go down at any moment.

"The ship's gone! " Ezra said, as they rose on the summit of a wave. When they came up again all looked round, but there was no sign of the ill-fated *Black Eagle*.

"We'll all be gone when we get among the breakers, " shouted Captain Hamilton Miggs. "Pull, ye devils, pull! Beat the mate's boat. It's a race, my lads, and the winnin' post is hell. "

Ezra glanced at his father, and saw that his lips were moving tremulously as they pattered forth prayers.

"Still at it! " he said, with a sneer.

"Making my peace, " the old man said solemnly. "My faith is now indeed a staff and a comfort. I look back at my long life, and though I humbly confess that I have erred, and erred grievously, still in the main I have walked straight. From my youth I have been frugal and industrious. Oh, my boy, look with candid eyes into your own heart, and see if you are fit to be called away. "

"Look to your own beam, " Ezra answered, keeping his eye upon the line of boiling surf, which came nearer and nearer every moment. "How about John Harston's daughter, eh? " Even at that awful hour Ezra felt a sinister pleasure at observing the spasm which shot across his father's face at the mention of his ward.

"If I sinned I sinned for a worthy purpose, " he answered. "It was to preserve my business. Its fall was a blow to righteousness and a triumph to evil. Into Thy hands I commend my spirit! "

As he spoke a great wave hurled the boat in upon its broad bosom, and flung it down upon the cruel jagged rocks, which bristled from the base of the cliff. There was a horrible rending crash, and the stout keel snapped asunder, while a second wave swept over it, tearing out the struggling occupants and bearing them on, only to hurl them upon a second ridge beyond. The peasants upon the cliff gave piteous cries of grief and pity, which blended with the agonized groans and screams of drowning men and the thunder of the pitiless surge. Looking down they could see the black dots, which indicated the heads of the poor wretches below, diminishing one by one as they were hurled upon the rocks or dragged down by the undercurrent.

Ezra was a strong swimmer, but when he had shaken himself free of the boat, and kicked away a seaman who clung to him, he made no attempt to strike out. He knew that the waves would bear him quickly enough on to the rocks, and he reserved himself for the struggle with them. A great roller came surging over the outlying reef. It carried him in like a feather and hurled him up against the face of the cliff. As he struggled upon its crest, he mechanically put out his hands and seized a projecting portion of the rock. The shock of the contact was tremendous, but he retained his grasp and found himself, when the wave receded, standing battered and breathless upon a small niche in the front of the rock which just gave him foothold. It was a marvellous escape, for looking on either side he could not see any break in the sheer declivity.

He was by no means safe as yet. If a wave had landed him there another might come as high and drag him away. Looking down he saw one or two smaller ones break into spray far below him, and then a second great green billow came rolling majestically towards him. He eyed it as it came foaming in, and calculated that it would come at least as high as his knees. Would it drag him back with it, or could he hold his own? He braced himself as firmly as he could, placing his feet apart, and digging his nails into the inequalities of the rock until the blood gushed from them. The water surged up upon him, and he felt it tugging like some murderous demon at his legs, but he held on bravely until the pressure decreased. Looking below the saw the wave sinking down the face of the cliff. Another wave overtook it and welled it up again, and then from the depths of the green waters Ezra saw a long white arm shoot up, and grasp the edge of the ledge upon which he stood.

Even before the face appeared the young man knew that the hand was his father's. A second followed the first, and then the old merchant's face was uplifted from the waves. He was cruelly bruised and battered, and his clothes had been partly torn away. He recognized his son, however, and looked up at him beseechingly, while he held on with all his strength to the ledge of rock. So small was the space that his clinging fingers touched Ezra's toes.

"There's no room here, " the young man said brutally.

"For God's sake! "

"Hardly room for one. "

The merchant was hanging with the lower portion of his body in the water. It was but a few instants, but the old man had time to think of many an incident in his past life. Once more he saw the darkened sick-room, and his own form standing by the bed of the dying man. What are these words which ring in his ears above the crash of the surf? "May your flesh and blood treat you as you treat her. " He looked up appealing at his son. Ezra saw that the next wave would lift him right up on to the ledge. In that case he might be hustled off.

"Leave go! " he cried.

"Help me, Ezra. "

His son brought down his heavy heel upon the bloodless hands. The old African trader gave a wild shriek and fell back into the sea. Looking down, Ezra saw his despairing face gazing at him through the water. Slowly it sank until it was but a flickering white patch far down in the green depths. At the same instant a thick rope came dangling down the face of the cliff, and the young man knew that he was saved.

CHAPTER L.

WINDS UP THE THREAD AND TIES TWO KNOTS AT THE END.

Great was the excitement of the worthy couple at Phillimore Gardens when Kate Harston was brought back to them. Good Mrs. Dimsdale pressed her to her ample bosom and kissed her, and scolded her, and wept over her, while the doctor was so moved that it was only by assuming an expression of portentous severity and by bellowing and stamping about that he was able to keep himself in decent control.

"And you really thought we had forgotten you because we were insane enough to stop writing at that villain's request? " he said, patting Kate's pale cheeks tenderly and kissing her.

"I was very foolish, " she said, blushing prettily and rearranging her hair, which had been somewhat tumbled by her numerous caresses.

"Oh, that scoundrel—that pair of scoundrels! " roared the doctor, shaking his fist and dancing about on the hearth-rug. "Pray God they may catch 'em before the trial comes off! "

The good physician's prayer was not answered in this case, for Burt was the only criminal who appeared in the dock. Our friends all went down to the Winchester Assizes to give evidence, and the navvy was duly convicted of the death of Rebecca Taylforth and condemned to death. He was executed some three weeks afterwards, dying as he had lived, stolid and unrepenting.

There is a little unpretending church not far from Phillimore Gardens, in which a little unpretending clergyman preaches every Sunday out of a very shabby pulpit. It lies in Castle Lane, which is a narrow by-way, and the great crowd of church-goers ebbs and flows within a hundred yards of it, but none know of its existence, for it has never risen to the dignity of a spire, and the bell is so very diminutive that the average muffin man produces quite as much noise. Hence, with the exception of some few families who have chanced to find their way there, and have been so pleased with their spiritual welcome that they have returned, there is a poor and fluctuating congregation. So scanty is it that the struggling incumbent could very well weep when he has spent the week in polishing and strengthening his sermon, and then finds upon the

Sunday how very scanty is the audience to whom it is to be addressed.

Imagine, then, this good man's surprise when asked to publish the banns of marriage of two couples simultaneously, each of whom he knew to be in the upper circles of life, and when informed at the same time that the said marriages were actually to be celebrated under his own auspices and in his own church. In the fullness of his heart he at once bought a most unwearable black bonnet with lilac flowers and red berries, which he brought in triumph to his wife, who, good woman, affected extreme delight, and afterwards cut away all the obnoxious finery and replaced it to her own taste. The scanty congregation was no less surprised when they heard that Tobias Clutterbuck, bachlelor, was about to marry Lavinia Scully, widow, and that Thomas Dimsdale, bachelor, was to do as much to Catherine Harston, spinster. They communicated the tidings to their friends, and the result was a great advertisement to the little church, so that the incumbent preached his favourite sermon upon barren fig trees to a crowded audience, and received such an offertory as had never entered into his wildest dreams.

And if this was an advertisement to the Castle Lane church, how much more so was it when the very pompous carriages came rolling up with their very pompous drivers, all of whom, being married men, had a depreciatory and wearied expression upon their faces, to show that they had done it all before and that it was nothing new to them. Out of the one carriage there jumped a very jaunty gentleman, somewhat past the middle age and a little inclined to stoutness, but looking very healthy and rosy nevertheless. Besides him there walked a tall, tawny-bearded man, who glanced solicitously every now and again at his companion, as though he were the bottle-holder at a prize-fight and feared that his man might collapse at a moment's notice. From a second carriage there emerged an athletic brown-faced young fellow accompanied by a small wizened gentleman in spotless attire, who was in such a state of nervousness that he dropped his lavender glove twice on his way up the aisle. These gentlemen grouped themselves at the end of the church conversing in low whispers and looking exceedingly uncomfortable, as is the prerogative of the sterner sex under such circumstances. Mr. Gilray, who was Tom's best man, was introduced to Herr von Baumser, and every one was very affable and nervous.

Now there comes a rustling of drapery, and every one turns their heads as the brides sweep up to the altar. Here Is Mrs. Scully, looking quite as charming as she did fifteen years ago on the last occasion when she performed the ceremony. She was dressed in a French grey gown with bonnet to match, and the neatest little bouquet in the world, for which the major had ransacked Covent Garden. Behind her came bonny Kate, a very vision of loveliness in her fairy-like lace and beautiful ivory satin. Her dark lashes drooped over her violet eyes and a slight flush tinged her cheeks, but she glided steadily into her place and did her share in the responses when the earnest little clergyman appeared upon the scene. There was Dr. Dimsdale too, with the brightest of smiles and snowiest of waistcoats, giving away the brides in the most open-handed fashion. His wife too was by his side in tears and purple velvet, and many other friends and relations, including the two Socialists, who came at the major's invitation, and beamed on every one out of a side pew.

Then there was the signing of the registers, and such a kissing and a weeping and a distributing of fees as never was seen in Castle Lane church before. And Mrs. Dimsdale, as one of the witnesses, would insist upon writing her name in the space reserved for the bride, on which there were many small jokes passed and much laughter. Then the wheezy old organ struck up Mendelssohn's wedding march, and the major puffed out his chest and stumped down the aisle with his bride, while Tom followed with his, looking round with proud and happy eyes. The carriages rolled up, there was a slamming of doors and a cracking of whips, and two more couples had started hand in hand down the long road of life which leads—who shall say whither!

The breakfast was at Phillimore Gardens, and a very glorious breakfast it was. Those who were present still talk of the manner in which the health of the brides was proposed by Dr. Dimsdale and of the enthusiasm with which the toast was received by the company. Also of the flowery address in which the major returned thanks for the said toast, and the manly demeanour of the younger man as he followed suit. They speak too of many other pleasant things said and done upon that occasion. How Von Baumser proposed the health of the little incumbent, and the little incumbent that of Dr. Dimsdale, and the doctor drank to the unpronounceable Russian, who, being unable to reply, sang a revolutionary song which no one could understand. Very happy and very hearty was every one by the time that the hour came at which the carriages were ordered, when, amid a patter ing of rice and a chorus of heartfelt good wishes, the happy couples drove off upon their travels.

The Firm of Girdlestone

The liabilities of the firm of Girdlestone proved to be less serious than was at first imagined. After the catastrophe which had befallen the founder of the business, there was almost a panic in Fenchurch Street, but on examination it proved that though the books had been deliberately falsified for some time, yet trade had been so brisk of late that, with a little help, the firm could continue to exist. Dimsdale threw all his money and his energy into the matter, and took Gilray into partnership, which proved to be an excellent thing for both of them. The firm of Dimsdale and Gilray is now among the most successful and popular of all the English firms connected with the African trade. Of their captains there is none upon whom they place greater reliance than upon McPherson, whose boat was providentially saved from the danger which destroyed his former captain and his employer.

What became of Ezra Girdlestone was never known. Some years after Tom heard from a commercial traveller of a melancholy, broken man who haunted the low betting-houses of San Francisco, and who met his death eventually in some drunken fracas. There was much about this desperado which tallied with the description of young Girdlestone, but nothing certain was ever known about the matter.

And now I must bid adieu to the shadowy company with whom I have walked so long. I see them going on down the vista of the future, gathering wisdom and happiness as they go. There is the major, as stubby-toed and pigeon-breasted as ever, broken from many of his Bohemian ways, but still full of anecdote and of kindliness. There is his henchman, Von Baumser, too, who is a constant diner at his hospitable board, and who conveys so many sweets to a young Clutterbuck who has made his appearance, that one might suspect him of receiving a commission from the family doctor. Mrs. Clutterbuck, as buxom and pleasant as ever, makes noble efforts at stopping these contraband supplies, but the wily Teuton still manages to smuggle them through in the face of every obstacle. I see Kate and her husband, chastened by their many troubles, and making the road to the grave pleasant to the good old couple who are so proud of their son. All these I watch as they pass away into the dim coming time, and I know as I shut the book that, whatever may be in store for us there, they, at least, can never in the eternal justice of things come to aught but good.

THE END.

.

Lightning Source UK Ltd.
Milton Keynes UK
UKOW040052030113

204317UK00001B/100/A